For everyone else who's late to the party.
Let's make up for lost time.

Queer people don't grow up as ourselves, we grow up playing a version of ourselves that sacrifices authenticity to minimise humiliation & prejudice. The massive task of our adult lives is to unpick which parts of ourselves are truly us & which parts we've created to protect us.

– Alexander Leon, 2020

PART ONE

PART ONE

ONE

Usually when someone's fondling my balls, I disappear. I try to pretend it isn't happening. The whole thing makes me so uncomfortable I don't know what to do, so I just vanish. Mostly they don't seem to notice, I think. But on this occasion I'm having to answer questions, which makes it trickier.

'And is this a monogamous relationship, duckie?' the middle-aged Irish lady is asking. I wince as her thumb slips probingly around the tender bit of the left testicle.

'Yes, of course,' I say to the beige-tiled ceiling. Why does everyone keep asking me that? It's just a normal relationship, like any other. 'Can you feel the lump? Does it feel bad?'

She ignores me.

'And are you top or bottom?'

I swallow hard.

'That's a very personal question. I don't really see why it's relevant.' She sets me with a look. 'The GP just said I had to come here because of – you know – the *area*.'

My heart is thrumming in my neck. This is maybe the worst place I've ever been. I'm never coming back.

'We ask these questions to everyone – to get a better idea of your sexual history.'

'But this isn't about sex. It's about . . .'

I nod towards my crotch.

Her blue-plastic-gloved hand – the one that's not currently keeping my scrotum hostage – lands on my arm and squeezes gently. It's strange to be held in this way, even for a moment – oddly comforting.

'I won't be sharing this with anyone, dear. Everything you say is confidential.'

I can't bring myself to look directly at her, or where either of her hands are, so I focus on my lightly haired, startlingly white thighs. Then on my calves, then on my ankles, where the navy Topman boxers sit loosely, inside the scrunched-up cave of my pulled-down jeans.

'Bottom,' I whisper.

'Thanks, dear,' she says warmly, removing the hand from the arm. Then, casually as anything, she says: 'Any fisting, choking or BDSM?'

I make a coughing, wheezing sort of noise and see that I've actually sprayed several flecks of spit onto the front of my pale-blue cotton shirt. My face heats up, even though the nurse hasn't noticed and wouldn't care anyway. She must see hundreds of scrotums a week. And globules of startled spit.

I try to get it together.

'No,' I say, as evenly as possible. 'I'm just really not into contact sports.'

'Any GHB, GBL, mephedrone or general recreational drug taking?' she goes on.

'No.' Then I think. 'What about coffee? Sometimes I have, like, three oat-milk lattes a day and I feel a bit' – I shake my head from side to side – '*floopy.*'

She ignores me again. 'Any chemsex orgies?'

'Is that a band?'

'Any animal play?'

I shake my head. She's lost me now.

'I don't have any pets . . . but I'd love a Shih Tzu.'

She gives Old Lefty another good squeeze. I make a 'Gah!' noise.

'Ooh, sorry there, dear,' she says, almost sings. 'And do you use condoms?'

Oh, so we are still talking about sex.

'Yeah, I'm not an idiot,' I say very quickly – too quickly. My tongue is dry. I swallow loudly and listen as the lie comes out. 'Well, we use them *most* of the time. But, like, a few times we've been a bit drunk, or it's the morning and it just sort of . . . happens. But it doesn't matter, because Tobbs would never cheat on me.'

I really can't remember the last time we used a condom – maybe eight months ago?

I glance up. This time, her stare is focused and intense.

'Do you often take risks like this?' she says in a low, serious voice.

'I'm in a monogamous relationship.' I hear this come out much more West Country than I would like. I'm an urban professional now, not the son of a couple who run a chippy in the arse-end of nowhere. I take a breath, I try to flatten my 'r's and shorten my 'a's. 'And I don't see what this has to do with, with . . . whatever's going on down there. This is . . . *something else.*'

The woman looks up. Jacqueline is her name, the laminate badge spearing her pendulous bosom informs me. I've been in too much of a whirl to notice anything until now, when this sudden, vivid realisation that I'm here, actually here, shakes my vision. This tiny square room I'm in with this woman, her frizz of dyed magenta hair beautifully illuminated by the blue

5

computer screen on the desk behind her, giving her an oddly religious aspect. I really am here, me, Danny Scudd, the most sexless man in all existence, spending Friday afternoon in the STI clinic, the place I've always avoided, because there didn't seem much point in coming.

I look up at Jacqueline, looming over me like a dishevelled Madonna. I feel bad news coming, not in my gut, but in my ball.

'There's something there, though, isn't there? A lump?'

After a few thoughtful facial expressions, Jacqueline says, 'Oh yes, darlin', they do feel a little boggy.'

'*Boggy*?' I gasp.

'Boggy.' She nods.

'Does that mean it's . . . cancer?'

She stands up, bins the blue gloves. She has a nice face, but it's tired, drooping like a St Bernard's. She must be in her late fifties, around my mum's age. I imagine the bleached barrel that is Mary Elizabeth Scudd spending eight hours a day inspecting young men's bits, and then coming out with a word like 'boggy'. She'd probably love it.

'Oh, heavens, no!' Jacqueline leans in and winks at me. I get a powerful waft of supermarket-bought geraniums. 'The bad ones don't hurt, and if it *was* cancer I'd feel a lump like a small hard pea attached to the testicle. What we've got here is either gonorrhoea or chlamydia. Rejoice!'

'Ohhh!' Is this something to rejoice about? That sounds pretty serious to me. I have an impulse to take out my phone and text my best mate Jacob. In fact, I wish they'd been able to come with me; it would have made this awful experience slightly less traumatic. 'Does that mean I can't have kids?'

Jacqueline blinks at me a couple of times.

'Now, wherever did you get that idea from?'

I shrug. 'Instagram?'

She shakes her magenta halo. 'You're all right, treacle. Never you worry.'

I lean up awkwardly on one elbow, trying to see what she's really thinking.

'Are you sure it's not cancer?'

Jacqueline smiles to herself, some emotion I can't quite work out.

'It's not cancer, dear. Not even close.'

She turns and goes over to a little plastic trolley, opens and closes its drawers, fiddles with packets of things. I notice for the first time she's wearing Crocs, also magenta, a colour that really fights with the pale-green scrubs.

I lie back on the white bed, pants and trousers still around my ankles, the low buzz of the strip light seeming to get louder and louder. There's so much spinning around my head I don't know which thought to settle on. What does this mean? What does any of this mean?

'How will we know which one it is?' I say.

'Which – testicle?' Jacqueline says, donning another pair of blue gloves.

'Which STI.'

'Oh yes!' she laughs. She actually laughs. Doesn't she realise this exchange is scarring me for life? 'We'll run some tests now, as well as treat you for both.'

She's standing above me again, this time brandishing a needle.

'Roll over.'

I do not move.

She smiles again, though with less patience. 'Roll over, there's a dear.'

'Oh – OK.'

I roll around like a giant worm, taking care not to knock the boggy balls. I stick my bare arse up in the air, wondering if this was indeed how I ended up here in the first place.

'Sharp scratch.'

My eyes are scrunched shut and every muscle I have is tensed as the pain centres in the middle of my right cheek.

'Try to relax,' Jacqueline says, in vain. Next thing I know, she's tapping me on the shoulder.

I jiggle back around, my feet still trapped in the boxer-jean shackles.

'That wasn't so bad, was it?'

'Not compared to choking or fisting, no.'

Jacqueline laughs with such force, I press myself back against the plastic bed, which rattles unnervingly.

'Oh dear, you boys do make me laugh,' she says, thumping her ribcage.

I ignore 'you boys'. But I know what she means, of course.

'Now, we've just got to take a few samples for testing . . .'

She peels open a little plastic bag and pulls out a little plastic spoon, sort of like one you might get in an ice-cream tub at the cinema. Fondly, I think of the time one Christmas when my parents took me to see *Little Women*. We had a chocolate-mint-chip each.

This lovely thought is fleeting, however, because then Jacqueline takes hold of my little bishop in a turtleneck with the same lack of interest I might grab a banana on the way out the door. She's obviously done this many, many times. It's disorientating, looking down and seeing a middle-aged woman's hand circling my poor guy.

'Another sharp scratch.'

I have no time to react, which is for the best.

This is *not* a sharp scratch. This is a popping open of the pee hole, an inserting of the ice-cream spoon, a terrible feeling, like it's too big and going to snag on whatever the hell is in there, and then a deep feeling of sickness. I don't want to look, and yet I can't look away.

Jacqueline peers at the spoon after she brings it out, her flaking scalp in my face.

'Oh dear,' she says darkly. 'Not enough gunk. We're going to have to go deeper.'

These are words you never want to hear.

This time, I lie back, crunch my eyes closed and try to hard-core dissociate. I wonder what Tobbs is doing. Has he also panicked in the work loos on a Friday afternoon upon realising his testicles feel bigger and lumpier than they ever have, started to hyperventilate, gabbled excuses to his boss and made an emergency appointment with his GP, who recommended he reroute to the nearest sexual-health clinic?

Unlikely, seeing as he barely washes. He's authentic and worldly like that. He's probably *too strong-constitutioned to get an STI anyway* – that's what he'd say. Although that does beg the question: if he doesn't have it, where the hell have I got it from? He's the only guy I've been with for over a year. More than a year. OK, he's the only guy I've ever *really* been with, if you get my drift. And, if he does have it, does that mean . . .

I'm good at drifting off, forgetting where I am. But Jacqueline isn't so hot on extracting the 'gunk', and makes heavy work as she dips in a couple more times. I can't help but be dragged back into this horrible little room.

With a whistle of glee, she decides there's enough to send to the lab. After that, I'm treated to a couple more jabs in the arm and some leaflets about HPV, and hep A and B, being, as I am, in a 'high-risk group' – an NHS synonym for 'homo'.

'The tests will come back in five working days or so,' she says over her shoulder. 'It could be either, or even a UTI. If it's chlamydia, then that'll probably have been gestating for three to four weeks. Bubbling away inside the balls, there. Symptoms of gonorrhoea typically show up shortly after exposure, so you'll have contracted that in the last few days or so.'

'No, no,' I try to correct her, thinking how Tobbs and I last had our typically brusque coitus on Monday night – unprotected. 'I can't have just contracted something. I'm in a relationship.'

She turns, clutching a plastic envelope containing tubes of my blood, poo, pee and 'gunk'. She smiles kindly, though something in the eye is sad. *Poor boy,* she's thinking. *Poor stupid boy.*

'And it's not an open relationship, is it? I know you boys are into that sort of thing.'

You boys.

When she says it this time, my brain fizzes gently above the eyebrows. But again I say nothing. I'm sure my facial expression doesn't even change. I don't want to make a fuss.

'No, no,' I say, though I hear my voice crack. 'That's not for me. It's just a normal relationship.'

Jacqueline shrugs and seals the plastic envelope with a rub of her thumb.

'Normal's different for everyone, dear. No judgement. But you do know you're more at risk being the receptive partner – *and* having unprotected sex?'

'Yes, I know,' I say, maybe too sharply. I'm not sure I did know this, though. 'Tobbs wouldn't lie to me; he's a really nice guy.'

'Nice guys can catch HIV, too.'

There is definitely some judgement in this.

'No, no – I didn't mean that. And, wait, who's talking about HIV?' I can feel the fuzz of distress growing, the electric fingertips grasping my temples.

Jacqueline smiles with a genuine warmth. 'Well, if you're not always using condoms, it might be worth thinking about PrEP. When taken daily, pre-exposure prophylaxis is ninety-nine per cent effective in preventing the spread of HIV. It's highly recommended if you're having risky sex.'

'I'm not having risky sex! I'm having consensual, loving sex with my monogamous partner!'

I realise I'm breathing quite hard, staring at her wide-eyed. As if this whole scenario wasn't embarrassing enough already, now I'm making a scene. Tobbs would hate it. He hates it when I get like this.

Jacqueline taps me on the knee. 'Well, let's wait and see, shall we? No use worrying about something that might be nothing, is there?'

'Try and stop me.'

She smiles again. 'Pop your pants back on, lovie.'

TWO

So – hi, hello there. I'm Danny Scudd. I guess we know each other pretty well already – although I wish we didn't. Welcome to my life. As you might be able to tell, it's all going swimmingly.

Though you might have an idea of what *parts of me* look like, let me paint a picture of the rest:

I'm twenty-seven, pasty-faced, with fine, lank light-brown hair, and am both skinny and fat at the same time. You know: arms like spaghetti but somehow still a belly. Basically, it's the body of a teenage boy waiting to develop into itself, to inhabit itself properly, to take ownership. That hasn't happened yet, and I've pretty much given up on it ever happening. Of course, I could exercise, but I just feel like that's not for me. I don't look good sweaty.

You might think I wear glasses, but I don't. I just have that demeanour. It makes sense, though. I squint at words all day long. I'm the content editor at this sort of culture app. It's called – wait for it – CULTRD. It's basically a listings app that you can filter by interest, location, price, etc., and then me and my team make these articles, photo galleries and videos that pop up to show you something vaguely related. They've been getting more and more ridiculous in the three years I've worked there: 'Food Diaries: Orgy Edition' and 'GoTHICC Abodes: 10 Hot Hotels to Die In' are just two of the pieces I've published this week. If you're wondering how this makes any money, at the end of the photo gallery it then links you to all the Hiltons in the area. When I was younger, I wanted to be Teri Hatcher in *Lois & Clark: The New Adventures of Superman* – you know, hunting down the story, exposing the truth, that kind of thing. Anyway, this is where I've ended up.

I dress like every other guy like me: long-sleeved cotton shirts in inoffensive colours, jeans and trainers. Sometimes I go wild and mix it up with a plain T-shirt in a pastel shade. If you saw me in a line-up, you probably wouldn't remember me if you had to identify me later. Not that I'd ever get arrested for anything. Except maybe lurking in plant shops.

In the waiting room of the clinic, however, I stand out like a sore pee hole. I'm fidgeting, shaking my leg up and down, sweating quite a lot around the neck (not a good look for me, as discussed).

It's even more depressing than the little cell where Jacqueline's been poking me. It's violently lit and reeks of ammonia. Sad plastic Halloween decorations span the tired beige walls: black and orange bunting, stencils of bats, witches and skulls. Is this what I'm paying my taxes for? There's no natural light, except from the sliding glass door onto the street that beeps as people enter and leave. A *Jeremy Kyle* rerun plays on a screen overhead, and the two guys sitting under it are loudly trying to work out if the woman on the show is lying to her husband about giving up crack. *What are you in for?* I wonder.

Even though it's my balls that are the issue, my legs felt wobbly when I left Jacqueline, and I sat down on the edge of one of the slidey chairs bolted to the floor in rows. She's given me a prescription to pick up from a pharmacy down the road, but I just need a minute to calm myself down. To rearrange the guys. To breathe.

Sometimes this feeling comes over me like my bones are rattling to be let out of their skin casings. Like some witch's fingertip is pressing my temples tight and shooting electricity through them. It happens at times like this. Or sometimes when I have too many oat-milk lattes. It's just one of my weird things.

I sit here, eyes closed, subtly feeling my hard left ball.

What if Tobbs really has cheated on me? I can't even entertain that. He's the one, I know it. He's everything I've always wanted but never managed to find. He's *much* cleverer than me, more worldly, more handsome – well, handsome if he tried, but he doesn't give a shit what other people think about him, so he doesn't really wash or change his clothes that often. It's part of his whole rugged-reporter thing. Unlike me, he's an actual journalist. He works at this lefty newspaper he refers to as 'the Factory', writing about things that really matter. He's brave. He's *authentic*. And he likes me. Me, Danny Scudd from the chippy in Whistlecombe.

What if I've had something for ages and given it to him?

No, that would be almost impossible. Tobbs is the only guy I've, like, you know, done *it* with. Don't get me wrong, I've done other things with people. Just not *it*. I did kiss that homeless woman last year at the work Christmas party at 2 a.m., when I was outside in the smokers' area, trying to smoke but just stifling coughs. I told her I loved her *and* gave her a tenner. Lucky woman. Possibly unlucky me. Can you get chlamydia from a kiss?

And when I was younger, there was someone – but that was a long time ago. It can't be him . . . can it?

I run over these scenarios again and again. Each time, my chest tightens and my guts do acrobatics. Maybe this is the sort of information I should have disclosed to Jacqueline. That, and one other vital nugget: maybe I should have told her that, in all my twenty-seven years, I've never been tested before. That this was it, my first time.

Maybe I should have told other people this vital information, too. Tobbs, for example. Or the homeless woman.

Or myself.

Maybe I should have told myself instead of putting it in that neat little box in my mind where I put stuff to forget about it.

There are some muted yelps, and I open my eyes to see the mother opposite hauling her little daughter off her seat and towards the sliding exit doors, scowling at me evilly. It's only then I realise I'm sitting here with my hand down my pants, heavily breathing.

Another win today.

I withdraw the hand and put it into my pocket instead.

My heart makes a tiny slope downward as I retrieve my phone: no messages.

I'd texted Tobbs when I was leaving work saying I was feeling funny and going to the doctor's. As usual, he's read the messages but not replied. It's fine. I've got used to it. He's a busy guy, and maybe I do 'over-text' a bit. He says it stresses him out, and I've tried to cut down. I'd only sent him a few earlier. Really short ones. Mostly a couple of words. He normally replies in one big block that he's really thought through, because he's a real writer.

I mean, it's totally fine. I know he likes me. Maybe even loves me.

Instead, I message Jacob, who replies immediately.

WTFs a boggy ball?

Gonorrhoea or chlamydia or maybe a UTI

WTF??!
Babe, how the hell do you get a UTI in your nut?

¯_(ツ)_/¯
I dunno
Ask Jacqueline

Who?

Nurse Jackie

Shut up that's her name

Just clocked that it is

I literally live for Edie Falco

You live for anyone called Edie

TRUTH
Edie Sedgwick
Little Edie Bouvier Beale
Edie Piaf
Every Edie is iconic
That's why we're both Edies

Anyway, can we just rejoice that I'm not dying

Babe, you're dying every week

In the Sylvia Plath sense we are all dying

HARH HARH Fight Club
SUCH an erotic film

Can we please not use the word 'erotic' right now

Sensual
Sexual
Sexy
Sex
Sexxxxxxxx

What are you doing now?

Oh, just sauntering about my fabulous life
I need to get some quail eggs
Where the hell does one procure quail eggs in Bow?

Wanna get drinks to celebrate my boggy ball?

As long as it doesn't come as a side order

I said no sexy talk

I cannot help but arouse the sentiment
Are you still near werq?
I'm in the area

Yas Gawd

We can sipple supple tipples in the post-gay media hellhole

17

of Soho

Yas Gawd

I'll be right there
Love You Little Edie
XOXO Gossip Gay

Love you too Jay
XXX

I click my phone to black and head out towards the pharmacy. The image of my parents battering cod behind their shop counter back in sleepy Whistlecombe floats across my mind.

Is this the sort of life they imagine I lead in the big city? Is this where they envisage I spend my Friday afternoons? Is this what they say when they brag about their son having a 'fancy job in London' to the Rileys next door?

Maybe.

Maybe maybe maybe.

Everything is maybe.

Boggy ball – maybe.

Cheated on me – maybe.

Going to text back or call me – maybe.

Nothing is certain. I wish they taught you this in schools rather than just the Second World War and bloody Henry VIII. No one prepares you for this stuff or how to deal with it. Which is why in this case, as in many others, I'm choosing to deal with it with my best friend . . . and eight flirtinis.

THREE

As usual, Jacob is not 'right there'.

Standing on Old Compton Street in the rain, I'm reminded how 'the gay district' is really now the bougie media profession-als' district with a gentle peppering of gays. Their square-toed wedding shoes and toothpick-thin heels dart across the slicked silver cobbles, hiding their last-minute Halloween costumes under daily tabloids. I press myself into the wet wall, and keep checking my phone. Still no response from Tobbs. I hate how I'm always waiting for people because I never have any reason to be late to anything.

Then, above the waves of media mediocrity, wades the heron. The stalk. The pink flamingo.

I see Jacob some distance away. Though already six foot four, with heels and hair they're scraping the mile-high mark. Jacob calls Halloween 'Gay Christmas', and is dressed appropriately: Naomi Campbell-thin body sheathed in a silver mini-mac with giant lapels and ten metres of bronzed, glossy leg sticking out the bottom – no evident clothing beneath – long black braids threaded with silver, falling from two bunches perched on either side of their head. 'Alien stripper realness', as they've previously described the look. Their entire being glitters in the street light and neon peep-show signs.

They walk straight towards me, then act like they've only just seen me.

'OH MY GOD, HI, ANGEL!'

They fold in half in order to wrap their long arms round me and kiss me on the lips with a MWAH! Then they are cobra-upright again, looking in the mirrored back of their phone.

'Prithee, my lip gloss!'

'"Right outside"?' I say with finger quotes.

They loop their arm through mine.

'*Très pardonne-moi*. I forget you don't like to go in alone.'

'Guys sitting by themselves in bars are creeps.'

Jacob tugs me towards two especially moody bouncers.

'Not guys as cute as you, *bébé*.'

Three drinks down, and I've almost managed to dissociate successfully. Even if the crowd in this gross, dark, loud, sticky, narrow little bar are making it difficult. They're all merrily milling around in their standard gay-guy uniform of a vest plus something else: a vest plus devil horns; a vest plus angel wings; a vest plus impressive *Buffy* prosthetics. One guy in a harness and an Alice band with little grey felt circles on actually said, 'I'm a mouse – *durh*,' when Jacob asked him what he was meant to be. On the bar behind us, an absurdly muscular go-go dancer wiggles about in only a jockstrap and Nike Airs.

With his buttocks directly over my head, I'm saying something like '. . . And she was, like, "Are you quite sure this isn't an open relationship? I know you boys like that." YOU BOYS! Why does everything have to be about sex the whole time?'

I'm not sure when exactly, but at some point, Jacob pulled

a selection of what I can only assume are alien instruments of torture from their clear plastic backpack and put them on the table between us. One is a purple tentacle. Another, a lifelike human forearm. Most, however, are more phallic in nature.

'Sex doesn't have to be this terrifying thing, you know, angel?' they say, stroking an unnervingly realistic vein on one *member*.

'I don't think you realise how traumatic an experience it was, Jay,' I say, unable to look away from the vein.

'Did she give you the whole "Have you been fucking seventy guys in a heroin squat again" chat?'

'Yeah!' I splutter. 'What's that about? I don't even know what some of those acronyms mean. BDSM? GHB?'

'OMFG? And did she poke you, too?'

My eyes scrunch shut reflexively. 'Jay, don't even. It was awful.'

'Totally heinous,' they say in Californian. 'And where did sweet Nurse Jackie pluck the term "boggy balls" from, one has to wonder? Are you quite sure she was an actual nurse?'

I consider this for a second. It would be very on-brand of me to walk into a vet's, drop trou, and ask them to examine my rock-hard plums.

I nod my head. 'Yep, that's what she called it. She also used the word "gunk".'

'*Shivers*,' Jacob says. 'Actual shivers. Why didn't you go to Dean Street instead of this weird, ratchet walk-in clinic?'

We're right around the corner from there now.

'What happens on Dean Street?'

Jacob tilts their head at me like a dog who's just walked in on you trimming your pubes in the bathroom. 'Dean Street Sexual Health Clinic, babe. The number-one STI stop-off for us queers. Come on, you've been there.'

21

'I don't think I've heard of it.' I shrug, as casually as I can. 'I mean, I've never been tested before today, so I'm not exactly a proper gay – or whatever.'

You never really know what Jacob will do next. And though you can pretty much bank on it never being subtle, it doesn't tend to be violent. On this occasion, however, they break precedent.

My left cheek is suddenly stung as if by a giant bee. Except the bee is the purple tentacle. It takes me a second to realise what's happened; they've smacked me with it. It's more rubbery than expected. Around us, several men cheer.

Before I can react, Jacob has me by the shoulders, shaking me.

'WHAT THE FUCKING FUCK, DANIELLE!' they shout. 'DON'T TAKE RISKS WITH YOUR HEALTH!'

I make an odd wailing noise and battle them off with a slew of little smacks.

'*Pleasecanyoujustsitdown*!' I hiss.

My heart is beating in my neck so powerfully I can barely hear the throb of the electronic music. I glance around, certain everyone is staring. Some actually are.

Jacob resumes their position on their stool, back straight, hands folded demurely in their lap – if 'demure' is a word that can ever be applied to Jacob. As usual, they don't even look around. They genuinely don't care what other people think of them or their behaviour. I fight inside myself about this: at best, it's inspiring, and I find myself doing and saying things I'd never normally do. At worst, it's this. This moment right now.

'Dan, I'm not joking,' they say in a steady, cautious voice. 'You've got to be careful. Especially because you don't know who else Tobbs is—'

'He's not cheating on me!' I whisper fiercely. 'He's a good guy.'

'Good guys get STIs, too, Little Edie.'

'I don't have an STI. It's just . . . just—'

'A boggy ball?'

'Exactly!'

We sit in silence for a few heartbeats. Maybe five for Jacob, fifty for me, as the organ beats its rapid pulse. We sip our drinks. The vest gays dance. My forehead buzzes with electricity. It feels like it's scrambling my brains. I really just want to scoot past this whole thing, pretend like this entire day never happened.

To cast the spotlight away from me, I look down at the mortuary of limbs and say, 'Why do you even have all these *thingies*?'

Jacob regards me carefully, possibly deciding if I'm in the right state for the truth.

'I just bought them round the corner,' they say. 'For my workshop at the Royal Academy next week. "Decolonising Colons – and Other Queer Sex Mythologies" – you can come if you want?'

'Hmm,' I say, and go back to sipping my flirtini.

They deliberately tried not to make it sound pointed, but how could it not? Jacob is oblivious to my discomfort, or pretends to be.

I know what you're thinking: how is a white-bread nobody like me friends with an extraterrestrial princess like Jacob? Well, we've always been friends, ever since we used to dress up at preschool in the Methodist church back in Whistlecombe. They come across as a skilfully crafted performance piece: Jacob Jamal Diaspora, artist, teacher, visionary, which is how they rebranded themself shortly after starting at Central Saint Martins, managing to carve out a niche in small pub performance spaces and the Twittersphere ever since.

To some degree, they've always been this person – they were

just never able to embody it fully while we were growing up. So I don't see them the way the world sees them, because I remember all the versions they tried on while on the way to this one. I remember their emo phase. I remember when they were just Jacob Jones, the only mixed-race kid in our school, town, county, it seemed. I remember when they were eye-catching for reasons beyond their control. I remember when I came out to them in the kids' play park, drunk on Scrumpy Jack. And when they didn't have to come out at all. I remember standing next to them at their mum's funeral, holding hands so tightly, even though we weren't speaking at the time. I remember when we watched the seminal cult camp classic documentary *Grey Gardens* over and over and over again and play-acted the leads: Jackie O's neurotic cousin Little Edie and her eccentric mother, Big Edie. Guess who played who.

I remember all of it, and then they aren't the character the rest of the world sees – they're my best friend. Alien strippers do not land on this planet in finished form; they evolve, just like us awkward Earthlings.

They're still staring at me as they sip their flirtini.

'Jay,' I say to them, 'I just want a normal life.'

Jacob's hand reaches out and squeezes mine.

'There's no such thing as "normal", babe.'

Are Jacob and Nurse Jackie in this together?

'Oh, you know what I mean! I just want a husband and kids and a flat, and do, like, arts and crafts with them on the weekend, and maybe go to a National Trust property and be able to pay for everyone to have one of those little ice creams in a cardboard tub.'

'The ones with the tiny plastic spoons?'

I shudder. 'That's what I want.'

'And do you think Tobbs is the one to give it to you?'

'Look, I know you don't like him—'

'I don't like the *sound* of him,' Jacob objects. 'How can I dislike a man I've barely met? You never let me near him!'

Is it any wonder?

'Please,' I say slowly, 'can you just support me in this?'

Jacob is visibly forcing their lips to stay shut.

'Of course, babes. All I want is for you to be happy. Same as any mother.'

'Yeah,' I say, sighing. It must be written across my face that I'm not even that.

Suddenly the dance floor seems to be crammed full of only couples. All beefy, all snogging in a hypersexual, carefree manner. Tobbs would never snog me like this on a dance floor. Tobbs would never snog me like this anywhere. Is it even possible for two guys to have a really happy relationship together, like straight people do? I don't know of any. Will I ever get to buy a branded tea towel at Hampton Court on the joint account?

I check my phone again. Still no reply.

'Where's that boy gone?' I say, sounding just like my dad.

I look up, and Jacob is smirking.

'You went proper West Country then,' they say, vowels slipping out long and tinged with hay and mackerel, just the same.

Despite how shit I feel, I'm smiling.

'Whatever, Alice Tinker!'

'Shh!' Jacob holds up a finger to my lips, silver acrylics glinting. 'They must never know our origin story.'

I grab the hand and thrust my other one out dramatically.

'Grown from the same shit heap, we was!' I gasp like an aged Devonian witch. This is a whole *bit* we do.

'Two roses, plucked from the pyre!'

'Two thorny sisters, flown from 'twixt they cometh!'

'That's enough now. Let's get shots.'

———

This is the part of the night that really starts to dissolve.

We have maybe four more drinks and three more shots, and next thing I know, Jacob is dancing in circles around everyone, waving the tentacle and forearm, spinning and loving it as people click their fingers, yell 'YAS, QUEEN!' and film it all on their phones. As ever, I stand there, semi-swaying along, until, eventually, I'm drunk enough to join in. When this happens, it feels like it's me and Jacob against the world. I'm proud to call them my best friend, proud to be lifted out of the *me* I feel so uncomfortable in.

Suddenly it's 3 a.m. and I'm staggering towards Tottenham Court Road Tube, Jacob swaying around in the street behind me having half-bits of conversations with anyone and everyone we pass.

'I mean, he wouldn't cheat on me, Jay,' I'm slurring. God, why am I saying this? 'He just wouldn't. On Monday, he nearly said he loved me. I'm sure of it. That was our one-year anniversary. Nope, nope, nope, he wouldn't do that. He's not like that.'

'Have a lovely evening, madam!' Jacob is shouting. 'Boris Johnson is my style icon, too!' Their arm is around my neck, their silver form pressed against mine, their sweet, citric breath in my face. 'What *is* he like, then? Seeing as I'm not allowed to kiki with him.'

'Well – you know – he's, like, a genius.'

'Oh yeah, is that why he doesn't reply to your texts?' Jacob snorts. 'Doesn't sound too clever to me.'

'He needs his space,' I say. 'To – like – think. And stuff.'

I fumble in my pocket for my phone. Two missed calls from MA & PA HOME.

'Still no reply?' Jacob says, a little too righteously.

I put the phone away.

'He's probably on a late shift and forgotten to tell me. Or, like, interviewing someone famous. Stop making such a big deal about it. There's no such thing as normal.'

'Ain't that the truth.'

My heart does feel heavy, though . . . but it could just be the shots.

'You know what you've never told me?' Jacob says as the wide, white entrance to the Tube looms.

'What?'

'Is how big Little Tobbs actually is.'

'Oh my God, Jay!' I shout, causing a cluster of budget Disney princesses to turn and stare. 'Like, I don't know. Not small, though! Why do you even want to know? That's the problem with gay culture. Everything is so oversexualised! All anyone wants to know is how big everyone's dicks are. No one cares how kind you are, or how often you call your mum.'

'When *did* you last call Mary?' Jacob laughs.

'That's not the point!' I snap as we unsteadily totter onto the escalators. The sudden movement takes us unawares and we hold on to each other. Around us, everyone is pressed together, laughing, shouting, singing.

'What is the point, Little Edie?'

'The point is . . .' I say, unsure what we were talking about now. 'The point is . . .'

'The point is, why are you so ashamed of it?' Jacob says, releasing me and staggering towards the barrier.

'Ashamed of what?' I shout after them. 'Jay! Ashamed of what?'

But they have scanned their card, waved a hand and marched off into the tide of people. Farewell to the pink flamingo.

FOUR

The room looms blearily into focus. Although much of it is obscured, and I immediately start to panic that I've had a stroke or my retinas have detached and now I'm blind forever. The electric fingers dance across my temples, as they always do on a hangover.

I sit up straight, and the darkness drops away. I blink several times and realise that I am not blind. I was just lying face down, like a corpse in a canal. I must have just fallen onto the bed and stayed like that all night.

Though the edges of everything seem watery, undefined, they are at least visible: the clothes being puked from the chest of drawers onto the small amount of floor around the bed; the white sash window to the left; the curtains that are barely tugged closed; and the plants. Oh, the plants.

If you popped your head in here, just for a second, you might not realise there's any furniture at all. In fact, you might not think this is a room used for human habitation. Most space, if not covered in clothes, is covered in plants. I've got a bit of a thing for them. I know it's got maybe *a little* extreme, but I like them. They calm me down, and they remind me of home.

Between the velvety foliage of the green-and-red calathea and the delicately patterned, church-window-like leaves of the prayer plant gazes the holographic triptych of Dolly Parton. It's one picture, but, depending on what angle you look at her from, Dolly can be seen doing different things: Dolly holding up her palms like the Virgin Mary, only dressed in a sequinned minidress; Dolly tending sheep in a meadow, lulling them to sleep with her guitar; Dolly typing at an altar in her *9 to 5* eighties get-up, with head turned to us, plastered with a knowing look – 'Yep, I'm about to bury my boss. Amen, children!'

Other than the plants, this is my best purchase to date. I got her at Brixton Village Market for a fiver. She's always there, watching over me benevolently. I wish I could say she's seen some ungodly things happen in this bed, but she's been mostly spared. She's never even seen a slither of Tobbs's bum cheek, because he doesn't like to sleep here. The worst thing she's seen is me going at it under the covers to some amateur stuff on my phone, like a teenager.

Speaking of which: I root around for my phone in the duvet. Tobbs has replied at last! Quite curtly, but at least he's acknowledged me:

What's with all the messages and calls, boyo? You know it stresses me out. Tell me at the screening later. T

Tobbs was really sweet last week and got these tickets for a documentary screening at the Curzon at 2 p.m. for our anniversary. I think he got them through work.

It could just be the booze, but the thought of actually confronting him about my trip to the clinic makes my stomach swirl. He always says I'm making drama, so maybe I don't have to tell him. Maybe we can just have a romantic afternoon out together. We so rarely do that nowadays . . .

The thought of Tobbs leaning in and kissing me with his smoke-infused breath starts to have, um, an *effect* on me, and I reach down and give Little Danny a tug.

'Morning, party animal!'

As often happens, because she owns the flat, Laura bursts in unannounced.

I scream and grab the bed sheets. She screams and walks into the door frame.

'Laura, Jesus Christ! Why don't you knock!'

'It's twelve-thirty!' she shouts, rubbing her forehead.

The wide whites of our eyes meet tentatively.

'Sorry,' she says, scanning the scene, my embarrassed expression and sheets drawn up under my chin. The brows of her round, Home Counties face furrow. 'Do you want breakfast – well, brunch?'

'Yeah, yeah. Thanks. I'll be out in a minute.'

She smiles and makes a big show of closing the door.

My hand stayed where it was throughout the conversation, frozen in encircled fear. I unfurl the fingers. In doing so, I knock my enlarged scrotum. I'd temporarily forgotten about that. God, still big, still boggy. Let's hope these antibiotics do the trick. Nurse Jackie's words roll around my mind again and I have to concentrate really hard to make them roll out again. *No use worrying* . . .

I untangle myself from the sheets, find my hoodie and pyjama bottoms, make a prayer to the hologram.

'Sorry you had to see that, Dolly. Please forgive me. Amen.'

————

'EAT IT, YOU SLAG!' Luke is shouting from the sofa.

Without needing to see more, I pull the drawstrings of the

hood tight, scrunching out the violently bright kitchen–living room before it fully comes into view.

Laura's decorating is nice, but not really to my taste – and not just because there aren't enough plants. The cream walls are sporadically interrupted with white hearts twisted from willow, and laser-cut beech words saying things like 'Family', 'Love', 'His & Hers'. There are even framed sayings that I had first assumed came with the frame: 'Love is an everyday practice,' 'Live the life you love' and 'The journey of life starts and ends with love.' Everything else is white or cream with hints of gingham, a dazzlingly twee palette difficult to deal with even when you're not on the verge of death.

'YOU TAKE IT IN THE ARSE, YOU KIWI BASTARD!'

Luke's clipped Surrey accent really brings out every word of his beautiful poetry.

'Lukey, stop it,' Laura sighs in that half-flirty-little-girl, half-tired-motherly way she reserves for him – and for the other men in her life.

My hands reach for the familiarity of the back of the IKEA kitchen chair, the edge of the IKEA kitchen table, the same weight and clatter of the IKEA knife and fork.

'Danny-boo, where are you?'

Laura seems to be prising open my protective hooded shield. I make no attempt to resist. Her face is in mine, all rosy cheeks and wholesome, tumbling brunette locks. Kate Middleton of South London, she is. Her summer-picnic-in-the-park sky-blue eyes sparkle, though there's a hint of worry in them, some clouds coming.

'There he is!' She smiles and 'bops' me on the nose with an index finger.

The movement is enough to make my stomach roll. I rub my

eyes and forehead. How does her hand smell so powerfully of potpourri?

'I made bats!'

Like the inverse of a night sky, the white IKEA plate before me displays two fat, softly ochre bats, their blobby wings fried motionless mid-flight. The rendering is genuinely impressive. Laura's level of domesticity is honestly startling to me, even after five years.

'Happy Halloween!' she sings with a slightly manic edge, waving the spatula a little too much.

'Oh, lovely,' I say. 'Thanks.'

'You're welcome!' Laura sings, picking up another plate of 'bats' and taking them over to the living-room area. 'I just thought it would be, you know, *nice*.'

Without needing to look, but still doing it anyway, I glance over to where Luke is sprawled on the sofa in just his loose chequered boxer shorts. His arms are up around his fair hair, hands dangling over one sofa arm, his legs spread wide, feet lolling off the other end. He looks like he's been moulded from Play-Doh – his whole muscly bulk is uniformly pink and matt. His massive frame makes the sofa look like a doll's-house item, a Sylvanian Family situation, slowly getting crushed under the sheer volume of this big pink giant. His chest and stomach glisten with a fuzz of golden hair, and I can literally see a slither of his dong through the gap in the boxers as he continually readjusts the guys. He really doesn't care who sees. In fact, I'm pretty sure he likes it. *All fun and games, Dazzer, just like at school.*

'PASS IT, YOU USELESS PRICK!' he belts at the flat-screen. Mountain-framed men that look exactly like him leap on top of one another on the green pitch. I do not follow the 'rugger', and it amazes me how he manages to find a game every single time he turns on the TV. Which is every minute he's in the flat.

'Here you go, my big strong man,' Laura says, sliding a plate onto the coffee table in front of him. 'Happy Halloween!'

'Ref's a fucking ponce,' Luke says in thanks.

'Lukey, come on.' Laura squeezes his thick, veiny anaconda wrist and glances over at me nervously.

I don't react. He's always saying stuff like this.

'Coffee, Danny-boo?' She's now sitting opposite me, dusting bat flour off her red-and-blue Cath Kidston apron. 'And there's blueberry compote. Your fave.'

She smiles with a lot of teeth and bobs her shoulders.

'Thanks, Laur.'

She really is a sweetheart, even if she is a bit overly gooey. We've known each other since secondary school, when we weren't really friends, but, she assured me, she knew we would be one day. She was in the Girls with Pearls netball crew. I existed on their fringes, trying to be as invisible as possible. Meanwhile, Jacob flitted between art-room weirdos and sexually ambiguous stoners, making everyone suspicious but generally keeping them amused enough to evade attack – not completely, but mostly. A bedazzled social butterfly from an early age.

It was only after uni that Laura and I ended up reconnecting, when I moved out of halls and needed somewhere to live. Luckily, her parents had bought her this flat as a 'starter home' for her and Luke. This is a term I have yet to fully grasp the concept of – it's nicer than my parents' house, and they've been there thirty-two years.

'How was your night on the razz?' Laura says as I drizzle the purple-blue syrup all over the cheerful wings and tubby torsos. 'With Jacob?'

Though my brain is dead and my eyes are heavy, they still flick to her, and she gets the accusation.

She holds up her hands. 'I didn't say anything!'

'They really aren't as bad as you think.'

'Oh, does he have a boyfriend now?'

'Laura.'

Her fingers flutter; she brushes hair back from her face.

'Oh, I'm sorry – I just don't get it!'

I munch the left wing of the first bat to die today.

'You know it's the gender-neutral pronoun Jacob likes to use,' I say in my usual timid form of protectiveness, while knowing full well that Jacob doesn't really care *that* much about pronoun specifics. Once, they said, 'He, she, they, gurl, kween, betch, mate – I'll take 'em all!'

Laura's arms are now folded.

'Well, if he wants to be gender-neutral, why doesn't he change his name?'

I suddenly feel under attack. I'm chewing the bat wing like it's made of iron.

'Because it's not about them adopting a fake identity, it's about being themself. You wouldn't refer to yourself as "he", would you?'

'No!' Laura scoffs. 'Because I'm a lady.'

'What makes you a lady?'

Laura sighs, looks heavenward. 'Oh, Dan, don't start this again.'

The immediate fear that I've gone too far dances wickedly around my skull. I've said too much, been too aggressive. This will just give her and Luke more fuel for talk before they go to bed – and for me to overhear through the wall. 'Jacob's a bad influence on him. Everything is always so complicated. I just feel like I can't say anything . . .'

I try to chew more calmly.

Maybe she's right. Maybe Jacob *is* a bad influence on me. I do always seem to pick holes in what she says after I've been hanging out with them. Like when we had that argument about coming out. Laura didn't get why queer people have to make a big thing about it, because straight people don't come out. I felt like the answer was obvious until I listened to her for a little bit. But then I told Jacob about it and they went mental and said this was why you can't live with straights. I said some of it to Laura, and she was like, 'Well, that's not very PC to straight people.'

It did confuse me, though. It made me question which I should be going for: be a gay version of Luke and Laura, try to get married, adopt a kid, etc. Or don some kind of sheer, glittery top and start voguing while yelling, 'PRIDE IS A RIOT!' like Jacob. Not that I'd ever do that.

'I hope you'll be perkier for our little soirée this evening,' Laura says with deliberate perkiness.

I look up.

Her face falls. 'You've forgotten.'

I make a big show of fake-remembering. 'No, no, of course I haven't. It's just, Tobbs invited me to this screening . . .' Laura looks bereft and furious simultaneously. It's actually quite scary. 'But I'm sure we could just come straight afterwards.'

Her expression immediately changes. 'Oh, good! That's sorted, then! Everyone's confirmed: Simone and Sim, Georgia and Gerry.' She raises an eyebrow. 'And Zain.'

Zain.

The right wing pauses on its fork halfway to meet its doom in my mouth. She waits to see my reaction. I purposefully try not to react, but I can feel my face heating up. How many times do we have to have this conversation?

'Oh, cool,' I say.

'Cool *and* single.'

Laura's sipping her coffee and giving me Emma Woodhouse vibes. Zain went to uni with her and the rest of her gang and will be the only other gay guy at the party. It's always just the two of us – and everyone else's whispers. Despite how clearly wrong we are for each other, Laura's been trying to matchmake us for at least three years. Something about him, or maybe just the situation, makes me feel deeply uncomfortable. Jacob has a term for guys like him: 'intimigays'.

'Apparently, him and Rufaro had a mega-blowout, and Rufaro was all like, "If I see you again, I'll kill you," and Zain was like, "Is that why you banged my brother?" Anyway, he's on the market again.'

'Laur, *please.*'

'Aaaand his play just got commissioned by the National. He's basically this generation's William Shakespeare. I've always thought you guys had a bit of a thing.'

And the wing is dust.

'I have a boyfriend.'

'Oh yeah, I know.' She's all dismissiveness, then suspicious, probing. 'How long have you been going out again?'

'A year!' I'm trying hard not to sound exasperated. 'We had our anniversary on Monday, remember?'

'Oh yes, the Chinese takeaway night.' Her eyes flick to Luke, letting me know how many more conversations I haven't over-heard. 'True romance.'

'He's who I've chosen to be with, OK?' Now I'm looking at her, trying to measure my voice so I don't sound as angry and upset as I'm becoming. This probably isn't the best time to mention the boggy balls. 'He's just got, like – stuff. He went to boarding school.'

'Nothing wrong with that, Dazzer,' Luke says in my ear, scaring the life out of me.

His bulk has loomed up behind me. I can literally feel his dick pressing in between my shoulder blades. Now his big clay hands are massaging my neck, my upper arms, in motions so powerful I undulate back and forth with their crushing rhythm. 'You gonna eat that, Flops?' He points at the second of Laura's bat pancakes.

She shakes her head and offers it up to him. 'All yours, Cotton Tail.'

These are just two of the many nicknames they have for one another. There's also some Enid Blyton ones.

'CALL YOURSELF A FLY HALF, PUSSY?' He's back on the sofa, yelling and chewing.

Laura looks at me.

'Danny-boo, I'm just saying this because I love you. *We* love you.' She reaches out a hand and takes mine. Why do I feel bad news coming? Those clouds over the picnic in her eyes are rolling in, heavier and darker. 'We'd love to see you settled, with someone, you know? Being with Lukey is honestly the best thing that's ever happened to me. And, you know, we're not twenty-two anymore.'

I'm not really sure what to say to that. I want to say, 'It's different,' but don't know how to, or even if it's true.

'We're only twenty-seven, though,' I say. My shoulders are now hurting, along with my head and balls, and soon, I suspect, my heart.

'Mama Clifford had me when she was twenty-one.'

I swallow audibly.

Something in my brain aligns. 'You're pregnant.'

Her other hand comes to join the first, squeezing mine with both thumbs. It's only then I notice the ring. The stone is actually startlingly enormous. The shine off it hits the back of my retinas, and my stomach swirls again.

'And engaged!' she squeals. 'Lukey popped the question last night! You're the first person we've told – well, except for our parents, obvs. And the work gang, I had to tell them. And, like, Andrea and Wills from school, because we always said we'd get married and preggo at the same time. And, well, they beat us to it with the wedding, but not the baby!'

I'm very aware of the roar of the crowd and the pithy statements from the commentators on the TV. Why do I get the impression this is the sort of news Luke might forget to share until he has returned from the honeymoon, holding his twelve-pound bruiser in the crook of one enormous arm?

'Oh – wow.'

'We're going to tell everyone at the party tonight!'

'Oh, Laur.' I smile at her. She was born to be a mother; I am genuinely happy for her. But I still feel uneasy. 'That's so great.'

'Thanks, Dan. Due in May. We don't know the gender yet.'

'The sex,' I say, without thinking.

'That's what I said.' Laura cocks her head.

'No,' I say. '"Sex" refers to the biological body; "gender" is socially constructed and ascribed at birth.'

Laura's face darkens. Here's the storm.

'Look, Dan, we need to talk to you about something.' I glance over at Luke. Again, he seems not so concerned with this announcement. Who came first, I wonder, the baby or the proposal? 'We want to make this place into a home, a *real* home, for our family, and we were just thinking, maybe seeing as you're not really, you know, at the same stage in life, if you'd be happy to, you know . . .'

She trails off.

'TAKE IT, ARSEWIPE!'

The crowd roars.

'You want me to move out?' I say.

'No, no, no!' Laura leans in, really presses into my hands. 'It's not that we want you to *move out,* it's just we need the space, you know? Like, to make a room for the baby.'

Weirdly, I say, 'But where will my plants go?'

This breaks the tension. Laura laughs and dips her face to the table, her brown hair spilling over the plate, now bat-free and blueberry-stained. She looks up, beaming.

'You don't have to go right now. Just, you know . . .'

'Over the next few months?' I proffer.

'Weeks.' She smiles. 'We've ordered the cot already.'

My mouth must be open, because then she giggles and bops me on the nose again.

'You *are* funny! More coffee?'

She's up and at the counter, busying herself. Then she's turned and is looking at me.

'In all seriousness, Danster, it might be good for you.'

With a horrible sinking feeling, I realise I've heard her saying this exact sentence to Luke through the wall. Only now does it make sense. How long have they been planning to say this to me? Well, how long has *Laura* been planning to?

'Being homeless?' I manage to say. I feel sort of in shock. 'That'll be good for me?'

'No, no, no!' She picks up my mug, pours in more coffee, even though I haven't touched it. 'Going out there, finding your way in the world, you know? Who knows who you'll meet.'

I have a job and a boyfriend and a life, you know! I want to shout at her. Everything is swimming. My stomach lurches. I'm going to be sick.

'OK,' I say. The only thing I know now is that I need to get to the bathroom immediately.

'So you're not angry?' Laura squeezes her fingers together with a pained expression I don't exactly buy. Or, rather, I believe she feels pained. Pained for having to tell me. Pained for the awkwardness, the fuss, the bother. Not pained for me.

I stand in a clumsy way, nearly knocking the IKEA chair over.

'No, no,' I say. 'I've just got to—'

But the wave in my stomach has me. I lurch from the kitchen into the tiny hall and all but fall into the bathroom, slamming the door behind me. I vomit powerfully.

'You'll still come to the party later, right?' Laura calls through the door.

After some more heaving and filling of the bowl, I steady my forearm on the wood of the seat, press my face into the soothing nook of my elbow.

'Yes!' I call back.

'Oh, great! I'll leave you to be sick in peace. We really are sorry, Danny!'

'It's OK!' I shout, then lay my head down and groan.

I should have known they were guilt bat-cakes.

FIVE

Between vomiting and trying to shower, brushing my teeth, and dressing without falling into things, it gets to one-thirty and I'm only just ready to dash out of the house. The thought of actually speaking to Tobbs fills me with an increasing sense of dread. I'm in no state to have a 'serious chat'. And he especially hates 'serious chats'. The heat of the Underground makes me woozy, and as I emerge from Leicester Square Station I see a message:

Already here, boyo. Just making friends with the sexy barman 😜 *T*

My brain is vibrating as I push open the Curzon's glass doors. I hate it when he says stuff like this. It makes me feel like the ground is cracking, like everything we have isn't stable. I know it's really just me being neurotic again, and I crush the feeling into my palms and the soles of my feet.

Is this the feeling the Brontës and other Victorian novelists were writing about? Mum used to get all the classics on Story-tape from the library when I was growing up, and it seemed like every one had a character in it going mad from love. Is this it? This intensity of emotion? This buzzing in my brain? How are you supposed to know?

42

I feel as out of place in an art cinema like this as I did in the bar last night. Everyone is sitting at a high metallic table intently working on their screenplay. Or they're discussing the merits of the Tarantino and Hitchcock posters that line the black walls while sipping espresso martinis on scarlet chesterfields. Or they're hiding somewhere in the crowd, perving on the barman, like my boyfriend is.

Spotting Tobbs in a busy space is an impossible task. I can never seek out his silhouette. His face blends into the others, like a background figure in an Old Masters painting: smudged, indistinct, unreadable.

All the same, I am twisting my head this way and that, looking for him, my face heating up as I catch strangers' eyes, when someone grabs my hand. I jump.

'Daniel!' I look down, sweaty and startled. A guy in a ratty old parka with messy brown hair is holding on to me. I tear my arm away; then something in my brain clicks: it's Tobbs. 'I was waving,' he says.

I blink a couple of times. Yes, it is him. The voice confirms it. The edge to it that makes my neck prickle.

'Sorry!' I say, trying to laugh, looking around for another stool. 'Sorry! I'm a bit . . . flustered!'

'There's no free seats,' Tobbs says, sipping his already half-finished IPA. 'I looked.'

'Oh, OK.' I broaden the search. There's one at the busy next table. I ask them if I can take it and continue with my excuse story. 'I was worried I was going to be late to meet you. And I was really looking forward to seeing you and now I'm all like this and . . .' I place the stool opposite Tobbs, shrug my jacket off, sit. 'Sorry.'

Tobbs takes another sip of beer. 'The doc's not on for another half an hour.'

'Oh yeah, true, true.' I shake my head like a wet dog. 'You're totally right.' Relief floods me, along with its best mate, embarrassment. I shouldn't have brought it up.

Tell him, a voice hisses in my head. *Tell him*.

'I'll get a drink,' I say, even though I can think of nothing worse.

Tobbs leaps up.

'No, I'll get it, boyo! I need another anyway – I've been here awhile.' He folds forward and kisses me. 'You look so cute when you're worried.'

He takes his glass and weaves through the crowd seamlessly, like a shadow, like a ghost.

I watch him ordering at the bar. There's an especially hunky barman – clearly a student, but massive, vast biceps and chest almost tearing open his skintight white T-shirt. This must be the one he'd said about in his message. He's got one of those dumb faces, like a model or an American frat bro, unremarkable if it wasn't on top of Chris Hemsworth's body. He could be Luke's brother.

My knee starts jumping up and down as I watch. Tobbs is saying something, and the Poor Man's Thor is laughing.

He's clever and funny and incisive and you never get much say with him. That's one of the things I liked about him when we first met. Whatever you say, he'll do his own thing. He doesn't cave to peer pressure or unreasonable landlords/friends, like I do.

He might not be traditionally handsome, but there's something about him. His features are sharp, eyes pretty and cat-shaped, lips thin and either tightly closed or tumbling open with opinions on politics in the Middle East. He's several inches taller than me and has a pretty epic jawline, usually thick with brown fuzz, which makes appearances basically everywhere

else, and I've come to really like it, wishing I was more hir-
sute to match. There's a triangle of it at the nape of his neck
that I think of as being very tender. I like to put my hand
there when we kiss and rub it, crackling the hair under my
fingers.

Though he isn't exactly skinnier than me, his frame hangs
looser, like a heavy coat on an old wire coat hanger. His shoulders have a jagged slope to them. He dresses somewhere between a dad and a teenager, in scuffed brown boat shoes, that
funny fit of jeans that's too baggy around the arse and too tight
around the thighs, and a series of striped pale-blue shirts that
swallow up what figure he has.

But I like this about him, too. He isn't self-consciously com-
posed like I am. He looks like he's just thrown on whatever, and
if you criticise it he doesn't care. Although that isn't exactly
true. Once, he asked me if I could tell if he'd been wearing the
same shirt for a week, to which I gently agreed it did kind of
smell, and he replied, 'You'd probably rather I was wearing a
peach bomber jacket or something media-y?' So I always just
say whatever he's wearing is nice. It is nice, really, that he isn't
a hipster like everyone else in London. He's different. He's an
original.

'God, I'd fuck the hell out of that hottie,' he says, placing two
IPAs down on the table. 'It's IPA you like, right?'

'*Tobbs*,' I say, 'do you have to?' My teeth are chattering for
some reason. I didn't mean to say this, it just came out.

'Oh, shit! It's IPA you *don't* like. Whoopsie!'

I glance at the barman. I have this strong desire to throw this
pint glass right at his big head.

'No, I mean, do you have to say that?'

Tobbs makes a face at me, sits down. The breath goes out of
my body.

'I'm just saying. Wouldn't you?' He sips the head off his ale. 'Don't be so vanilla.'

I say nothing. Instead, I sip my ale, which turns my stomach, but I don't want to start something else.

'I fucked a guy in the loos here once,' he says, as if this is a lovely topic we're both enjoying discussing. 'Best sex of my life.'

Just fucked a guy in here once, no biggie. He doesn't say it like he's trying to boast exactly – the tone is very neutral. All the same, my head starts buzzing, and I can actually feel the ground shaking beneath me.

'Mmm,' I reply, taking a deep glug of the horrible malty drink.

Around us, everyone else's conversations seem to be louder, more animated, more fun. Are they looking at us, thinking, *They don't seem to be having a very good time*? It feels like they are.

Tell him, the voice hisses, and something about this last comment makes me bold. I decide to risk it, and broach one of the topics I need to talk to him about.

'Hey, did you see my message?' I say.

'Which one? You sent about a hundred,' he laughs.

'About Laura.' I swallow. I feel like I'm bothering him. I desperately don't want to cry. 'About her, you know, evicting me?'

Tobbs's eyebrows shoot skyward, as if this is the most surprising news he's ever heard.

'Who?'

'Me.'

'Me who?'

'Me *me*! Laura's having a baby and throwing me out.'

'Fucking breeders. They're literally the worst. They always

like to have a little pet faggot around to show off to friends, but then, the minute you aren't fun anymore, you're dead to them.'

'Laura's not like that,' I say. Although it does feel exactly like that.

'You'll be all right.' Tobbs sounds like he isn't even really listening. He's bored of me, that's why. Just like Laura. 'It's not like you're getting bombed by ISIS.'

'I know that. I'm not saying I am. I just don't know what to do right now.'

'This is the problem with private landlords,' Tobbs says in his lecturer voice. 'You pay them all that money, and, ultimately, they have the power. I'd never pay a private landlord. At worst, I'd stay with a friend.'

'She is my friend.'

'Doesn't sound like it.'

'Look,' I say, trying to reason with him, 'I'd love to stay with another friend, but I don't have any that own their own property, do I?'

Silence. I try not to get snarky with him; he doesn't know how to deal with it. But that's easy for him to say when he owns his own flat.

'You'll find somewhere,' he says coldly, his face impassive, emotionless. I knew it: I've gone too far already. And I'm still only on Point 1.A of the agenda.

'Well, I was sort of hoping you'd offer me to stay at yours, for a bit.'

'Oh,' Tobbs says after way too long, blinking at me, startled. 'When do you have to move out? Next month?'

'ASAP. Like, now.'

'Fuuuuuuuuck.'

'Is that a no, then?'

47

'Thing is, Daniel, you know I like my own space. I get stressed out if I have people around me all the time.'

'Yeah.' My stomach twists. *But you're my boyfriend.* 'I know that. I just . . . I just have nowhere else to go, Tobbs.'

'What about SpareRoom?' He looks genuinely puzzled.

'OK, well, whatever, don't worry about it.'

'Hey,' he says, in his pillow-talk voice. 'Don't be so dramatic. It's not that bad.'

I'm finding it harder to breathe. My stomach is swirling all over the place.

'Yeah,' I say. 'Jacob might know someone with a spare room.'

'You always talk about Jacob,' Tobbs says immediately. He's jealous of Jacob, even though he's only met them a handful of times.

'They're my best friend,' I say.

'It's not primary school,' he says, and that's the end of that.

We go back to our IPAs. I hate it more with every sip. Now my head is throbbing.

'How was your week, anyway?' I say after a bit.

He's looking towards the bar.

'Back at the Factory,' he says, glancing at me.

'Oh, shit, how was that?'

Tobbs always makes it seem like it's against his human rights to actually be in the office. I can never work out if I'm weak for not being bothered that I, too, am in an office all day, or if he is just this kind of creative, misanthropic genius who needs to be left free to roam.

'Pretty fucking brutal, mate,' he says. 'When I'm locked in there, I remember how fucking privileged everyone is. If a bomb fell on that building, you'd wipe out half the Eton alumni.'

So Tobbs is kind of posh, but not like *real* posh. Well, he did go to Cambridge, then got a master's at City, then someone-he-went-to-school-with's-uncle got him an internship at *The Times*. He's also twenty-nine and has his own flat in Dalston. Once, I showed him a picture of my parents' fish-and-chip shop and he said, 'Oh, wow, is that building derelict?'

'That's how privilege works, I guess,' I say, really straining my brain to come up with something intelligent-sounding to atone for my emotional outbreak. 'Journalism is pretty tough to crack unless you've got money behind you.'

'Not if you work hard and have the skill,' Tobbs says.

The way he says it makes it seem like *I* am one of said journalists who *do not* have the talent or the skill. I don't like to talk about writing with him, because he flies to Israel and Lebanon to cover stories and I write articles like '5 Big Red Fruits to Give You That Bank Holiday Horn'.

'Yeah, true I suppose,' I say into the glass.

Tell him, the voice says in my head. *Tell him the other thing, Agenda Point 1.B.* God, he's going to flip. But I have to tell him. It's a health issue. I'm doing it *for* him.

I clear my throat.

'Hey, so, Tobbs, something weird happened the other day.'

'Was it actually weird? Or just weird for you?'

'Ha ha, no. I . . . um . . .' I don't know how to say it. 'You know how I said I was ill yesterday?'

'No? You never tell me anything.'

I messaged you, I say silently, but not aloud this time. I need to be extra delicate.

'Well, I got tested.'

'For what?' He doesn't seem bothered at all. In fact, he's looking at the barman again, which makes me bolder still.

'For, like – STIs.'

'So what? I get tested all the time.' Tobbs makes his lips *brrr* together dismissively.

I swallow hard. That's weird.

'Well, I haven't before. Like – ever.'

This was the Bombshell Moment. At least, I thought it was going to be, but Tobbs just waves a hand.

'Who cares, they put you on pills for everything now anyway.'

My hands fiddle with my pint glass. I can't tell if this is making it easier or worse.

'Yeah, well, here's the thing: I've got something.'

Now he stares directly at me. 'What have you given me?'

'No – nothing,' I shake my head. My pulse quickens in my neck. 'It's actually . . . it's the other way around. I don't know how, but . . . you've given *me* something.'

His eyes are as round as his flaring nostrils. He's absolutely furious. 'How the fuck do you know it's me, boyo? It could be anyone.'

I can feel my facial features make some tight, rapid, ugly dance.

'No, no, it couldn't. I've only slept with you for the last year, haven't I?'

His lips roll together, making the *brrr* sound again. '*Why*?'

I blink at him. The casual jollity of everyone else's laughter is especially grating right now.

My throat is so dry I can barely force out the words.

'What do you mean, why?'

The intensity of his stare is freaking me out. This must be the way a CEO looks at an intern who's dared to speak up during an all-staff meeting.

'Why have you only been sleeping with me?'

My forehead is sparking up like mad.

'Because we're in a relationship.'

'We never said we were monogamous. That's such an out-dated idea.' And he sips his drink like it's nothing. 'We aren't Luke and Laura.'

The ground feels like it's moving again. My fingers are now splayed out on the sticky tabletop to steady myself.

'Do you mean you've . . . been with other people?'

Tobbs nods like I'm an idiot. 'Obviously.'

'Why obviously?'

He shrugs.

'Monogamy is a heteronormative paradigm steeped in misogyny, designed to control. As queers, we get to define our own relationships.'

My head has bowed. I'm staring into my drink. I'm trying my hardest not to cry, or show I'm as upset as I am.

'I thought it was just you and me.'

'Hey.' He takes both my hands. My eyes dart around: it's OK, no one's looking. It amazes me how, even in this moment, I'm still checking to see if someone's going to gay-bash us. 'It is. *You're* my special guy. The others are just wanks with perks.'

'OK,' I say, quietly, barely at all. *Wanks with perks?!* 'But you know I've only ever been with you. Like *properly* been with.'

'Yes, you keep saying. And I've never understood it.' He lets go of my hands, leans back, whistles. 'This has got really heavy. It always gets really heavy with you. You're just, like, such an intense guy.'

'You've just told me you've been sleeping with loads of other guys while we've been together. How do you expect me to react?'

Tobbs holds out both his palms towards me, like he thinks I'm about to launch myself at him. 'I'm getting a really hostile vibe from you, boyo, and I just think blame is the last thing we need in the LGBT-Plus community right now.'

'Yeah, no.' I hear my voice slope around back to Devon, making me feel even more basic and provincial than usual. 'I'm not blaming anyone. You just could have said, is all.'

I hate the feebleness with which my words are coming out. Am I angry? Am I hurt? I genuinely don't know. One thing is clear, though: I can't lose him. I need to rein it in. Who's bothered by this sort of thing these days, anyway? We're all liberated, aren't we? It's fine. I'm chill.

'Look,' I say, leaning in, trying to take his hands, but he pulls them away. 'It's cool. I'm cool with it.' I wave a hand and make a sort of farting noise from my mouth. 'Monogamy is so over.'

As if the scene has changed, his messy eyes go cold. They look through me, like I'm a stranger. This always happens when we argue. He detaches; I cling harder.

'You're always making me feel bad, do you know that?' His voice comes out low and sinister, crawling across the floor, over the chairs and tables and circling around me. 'I always feel under attack with you, and I don't think I can do it anymore. You're basically gaslighting me, and that's a form of abuse, Daniel.'

'Tobbs, I—' I try to start, but he cuts me off.

'I think I'm gonna see the doc by myself.'

My head flicks up.

'Wait – what?'

'I think you should go.'

I just want him to hold me, to give me some reassurance. Out of desperation, I say: 'But what about the party?'

'If I wanted a ticket for Straight Pride, I'd get one free from work. Boyo, I think you should go. I can't do this anymore.'

'Wait, are you dumping me?'

'I need some time alone.'

I am fraught with panic. 'Do you mean this evening, or this period of our lives?'

At this horrible moment, the table starts vibrating. For a second, I think it's the ground falling apart beneath me, or the curtains coming down on this year-long romance.

'Your mum's ringing again,' Tobbs says, downing the last of his pint.

'Oh, it's OK,' I scrabble for the black rectangle. 'I can just call her later.'

'Don't be disrespectful. Talk to her.'

He's already got his parka under his arm and is looking for the right screen to head towards.

I stare from him to the phone, where it's zzz-zzz-zzz-ing on my palm. My chest is so tight I can barely breathe, let alone speak to my parents, pretending everything is normal.

He swoops down and kisses me on the mouth. Though it's brief, my spine melts. He's an amazing kisser.

'Bye, boyo.'

He turns and slips away, with that funny swoopy walk where he sways from side to side with each stride, like a sprig in a breeze. And I feel my heart break a little.

SIX

Sitting alone at the table, I stare into the nothing for a while. I don't cry. I don't even really feel anything.

It takes me a while to notice my phone's stopped ringing. Before I can unlock it and call back, MA & PA HOME pops up on the screen again. They always ring twice.

I look at it for another few seconds. I can't quite get my head around what I'm supposed to do. Then, all in a rush, I answer.

'Hi, family.' My voice cracks.

'No, that's the right button, Mary,' I hear my dad's muffled West Country voice say.

'Don't you take that tone with me, Joseph Michael Scudd. I'm not an old-age pensioner yet!' Mum snaps back, sounding broader than ever.

There are several electronic tapping noises, and a buzzing.

'Can you hear us, son of mine?' Dad's voice echoes as though from the bottom of a well.

'Sort of,' I say blankly.

'We've got you on the speakerphone.'

'Yes, I realised.'

'Ha ha! Good week at work?'

'I s'pose.'

More electronic tapping.

'Would you leave it alone, Mary!' Dad's voice reverbs. 'I'm trying to talk to the lad.'

'If you want a quiet, obedient little wife, Joseph, I suggest you order one from Taiwan!' Mum says with even more vitriol.

'Mum!' I hiss. 'You can't say that!'

'Oh, now you're at it, are you?' she says.

'See the Spurs game yesterday?' Dad says, as if the rest of this interaction hasn't happened.

'I was at work,' I reply in the same voice I always use when he tries to engage me in football chat.

'Didn't they put it on?'

'Who?'

'The CEO.'

'Did the CEO of my company put the football match on the TV at the office yesterday? Is that what you're asking me?'

'Yes.'

'No, Dad, she didn't.'

'Bastard.'

'The CEO is a woman, Dad. Sophia LeSwann. Remember I sent you that news story about the embezzlement?'

'Bastard woman.'

'I expect you're busy, aren't you?' Mum pipes in, wildly loud and muffled at the same time. 'Living your fast-paced London lifestyle.'

'Not really, no.' I almost laugh, thinking how I'm not really 'out', now that my boyfriend has vanished. 'I was just having a drink with Tobbs.'

Mum tuts like she knew it, she just knew it.

'Who?' That's Dad.

'Tobbs,' I say. 'My BOYFRIEND.' God, my nerves are fraying, just like Jane Eyre's. Where are my smelling salts?

'Oh yes,' he says. It sounds like he's rustling papers, although I don't know what papers he would have on the living-room sofa, which is where they always call me from.

'You can ask me about him if you like,' I say.

'All right,' Dad replies. Then says nothing.

'How are his parents?' Mum attempts, after a pause.

'I don't know. I don't know his parents. And he doesn't see them much, because he doesn't get along with them.'

'Oh dear, dear. That's a sorry state of affairs.'

'They alkies or something?' This is my father's attempt at humour.

'Yes, actually.'

'Bugger,' Dad says. 'That is a bugger.'

'I've told you this before.'

'Yes, well I can't keep up with all your friends.'

'He's not my *friend*. He's my *boyfriend*,' I say. Although, as I say it, I wonder if it's even true anymore.

'So you've been out with him? That's nice, isn't it, Joe?' Mum says, trying to scoot over everything. 'This, then, maybe explains why you've failed to respond to my many, many urgent voicemails.'

Urgent voicemails? Had she left them? With a panicked feeling, I recall the missed calls from last night. I've really been in my own head recently.

'Shit, is everything OK? Has someone died?'

'Daniel! Watch your language, please!' Mum scolds.

'Dad just said "bugger"!'

'That's different!'

'How is it different?'

'Because.' Silence. A sort of scuffling noise, as if she's trying to hang up. 'Anyway, I'll spare you the bother of having to listen to my voice and just tell you.'

'Bit ironic,' I say.

Either she doesn't get it or she ignores me, because she carries on.

'We – your pa and I – were wondering what your Christmas plans are?'

'Mother, it's only just been Halloween.'

'Which is why I'm getting things organised now. We've got lives as well, you know, Daniel.'

'Your ma's been on it since June,' Dad chuckles. I hear some loud, crackly sound, and I know Mum's just smacked him on the arm. His chuckles intensify.

'We're planning on having some more of the family over, you see.' I can tell Mum's saying this through barely moving, aggravated lips.

'Oh God,' I say. If you think Mum and Dad are a lot, you wait until you meet the others. 'Is Old Dave out of prison, then?'

'It wasn't prison, Daniel,' Mum replies curtly. 'Uncle David was under house arrest. That's very different.'

'Apparently.' Dad chuckles again.

'Anyway,' Mum says after another audible thwack, 'we wanted to check if you're bringing your *friend* for Christmas? And is he vegan or something stupid like that?'

'What else happens over Christmas?' I hear myself parrot Tobbs's exact tone.

'Joy and togetherness with your loving family, you cheeky boy.' Mum's really on the warpath today. 'And tell Jacob him, Amadi, and the girls are welcome on Boxing Day, as always since . . . you know.'

'Yes, Mum, I know.'

'Well it must be hard for them, this time of year, is all I'm saying.'

'Yes, Mum, I know.'

57

'Have you been seeing Jacob recently, lad?' chimes in Dad.

Even though Jacob is just about the gayest person you've ever met, my parents have always been mad about them. They are arty. They are eccentric. And they always compliment my mum's dodgy blonde dye jobs she gets for free off her mate Linda, who is a veterinary nurse with coiffeuse aspirations.

'I saw them last night. And I'm having lunch with them on Monday.'

'Oh, does he have a friend, too?' Mum says, with effort.

'No. Jacob's non-binary, Mum. We've had this chat. They don't like gender-specific pronouns.'

'Oh yes, it's all about that now, isn't it?' she sighs.

'You're not going to work, then?' Dad says, but in a vacant voice.

'Yes, Dad, I'm going to work. Jacob's coming to the office for lunch.'

'And they'll just let him in?'

'THEY, DAD. AND YES. THEY AREN'T A TERRORIST.'

Several heads turn to me and cut their eyes. Sometimes I forget there are certain words you can't just shout out in central London.

'Oh, does he work near you now? Isn't that lucky!' Mum says, her voicemail-induced rage totally forgotten. Growing up, I often wondered if she'd have preferred to swap me for Jacob. 'He's such a sweet boy. I always liked him— bollocks, I mean, a sweet boy *or* girl.'

'No, they're a performance artist, remember? They're doing an artists' workshop nearby for the week,' I say.

'A what?' Another concept that's beyond my mother.

'GO ON, YOU BEAUT!' Dad yells.

I realise now why he sounds vacant. He's lost interest and is watching the football catch-up. He's probably got the sports pages of the paper open on his lap, too, accounting for some of the extra crackling. This is routine behaviour: often he calls me, then gets immediately bored. It's like he just wants to check I'm still alive, but doesn't actually require any of the details.

'JOSEPH!' Mum yells. 'We're still on the phone to your son and heir! Would you stop acting like you were raised in an outhouse?'

'I bloody well weren't,' Dad mutters.

'Anyway, I've got to go,' I say. 'Love you.'

There was the usual pause.

'Oh yes, Daniel, you, too,' Mum just about forces out.

'We lost anyway,' Dad says, as the line goes dead.

I sit and breathe deeply for a bit. Then get my jacket and go out into the street, feeling like a total loser that my boyfriend has left me to have a call about nothing with my parents. It isn't even properly dark yet.

As I walk to the Tube, I can really taste the pollution in the air. It's clogging my throat, filling my lungs. So many people are out, in fancy dress again, heading into restaurants, filling the pavements, arms linked, laughing with mates at in-jokes. All of them enjoying the time they're spending together. I realise I hate each and every one of them.

The Tube carriage is crammed. I wonder how bad the air pollution is down here, because my chest is getting tighter and tighter. *Only three more stops*, I say to myself. *Then you can get out into the slightly less polluted air.*

Pressed right up against me is a girl with a high ponytail sucking face with a finance bro in a miniature shiny suit and messily loosened tie. They're so close I can smell the apple sours they've been necking. They're so close I'm basically having a threesome with them. *Just like Tobbs has been doing.*

As I'm climbing up the steps at Brixton, my vision goes

dotty. My heart is thudding like crazy, my breathing coming really fast. I'm having to hold on to the metal railing and stop, bent over. The next step seems impossible. They really need to clean up the air in this damn city. My whole body is trembling.

I'm gripped by the most terrible sensation of dread. It's like I'm falling towards it. I just know it's going to happen. The worst thing imaginable. *It's over, it's over, it's over.*

'You OK, fella?'

One of the Tube staff, a middle-aged Jamaican man with a paunch and a kind, gap-toothed smile, leans forward at my elbow, peering at me.

'You on something?'

'No, no.' I try to say, *It's the air.* But I can't get it out.

'You need help?'

The man is holding on to my shoulders. He's really got a very kind face. It's so nice of him to be concerned. I could be on crack – he doesn't know.

'No, no,' I gasp again, but he's sat me down on the top step of the Tube entrance and is beckoning behind him. A younger woman with an eyebrow piercing and neon clothing far too big for her appears beside him with a paper cup.

'Blimey, he looks funny,' she says very loudly and hands me the cup.

'You sick?' the man says.

'I'm just,' I half say, 'I've got something' – I gulp down the water – 'something wrong with my balls.'

The woman looks at the man, then turns around and walks back down into the station.

'Sit here a minute,' he says, resting a hand on my shoulder. 'You'll be OK. You'll see.'

I sit here for a little while with him and listen to how this also 'happens' to his oldest daughter, apparently. His name is

Maurice (but pronounced Mohr-EESE).

'She lets things get on top of her,' he says. 'She's a sweet, sensitive girl. Too sensitive for this world, we say sometimes.'

I'm not sure how long I'm here for, but the crowds keep coming past, getting thinner and thinner. Lots of faces stare. Some scowl – they probably think I'm some drunk young professional, gentrifying and then vomiting on their area. I suppose they're half right. After my heart rate slows and my breathing clears, I try to get out of there as quickly as possible.

Embarrassment returns, and I gingerly get up. Maurice looks not so sure I'm ready to go, but I say cheers a lot and walk slowly home, making a mental note to get him a thank-you card and tweet at TfL about how great he's been. I know I'll forget to do both.

SEVEN

Jay, I can't do it

You've got this, Little Edie, truly, I believe in you

I can't believe he just dumped me
Or did he even?
I genuinely don't know!

**Babe, stay strong, just make an appearance then hide in
your room
Or better still come to mine and get off your nut on slagtinis**

MY NUT??

**No!
No, I didn't mean that!
Look, sweet angel, I have to go**

Can you believe he dumped me??

Babe

Get it together
Sack them off and come to my party instead
There'll be genuine high-quality queers for you to have your
weird, stilted conversation with

> *Bit harsh*
> *And I can't, can I?*
> *I promised Laura I'd be here*

Danielle, you need to liberate yourself from the shackles of
the straight world
Seriously

> *I know, I know*

Look, I gotta go OK
I have to get this Thatcher wig on and you know this lady's
NOT for turning
Go out there and show those straights you aren't ashamed
of who you are

> *I'm not ashamed!*

Love you, angel
XOXO Gossip Gay

> *K*
> *Bye Jay*
> *Have a good night*
> *Love you too*
> *XXX*

Fortunately, I have time before everyone arrives to lie in bed and cry my eyes out. I do some deep breathing as well, which is when Laura comes in wearing just her underwear and thinks I'm at it again. After establishing I'm not, she sits on the edge of the bed and says, 'Have you boys had a widdle fight?'

'He just has a deadline,' I say into the pillow.

'Oh, great! So no drama tonight, then.' She smiles. 'Is that what you're wearing?'

I look down at my pastel-blue T-shirt and navy jeans.

'What else would I wear?'

'It's a Halloween party, Danny-boo. Everyone will be dressed up. I'm going to wear The Dress.' She gasps at her own gall. The Dress is what she calls this black fifties cocktail number Luke bought her for her birthday last year under strict instructions from her mum. 'Can't you wear something flashier? Or, like – fetishy-er?'

'Fetishy-er' isn't a word I would imagine ever hearing Laura utter.

'Fetishy-er? Like what?'

She scrunches up her face. 'Ooh, what about this!'

Her cream thighs dance out of sight, then back again. A garment is thrust towards me. I take it and hold it out, trying to work out what it is.

'No, no, like this,' she fusses.

She presses it to my neck and tries to spread out both arms so I can see the full glory. It's a black sheer shirt with narrow sequinned stripes. Not even a nipple could hide in this and certainly not a belly roll.

'Umm . . .'

'I know, I know, it's a bit *out there*,' she says, waving a hand. 'But I think you can pull it off.'

I gently fold my hands around the shirt's shoulders and push it away. The shirt resists. Laura's eyes meet mine. The twinkle in them is unnerving.

'It's just, it's not really my style, Laur . . .'

Her eyes roll and the twinkle falls out.

'Oh, come on, Dan-Dan! Do it for me – it's a special night! And it'll look fan-dabby-dosey!'

'Laura, no.'

'Go on, Dan, do it for me. It's our last big hurrah,' she says and then stares at me for an uncomfortably long period of time.

'OK, I'll wear the shirt.'

'Oh, yay! Great. Love you, Danny-boo.' And she's hugging me. 'They'll be here in twenty minutes, OK?' She darts back towards the living room, turning in the doorway. 'Ooh, now you can chat to Zain!'

—

Quivering from the bones out, I creep around the corner from my room to the living room. Laura is holding court with all her uni friends, sedately sipping home-made cocktails and nibbling on sea-salt Kettle Chips. The beautiful street lamp that is Simone is gesticulating with her mojito in the centre of the circle.

'And my brother was like, "Well, you're just saying you don't believe in marriage because you live in London and think you're better than everyone else",' pointing it firmly at her invisible brother's chest. 'And I was like, "Um, that's not it at all, Michael Roy Xanadu Davidson, it's actually that I don't abide by your outdated patricidal standards of love." Why should Sim and I *have* to get married – know what I mean?'

'Yeah,' Simon agrees, pretty drunkenly, his smirk hiding whatever he's really feeling. 'Wake up, sheeple!'

Simone makes a face at him. 'Simmy, that's my brother.'

The electric fingertips are out with relish, zapping my temples like Winifred Sanderson. I swallow hard and try to embody some of Jacob's confidence, but I'm not sure how to find an inroad with this conversation. Possibly because the Sims are dressed as low-effort Khaleesi and Khal Drogo, and still look violently stunning. Possibly because everyone is discussing which financial firms their skiing friends work for. And possibly because it's hard to speak when you're sucking your stomach in and your heart is breaking in your chest.

Plastic witches and ghosts hang in swathes across the walls. A pumpkin grins on the nibbles table in the bay window. The affair is mild. I imagine Jacob is projecting horror films in their house, or staging the prom scene from *Carrie*, only told through the medium of contemporary dance. Highly political queer people will be laughing at something topically satirical while wearing pleather. Someone will certainly be naked. Tobbs would love it.

I have the final sip of my G 'n' T, which I've been nursing for a while, fearing the moment it's gone and I don't have a prop anymore. I try to remind myself: they're all nice people. Simone is always very interested in my sex life. Simon is just sort of there, like a dog.

Is that how people view Laura and Luke? Laura's having a party with her massive, bored Doberman. How do they view me? As their gay little poodle in a handbag? *Oh, look, the L's have still got Danny, I wonder who he's humping* . . .

'Wait.' Laura holds out both hands. 'Your brother's middle name is *Xanadu*?'

Simone rolls her stunning grey eyes.

'You know my dad was that movie exec?' The circle of heads nod. Simone's dad basically ran the British film industry for the whole of the eighties. 'It's just him and Mum being twats. Anyway, we had a *massive* blowout about it, and now I'm leaving all his WhatsApps on "Read".'

She downs the last of the mojito and stares at us triumphantly,

Daenerys stepping out of the fire naked with her dragon eggs.

'Guys are so reductive,' Georgia says, sighing, her arm looped leisurely through Gerry's. Gerry is her boyfriend of six years. They've come as Kurt Cobain and Courtney Love, which is kind of funny, because they're getting married next August. I'm invited to the evening do at Shoreditch Town Hall, but not the ceremony.

'Yeah, look it up,' I say, to which no one responds. The air is tense around my face, and I wish I hadn't said anything at all, I wasn't here at all. I sip from the empty glass just to do something.

Straddling one arm of the sofa opposite, Luke inhales a Corona in one tilt-back of the bottle. He's in the shiny grey suit he wears to the recruitment firm, only with blood applied minimally to the throat, to match Laura. It strains around every part of him, particularly the upper arms, thighs and crotch. He adjusts his bulge for the eight hundredth time, and I try not to look, the fuzz of electricity singeing as I imagine the way Tobbs would gawp. Laura sips at a Shloer.

'Would you ever get married, Danny?'

In horror, I realise Simone is staring at me. She really is very beautiful, like a cardboard cut out of a celebrity.

The ring of couples stare at me. Why does this have to happen tonight, of all nights?

'Well.' I cough several times, tipping the empty glass to my mouth again, causing the wedge of lime to slip up against my lips and somehow find its way out onto the Union Jack rug. Everyone's eyes slide after it, then back to my face, awaiting an answer. 'Well,' I say, wiping my lips. 'Yes. Yes, I'd like to.'

'But don't you think it's an outdated form of imprisonment designed to control, rather than empower?' Georgia leaps on me immediately. She's doing a PhD.

Laura's hand goes to Luke's forearm.

'Well,' I say again, 'we've only been able to get married for a few years, so it seems all right to me.' I really don't want to be forced into saying the words 'gay marriage' – the us-and-them dynamic is already at its most tangible. Well, *me*-and-them. I can feel my vowels slipping around all over the place, alcohol and nerves forcing an embarrassing West Country appearance. No one can take someone who sounds like a farmer seriously, not at a bougie gathering like this.

For a second, the couples do not react. They blink at me blankly.

'Oh yes, yes,' says Simone, twigging what I mean.

'At least now you can get bored of each other and stop having sex within six months, like the rest of us,' Luke says in a sudden, unexpected display of wit.

'Lukey!' Laura cries, smacking him on his big, big chest.

He winks at me. I sort of half smile back, then fumble for the nearest bowl of Kettle Chips. I can't tell if he's done that to help me out or as an opportunity just to be an arsehole to Laura. It's hard to tell with him.

'No, no, the gays are all in open relationships,' Georgia says firmly, as the shrieks and laughter abate. 'My cousin Zac and his boyf, Martin, are always shagging around. They say it keeps it fresh. Right, Danny?'

For some reason, I nod. I NOD. And I agree with them, even though I seem to be the last person in the world to realise this fundamental truth. Monogamy? How passé! How is it Georgia knows more about gay relationships than me? How is it *every-one* knows more about gay relationships than me?

'Sounds pretty good!' Simon says like an overly familiar uncle, cheersing the other boys in the circle, all of whom are now riled into activity. Like stags, they take up the fraternity gesture and return it. Luke yells, 'Oi! Oi!'

'Well, my hairdresser has, like, three actual relationships on the go *and* a husband,' Simone goes on. 'They even have two kids together, and the other boyfriends all come round theirs on Sundays for play dates. It's like a big gay crèche . . .'

This continues for a while, until they get so caught up on how liberated and carefree the gays are they stop asking for my input altogether. I can't hack it anymore, so slip away to the bathroom to get another drink. No one notices me go.

Luke has filled the bath with ice, and an array of bottles merrily bob away there. I riffle through for a bottle of Bombay Sapphire I'd seen earlier. The asparagus fern on the edge of the bath is going yellow and needs more light, so I swap it with a small fig tree on the windowsill.

'Wouldn't expect to find you with your head in a bush.'

I am somehow tangled in its wispy tendrils, and try to free myself.

'Hi, Zain.'

He's leaning against the door frame with a glass, unscrewing the bottle of Bombay Sapphire. His incredible jawline really pops at the centre of its shroud of matching black; he's still wearing his black leather biker jacket and enormous black scarf, making it look like his head is floating above the darkness. The single gold hoop in his ear catches the light, but the nasty twinkle in his deep-brown eyes is brighter still. No costume, of course.

'Hi, Danny.' He pours the gin into his glass, barely looking at me. The light bounces off his shaven skull.

I think he's going to ask me how I am, out of politeness, when I remember how he has never once, not in five years, asked me how I am.

'How are you?' I say, trying to force him to reciprocate.

'Oh yeah, fucking fine. Is there ice?'

'Laura told me your play got taken on by the National Theatre?'

In a swish of black that fills the room, he reaches past me into the bath. He pops cubes one by one into his glass.

'Oh yeah, sick, no? What about tonic?'

I nod towards the bath while biting back the urge to ask him how things are, re. his break-up. But it doesn't really matter, because when he finds the tonic, he turns and says, 'Laura says you're single again.'

Points to Zain: One Massive Bitchy One.

I always shrink to nothing when he's around. Why do I make myself smaller to make him more comfortable? I don't even like him, and I sure as hell don't owe him the truth. So fuck it.

'No, I actually have a really great boyfriend,' I say, much more confidently than I'd ever speak to anyone else. 'We just had our one-year anniversary.'

'Oh yeah?' Zain glances up at me as he pours the tonic. Challenge accepted.

'Yeah. His name's Tobbs.'

Zain's lip dances.

'Posho?'

I swallow. 'He's, like, a journalist. He covers big stories in Syria and the Middle East.'

'Pretty dangerous out there.' Zain's now screwing the yellow cap back on the bottle. 'That BBC journo got killed last week by an unexpected ambush. Legs and arms blown forty feet from his body.'

'I didn't hear about that.'

He stares at me. 'They never found the head.' Raises his glass, and drinks.

Points to Zain: A Billion Humongous Evil Ones.

'Nice top,' he says, but in a tone that really means, *That is the ugliest effing top I've ever seen.*

'No one's ever said that to me before,' I reply without missing a beat. Sometimes I amaze myself at my own wit.

'No doubt!' he snorts, and somehow the ball is back in his court. 'Your whole vibe reads *bottom*.'

I'm very aware I don't have a drink to swirl like a gay Bond villain. All the same, I smooth down this stupid Liza Minnelli top, suck my stomach in again and put my hands in my pockets. I'm nonchalant, I'm breezy. I go in for the kill.

'Sorry about Rufaro. Getting dumped bites.'

Try as he might, Zain cannot hide the flash of anger that momentarily splits his eyeballs. Then he's all throwaway hand gestures.

Points to me: Uno. But it's a good one. I might actually be winning.

'His schedule was impossible to work with.' He gives me the Lucille Bluth version of a conspiratorial stare: cold as hell, the actual opposite of what it's pretending to be. 'Dancers. You know?'

'Yeah, I heard they're a nightmare,' I say. 'Total narcissists, too.'

'But if that body's ripped and that D's good?' He shrugs. 'Know what I mean? Or are you more into guys who, like, play World of Warcraft?'

'Tobbs is more of an intellectual,' I hear my voice say, drunk on its own lies, unable to stop. 'But not like a stuffy one, one that really cares about the world, you know?'

'Ohh,' Zain says, looking wickedly over the rim of his glass. 'A do-gooder. They're the worst. They cheat on you – but they do their recycling.'

Points to Zain: Another Fucking Billion.

'Tobbs isn't like that. He's just a really good, decent guy.' The façade is cracking. 'And he's super-interesting and sexy.'

'Mm-hmm.' Zain takes a big swig. As he does, his jacket gapes open. I nearly lose my mind. Under it, he's wearing a sheer black top with sequinned stripes. 'Anyway, nice chatting, babe.' He grins and waltzes out.

I'm left there, holding on to the edge of the bath, pulsating with rage. Jacob says gay guys are like cats: if you put two in a room, they'll either scrap or have sex. I've always thought that's a pretty *reductive* thing to say, but maybe it's true.

There are whoops and cheering from the living room. A burst of electricity jolts across my forehead, and I panic that Zain has made some comment about me to the room. I'm suddenly very aware that I'm hiding in the bathroom by myself again, like at every party. I grab the Bombay Sapphire, pour myself a big shot and neck it before heading through to the living room.

Everyone's standing around Laura, clapping, like she's won an Oscar. Luke's standing back, by the curtains, doing his best smug fiancé cosplay. I pause in my step: Zain is actually hugging Laura, her hands are clasped around his head, her eyes squashed shut tearily, pressed between his cheek and his shoulder. I thought I was her gay best friend?

A swell of emotion blooms in my stomach, rises up through my chest and into my throat. Everything is rushing towards me all at once: me getting evicted, Laura entering that next stage of life, Zain cutting me down, and Tobbs – oh, Tobbs! Everything. Shit, I'm going to cry.

'To Laura and Luke!' Simone cries.

'To Laura and Luke!' everyone intones, raising their glasses.

'The first of our group to get chained to a child!' Georgia adds, and everybody laughs, except for Laura, who is still crying into Zain's shoulder. For people who hate conventional marriage, these guys seem pretty into marriage and babies.

I cheers. I drink. I stand by the wall wishing I was anywhere but here. Not since the school playground have I felt this alone. I didn't fit in then, and I still don't now. Not here, not anywhere. Not with the married straight people, or the chic city gays like Zain.

Jacob will be thrilled, though. I've been liberated from the straight world, whether I like it or not.

EIGHT

The only thing that makes Monday morning bleaker than it already is, is waking up to remember you've been dumped, and then getting waved off to work by your friends who are evicting you.

'Have a lovely day, Danny-boo,' Laura says, kissing me on the forehead, then going back to the sideboard, where she's finishing off packed lunches for them both.

'Fuck 'em up, big boy!' Luke yells from the sofa, where he's leaning forward tensely in the same suit as Saturday night, trying to get in the last bit of yet another game.

'Found anywhere yet, Dan-Dan?' Laura says, almost like it's by accident.

My hand is on the latch. I don't turn.

'No. Not yet.'

'You can check out SpareRoom on lunch,' she suggests helpfully, nodding and smiling.

'Yeah.'

Does she not think that's what I'd spent all of yesterday doing and that's why I couldn't come and watch her mate playing Quidditch on Clapham Common?

'Want me to ask around some of my friends? I think Zain

might be looking for someone, now Rufaro's moved out—'

'Thanks. But I'm on it.'

'It's just . . . the cot's arriving tomorrow.'

I turn and stare at her. She looks genuinely troubled.

'I mean, we can keep it flat-pack in the living room. No pressure.'

'EAT IT, YOU SOUTH AFRICAN BUM BOY!' Luke screams.

'It's cool,' I say. 'Honestly. I'll sort something out.'

'Thanks, Danny.'

'Have a good day, guys,' I say, and leave.

———

The bus is packed, and I end up spilling my oat-milk latte down my shirt. Typical. *Why am I such an idiot?* I'm checking my phone for a text from Nurse Jackie to find out which STI I have and forget about the paper cup. What a fun little waiting game this is.

I wonder what Tobbs is doing now? *Probably already fucking someone else, someone less neurotic than me.*

I get to Oxford Circus, squeeze off the bus, through the street of commuters, across the lobby and into the lift, where I stand shoulder to shoulder with people I see every day but never speak to. We're on the fifth floor. The frosted, blocky letters CULTRD part as I walk through the glass doors into the office, revealing the half-pipe that takes up much of the space, the graffiti wall and neon signs. When I started here three years ago, I remember this feeling of excitement rise in my stomach as the doors slid open. I couldn't believe I had a real writing job in a tall building in the city. But, as Tobbs liked to point out, what I write is just paid-for content bullshit, not real journalism. It's just capitalism for the sake of it. It doesn't mean anything.

To say I'm not feeling chatty is an understatement. I head straight to my computer and start busying myself. I want to just keep my head down and get my work done in peace, then go home, run a bath and listen to *Blue Smoke* from start to finish.

'Oh my God, Danny, I'm so glad you're here!'

No such luck.

I minimise the eight SpareRoom tabs in a manic spasming of the index finger.

Callum is already perched on my desk, just left of my elbow. Gorgeous Callum. The fresh-faced twenty-two-year-old media grad with the Cardiff lilt and attitude stolen from *Beauty and the Beast*'s Gaston – if Gaston stumbled out of Shoreditch House every Friday night with his bulging arm around a different cherubic twink. He's the video editor, making me his unofficial boss. Not that I've ever disciplined him on his perpetual underperformance.

Callum sets me with a concerned stare.

'Danny, will you be honest with me about something serious?'

I sigh deeply.

'Of course, Cal. Is it the "Best Sunday Roasts for Your Pets" feature?'

'No, no.' His refrigerator-white teeth reflect how shitty I feel. 'It's just: does it look like I have four buttocks? I'm wearing a jockstrap, aren't I.'

Trying to be professional, I briefly glance at them. They look even higher and rounder than usual. His neck is twisted so he can still be in view of his perfect posterior, squeezed, as it is, into a pair of ripped skinny jeans. Everything Callum wears is two sizes too small. His friends are identical to him. He's always showing me pictures of their week-long benders on Mykonos.

'You look great, Cal.'

He tries to twist around the other way, flailing his arms like an impossibly muscular baby.

'Really?'

'Really.'

'Got a date again tonight, haven't I.'

'Who's the lucky fella, James Dean?' I ask.

Callum narrows his eyes. 'That's not his name.'

I wave a hand. 'Of course not.'

'He's some rich sugar daddy, isn't he,' he continues, unfazed. 'I like 'em when they can treat you proper. Proper old-fashioned romance, you know?'

The irony isn't lost on me that last week he merrily sent around an all-staff email asking people to subscribe to his OnlyFans for 'exclusive cheeky content! 😜'.

'What happened to that barrister?' I ask.

Callum rolls his eyes. 'He had to be up at five every day to make all those cappuccinos, and I'm just not an early riser, you know?' Then he catches himself and does a little smile. 'Well, I can be, in a naughty way.'

'So he was a *barista*, not a barrister?'

'That's the one!' he laughs, all dimples and stunning blue eyes. 'I always say it wrong. Honestly, Dan, you're so clever, I bet you're a laugh on dates.' He runs his fingers across his gelled-rigid little blond quiff. 'I never know what to say, so I normally just take my shirt off, to be honest. That usually works.'

As so often happens, I automatically look at his huge chest. I can actually see both nipples through the fabric of his navy River Island polo neck.

'Sure.'

He leans in conspiratorially, but keeps the volume of his voice the same. 'And just between you and me, don't tell anyone I'm going on the date.'

This sudden modesty strikes me as amusing.

I smile back softly. 'My lips are sealed. Have a great time.'

Callum grins like I've just given him a gold star in show-and-tell. 'Thanks, Dan!'

And he bounces off in his box-fresh Reebok Classics.

Callum is perpetually asking people how he looks, and then flexing. He's like a nervous puppy that chugs protein shakes. Every man and every woman who has ever seen him then comes over to me to ask if he's single. Callum, the most basic, cookie-cutter gay.

Tobbs would like him, I think. *Big boy like that. Mmm, lovely. Slurp, slurp!*

I crush my eyes shut and try to breathe through the feeling.

Just get your work done and go home. That's all you need to do today.

'Morning, Scudders!'

Oh no, not another one.

If anything's going to push me over the edge, it's Stan, the creative director. He's bounding past. 'Scudders' is what he calls me. It's just, like, a *thing* he does.

He points at the brown stain down the front of my shirt. 'Ooh, had an accident? Forget to douche?'

I throw up my hands in mock shock. 'When will I learn, ehy?'

When have I ever used the word 'ehy' before?

Stan punches me in the arm. Why do straight guys love to do this so much? 'Gotta douche, Scudders. Otherwise, your breakfast is lunch.'

I shudder but try not to show it.

'Speaking of, how does my arse look in my new threads?' Why is everyone in this office constantly asking me this? He pivots his cheeks towards me like a coquettish baboon.

As always, Stan looks like he's been dressed by his fourteen-year-old son to go to a Kendrick Lamar gig. The way his paunch looms beyond his peach bomber jacket never ceases to unnerve me. It reminds me of a shark's nose lurking behind a coral reef. At least, unlike some men his age, he's embraced male pattern baldness, and shaved it all off. Not that it really matters, because he's seldom seen without his matching peach cap emblazoned with 'boss' in rhinestones. His Adidas hi-tops reflect the same colour scheme. If aliens made up what they thought a 'young person' looked like, it would be Stan.

'I'd tap that!' I say in a strangled cry. Stan absolutely loves it when the office gays give him attention. Just the way Luke loves it when he catches me glancing at his massive wang flopping around in his boxers. It doesn't stop him making inappropriate comments to every woman in the office, too. Last week, he called Nadia from PR 'an exotic little madam'.

'You'll have to fight it out with the missus, mate,' Stan says, winking, then turns to the office, where his employees are mostly not working. Instead, they are: arriving late with enormous coffees and enormous bags under their eyes. They are: chatting by the Newquay surf kitchenette while peeling open protein-ball breakfast snacks. They are: in the Brixton Skatepark 'breakout' space, comparing whose trainers are the most vintage. 'Excited for another week at one of *TimeOut*'s Top Fifty Art and Culture Apps, snowflakes?' he belts, arms crossed, feet spread wide, in a pose I imagine he's copied from a Justin Bieber music video. 'Remember, subscription rates have been down the prison shower drain in the last quarter, and our parent company, Dying Swann PLC, are getting a *little* antsy about it. Which is why I've entered us in a few upcoming awards . . .' He takes out his giant phone and scrolls. Tupac smiles meekly from the back of the case. 'Most Subversive Voice in Tech Award. Highest Third-Party Data Harvesting Award. The British Journalism Awards—'

'Shitfuck!' I say, without meaning to. 'The British Journalism Awards?'

Every head pivots to me.

'Got a problem, Scudders? Come on, outside!' Stan's got me in a headlock, knuckles rapping across my skull. 'I'm just joshing with you, princess! Yes, the British Journalism Awards.'

I struggle free and straighten my collar.

'But – but – how can we be nominated?' I stutter, hearing Tobbs's voice in my head. 'We're not journalists.'

'Who says we are not?' Stan cries. 'We're storytellers. Soothsayers. The Shakespeares of our era. He wrote for money, and so do we – while drawing in new Cult Members and pushing them through to our business partners. "Drink the COOL-aid. Join the CULT." That's what we're all about.' He starts walking in a little circle, hands held out wide like a benevolent Charles Manson. 'We want the truth from all of you. That's why we hired you. We want to hear your unique stories – that's what our users resonate with. Troy!' Stan points forefingers like pistols at Troy from Development as he rams a protein ball into his mouth. 'You identify as black, right?'

Troy starts coughing violently.

'Um – yep.'

'Safe, bruv. That's just the sort of perspective we want here. Modern, diverse stories. We love that at CULTRD. We champion it. Nothing at CULTRD is anyone else's problem, so if you have an idea, it could be our next big thing! Think real, in-depth storytelling. Really sliding in under the surface of people's lives. And I know you cool cats and kittens have what it takes to produce the stellar content we need to get nominated for these awards. You got this, homeys!'

A low moan ripples through the collection of hung-over twenty- and thirty-somethings.

Willowy Robyn from Strategy walks past, and Stan whistles and shouts, 'Gettit, girlboss!'

She scowls, but he doesn't notice.

'Bet you've got some inroads with the LGBTXYZers, haven't you, Scudders? Some out-there drag queens and gender-fluids?'

Christ, he's talking to me again.

'Totally,' I say.

'Because the pink pound is a BIG market, Scudders. People love it *faggy* these days.'

'Erm . . .' This word hits me like a breeze block. I'm too slow to react.

'Really flaming *faggy* stories, that's what it's all about now.' His arm's around my shoulders. 'And it's good to have people on the inside, Scudders. I'd love to hear your ideas – you know, as an equal-opportunities employer.'

He stares at me with his bright, piggish face. His nose is wide and slopes to the left. Across it are splayed broken purple veins – from alcoholism or stress, or painted on to look alcoholic as part of his whole ironic comedy thing.

'Well, I was really happy with that piece last month about the bonsai microclimates.'

Stan's face is a computer searching All Documents.

'Oh yeah, the Dalston Plant Dads interview,' he says. 'It's not very exciting though, is it, Scudders? We want click-through. We want subscribers. We want stories bright young things connect to. Know what I mean, mate?'

'Young people like plants,' I say weakly.

'That piece was embarrassed of itself,' he goes on. 'We want content that's proud to stand up and be counted, diva.'

He pulls the arm away and claps me on the shoulder. More of this man tapping. Through my shirt, I can feel the dampness of his palms.

'Absolutely,' I say. And then I add, 'Thanks, Stan.'

I actually say thanks. Why the hell do I say thanks? Tobbs would have had him before a tribunal already. Maybe because I sort of feel sorry for him? He's so desperate to be twenty years younger.

'Stan *what*?' he says, pointing at the cap.

'Stan Boss Man,' I say. AND THEN I SALUTE. WHAT IS MY PROBLEM?

Basically spunking his pants, Stan salutes back.

'Righty-ho, Roger the Cabin Boy!' And lollops off to the Grime Music Studio room.

For a second, I sit there and blink. What just happened?

As I do, I feel my bones start to tremble. The ground beneath my feet becomes unsteady. The foundations of the building move.

'Seven eleven, seven eleven, seven eleven,' I whisper to myself, breathing in for 'seven', out for 'eleven'.

Then I shake my head violently, turn back to my screen and try to get on with some work – those houses with two-to-three Dolly Parton fans and plenty of pot-plant-friendly windowsills aren't going to find themselves.

———

The rest of the morning passes without drama. I am left to just get on with my work, which I manage to get into, despite everything – or maybe because of it. It reminds me of the thing I used to love about writing: it's calm, it's engaging, and you don't have to worry about anyone else while you're doing it. It's oddly cleansing. I remember this feeling from when I was desperately trying to get into journalism school. Then when I was desperately trying to get an unpaid internship. Then, after that, when I was desperately trying to get a job. All before Tobbs, when I had some ambition, when I was desperate for myself, not just for him.

I'm lost in my work, unaware that people around me are breaking for lunch, when, all of a sudden, I hear my name screeched across the office at full volume.

'DANIELLE? WHEREFORE ART THOU, DANIELLE?'

My heart thrums in my neck. My spine crumples to dust. I'd know that screech anywhere.

Standing on the edge of the half-pipe, easily a head higher than any of the bemused, pastel hipsters rolling past on skateboards, is Jacob.

Without so much as a breath, I leap from my desk and race towards them, but the peach shark intercepts me.

'Woo-eee! Friend of yours, Scudders? Knew you'd pull it out of the closet!'

The thought of interviewing Jacob for some 'diversity' piece to con Gen-Z-ers into clicking through to corporate brunch offers is too much to bear.

'Jacob doesn't need any more attention,' I say, perhaps more bitterly than I'd meant to, because the dopey grin falls from Stan's face as I speed away.

'THERE'S MY ANGEL!' Jacob calls, kissing me on both cheeks and the lips.

A gasp goes around the crowd of gawping millennials.

'I said I'd come down and meet you,' I hiss.

They shrug.

'I wanted to see inside, didn't I? You've never let me through the door before!' They lean in close. 'It's like Nathan Barley's wet dream in here.'

My eyes travel up and down my friend's body. 'I see you've gone for a subtle, working-girl kind of look today?'

Jacob clutches one silk opera glove to their sheer silver top and uses the other to fan out the long gold skirt. I actually have to shut my eyes, it's so bright. Is it any wonder I'm not keen on having my vinyl-loving, puffa-jacket-wearing colleagues meet the human glitter ball? 'What, this old thing?'

'Wouldn't want to distract your students, would you?'

They strike a pose. 'Babes, I'm the inspiration.'

Behind the skirt's glistening pleats, I spy a garden trolley filled with what looks like the contents of a dustbin.

'What the . . . ?'

Jacob twists to look and rolls their eyes.

'They've got no security at the venue, so I had to just bring all my props. One can't get the staff these days.'

'Is that a bust of Elvira?'

'Mistress of the Dark. Yes, sweetness.'

'And are those' – I lean closer, lower my voice – 'quartz butt plugs?'

They peer at me over the rims of their triangular vintage Gucci sunglasses.

'The workshop is about our changing relationship to sexuality and its many shifting paradigms in response to the Web 2.0 era, Little Edie. A minefield for the younger generation! I'm doing them a service, helping them articulate their feelings. Don't you get shady with me before I've eaten your work's free food. Mother's famished.'

'What?' Panic floods my system. 'No, no, no. We're going out for lunch.'

Jacob's fake lashes waft up to their arched brows as their eyes widen. 'Sweet angel, I won't be invoicing for this job for another few days, and won't get paid for over a month. The Bankquese of Diaspora is dry! Plus, you're always saying how lush the lunches are.' They take hold of the trolley's handle and pivot Elvira around. 'I'll leave Old Spooky Tits by your desk – all right, girl?'

NINE

This is a waking nightmare.

It's not that I'm embarrassed of Jacob, per se. They just don't know how not to be the centre of attention. And in a place like CULTRD, this is the primary currency.

After we deposit the trolley at my desk, we head over to the surfboard sideboard, where the kitchen staff downstairs have laid out the usual impressive display of driftwood bowls piled with leaves, pulses and vegan 'sandless'-wiches. Jacob's Beyoncé-at-Coachella-inspired silver tinsel boots scut-scut across the polished floor louder than the entire chattering workforce.

In the queue, they make friends with everyone, including, to my absolute horror, Stan.

'You go target those influencers, stud!' Jacob sings.

'You know it, kween!' Stan replies, wiping the forever-sweat from his forehead before walking away with an affected skip.

The office is mostly open-plan, divided up thematically: the Brixton Skatepark Discussion Point at its centre; the Luxury Loft Hot-Desking area towards the loos; the Cottege-Core Sofa Zone half ensconced by the living wall that glimmers with neon signs in handwritten fonts declaring 'MAKE IT HAPPEN!' and

85

'COOL BRITANNIA'; and the 'real' East End Market, where the Eely Pie Stall is still unoccupied.

We draw up chairs to the scaly, laminate tablecloth, which is in the farthest corner. But we might as well be naked onstage right in the middle. Everyone is glancing over and whispering. The electric fingers are out in force, and I'm finding it hard to eat my (mostly pasta) salad.

'They're just so scared of being embarrassed,' Jacob is saying over their mound of bok choy and roasted pine nuts. 'They refuse to loosen up and let themselves out. I mean, all I'm asking of them is to show the group what pleasure looks like to them – I even provided the props! What more do they want? God, aren't you glad you're not a student anymore?'

And yet a student is exactly what I feel like. This is what it was like being Jacob's friend at school. Everyone looking and whispering the whole time, and Jacob just carrying on blithely, as if they really don't see and hear it. Although I know they do, they just choose not to let it affect their behaviour. Whereas I've always been strangled by it, stupefied by it. Even now. Especially now.

We did everything together until we were fifteen, when I suppose we had a blip. There were a series of *incidents*, after which I distanced myself a little. One involved Rory McClure, Laura's first obnoxious boyfriend. He stole Jacob's uniform from the changing room after PE and replaced it with a frilly floral gown from the drama cupboard. To their credit, Jacob put it on and waltzed to Double Maths, somehow making it work until they and Rory were called in to the head teacher's office and their missing uniform mysteriously reappeared.

'He thinks he's a lady,' I remember Laura whispering to me. Everyone was whispering, and all I could think was how lucky I felt that it was Jacob they were laughing at, not me. It was a rocky year, but we made up at sixth form; it's all in the past.

My chest is heaving up and down way too quickly. The screech of chairs against the floor, people talking and laughing, and the piped-in Dizzee Rascal is making my head edge closer towards explosion.

A pale-yellow silk glove wraps itself around my non-eating hand. It's the colour of Belle's dress from *Beauty and the Beast*.

'It's happening, isn't it, babe?'

I look up. Jacob's deep-mocha eyes are gazing at me, concerned. They're outlined in pale yellow to match the gloves, and the cheeks are speckled with gold. Cute.

'It happened Saturday night on the Tube, too,' I say. Then I shake my head. 'But it's fine. I think it's the air quality in London these days.'

The Belle glove tightens around my fingers in a firm, soothing way.

'You honestly should go and talk to someone about it,' they say in a slow, mellow voice. 'It's been getting worse.'

As a response, I ram too much pesto fusilli into my mouth and chew for a long time. How am I supposed to tell them they aren't exactly helping? That as soon as they're gone everyone's going to ask me about them, tell me they love them, snap their fingers at me EVEN MORE, and maybe ask me to screenings of *Drag Race* at their best girlfriend's flat next weekend.

'I'm fine, Jay.'

Jacob presses on. 'Honestly, angel, my therapist is like a surrogate ma to me. I love her. I couldn't do it without her.'

'Please, can we just talk about something else?'

'Look, I'll text you her number. She's an absolute babe. AND she has *the sickest* fashion, like, absolute icon – and I'm not even misusing that. Honestly, hon, she'll turn you straight . . .

though she's a straight-up dyke, of course. BA-HA!' My phone vibrates. Jacob winks at me over the rim of the glasses. They're still wearing them inside. 'Got you covered, girl.'

'Jacob, please.'

They throw their hands up, a paper napkin fluttering between the middle fingers of one, looking oddly elegant.

'What? I'm being discretion herself!'

My phone vibrates again. Oh God, what have they texted me now?

I peer at it.

Hello. You've tested negative for chlamydia, gonorrhoea, syphilis and HIV. But there are signs of a urinary tract infection. Please continue to take the antibiotics prescribed and symptoms should clear within the next 24–48 hours. Thanks.

'*Fuck,*' I breathe.

The buzzing gets louder through my skull. The fusilli swirls in my stomach. When I look up, their eyes are on me again.

'It's the clinic.'

'Shit, what's he given you?'

'Nothing.'

'Nothing?'

'Nothing!'

'How can it be nothing when your balls are boggy?'

'It's a UTI.' I roll my eyes, trying to make a joke of it. '*Classic me*, getting an STI that isn't even an STI.'

Jacob is not amused. They've gone full Disapproving Mum. 'How did you even get a UTI?'

'Apparently, you can get them from a blow job. Just, like, the saliva of the other guy can get up your urethra and, like, stress out your dick enzymes or something.'

'Further evidence that every part of that man is toxic.' Jacob shakes their head. 'At least he's not cheating on you.'

'Well,' I say slowly.

'*Well*?' Jacob folds their long arms.

'He thinks we've been in an open relationship this whole time.'

'This. Whole. Fucking. Time?' They say every syllable with absolute precision.

'Yes, for a year.'

'And you didn't know?'

'Of course not!'

'He's a psychopath.'

'No, no, no!' I say, feeling guilty, like I'm dobbing him in. 'He's not. He just has, like, really intellectual definitions of things. Like, why do we even need to be in monogamous relationships? It's so outdated and heteronormative.'

Jacob's eyes roll to the right. 'Of course he does. Typical overeducated Oxbridge bullshit to excuse his selfish fucking behaviour.'

'No, no! Honestly, Jay, he isn't a monster. He's just a really complicated person.'

'We're all complicated people, Danielle.' I look at Jacob. That is certainly true. 'Is that what you want? To be in an open relationship?'

'I dunno. Maybe. Isn't that just what being gay is all about?'

Jacob stares at me like I'm a complete and utter idiot – which is exactly what I feel like.

'A relationship is what you both want it to be, not what one of you wants it to be and then doesn't communicate it.' Jacob sits back. 'Does he ever make you feel special?'

'Yes! All the time.'

'How?'

'Well,' I say, finding it hard to think of specific instances, 'he does thoughtful things, like brings me copies of books they get sent at work he thinks I'll like.'

Jacob is nodding. 'Uh-huh, freebies.'

I plough on, feeling increasingly pissed off at having to explain myself.

'He got those tickets for that documentary screening about being queer in Algeria.'

'Uh-huh, freebies.'

'He says I'm his special guy.'

'Because you're his boyfriend!' Jacob's arms are out wide. 'That's normal fucking behaviour, Danny. That's the base-fucking-line for a relationship. You know, you're lucky he hasn't given you anything. It could be a lot worse.'

'Yeah, I know that, Jacob.'

I swallow and go silent.

Jacob's head tilts at an angle. Their pink Perspex question-mark earrings jangle as they come into contact with the sunglasses.

'So what are you going to do?'

I shrug. 'I dunno. I don't know if we're even still together. I never know with him.' I gaze at them and realise my vision is going shaky again. 'I don't know what I want, Jay. I think there's something wrong with me. I get so freaked out by everything he does. It's like he's always running away from me. I feel so desperate and pathetic, chasing after him. Every time he looks at another guy, I feel sick. Maybe I'm one of those gay guys who just can't do love, even though I want it so much.'

Jacob's hands go to mine, squeezing them hard.

'Babe, you *can* do love,' they say, in the sincerest voice they've ever used. 'I love you and you love me. Mary and Joseph love you. Even Basic Laura loves you, in her own artificial way. You don't just have to put up with someone's shitty behaviour because you don't think you can get someone else.'

'Well, I haven't had it before, and it's not like I've got suitors lined up for my hand, is it?' I sniff.

'Angel, you're a catch, a dream – a dreamcatcher! You need to think about you, not about him all the time, OK? Think about what *you* want and how *you* feel.'

I sniff hard again and glance around. Fortunately, everyone seems to have lost interest in Jacob, and they're tucking into their lunches instead.

'Well, Stan's actually putting us forward for the British Journalism Awards, so we've got to come up with some really great content.'

Jacob's mouth pops open and arms spread out wide. 'There we go! That's just what you always wanted to do!'

'Yeah, I s'pose.'

'You'll write something amazing, I just know it.'

'Maybe I could write something about being homeless.'

Jacob peers at me quizzically. 'Don't fox Mother with riddles.'

'Laura's evicting me.'

'WHAT? Capitalist pig landlords!'

'She's not a capitalist pig. She's pregnant. And her and Luke are getting married.'

'Oh, shotgun wedding, is it? I suppose people like them can always be counted on to uphold traditional values. This is just the sort of thing she'd do. Bloody Basic Laura! I never liked her! Do you remember in Year Eight there was that massive turd that appeared in the girls' loos every day?'

'Yes.' I don't know what this has to do with anything, but I do recall it. 'As wide as it was long.'

'Well, she told everyone it was me, that I was the Phantom Logger. And you know what? Years later, I heard from her friend Jessica Smyth that it was actually her. Can you believe that? I'll never forgive her for it, not till the day I die.'

I can't help but laugh.

Jacob smiles at me warmly. 'Dan, I hope you realise you're moving in with me.'

'What?'

'Babe, you're moving in with me, to the Centrefold. The house is massive. Plus, we actually have a free room! We were going to put in on SpareRoom this week! Coinkidink?'

'The Centrefold' is what Jacob calls 29 Tenterfield Road, the massive, dilapidated Victorian townhouse where they live in Bow. It's crammed full of 'creatives' with shaved neon heads and revolutionary ideas. It's the sort of place a lawyer's or doctor's family would have lived in in 1886 and be absolutely horrified now at how standards have slipped. Jacob refuses to refer to it as a commune, despite there being a minimum of seven house-mates at any one time and sometimes upward of thirteen. I don't really like going round there, but I did go to this party they had in summer that turned out to be a naked rave. They played hardcore techno until 6 a.m., when the neighbours formed a syndicate and came around en masse to physically unplug the speakers and scream at absolutely everyone.

The idea of moving in terrifies me. I think about the radical anarchist posters. The conversations about deconstructing gender norms. The bowl cuts.

'Jacob, I *can't*.'

'You absolutely must.'

I breathe deeply a few times. What other option do I have?

'OK, but just for a bit, while I get myself sorted.'

'Sure thing, hon. We'll be ready for ya. I'll even leave mints on your pillow.'

'OK. Shit. Thanks, Jacob.'

'One condition, though.'

Full make-up at all times, perhaps? Orgies of six or more only?

'What?'

'Go and see Nina.'

'Oh.'

'Danny, fucking do it. These panic attacks are a warning sign.'

'These *what*?'

'You're at a crisis point. Go and get help.'

'Whoa, Jay, I'm not—'

'DO IT, YOU BITCH.'

'OK!' I say, mostly to shut them up. 'I will! Jesus!'

'Oh, Danny, Mary and Joseph!' Jacob shrieks all of a sudden.

'What?!'

They're staring at their phone.

'I'm going to be late for the virgins!' They jump to their feet, their head almost going through the panelled ceiling. They kiss me on both cheeks and squeeze me around the shoulders. 'Love you, babe, mean it. Look after yourself.' And they race from the office like a gazelle.

Seconds later, they race back in, heads turning in a Mexican wave.

'Shit, I forgot Old Spooky Tits!'

TEN

'This drunk old shepherdess is the last of it, Snuffle-bunks,' Luke says, padding out onto the pavement in just tartan boxers and a grey Westminster School Rowing Club T-shirt. It is November.

'That's Dolly Parton!' I say, grabbing the triptych from him. 'Not some "drunk old shepherdess", thank you very much.'

'All right, Dazzer! Time of the month, is it?'

I clutch Dolly to my chest. 'No.'

'Oh, Danny-boo!' Laura says with a sigh, throwing her arms around my neck. 'I can't believe you're really going? I'm seriously devo!' *Not devo enough to let me stay, though*, I think. 'Now, do you have everything?'

'Because you don't want me coming back for anything?'

'Too right, mate,' Luke says, punching me in the shoulder.

'No! No!' Laura coos. 'I just want to make sure you're all set for this exciting new adventure.'

I twist my neck to scan the pavement, which is almost totally hidden under cardboard boxes and plants. Now they're out in the open, there seems to be an absurd number of them. Maybe I do have a problem?

'No, I think that's everything.'

'OK, great!' Laura says, with cheerful finality. She's in her fluffy pink dressing gown with the bears' faces on it. She shivers dramatically. 'Well, we might pop back in, then. It's quite chilly, isn't it, Bumblekins?'

Luke fondles the junk and shrugs.

'The Old Man's still at half mast, if that's what you mean.' And he laughs.

'*Lukey.*' She gives him a petulant, big-eyed pout. How would that ever be what she means?

As if on cue, a car horn echoes down the street, no doubt waking up every single person in these sleepy suburban terraces. It's still before eleven on a Saturday morning, bright and sunny and silent. It resounds three more brassy times. Laura and Luke turn, Laura with fear pressing her eyes wide.

An ancient Mini roars up beside the little jungle and stops. We all stare. It is glossy black with giant bright-pink upside-down triangles on the roof, bonnet, doors and boot. Under the one on the bonnet, just above the lights and grille, is the word 'QUEERS' in Gothic script.

Jacob leans out of the window, grinning broadly.

'Get in, loser, we're going cruising.'

'Oh Jesus,' I say under my breath.

Jacob shakes the door handle violently several times, then just bashes it with their forearm. In the end, a powerful kick gets it squeaking open – slowly at first, and then it drops to the pavement with a loud metallic clang, waking the last few remaining sleepers in the street.

Glancing at it briefly, they fold themself out, like a spider unspooling from a tiny crack in the wall.

Today, a day of physical labour, Jacob has opted for a double-breasted pinstripe suit with vast shoulder pads, a wide black fedora with pink satin do-rag beneath, and accompanying pink stage jewellery, which glitters in the morning sun. Stepping over the door, I see pink satin heels completing the She-Wolf of Wall Street ensemble.

They jangle back from their tiny vehicle, gazing down at the fallen door.

'It's fine.'

'Is it?' I say.

'Don't you just *love* her?' They swivel towards me with hands outstretched. 'She was left over from Ange's work's Pride float last year. I said, "Ange, we have to adopt her!" And we did.'

'I mean' — I glance around the street, which is mercifully mostly empty, despite the wake-up bell — 'it's very, um, *iconic.*'

Jacob flips the do-rag's silken tail over their broad, angular shoulder. 'Just like Mother, darling.'

'Oh golly-gosh,' breathes Luke.

I turn. Both he and Laura have retreated, their backs up against the door to the flat. This is exactly what Laura was hoping to avoid.

'What you call me?' Jacob says, then laughs. Luke does not respond in any way.

'Jacob,' Laura says.

Jacob peers at her, as if they barely recognise her. 'Laura.'

'Lovely to see you.'

'Likewise.'

'Thanks for picking up Danny.'

'The pleasure is all mine.'

'Hope the move goes well.'

'It will, thanks ever so.'

Laura turns to me and starts cooing again. 'Going to miss you so much, Dan-Dan! Safe journey!'

She scrabbles for the door handle and opens it.

'What's with the pink triangles?' Luke says, scratching away.

Laura smacks him on the arm. They were almost away scot-free.

Jacob leans back on the car's roof.

''Twas the symbol Hitler sewed onto the fine *vêtements* of our LGBTQIA forebears in the death camps.'

All the features of Luke's doughy face squeeze themselves into the centre as he tries to understand what this could possibly mean.

'So why have you got it on your funny little car?'

'Luke, honestly, don't start him off,' Laura hisses.

Jacob jerks their upper body off the car, in order to stare him in the eye.

'We've reclaimed it, sweet Sean. It's ours now.'

The dough face squeezes even tighter.

'Who's Sean?'

'Sean Cody.'

'Who's that?'

'Your employer.'

'What?'

'Bye, Danny, love you!' Laura calls, then pulls Luke inside and firmly slams the door.

I can't help but glance after Luke's boxers, with a mixed sensation of longing and relief. Simultaneously, a lump rises in my throat. That's the end of that portion of my life, then, just like that. I'll miss them both, in a funny way, I realise.

'Bye, guys!' I call to the door, before turning to Jacob. 'Glad you've buried the hatchet with Laura.'

'How'd you like being known as the Phantom Logger right up until Sixth Form, huh?'

I shrug, feeling very much like I've just been left at the school gates by one mother and am being picked up by someone else's, a scary Joan Collins mum who drinks too much. There's no going back now.

Bending down and picking up a box of special-edition Dolly vinyls, I try to do a Laura and smile brightly in the face of this whole situation. 'Where should we start packing, Big Edie?'

Jacob staggers towards me in the guise of an old woman. They peer at the box suspiciously. 'Welcome to Grey Gardens, Little Edie! The cat food goes in the back and the kimonos in the front.'

They grab the box from my arms and throw it through the open door into the passenger seat.

'How are you feeling, angel, about the whole, you know, Tobias thang?'

Just the mention of his name makes my heart sink.

Jacob further arches their drawn-on brows.

'You haven't heard from him?'

I drop the act. 'Not really. Well, he did maybe text, and I did maybe text back and told him what was going on.'

Jacob leans against the side of the car again, which creaks on what must be a hundred different rusting parts. They fold their arms and glare at me.

'Daniel Christopher Reginald Scudd.'

I gasp in horror. 'How dare you invoke my full name!'

'Daniel Christopher Reginald Scudd, I'm only going to say this once more: Cut. Him. The. Fuck. Out. He's no good for you.'

'I'll just put this cheese plant in the back.'

'They always want what they can't have. He'll reel you back in with his two-faced slippery snake wilds.'

'We were just chatting. He's not Hitler.' I wrench open the boot door and slide the plant in carefully. Inside, there is already: a large purple lampshade fringed with gold, a selection of Venetian plague masks, a startling number of empty Gregg packets and the naked bust of Elvira. Her rosy nipples stare at me. Why didn't Jacob clear all this junk out before leaving the house?

I come back around and pick up the Comedy Wig Box. I hand it to Jacob. 'I thought you were here to help me move, not give me a lecture?'

They take it and lob it in.

'Why do you keep defending him?'

'I'm not.'

'He lies to you. He belittles you. He cheats on you. He ambiguously breaks up with you when you call him out on it. He's no good for you!'

Despite trying to sidestep them, the unseen fingers creep across my forehead with their prickly touch. 'He's doing the best he can.'

Jacob gawps at me. 'What the hell does that mean? "Doing the best he can"?'

'He hasn't had what we've had,' I say, feeling a lump rising in my throat. I bend down and pick up the next box: the Unnecessary Post Sent from Mum Box. 'He didn't have a great start in life. He finds it hard to just, you know, be alive.'

Jacob's eyes and nostrils grow to mammoth proportions. They look close to explosion. They draw splayed fingers up and down their person, then wave them at me again. 'And you think *this* is easy, do you?' they say. 'You think being a six-foot-four black non-binary artist is easy? You think I just waltz through the world with no problems at all? Come on, Danny, we grew up together, you know it wasn't easy for any of us.'

'But he's had a really bad shot—'

'IT'S NOT YOUR RESPONSIBILITY!'

Jesus fucking Christ, now they're shouting. Net curtains twitch next door, I'm certain of it.

'You can't compare pain, Danny,' Jacob continues, at a lower volume. 'We're queer people, we've all suffered. There's not some Register of Pain where some lucky member comes out on top. You need to look after yourself and find someone who treats you like the magical queen you are. Not some second-rate gossip columnist who gives you the boggy balls!'

'Speak of the Devil,' comes a crisp, low voice to my right.

Jacob and I both leap out of our skin.

Tobbs is standing there, a stack of empty boxes under his arm and three takeaway coffees in a plastic holder in his other hand.

'Thought you might need a break,' he says.

'Oh, bloody Nora,' Jacob breathes.

———

Three takeaway coffees and fifteen minutes of awkward to-me-to-you-ing later and nearly all my shit is crammed into the Pride Mini.

Conversation, as you might imagine, is stilted. Tobbs and I mumble some meaningless fillers to each other as he passes me the last box – the Old Plant Pots I Don't Use but Might One Day Box – and I ram it into the side door. Jacob has said nothing to Tobbs directly but has been huffing very, very loudly, making talking impossible. Now they're clambering into the driver's seat, their knees up around their ears, swearing at the wheel, so I take my opportunity.

'Thanks for helping, Tobbs. You didn't have to.'

'I know,' he says back. Then, with evident effort, he adds, 'I wanted to.'

'Is that an apology?' Saying this feels very brave.

Tobbs looks up at me, the messy hair, the unironed stripy blue shirt, the afghan neckerchief hanging limply around his narrow neck. His smudge-coloured eyes glare at me, wounded and angry. 'Guilting me again?'

'Come the fuck on, Danielle!' Jacob's head is sticking out

the window. They shoot Tobbs a look of daggers. 'Mother's got appointments.'

'Tobbs,' I say, 'what are you doing here?'

He looks at the ground, and shrugs. His shoulders are sloping even more than usual, and he looks waifish and contorted. In this instant, he's transformed into a little boy. My heart aches for him.

Then, quick as anything, he darts into the passenger seat and pulls the door closed.

'What the shit?!' Jacob screeches. 'You get the fuck out of this car right now!'

'Jacob!' I shout through the window. 'Will you just drive, please?'

Jacob gazes at me and I don't think I've seen them ever look so furious.

'Please?' I repeat.

'In the back,' they order. 'With Dolly and the wigs.'

'My drag band,' I say in a voice of mild hysteria, squeezing myself into the minuscule space remaining in the back seat.

'If only,' Jacob says, pulling the door back on.

———

We drive without speaking. A seventies soul station provides a helpful, and incredibly jolly, distraction. Tobbs sits with a straight back, head bent over his phone. I keep having to steady myself between the Dolly vinyls and Elvira's nunga-nungas, worried for my plants. Worried for this tension I can't bear.

Then, out of nowhere, Jacob says: 'You know, you haven't asked me what my big break is yet.'

'What big break?' I say, with so much false enthusiasm I want to slap myself.

'The one I keep messaging you about and waiting for you to reply.'

'Doesn't sound like you,' Tobbs snorts into his phone.

'He's been very busy recently, actually,' Jacob snaps.

'What big break?' I ask. I genuinely don't recall reading any of these messages.

'Well . . .' Jacob lifts their hands from the wheel and turns to look at me. 'I've been asked to perform at the most exclusive club in this whole depraved city. Klub Klutch!' They pause for a reaction that does not come.

'Never heard of it,' Tobbs says.

'Jacob, watch the road!' I shout as a bus goes past beeping its horn.

Jacob turns back around and grabs the wheel, unbothered.

'It's only the most iconic underground queer club in town. It's a big deal to perform there, Little Edie. This is the high point of my career thus far!'

'Why do you call each other that?' Tobbs snarls.

'Call each other what?' Jacob says back with equal menace.

'Big and Little Edie.'

Jacob stares at him. 'From the seminal cult *classique Grey Gardens*.'

'It's just this silly thing we do,' I say hurriedly. 'Big Edie and Little Edie are the main characters. Big Edie is the elderly mother, and Little Edie is the adult daughter.'

'What's it about?'

'It's a documentary,' I try to explain, then immediately regret it.

'What sort of documentary?'

'Nothing serious,' I clarify. 'It's just these two mad women in this broken-down house in New England. It's stupid, really.'

'DANIELLE!' Jacob shouts. 'This is blasphemy! Do not speak ill of the Bouvier Beales!' They glare at Tobbs. 'It's our favourite movie. We used to watch it over and over again at Danny's parents' when we were growing up.'

Their use of 'we' makes me cringe. Tobbs never refers to him and me as 'we'.

'Oh, it's that one about Jackie O's cousin,' he says, deliberately ignoring anything else Jacob is saying, as if the name gives it more credibility, allowing his commentary. 'I've heard of it but got too many other docs on my list. I'm going to watch *Taking On the Taliban* tonight. It won Best Documentary at Sundance.'

The car jolts violently as Jacob turns us onto a suburban street of sixties high-rises and tired Victorian tenements.

'Well, we like this one,' they say. 'Don't we, Little Edie?'

'Yeah . . . it's OK. You'd find it funny, too, Tobbs. I know you would.'

'Mm-hmm,' he says, gazing out the window. 'Where was Luke today? We could have done with his muscles moving everything around. Typical selfish straight guy.'

Jacob catches my eye in the rear-view mirror. Their pink diamanté earrings jangle as they shake their head. I look away. How I long to be back on the clinic table with Nurse Jackie fondling my plums – a stroll in the park compared to this.

Without warning, Jacob careens violently into a narrow driveway, causing everything to tumble everywhere, and trills loudly, 'We're home!'

'Fucking hell, Jacob!' I yell.

They spin in their seat and regard me coolly.

'Welcome to the Centrefold! Our house of love and respect, where we welcome all open-hearted queers who do the right thing by each other.' They smile at Tobbs frostily. 'Shall we?'

I peer out of the window. I haven't been to the house in a while, because it terrifies me, and I've forgotten how vast it is. It's a grand but dilapidated Victorian villa, red bricks now mottled brown, with a huge curving bay window half eaten by foliage and a matted lawn springing with thistles and gone-over dandelions. Tall arched windows look out like startled eyes, and a crooked finger of a turret (how had I forgotten the turret?) scratches the underside of the sky with a nail of flaking tiles. Like a tired earl in session, it squats at the centre of the street, the East London Addams Family abode.

'Go to! Go to!'

Jacob has already leapt from the vehicle and is fiddling with a series of keys at the chipped black door, where the copper number '29' discolours at the centre. Eventually, the door swings open into the tiled hall beyond, where I can just make out a 'BLACK QUEER LIVES MATTER' placard and a long, sequinned *something* hanging from a coat rack.

They twist their head back over their shoulder.

'You, bring those Dollys.'

I look around for the box of vinyls, before realising they're talking to Tobbs, who isn't reacting.

'Bring those Dollys, I said,' they repeat.

Tobbs struggles out of the seat with the box, which Jacob seizes.

'There's an eighth layer of hell for bastards like you.'

'Jacob!' I shout, desperately trying to fight myself free of the wigs and giant fibreglass jugs and leap after them.

'This man is the most wonderful man in the whole entire world, and you've treated him like shit for the last year. Which is just typical white, cis, straight-passing, private-educated privilege. And now you think you can just swan back into his life after giving him the boggy balls. Are you actually a psychopath?'

'Jacob!' I shout, grabbing their arm, my eyes flipping between the two of them. 'Please.'

Jacob's entire body is bristling. Their chin is held high. For a second, I'm convinced they're going to lob my Dolly collection at Tobbs, who is sheepish, in a way I've never seen before, cowed before the ultimate force of nature that is Jacob.

'Are you his mother or something?' he says unwisely.

Jacob's eyes essentially shoot lasers into his skull. 'I love him the way he deserves to be loved.'

'Jay,' I say, 'please, can you just give us a bit of space?' The lasers swivel to me. 'To talk?'

They breathe three deep, livid breaths, and hand me the box. They look back at Tobbs. 'Lucky for you I have to run off to rehearsals.' Then back to me. 'One of the exquisite little tarts in there will be happy to help.' They lean their head backward into the darkness of the hall. 'FRESH MEAT'S HERE, HOOKERS!' They give me a little peck on the mouth. 'Love ya, babe.' Then walk away, not breaking eye contact with Tobbs until they've vanished beyond the overgrown bush.

'Now, that's someone to respect,' Tobbs says, like we're discussing a documentary about a Mongol warlord. 'Someone who really doesn't give a fuck.'

'Tobbs,' I say, Dolly's *Halos & Horns* album between us, 'Jacob's right, you should really go.'

He looks back at me with the face that made me mad about him in the first place. It's a wilted, vulnerable face, one that isn't trying to get away from me, one that's trying to get closer but doesn't quite know how. At least, that's what I think it is.

'Daniel, I'm sorry for the other day. You know I get stressed out. Maybe we could . . . give it another go?'

This pours through me like a wave. I'm doomed the minute he says things like this. But I'm determined to stay strong.

'Well, I don't know, Tobbs, I don't know what you think half the time.'

He stares at me, looking a mixture of angry and hurt. 'What's that supposed to mean, boyo?'

'You confuse the hell out of me,' I say, blood starting to pump in my neck. I really wasn't expecting to say this. It's dangerous, but I just can't take all this uncertainty anymore. 'I don't know whether you like me or are bored with me, or whether I'm just another conquest that you won't stop going on about. You don't want to see me, text me back, or have sex with me. What the hell am I supposed to think?'

The brown of his eyes is taking over the blue. He blinks and looks towards the street again, his sharp jawline even sharper as his thin lips draw tight.

'You know I'm mad about you,' he says.

I'm emboldened by this victory.

'Yeah, well, you say that, but then you never want to see me.'

'I *do* want to see you. I'm here, aren't I?' He sniffs loudly and looks back at me. Now the eyes are glossy and wet. 'This isn't easy for me, you know? I'm not – like – used to opening up to people.'

I move a pace closer and try to take his hand, but he draws it away before I can.

'I know,' I say. I can hear the pleading note in my voice. And the more he recoils, the more urgent it feels to get to him. From the top of the house, I hear footsteps growing louder.

'I'm doing the best I can. The reason I only want to see you for a few hours at a time is because I find it really over-whelming.'

'What?'

'After I see you I have to go and lie down.'

'Why?'

'Why?' He stares at me, annoyed now. '*Why?* Because it's so intense. Because *you're* so intense. You want to see me all the time and text all the time and fuck. All. The. Time. I'm trying, you know, but you're very—'

'Open and loving?'

'Smothering.'

'Smothering! Tobbs, I want to' – I lower my voice – '*fuck* once a week because you only let me see you once a week. Meanwhile, you're off fucking anyone and everyone, leaving me wondering what the hell is going on between us. Me, your boyfriend. If I even really was your boyfriend.'

His lips do something ugly, and he steps away from me. 'Why can't it just be easy? Why does it have to be this, like, formal, serious thing?'

I stare around the overgrown garden as if it's an audience that'll agree with me.

'Why did you have to keep running away from it being *anything*?'

An Asian man appears in the doorway. He's wearing a floor-length sheer black dress with a leather thong underneath and pink, fluffy rabbit slippers. His arms are enormous. His pants are not.

'Fresh rump steak for the grill?' he says cheerfully.

We both jump, and stare at him. Tobbs looks him up and down, and I feel a rage burning inside me. The urge to drop the Dollys is strong.

'Oh, nice,' I say. 'You don't want to fuck me, but you'll fuck him, right?'

Tobbs glowers at me. 'You can be a real stone-cold bitch sometimes, you know?'

'And this is you trying to win me back?' I shout.

The Asian guy looks from face to face, his own lighting up with the drama of it all.

'You know what?' Tobbs says, backing away. 'You're already in a relationship I'll never be a part of, so I don't know why I even bothered.'

'What the fuck, Tobbs? Jacob is my best friend.'

'Well, lucky fucking them, they get to hang out with the best person I've ever met in my life.'

We stare at each other, and the traffic silences itself, the world falls away. Even the guy in the thong and slippers disappears.

'I can't deal with this anymore,' he says, then turns on his heel and crunches to the end of the driveway.

'Tobbs,' I say, suddenly full of fear and regret. 'Tobbs, wait!'

But it's too late. He's already vanished behind the overgrown hedge. And I'm left standing there with a boxload of Dollys.

PART TWO

ELEVEN

I'm in another waiting room. My knee is at it again. Thumping up and down.

This one is small, pale, anonymous – once the living room of a three-storey Islington townhouse. Now it has a reception desk with a mauve orchid but no receptionist, two cream leather sofas and a selection of pastel magazines called things like *De-stress* and *Calmness World* fanned out on a coffee table between them. A pale blue square glows softly on the wall behind the desk, laser cut with the words 'The Getting Better Centre' in cursive script. The street beyond the muted blinds is quiet and dark. There seems to be no one out there, and no one in here. The world is empty. I pressed the '7' on the buzzer, as instructed, and was let in, but have yet to see another soul.

Who knew it was so easy to get a therapist during 'unsociable hours'? I just rang the number Jacob gave me as soon as I'd got everything into the house and had an appointment booked straight away, for 9 p.m. this evening. And it's even reduced-cost. It turns out people don't want to spend their Saturday night talking about their childhood trauma. Other than Gin, the thong guy, I'd managed to avoid all my other new housemates and creep out. Sweet mercies.

111

I'm deep down in a phone hole, scrolling through articles about therapists doing batshit things to people. In Scarborough, one guy saw this therapist who put him into a trance, and he got stuck there – as his childhood pet Sphynx cat. His wife had to stroke him every day while he prowled around the house on all fours, naked.

'Danny Scudd?' a twangy American voice calls down the stairs in the hallway.

I leap up, knocking a copy of *Mindfulness Today* to the wheat-coloured natural-fibre flooring and race out into the long, dark corridor.

Standing in the low light of an open doorway at the top of the stairs is a woman. She has short hair and seems to be wearing a suit, but she's backlit, a silhouette, and I can't make out the rest.

'Hi, I'm Danny,' I say, remaining at the bottom of the stairs.

'I know,' she says. 'I called your name.'

'Oh yes.'

'Are you going to come up?'

'Yes. Sorry. Yes.'

The stairs squeak, which I find achingly embarrassing in the silence. As I get closer, the woman's features gradually specify. She's a little shorter than me, with big hips and a round, piggy face, very pink. She's maybe just shy of forty, with a black pixie bob parted in the middle and black, thick-rimmed glasses. She is, as Jacob described, dressed immaculately: black jeans, black satin blazer, white silk shirt tied at the neck with a black ribbon in a low, drooping bow. She exudes strong lesbian dominance.

For a second, we're lodged together in the narrow doorway. We look at each other, uncomfortably close. She smiles like I'm a fond but forgettable memory she's had while brushing her teeth. I edge past her into the room. It is tiny, with sloping ceiling and low window shuttered absent by a beige venetian blind. Two cream, coffee-shop-style leather armchairs face each other at alarming proximity, and under the window is a table sporting another mauve orchid and a box of Mansize Kleenex – odd choice for a therapist specialising in gay issues.

I stand in the centre of the room, feeling both too large and too small.

The woman looks at me with an effortless, practised kindness. 'I'm Nina Leibovitz,' she says. 'You can sit down.'

'Oh yes.' I immediately perch on the edge of one of the chairs. 'Sorry, I'm a little nervous. I've never, um, done anything like this before.'

Nina gently closes the door. She seats herself opposite and gazes at me over the thick rims. The overhead light renders her facial features as monochromatic as her wardrobe: pink skin now white, small eyes as black as her glossy Oxford brogues.

'That's completely understandable,' she says. 'But the important thing to remember is that you're leading this session, and you can stop it at any time.'

'OK.'

'If you could just fill out this questionnaire before we get started?' She hands me an A4-sized form on a clipboard and biro. 'Don't worry, it's just something we have to do for the Centre.'

Hands shaking, I scan the questions, all of which I have to circle on a scale of 1 to 10. In the last week, have you made plans to end your life? In the last week, have you had trouble sleeping, concentrating, been talking too fast or too slow? In the last week, have you felt life is overwhelming or meaningless?

'Pretty fun little quiz,' I say, circling several tens.

'It's a great way to break the ice, huh?' Nina says with a smile, a real one.

'Are you American?'

'Canadian.'

'Oh, shit, sorry.'

'Don't be; everyone says that.'

'Did you go to uni in this country?'

Nina clasps her hands around one knee. 'This time is for you.'

I glance up at her. 'Go on, where'd you go? I won't tell anyone.'

She stares at me over the top of the glasses so unflinchingly I have to look back at the questionnaire.

'I can tell you,' she says, after a long pause. 'But a more interesting question is why do you want to know?'

I roll my eyes and look back up at her. 'That's such a shrink answer.'

'Well . . .' She holds out her hands expansively and laughs.

I can't work out if I like her or hate her.

'There you go.' I hand back the questionnaire and pen. 'Got some high-scorers!'

Her eyes run down it, while her head nods sagely. She places it on the table between the orchid and the Kleenex. Then the eyes are back on me, two black crystal balls.

'So . . . what brings you to therapy, Danny?'

And, lo, the knee is at it again. I put a hand out to steady it. Nina calmly watches.

'Um . . . I've, sort of, got a lot going on at the moment.'

'What sort of things?'

'Like work and love life and home life and stuff.'

'Well, that's all of the things.'

'I haven't got cancer or anything, though, so that's good.'

Nina nods slowly. 'Absolutely, that is good, but let's focus on the things that are causing you distress.'

'OK.'

'I can see from your questionnaire that you're having panic attacks and trouble sleeping. What sort of thoughts are keeping you awake?'

The electric fingertips are back, along with the juddering knee. I rub my forehead with the hand that isn't holding the leg still. The orchid smells sickeningly sweet.

'Like, I don't know, really . . . *Everything*.'

'Can you be more specific?'

'My boyfriend. Well, *ex*-boyfriend,' I say. And then, as if this needs clarification, I add, 'I'm gay.'

'Yes,' Nina says. 'I'd guessed.'

'Oh – yes.'

'What about your ex-boyfriend keeps you awake?'

'Well, not his dick, that's for sure!' I say in an explosive wail. She doesn't smile. Tough crowd. I cough, and continue. 'Well, he just dumped me – twice, kind of. Which I feel – I dunno about. I sort of feel like he never really liked me anyway. Like he was forcing himself to hang out with me.'

'What makes you think that?'

'Well . . . he avoided me. Didn't text me back for, like, *days*, only saw me for a couple of hours at a time, didn't like sleeping round mine, or having sex anymore, really . . . although he loved having sex with other guys, it turns out. And, like, I know that monogamy is a heteronormative construct, but I wish he'd told me, because then he gave me this UTI and my ball swelled up and I thought it was cancer. And whenever we actually got into bed he'd be, like, "God, you're such a nympho." And, like, nymphomaniac isn't even a term you can use for a man.' I glance at her quickly. 'Not that that matters. Gender is also a construct.'

Nina visibly tries to hold back another smile. Weirdly, I feel like I'm winning.

'What's your ex-boyfriend's name?'

'Toby Stethel-Thwaite. I know, what a name, huh?' Then I have a freak-out. 'Wait, you're not going to put this on record or something, are you? Like, is he going to find out I'm bitching about him?'

'Everything you say here is confidential.'

'OK. Everyone just calls him Tobbs anyway, so.'

'Great, thank you. And how long were you together for?'

'Just over a year.'

'Perfect. Would you mind telling me a little bit about things Tobbs did that you liked?'

Oh no, not this trick question again.

'Ummmm.' I think hard. All I can hear is Jacob saying 'free-bies' over and over. 'Well . . . he was very thoughtful in some ways. He brought me books he thought I'd like from work and took me to documentary screenings he thought I'd find inter-esting. He texted me nice messages, too, sometimes, although every time he did I felt sick.'

'Every time he texted you nice messages you felt sick?'

'Yeah, I know. It's fucked up, isn't it?'

'I wouldn't say that. What did you say back to these texts?'

'I'd wait a bit – like, a few hours, because he normally doesn't – didn't – reply for a day or two, or sometimes not at all, so I didn't want to smother him—'

'I wouldn't say replying to your partner's text was smothering.'

'No, right. Yeah, agreed. Anyway, I texted back a few hours later and said something similar, but not too gushy. And I NEVER called him. Well, except sometimes.'

'Why not?'

'Because that stressed him out. He's got a really hardcore job – he's a journalist – so sometimes he'd be away on assignments in the Middle East. Although most of the time he's in London.'

'So he doesn't reply to your texts when he's in London, as well as the Middle East?'

'No. He's a real writer, though, so he needs the headspace. That wasn't a big issue, I get it.'

'What do you do as a job?'

'I'm a content editor for this stupid culture app.'

'So you're a writer, too?'

'No, no. I just do stupid articles about skate parks to have sex in and "edgy" places to eat at.'

'That sounds like writing to me.'

'Yes, well, it is *technically* writing. But it's not, like, *real* writing, like what Tobbs does.'

'What makes his writing more "real"?' She air-quotes with her fingers.

I shuffle uncomfortably in the chair, which squeaks like a tiny mouse fart.

'Well, you know, it's, like, hard-hitting journalism, not just fluff like I do.'

'What sort of events does he cover?'

'He writes these opinion pieces about – well, anything really, but it's mostly celeb stuff. He's actually only been to the Middle East twice, I think. And that was for Eurovision. Tel Aviv.'

Nina properly laughs. A real belter that's madly loud in this tiny, silent attic room.

'So he writes about celebrities and you write about food, but his writing is more *real* than yours?'

I stare at her. Is this woman an idiot?

'Yeah. He works for a *real* newspaper, not a stupid app like me.'

'What makes it stupid?'

I think of Stan in his Burberry twinset, the boys playing VR volleyball every lunch break, the PR girls' staggering ability to do absolutely no work whatsoever.

'Oh God – *everything*!'

Nina fixes me with a slightly more interrogative stare. I don't think she's blinked since I've been here. Does she even have eyelids under those glasses?

'Danny, have you heard of the concept of "boundaries"?'

'Like, between Israel and Palestine?' (This is the sort of thing I said to Tobbs, so he would know how worldly I was.)

'Not exactly,' Nina says, smiling kindly again. 'I mean between people.'

'Um, I suppose no, then.'

'So, Danny, my modality as a therapist is compassion-focused, but from a psychodynamic background. That means I concentrate on helping my clients be kind to themselves, to heal their trauma and understand what's led them to reaching out for help. I don't provide solutions, I help guide you to realising them yourself.'

'OK.'

'When we talk about boundaries, we mean rules we set down for ourselves regarding what behaviour from others we are willing to accept.'

'OK.'

'So . . . may I ask you, when Tobbs texted you, how would you have *liked* to react?'

'Texted him back.'

'But you didn't feel like you could?'

This woman has obviously never had a serious relationship.

'No, because he'd either ignore it or tell me I text him too much.'

'Has he said that to you?'

'Yeah, when he was dumping me – the second time.' I shrug.

'He always said how me and my best friend, Jacob, text so much and it'd stress him out having to do that with someone. Anyway, it doesn't matter now, does it? He's dumped me. I'm alone again. Like always.'

'Right, right.' The Nina Nod is back. 'I think it matters a great deal, actually, Danny. What it sounds like to me is that Tobbs's behaviour overstepped your boundaries of what's acceptable.'

'Yeah, but I'm neurotic like that,' I say, sitting up straighter. 'I just get anxious and weird. It's probably because of my parents. Honestly, even if they weren't called Mary and Joseph, they'd still crucify me like I'm the bloody Son of God.'

Nina's cheeks swell up. She presses her lips together. Her fingers go to her nose and she snorts.

'I'm sorry!' she says. 'Are your parents really called Mary and Joseph?'

'Yes. Please, don't.'

'Well, let's discuss that in another session.' Her face has gone puce. I can't believe this: even my therapist is laughing at how ridiculous my life is. 'Just – um – going back to the texting – there isn't a level of acceptability. What's acceptable behaviour varies from person to person. It sounds like what might have been acceptable for Tobbs might not have been acceptable for you.'

'But why wouldn't he want to text me back?' I say – shout, actually, at amazing, sudden volume. Nina's tiny pig-eyes go as wide as they probably can. Where'd that come from? 'I *loved* him – I still love him – I *wanted* to talk to him. I *wanted* to see him and have sex with him. Am I fucking crazy for wanting that? Like, what was I doing wrong?'

Nina is nodding again like she knows exactly what it was.

'Why do you think it's you who's doing something wrong?'

'Because otherwise why would he be acting like that?'

'Well, Danny, it's interesting you mentioning how he only likes to see you for a few hours at a time.'

'He's got a busy life, he gets stressed out. I get it – I can be quite intense sometimes.'

'To be honest, Danny, he sounds like the intense one, not you.' Nina covers her mouth with a hand. 'Sorry, that's reassurance-seeking; I shouldn't have said that.'

I furrow my brow. This psychobabble is all very much beyond me. Whenever people say stuff like this, I normally don't ask them to explain, so they won't realise how butt-fuck ignorant I am.

Nina clasps her hands around her knee again and looks at the clock, which is behind me. She's getting bored, I know it. My trivial problems are tedious and stupid to her. Because I am trivial and stupid.

'I think what we might be dealing with here is some significant trauma around intimacy,' she says.

'Well, yeah, that's exactly how I feel. Whenever I tried to get close to him, he pushed me away, but then kept me around. It *was* pretty traumatic.'

'No, Danny, I mean in Tobbs's past.'

I blink at her for precisely forty-two years.

'Oh. What makes you say that?'

'The emotional distance. The confusing behaviour of both wanting intimacy and then avoiding it. What's his relationship like with his parents?'

I swallow hard. Why didn't anyone think to put a jug of water on that stupid little table?

'It's bad. He doesn't see them. They're both alcoholics.'

The nod. The nod is in full flow. She cannot stop nodding.

'I think that's what we're looking at, Danny. Some kind of significant past trauma where his needs were not met.'

I feel sick and guilty and confused, all at the same time.

'He told me a lot about the other guys he's fucked. Like. All. The. Time.'

'Right, right.' This in an 'of course' voice.

'So what does this mean? I'm not mental?'

'No, Danny, you're not mental.' I'm starting to warm to the smile. It's kind, not mocking, I realise. 'Not that I'd use that term.'

'But Tobbs is?'

Nina looks like she's weighing up how to answer.

'It certainly sounds like he has a lot of activated trauma around intimacy and relationships, which is, sadly, not uncommon among gay males.'

'I guess we can't all move in on the second date like you dykes, can we?' I say, in a Stan-style 'risky comedy' moment.

Nina just stares at me. I instantly regret it.

'Well, that's a stereotype, Danny, and quite a reductive one.'

'Yes, sorry. So reductive. Sorry.'

'Tobbs's emotionally abusive behaviour sounds like it has really badly affected you, and I think you maybe haven't fully acknowledged that yet?'

She says this like it's a question, though I don't know how to answer it. Instead, this impulse in me rushes up. 'Whoa! Whoa! I wouldn't say he was "emotionally abusive".' Although, as I say this, I realise I haven't even mentioned the worst bits. Can she tell? Does she know I'm protecting him?

'Danny, it sounds like his trauma and emotional distance were really activating your anxiety – as it would with anyone, because his behaviour was inconsistent and confusing.'

I stop listening after that word.

'My what?'

'Your anxiety. It sounds to me like you might have an undiagnosed anxiety disorder.'

'Everyone gets stressed out from time to time.'

'Yes, but this isn't just "getting stressed out", is it? It's a dominant force in your life.'

I flop back in the chair. It squeaks with a huge fart noise.

'Fucking hell, this got heavy quickly.'

Nina smiles again. 'Have you ever considered journalling?'

'I'm not a fourteen-year-old high-school girl, so no.' These lines I'm coming out with here are wild.

Nina's perfectly plucked black eyebrows raise above the glasses.

'It's proven to reduce stress and aid processing troubling thoughts and emotions.'

'So you're saying I should keep a diary.'

'I'm saying it might help you make sense of what you're experiencing.'

I lean in really close all of a sudden.

'OK, I know you're not supposed to prescribe me things or whatever, but, off the record, can you just tell me: should I get back together with Tobbs? I feel so guilty now. Like, he wasn't that bad, and everyone deserves love, don't they?'

Nina does not move a muscle.

'You know I can't tell you what to do,' she says calmly. 'But writing it down might help you understand what you want more clearly.'

I sit back heavily again. This time, I don't even register the fart.

'What the hell is the point of this if you can't tell me what to do?'

'I could tell you, but I don't necessarily know what's best. That has to come from you.' Nina is looking at the clock again.

'And I'm afraid we're out of time, Danny. I'll see you same time, next Saturday.'

My eyes bulge at her. 'Wait, next Saturday?'

'Yes, and every Saturday after that.'

'I have to be here, 9 p.m., every Saturday?'

'You can always choose to leave.'

I cross my arms. Then wave them in the air. 'Whoop! Whoop! Saturday night!'

'You made a really big step today, Danny,' Nina says, standing. 'See you next week.'

She opens the door and smiles politely, but leaving me in no doubt that she wants me to get the hell out of there.

'OK,' I say and edge past her awkwardly. 'Bye, then. Have a nice weekend.'

I start down the creaking stairs.

'Oh, and Danny!' Nina calls after me.

I turn. 'Yeah?'

'Brown.'

'Huh?'

'That's where I went to school.'

I grin up at her. 'I knew I'd crack you.'

She grins back. 'Not exactly. It's on the Centre's website. Have a nice week.'

TWELVE

I've been crying for almost two hours. But I've also managed to multitask and call Nina Leibovitz three times, and she hasn't picked up any of them. After the third call, she texts:

> *Danny, remember the conversation we had about 'boundaries'. I'll see you on Saturday.*

Something about talking to her last night has really opened me up. I feel red raw, like a fresh wound – although she kept insinuating it wasn't fresh at all, just buried.

At a loss to know what to do next, I stare around the room: it is empty except for the bed and an island of boxes and plants. The mid-morning sun streams in in swirling yellows and browns through the tired seventies floral curtains. The room is wallpapered with peeling strips of a similar ilk – some flock, some paisley, some abstract rectangles – each patterned with not just a different loud print but blooming with bubbles of damp. I can hear the voices of people moving around downstairs. The thought of even popping my head out to find the bathroom and potentially bumping into one of them is too much. *What am I doing here? What is going on with my life?*

Heaving myself up, I think how these are the sorts of thoughts you put in a diary. Or, at least, people used to. Now when people are sad, they post shirtless selfies on Instagram with captions like 'Love my new mug! 😊'. But Nina would probably be happier if I stuck with the diary idea.

I root through the boxes. Jacob bought me this A5 ring-binder with an illustration of Dolly on the front, only with the body of a rearing pink horse. 'WHAT WOULD DOLLY DO?' it says above it, in a hand-drawn font. I find it under a copy of *On Palestine* by Noam Chomsky and Ilan Pappé, one of the 'free-bies' that Tobbs gave me and I still haven't read. What, indeed, would she do?

Back in bed, I draw my knees up to my chin and try to write something. Anything.

'Sunday 4th November,' I write. Then I put a bullet point beneath it. Something about writing a list feels less intimidating than trying to spew my heart out in perfectly formed sentences.

- *Writing a diary for the first time since I was a closeted emo teen.*

And then I set down my pen on the mattress and stare at it. A bizarre sense of pride fills me. When was the last time I wrote *anything* just for me?

Against my better judgement, I root around for my phone and go through the album titled 'Me 💚 Tobbs.' Considering we were together a year, I really don't have many photos of us. There's a few when we started going out. One of us sitting on the South Bank with beers in plastic cups, smiling in the sun. There's another of him on the shingled Brighton beach from when he agreed to go away with me. He's smiling in the photo, but he spent most of the time we were there on Twitter.

Then there's one of us in bed together, me cuddled up to his darkly haired chest, doing the long arm from above as we both grin with tired smiles and puffy morning-eyes. This one sticks in my throat. For all his flaws, we had some lovely moments. For all the unhappiness he brought me, I did love him. I stare at this picture, at the edge of nerviness in his eyes, in mine, for all the elation and even careless abandon we were feeling in this moment.

But did I really love him? Or was he just someone there for me to try to love?

The minute I think that, the floorboards creak and the wallpaper tears apart. The familiar feeling of dread starts to destabilise everything as my vision swims.

I pull the covers over.

Seven eleven. Seven eleven. Seven eleven . . .

A knock comes at the door.

'No, thank you!' I call from under the duvet.

It squeaks open.

'How's my angel?' Jacob says brightly. '*Where's* my angel?'

I hear their slippers shuffle in, and then a hand rests gently on my arse.

'Hey!' I shout, twisting around, emerging from the duvet.

'I thought that was your shoulder!' Jacob cries.

We stare at each other for a second, wide-eyed, and then I burst into tears.

'Oh my God, Dan, I'm sorry!' Jacob says, wrapping their arms around me. 'I really thought it was your shoulder.'

I want to tell them I'm not crying because they touched my arse, that I'm not actually sure why I'm crying, that the world is unstable and I can't even write more than one sentence about how I'm feeling, but all that comes out is a horrible '*Gah*!' noise.

'Shh! Shh!' Jacob says. 'It's OK. It's all going to be OK.

Things are just a bit rough right now, Dan.' Honestly, they are so soothing, they're basically a houseplant. If only they could photosynthesise.

We sit like this for a bit, them cradling me in my duvet chrysalis, as we've done for each other many times throughout our lives. After a while, I sit up properly and wipe my eyes. I wonder what time it is. Midday? Later?

Jacob passes me a chintzy teacup.

'Oat-milk latte?'

I take the cup.

'Bougie.'

'Essential.' Jacob takes a sip from their own blue-and-white Wedgewood knock-off. 'And quite tepid now.'

'Thanks, Jay. And thanks for all this. I don't know what I'd do without you.'

'Don't mention it, babe,' Jacob says. 'I know you'd do the same for me.'

They're in a tomato-red boiler suit that says 'Fı' on the lapel. Because they are so long, their thin, tawny ankles stick out at the bottom. Their feet are hidden by heavily beaded, over-sized Moroccan sandals with a dramatic toe curl. They perch elegantly at the end of the bed. They're wearing a headwrap of yellow and purple. I really am so lucky to have such a wonderful friend. Who else can say they are as close to a magical person such as this?

Between us sits the Dolly Diary. If Jacob had been anyone else, I'd have hidden it beneath the duvet. But I don't mind so much with them, even if they comment. Their eyes glance over it knowingly, but they say nothing.

'How was sweet Nina?' Jacob asks.

'Yeah,' I say, settling the cup on my knees. 'Pretty, um, mind-blowing.'

'She's incredible, right?'

'It happened so fast. Like, it just feels like she got right inside me.'

'Ooh, gurl!' Jacob smirks. 'Serious serious, though, that's how it is at the start.'

'What?'

'Therapy. Every session feels like a revelation.'

'Really?'

'Yah, hon. Then it starts to slow.'

'Oh.'

'Which is when the really hard work begins.'

'What hard work?'

Jacob lets their head fall forward, their eyes staring up like those of a monster crawling from a pit.

'The Untethering,' they say in a mutant slur.

'What?'

Their eyes dart to the window. 'The Untethering,' they say again.

'What's that?'

They sit straight, pat their headscarf. 'Perhaps a better phrase might be "the Unpicking".'

'Unpicking of what?'

Jacob sips their coffee.

'Of, well, everything, babes. Every part of you. The Unlearning. The Unmaking.'

A shiver flows through me.

'I don't like the sound of that.'

Jacob reaches out a hand and squeezes mine. Today their acrylics are a good two inches long, sheeny black, talon-like.

'We all have to do it, Little Edie. Growing up gay in a straight world plays havoc with your rainbow matter.'

'You mean grey matter.'

'Not anymore.' And they wink scandalously.

'You know, it was the weirdest thing, Jay.' I'm staring down at the one line I've written in the Dolly Diary. 'I was a different me in that room. I said stuff to her I would have never said anywhere else – well, maybe to you.' I turn my head to the window, crunch my eyes shut. 'Or maybe not.'

'You look like Kombucha Girl.'

I think of the quick-witted, expressive me in those moments with Nina, so different from my usual, mild-mannered, white-bread self. Where did he come from? Who let him out? All in one breath, the world is exciting, as opposed to scary. I feel its potential, rather than its traps.

I look at my friend and squeeze their claw hand. The warmth in this room is magical.

'Did you go after . . . after your mum?'

Jacob's face tightens.

'No. I should have done though. Dad can talk to anyone about anything for hours except for – that. Me and the twins didn't even talk that much about it.'

'Sorry, Jay.'

Something slithers between us. A snake. A brittleness we both try to ignore.

Jacob sniffs and smiles artificially.

'Are you going to keep going?'

'Yeah. It feels good.'

They lean forward and hug me loosely around the neck.

'I'm glad to hear it, Dan. It's honestly the right decision.'

I go full Kombucha Girl again, and tilt my head in the other direction.

'Is it weird that we have the same therapist?'

'Babe.' Jacob looks at me flatly. 'If you think that's weird, you're in for a treat in this house. A real, glittery, thongless treat.'

From the door comes distant laughter. Somewhere in the bowels of the Addams Family house, events are unfolding.

'Want to come down and see everyone again? You remember Melania, don't you? And Ashraf? He's the dishy one.'

I swallow. 'Maybe not yet.'

'Fair play, babes.' Jacob stands. 'You'll meet them tonight, anyway. You're coming, right?'

'Absolutely,' I say automatically. What have I forgotten now?

'Shamazing,' Jacob grins. They head for the door, then hesitate in their step, and turn. 'And, babe, I just want to check something?'

'Yes, Big Edie?'

They look momentarily pained. Their lips twist all around their face. This isn't something you usually see from Jacob.

'You don't hold any *vexatious feelings* towards me, do you?'

'About what?'

'About what I said to Tobbs?'

That name. I've been stabbed.

'No.' I'm not sure if I mean it or not. 'Of course not.'

'Phew!' They grin with relief. 'I was worried you were holding *vexatious feelings* towards me. You know I do these things to look after you?'

'Of course, babes.'

'Love you, Little Edie.'

'Love you, too.'

Jacob waltzes out and pulls the door to.

In this moment, the sudden potential of life is gone. I fold myself into the duvet again and ache and ache and ache.

—

I must have fallen asleep AGAIN, because, next thing I know, Jacob is standing at the foot of the bed in a black PVC trench coat and silken do-rag, looking stressed.

'What the fuck are you fucking doing?'

'Um – journalling,' I say, blinking.

'Not tonight you're not, missy. It's nearly nine o'clock!'

I sit up, gaze at the curtains. Sure enough, it's dark out.

'What happens at nine o'clock?'

Jacob starts battering my legs.

'Are you stupid? Only the biggest night of my life!'

'Topping for a change?'

More battering.

'You little bitch! I'm headlining at Klub Klutch!'

I roll over and stare at them. 'Shit. That's tonight?'

'Where do you think I had to run off to yesterday? I was setting up, mic check, all that.'

'Oh, shit.'

'I'm a fucking professional, Daniel.'

'But it's Sunday!'

'All the best queer nights are on Sunday! Don't you know anything?'

Evidently not.

'How long do I have?'

'Minus ten minutes.'

THIRTEEN

Klub Klutch is underground. I mean that literally. But also, it isn't well known yet. Probably because it's disgusting and small and, I'm pretty sure, doesn't have a licence for selling booze – or any of the other things that pass between hands down there.

Jacob drags me along the Kingsland Road, shouting, 'Out of the way, bitches! A star is about to be born!' every two minutes.

It's startlingly cold, with sleet dagger-stabbing us, and I only had time to pull on a denim jacket over my T-shirt. We take some turns until I'm totally lost. I'm dazed from sleep and not certain if I've put on underwear. People are staring. Can they tell?

Next thing I know, Jacob is half flirting, half arguing with a man dressed as a cowboy leaning against the door of an old shop coated in flaking bottle-green paint.

'I was here an hour ago, you big clumsy man,' they drawl like a Southern belle, running a finger up the man's Friesian chaps.

'I ain't never seen no gal as fine as you here before,' whistles the man from under his white Stetson, his face hidden by blue cigar smoke. 'And I'd remember a dame like you, yes sirree!'

Suddenly Jacob's had enough. 'Come on, Sam, stop being a dick and let me in.'

The man exhales noisily. 'You dancing hot-and-tot girls sure gotst spunk, that's all I know.'

He leans back on the door, and it creaks open. Jacob rolls their eyes and kisses him on the cheek. I follow past meekly.

'Cheers, then,' I say, going embarrassingly West Country.

—

Inside is a small room lined with books and trophy-animal heads. A wild boar snarls dustily above a large desk, behind which recline two men dressed as seventies American cops, complete with moustaches, aviators and teeny-tiny shorts. Both have their legs on the desk, both are smoking cigars. One is in khaki, and the other in pale blue. Pale Blue's tanned, muscular legs are *incroyable*.

'Back again, are we, Miss Thang?' Khaki says to Jacob.

'Fuckssake, you little bitches, I need to get in,' they say back. 'Knock it off for five minutes, wouldya?'

'One red token for you both!' cries Pale Blue.

Khaki turns to him. 'Jacob goes free. They're headlining tonight.'

'One green token!' cries Pale Blue, looking at me.

'Danny, Mary and Joseph!' huffs Jacob. 'Just give him the token.'

I stare at them incredulously. I do *not* want to be here, I realise violently.

'You never said anything about any tokens?'

'One green token!' repeats Pale Blue.

'Yeah, I heard you, didn't I?' I snap.

Jacob's eyes bulge at me like I just said I'd murdered the Queen.

'One green token from your back pocket!' he says in the same annoying, commanding tone.

Then I twig. 'Ohhhhh!' I reach into the back of my phone case and pull out a five-pound note.

'*A-doi!*' says Jacob, smacking themself on the forehead.

'Token accepted!' cries Pale Blue, getting wearily to his feet.

Turning from us, he pushes one end of the bookcase behind them. It starts to rotate, opening up a dark passage beyond.

'Down you go, gals!' he says. 'And, please, drink irresponsibly.'

'You know, physical money is over,' I say as I brush past, smelling his thick armpitty scent. 'Get with the times.'

———

The corridor is pitch black and at a sudden, unexpected point turns into uneven, creaking stairs leading down.

'Ooh, Nina's letting out a sassy little dragon,' sings Jacob, in a better mood now we're actually inside.

'What do you mean?' I say to the darkness.

'Flirting with sexy Kristoff – well, I never,' Jacob goes on, almost as if they think I can't hear them.

'I wasn't flirting; he was being a twat.'

'A sexy twat.' They laugh.

'Where are we going?'

'Follow Mother down her back passage!'

We stumble down into a low basement room of surprising size, complete with bar made out of half a fuselage and a series of old cinema chairs dotted around small tables of every description. Candles and fairy lights flicker, and people mill around with Babycham glasses; a small red-curtained stage sits at the far end. There's a distinct Prohibition feel.

'Jacob!' an Eastern European voice calls.

A very beautiful girl with a short peroxide bob is sitting at a low red plastic kids' table in a corner at the back. Several other dark figures sit around the table with her.

Jacob strides over and looks down at them all.

'Skanks, say hello to your new boo, Danielle Virgin Mary Edie Bouvier Beale Dollius Partonius Flower-Dad Scudd.'

'Hello!' intone four voices.

'Stay here, Little Edie,' Jacob says, pushing me down next to the girl. 'This queen's gotta get her hair did for the big performance. Watch out, children, Mother has arrived!'

And away they float.

My heart is thumping. Here it is, my new life, looking exactly as terrifying as I imagined it would. The question is, when can I get a drink?

'Hello, my precious lamb, so magical to see you again,' the girl says, kissing me on both cheeks like we're old friends. We have actually met a few times. But, like all the other housemates, she's often out when I've been round, doing something cool and intimidating, like activism or three-day raves.

'Hi,' I say, without adding a name.

'Melania. She/her.' She taps her breastbone. 'We met at the Midsommar Ritual party we had a few months ago – *please*, don't make any jokes about the name!'

'Cross my heart.'

'Yes, I'm Slovenian. Yes, I'm beautiful. No, I'm not a hooker or a spy OR married to a revolting orange cretin.'

She's dressed very chicly in black high-waisted suit trousers and a floor-length black trench coat. Her lips are small and puckered, rosebud red. If the look she's going for is 'not spy', she isn't doing a great job of it.

'Noted.'

'You can just call me Mel. Or Ania.'

'Also noted.'

'Let me introduce you to the family.' One hand holds a long

pink cigarette, its filter glimmering gold in the tea lights. Everyone is smoking. *Inside.*

'This is Gin. They/them. Fashion designer and sculptor extraordinaire.' Melania waves the cigarette towards the Asian guy who opened the door yesterday. *Person*, I correct myself silently. Apart from the pink bunny slippers, which are now black Doc Martens, they're dressed identically: just a sheer shift and a thong.

'*Konichiwa*, cunt.'

'GIN!' Melania scolds. 'We are breaking the lad in gently! E-hem! So this is Ashraf. He/him. Underwear model and actor extraordinaire.' A hugely muscular guy with piercing catlike eyes in a striped vest and white sailor hat reaches a giant hand across the table. I've seen him doing press-ups in the living room before, and tried not to stare.

'Actor and model,' he says in a strong Australian accent, crushing my hand with his. 'Welcome to the Centrefold. I love English boys.'

'H-hiii,' I say back awkwardly.

'Moving on!' Melania trills. 'And last but certainly not least is—'

'All right, twat, I'm Ange,' says a woman with an aggressively blunt fringe of dyed burgundy hair, and thick black eyeliner with wings heading for her ears. She has one fag in her mouth and another in one hand. She's squeezed what was probably once quite a svelte frame into a little leopard-print dress. Sailor tattoos embroider her arms, and her hands are surprisingly large and calloused. She's usually been in whenever I've come round to see Jacob, and often ended up volunteering a story about someone doing wrong to her. Last time, it was a thieving postman called Rod. 'Don't let any of these posh fuckers lead you astray. Brunch has never been a meal, not in *real* East London.'

Melania turns her head to me and smiles. 'Ange is actually *from* London,' she says, as though explaining an impossible concept.

'Born under the chimes of Bow Bells!' Ange cries, replacing the first cigarette with the second and offering it to me. I politely decline. 'I was! I really was. One of the last true Cockneys before the middle class moved in, with their avocados and gender non-conformities. My old dad would've died of shock if Ma hadn't already put a toothbrush in 'im.'

'A toothbrush?' I can't help but say.

'Broke-off toothbrush,' Ange says proudly. 'That's how she done it.'

I stare at her – not directly – trying to work out how old she is. I settle on somewhere between twenty-five and sixty.

'So this is the gang!' Melania beams. 'Welcome to the family, Danny. I know you will slot in just like a strap-on.'

I swallow hard, thinking what a shock they're in for, but smile as they cheers nonetheless.

They go back to chatting, and Melania takes both my hands in hers. For a second, I think she's going to tell my fortune. She has that vibe about her.

'I heard you are recently single also?'

'Shit, you too?'

'I know!' Now the hands are up in the air. 'Single, me, Melania! Can you believe it? Aw, women! They're the worst!'

'I wouldn't know,' I say, laughing. I've really gone through the looking glass now.

'My girlfriend, Titty, dumped me last month,' she goes on. 'She was a real English rose. Her name was actually Titty, can you believe it? I thought I was going to marry that Titty, but Titty had other plans.'

'Ran off with Clitty?'

'No!' Melania stares at me wildly. 'Dick!'

'*Dick*?'

'Dick the barber. He runs this shop in Dalston, and she went there for her crew cuts. Next I hear, Titty's moving in with Dick.'

'Plot twist!'

'My cold socialist heart was red and broken,' she says very seriously. 'And I do not love easily.'

'Who does?' Ange says, through a cloud of smoke.

I answer immediately in my head: *I do!*

Melania slaps me on the thigh with surprising strength. 'You will get over him. There are many better men . . . though not Dick.'

'Thanks. And you'll feel better about . . . Titty.'

Melania cups both breasts and smirks.

'I already do.' She raises her arched eyebrows and smiles devilishly. 'We shall be great friends, I feel this. And we shall have a good time tonight. Welcome to the madhouse!'

Triumphant tuba music resounds around the tables, and everyone looks towards the stage. The curtains are now drawn, and a small woman dressed as Charlie Chaplin but with a giant Dalí moustache is bowing to us, doffing her bowler hat, revealing a shaved head.

'Ladies, gentlemen, and everyone who ignores that pesky thing called gender, welcome to Klub Klutch! London's premiere avant-garde queer performance space!' She leans around her hand conspiratorially. 'And *shhh*! It's a secret!'

Everyone cheers. The barmen hammer fists against the fuselage, and I swear to God the wonky beams in the ceiling start wobbling.

'What a line-up we have for you tonight!' Charlie Chaplin goes on. 'Period prom queens, dapper dick impresarios and one uniquely unique spoken word extravaganza!' I clap wildly, knowing this must be Jacob. 'So, without further ado, give a warm, sticky Klub Klutch welcome to Mizz Taken!'

From the wings, a blonde woman in white 1950s underwear comes out and grins to us shyly. She whips out a pair of white ostrich-feather fans from behind her and starts to do a little routine to some crackly wartime Anderson Sisters track. *This is nice*, I think, bopping my head along to the tune.

As she draws the fans away again, everyone cheers. She's not only seamlessly lost the underwear, but something *funky* is going on in the crotch area. I keep staring. I can't look away. This is maybe the longest I've ever looked at a naked woman. Her hand goes between her legs and comes out red and dripping. She stares at us in horror, then continues with the dance. The blood is flowing faster, all down her legs. Its glistening red drops are staining the ostrich feathers, and as she flutters them from side to side, they flick off into the crowd, to rapturous applause.

As the song builds, she drops the fans altogether and writhes in the pool she's made, howling noises somewhere between an orgasm and a wolf attack. The song ends, she stands, totally bloodied, and bows.

'Mizz Taken, everyone!' cries Charlie Chaplin, back on stage. 'Can we get the cleaners up in here, please?'

The red naked woman grabs a pile of papers from the wings and leaps down into the crowd with it. She goes from table to table, handing them out, each marked with her gory handprint. When she gets to us, I can do nothing but stare at, well, *everything*. She smiles shyly again and slides a sheet of A4 onto our table. It's a feedback form.

'How's she gonna get them fevvers clean?' Ange says loudly.

'Wool detergent,' Gin replies, pulling out a pen to fill in the form.

This is when I go to the bar for the first time.

———

Next thing I know, I'm three drinks in and starting to loosen up. Conversation with the new homeys seems to be flowing.

'. . . And that's when the bastard dumped me!' I hear myself say.

Melania's hand is on my shoulder.

'Let it out, sweet lamb, let it out,' she says. 'Then you will be ready to move on. There will be a man tonight, I feel it in my brassiere. And you shall be ready to receive him.'

She isn't looking at me, she's watching the stage. Now a large, bearded drag queen in a blue tutu and studded choker is singing an operatic tale about masturbating to the sounds of rats having sex in the walls. She's accompanied by a skinny white naked man on electric guitar. Between his legs crouches a woman in a sort of chain-link bikini. Carefully, she moves his junk around to make various elements of the song: the rat, the wall, and – of course – the happy-time penis.

This is when I go to the bar for the fourth, maybe fifth time.

Leaning on the fuselage, I order six Negronis – one each, and an extra one for me to down right now.

'Fucking shit. Am I in Clapham?'

I turn to my left and nearly scream. Zain is propped up on the bar next to me. Zain, my nemesis. Zain, who is still the coolest person in this room of very deliberate coolness. His face is even more sculpted-looking than normal, in his black biker jacket and with a liquorice rollie hanging out the side of his mouth.

'Jesus! Hi, Zain.'

He raises an eyebrow. 'Didn't expect to see you here.'

I point towards the stage. 'I'm just supporting Jacob, so.'

'Oh sure.' He frowns at me like he still can't believe it. 'Do you like clubs like this?'

I giggle. I'm drunk. I feel reckless.

'Oh, you men with your big, dumb hands,' I drawl in what I'm pretty sure is quite a good Blanche Dubois rip-off. 'I've never been to a club like this before.'

He remains as he is. Unmoved. Unbothered. Looking down his nose at me.

'Sure. You're more of a Two Brewers boy, huh?'

As he says this, my mood flips. I've had enough of his snark. It seems to be his life's work to belittle me, and fuck him if he thinks he can keep doing it.

'How's single life?' I say, swaying around. 'Sad? Lonely?'

'Got a new one now,' he says back without missing a beat. 'A big muscle dude with a penis the size of your forearm.' Reflexively, I look at my forearm. *Jesus.* 'I heard you got dumped then Laura kicked you out?'

That catches me off guard. A toothbrush in the ribs.

'Actually, I chose to move in with Jacob and those people over there.' I wave an arm at my undeniably cool group. 'Ashraf's a model *and* actor.'

Zain glances over like he couldn't give a shit, then picks up his drinks.

'Sweet, sounds exciting. Well, enjoy the show.' And he strides off to the opposite corner, where a squadron of identical gays in black huddle at a low table.

I stare after him. The rage is building. How does he do this to me?

'You could start your own bar with that many Negronis,' says a man next to me.

I stare at him blearily.

'I got dumped,' I say.

'By that guy?' He points at Zain's posse.

'Fuck no!'

'He's that bad, huh?'

'Couldn't pay me to go out with the bastard!'

'Well, that'll drown your sorrows for sure,' he says, laughing. He's a little shorter than me, in a black T-shirt tucked into black high-waisted Levi's, a silver chain glittering around his neck. He's got short, messy hair and a nose piercing. He isn't smoking.

'Oh!' I say. 'They aren't all for me. They're for my new house-mates. I just moved in yesterday. After I got dumped.'

'What a weekend!' the guy laughs. He's got a lovely smile. Not mean and loaded, but joyful and light. 'Want a hand with them?'

'No, I can manage.' I pick up the drinks and spill one. 'It's OK. That was my extra one.'

'I'll take these.' He carefully extracts two of them from my hands and we head back to the table.

'You've met Raj!' cries Melania with evident glee.

'He's just some guy from the bar,' I say, slumping down onto a leather pouffe.

'Hi,' Raj says politely, with a little wave. 'I'm Raj.'

'Hello, Raj!' everyone intones.

Melania leaps up and hugs him, kissing him on both cheeks. I think they actually *are* old friends. She turns back to the group.

'Raj and I studied international finance together before he realised it wasn't for him.'

'No shit!' I hiccup.

'I haven't seen you for five hundred summers!'

'I know!' Raj beams. 'I gotta get back to my friends, but let's catch up! And' – he nods towards me – 'look after this one.'

'Thanks, Raj!' I yell, toasting to him.

Raj smiles and walks away.

Melania sits back down and bumps shoulders with me.

'Told you.'

—

By the time Jacob comes on, I'm so drunk I can barely cheer and clap, although apparently I do so with impressive gusto.

They stand there, head scraping the ceiling, dressed like a mirrorball Grace Jones in silver sequinned catsuit with lamé hood and giant black sunglasses spelling the word 'no' across the lenses.

'Good evening, sweet, wonderous angels,' they drawl into the microphone. 'And a very special good evening to my best friend in all the world, who needs a little bit of love this evening. Let's give it up for Danny!'

More cheering. I seem to be very high up; every face is turned to me. I raise my empty Negroni glass and shout something like, 'You can't always be the centre of attention!' Then Melania and Ashraf are peering down at me. The back of my head is cold. I'm on the floor.

'Good job, Danielle,' I hear Jacob sigh into the microphone.

'I said take care of him!' shouts a voice from somewhere near the stage.

'Raj!' I call from the floor. 'Raj! You have such a nice smile!'

'Come on, dear lamb.' I'm now back on the pouffe, with Melania holding a glass of water to my lips. Ashraf is hugging me to him – or just holding me up. My hands run along his forearm. It's so . . . *hard*.

'Now, listen, all of you.' Jacob's voice reverberates around me. 'Who here is sick of seeing the places we love changing? I'm talking parts of London – like this very bar, this very hub of creativity in our community – being destroyed, priced out, and sold to property developers who don't give a shit about LGBTQIA-Plus history and liberty. Who's fucking sick of it?'

The crowd goes wild. Beside me, Ange leaps up and beats her fists in the air, chanting, 'Tory scum! Tory scum!'

'But quiet down, babies, don't panic,' Jacob says laconically. 'Mother's here to host a rally cry.'

And the rest I can't really recall. Don't tell Jacob. There's audience participation, possibly a Mexican wave, possibly salsa dancing. *Definitely* more chanting. And at one point I'm pretty sure Jacob starts snogging one of the seventies cops. All I know is next we're all cheering, taking over the stage, raising Jacob up, and singing along to a Bond theme tune, I forget which one.

Then Raj's face is in mine again, and I'm saying something like, 'And he was fucking other guys and not telling me. What's with that?' Until hands are tugging me away from him, and then I'm moving down the Kingsland Road again.

'Excellent show, Mother!' Gin says from somewhere in front of me, or possibly behind me.

'Thank you, angel,' Jacob's voice floats back. 'Even if I was upstaged by this little prima donna. He better sleep in the living room tonight with the big pan.'

'My moon-cup pan?' Ange says indignantly.

'Your what?' several voices cry at once.

'Don't worry, I'll look after him,' comes another, weirdly familiar voice.

I look to my left and spy a dark silhouette, a chiselled jawline.

And that's when I puke.

FOURTEEN

Distantly, some metallic rattling feeds its way into my head.

I blink a couple of times, but my eyelids are slow on the uptake.

Everything around me is strange. Grey light creeps in dimly around barely tugged-closed curtains. This is not my room at Laura's, but some grandly squalid space with crazy wallpaper, an ocean of pot plants under a tall window, a pile of boxes in the middle, and a large cooking pot filled with something that looks like soup, but that I know from the smell isn't. Beside it, a man's dark silhouette struggles urgently with his jeans. My forehead dances with electricity as my stomach lurches.

The shapes start to make sense. This is my new home. But who the fuck is this? Tobbs? Luke? Jacob??

'Shit, you're awake.'

It's Zain.

It's Zain Porowski.

Zain Porowski is doing up his flies in my bedroom.

I rub my eyes, but it doesn't help much. Everything is still blurry, like I'm underwater.

'What's going on?'

He freezes. A thumb points towards the door. 'I've gotta get to work, so.'

'No, no.' I sit up. Still no sheet on the mattress, and now Zain knows how I live. 'I mean, what are you doing in my room?'

The thumb drops to his side. He's still in silhouette, but I can sense his Adam's apple dancing in his throat from the pause.

'Oh God, you *were* that drunk – I mean, we both were. Everyone was.'

'*Everyone*?'

'No, no!' Zain moves towards me and his face takes on features I've never seen. Deeply pained, incredibly handsome, uncomfortable features. Tentatively, he sits down on the edge of the bed, on the raw mattress. 'Do you . . . really not remember?'

I draw up my knees and rub my forehead. It's aching, but it's not the only part, I'm realising now. Memories pool across my brain like oil on water. Naked elbows toss this way. Naked knees stick up that way, then roll forward and hit me in the face. Someone's lips bite mine. Someone with a lot of stubble. Someone who is sitting in front of me right now.

'Fuuuuuck.' I press my head into my knees – again. 'And I thought I was going to get off with Raj.'

'No, my name is Zain.' And it's back to his usual abrasive self. 'But thanks for giving me some generic brown-boy name. By the way, my family are Muslim, not Hindu, so that doesn't even work.'

'No, no!' This seems to be the only word I can say this morning. 'There was this guy, this gorgeous guy, called Raj. He was Melania's mate. I'm not being . . .' I trail off and just stare at him.

'Racist?' Zain proffers. 'You can say it, you won't burst into flames.'

'Look.' I'm back to rubbing my head. 'I'm sorry, Zain, this whole thing has just taken me by surprise.'

Zain crosses his arms and glares at me. 'Well, you were pretty insistent on it last night.'

'Was I?'

He nods. 'Unless, of course, you thought I was your precious Raj.'

I dive deep into myself to see if I can remember more.

Oh God, it's coming back to me.

Zain helping me home. Zain helping me up the stairs and shouting goodnight to Jacob. Zain putting a big cooking pot by the bed. Me grabbing hold of him by the shoulders, pulling him on top of me. Me kissing him as hungrily as a cannibal. Me telling him I'd always wanted it from him, that's why I'm weird around him.

'Fuck,' I say again. 'What's Laura going to say?'

Zain laughs a high, cruel note, and that familiar feeling of smallness returns. As a cloud covers the sun, so any possible warmth and connection is gone. Poke a man too far, and the walls come up. How am I so good at pissing people off? I should win an award for it.

'It's just sex, Danny, it's not a big deal. Don't be such a drama queen about it,' he says nastily. 'Thought you were clinging to Jacob's apron strings now anyway, not hers?'

'Thought you had a new boyfriend?' I hit back without a pause.

He looks genuinely shocked, and I feel a stab of guilt somewhere in my undercarriage.

'Don't shame me!' he shouts suddenly. 'You white gay guys are all the same. You all want to be straight, but you won't admit it. Lanze and I are open, anyway.'

'Does he know that?' God, I'm sassy.

147

Zain leaps to his feet and grabs his black leather biker jacket. I can see Tobbs do the same thing with his ratty parka, and it's darkly poetic, like a line on a gravestone.

'You should feel grateful you got it from me,' he spits. 'Not the other way around. There's no way in hell I'd shag a guy like you if I was sober.'

'I thought Muslims didn't drink?' I literally hate myself.

'I'M NOT FUCKING PRACTISING, YOU FUCKING ARSEWIPE!' He pulls on the jacket and storms out the door. Then, seconds later, he's back, pointing a finger at me. 'And don't you DARE tell Laura or Luke or Simone or any of my mates about this, do you understand?'

'I thought it wasn't a big deal?' I mime a horrible baby version of his voice. 'It's just sex, Zain.'

'IT ISN'T A BIG DEAL!' he screams, and storms out again, slamming the door so loudly it'd wake the dead.

'Drama queen,' I say to the triptych of Dolly, the top of which is peeping out of the box of vinyls. She doesn't laugh back, and I feel guilty again. Who am I trying to impress? 'Sorry you had to see that, Dolly,' I apologise, struggling to my feet. 'Please forgive me. Amen.'

———

With my hoodie tied tight around my face, I stagger down the miles of creaking stairs into the dark, Gothic hallway and peer around. Zain must have left, just like that, slipped out between the cracks in the walls, like a ghost. I must say, I'm impressed with my consistent ability to repel men.

'Well, well, well,' a voice calls from the living room. 'If it isn't Lady Chatterley *himself.*'

I loosen the hood and shuffle to the wide double archway that falls into the huge, high-ceilinged room crammed with weird crap. Beanbags are dotted around an array of threadbare Persian rugs, different sorts of timber are stacked against one wall, and a sculpture of a naked man with a wolf head leers at me from a corner. Crimson Chinese lanterns hang from the ceiling at different heights, drenching everything in a brotherly glow, and massive canvases cover every bit of wall space. The one directly opposite is a close-up of a pink orchid. Wait – it isn't an orchid.

Grinning at me from one of two dog-eared sofas is Melania, in a pink robe, with messy blonde hair. The others sit around the breeze-block coffee table, cheerfully drinking coffee and taking forkloads of round, poufy circles of browny-beige from a pile on a central plate.

'GODDESS!' comes a piercingly high voice from behind me. I jump. My stomach gurgles.

Jacob is standing in the other archway, in a cherry-blossom kimono and strappy red heels with pom-poms, brandishing a plate of more beige poufs, like a waitress at Hooters.

'SHE LIVES!' they cry to the whole world. Then they regard me with a stare. 'So how's Mr I'm-gonna-drink-ALL-the-drinks-and-make-my-best-mate's-most-important-evening-in-their-life-all-about-me-and-my-break-up feeling this morning?'

'Huh?'

'Fancy Japanese pancakes?' they continue in the same brisk tone. 'Gin always makes them when we're hanging out our arses.'

They saunter in, perch genteelly on one of the sofas, next to Ashraf and deposit the second plate, which the others immediately lunge for.

Hesitantly, I shuffle in and take a seat on one of the beanbags, which sinks back into the floor, making me flail about. Winning already today.

'Morning, Fresh Meat,' Ashraf says with a wicked little smile. 'How's your head?'

'Not good,' I slur.

'A bit teethy, ehy?' he says, the smile broadening as I miss the joke.

'Some special tonic,' Melania beams, passing a Charles and Diana memorial mug of coffee to me.

'Get 'em while they're hot,' Gin sings, simultaneously passing over a plate piled with the tiny, thick golden-brown wheels of deliciousness, drowning in maple syrup.

'Where's Ange?' I ask, noticing her absence with some relief, tucking into the coffee, happy to get the taste of *something else* out of my mouth.

'She doesn't get up before midday,' Melania says.

'Says it's bad for the womb,' Ashraf snorts. 'Although the smoking's bonzer, apparently.'

'Welcome to your first Centrefold house meal, babes,' Jacob says, raising their jam jar of green tea. There's an edge to their voice this morning, but maybe they're just hung-over, too. 'We're wet as English summer rain to have you.'

'Thank you?' I grimace, unsure if this is a good or a bad thing.

'How long were you in your old place?' asks Melania.

'Erm – five years.'

'Oh, wow!'

'With a straight couple,' Jacob says with several waggles of the head.

Everyone whistles.

'Terrible,' Melania tuts. 'Just terrible.'

'Did they treat you like a little pet possum?' Ashraf asks.

'Erm . . .' I'm unsure how to answer. 'Not exactly.'

'Good to be out of there, though,' Gin says.

'And with your own people.' Melania smiles.

I blink at them. Are these my people?

'Try as they might, they just can't understand what it's like to live in a world not made for them,' Ashraf says.

'Plus, their taste in interior décor is always *dégoûtant*.' That's Jacob.

'And they want always to watch football and sporting things such as this.' Melania shakes her head, like she just cannot understand this alien mindset.

'Luke was addicted to the rugby, wasn't he, Little Edie?' Jacob says to me, forehead raised – they haven't painted their eyebrows on yet.

'He was, Big Edie. He was.'

'*Grey Gardens* is *literally* my favourite film of all time! Of. All. Time!' Gin says, tapping my wrist. 'That and *Texas Chainsaw Massacre*. Original 1974 version, *obviously*.'

'Bloody hell, Ginny loves that more than me!' Ashraf laughs.

'True,' Gin replies.

'You've seen *Grey Gardens*?' I blink.

Everyone erupts into laughter.

'Next he'll ask if we've seen *Priscilla, Queen of the Desert*!' Ashraf howls.

I titter along. I have heard of that film, I just haven't got round to watching it yet.

'Leave Little Edie alone!' Jacob scolds. 'She's not well right now.'

'After his night, I'll say,' Melania cheerses to me again with her espresso glass. 'Christening your bed on only your second night here is absolutely an iconic move.'

Jacob's eyes flash with sinister glee. The pom-poms bounce as their foot taps excitedly. I can see the brief internal battle in which they're deciding whether to downplay the drama for my benefit, or launch into it for their delight.

'And with Zain Porowski. Well, I never.' The more thrilling option wins.

'Urghhh!' I lean forward, nearly braining the pancakes.

'He did not light a fire in your loving oven?' Melania asks with all seriousness.

I stare up at them, this strange group of absolute fruit loops who I now share life with.

'Why are gay men so awful to each other?' I say through my fingers.

Gin and Ashraf both shake their heads as if I were asking, *But what is the meaning of life?*

'If you ever find out, let us know, mate,' Ashraf says with a broad, toothy smile, and consumes a whole pancake in one go.

'Well, we know why, don't we?' Jacob says in a voice I imagine their students recognise all too well. 'Internalised homophobia. They attack in others what they hate in themselves. It's basic stuff.'

'Come on, *Velvet Rage*!' Gin cries.

Jacob's eyes briefly slide in their direction, then back to me with pursed lips.

'That's why I could never be a gay man.' Jacob pops half a pancake into their mouth. 'I love myself too fucking much.'

'And we love you, sweet lamb,' Melania says, kissing them on one angular shoulder.

'White gay men are the worst,' Ashraf says, going in for more pancakes. His eyes flick up to me hesitantly. 'No offence.'

'None taken.' I swallow.

'They're at the exact intersection of toxic masculinity and white privilege.' Gin is holding half a pancake in each hand, like a schematic. 'The oppressed becomes the oppressor. The bullied becomes the bully.'

I blink at these phrases just casually rolling off their tongue. This is not like breakfast at Luke and Laura's.

I must look totally nonplussed, because then Gin adds,

'Meaning the cis white straight-passing gay men shit on every-one else in the community.'

Jacob sips their green tea.

'Those that feel powerless seek to exert power when they can,' they say. 'And who better to do it on than those already in the firing line.'

Jacob and I have had discussions like these, but it's very different when three other queer people are staring you down. It doesn't feel wildly different from being in the ring of straight couples asking me if I want to get married.

'What about Zain?' I say. I'm hoping I can deflect without going into details.

'Ahhhh!' Jacob taps me with their toes, the nails painted in white and green stripes today. 'Well, that sweet angel is still on the hunt for his identity. Or, rather, how to marry up his divergent identities.'

'And he tries to find it in *a lot* of other people, from what I hear,' Melania says, looking over the rim of her glass naughtily.

'He tried to find it in me once,' Ashraf says.

'WHAT?' Gin's eyes are aflame beneath the straight line of their black bowl cut.

'Before we were together, babe,' he says. 'Years ago. He'd never been with a trans bloke before, and it blew his fucking mind. I was honestly just laying there laughing.'

'You never told me that. I'd have scrubbed you top to bottom if I'd known you'd been with him.' Gin grins and kisses Ashraf on the lips.

So Ashraf is trans and is with Gin, I think. *And exclusive, from the sound of things.*

As if hearing my thoughts, Ashraf turns to me. 'What's your ex's name, Danny?'

My stomach immediately swirls, and the beanbag begins to

engulf me. My eyes flick to the high corners of the room, to see if the cracks are forming. If he's slept with Tobbs, I'll go full Bertha in the Attic. Already, the idea we've inadvertently tag-teamed with Zain is too much for a hung-over Monday morning.

'You wouldn't know him,' I say. 'He sort of keeps himself to himself.' *Except for when he's shagging a whole bunch of other guys.*

Ashraf nods and looks back to his plate.

'What about my startlingly beautiful little friend Raj?' Melania says, tapping me on the knees. 'I swear I saw love blossoming between you two – before you fell on the floor like a drunk old shepherd woman.'

'Yeah, he's very . . . *cute.*' Truth be told, I can barely remember what he looked like.

'And he is kindly and very active in the activist community,' Melania goes on. 'In fact, he is organising a protest outside the Russian Embassy to highlight abuses to queer people in Chechnya.'

'What time is it?' I say suddenly, with a start.

'Next Friday, twelve noon,' Melania says, thrilled.

'No, no, I mean now?'

'Eight-thirty-two, angel,' Jacob says, standing. 'I'd better get my act together for the seminar I'm running at the RCA at two. Decolonising Biased Bindings and Biased Binaries – don't you just *die* for it?'

'I'm dead,' Melania says.

'Shit!' I struggle to my feet out of the beanbag. 'I'm going to be fucking late!'

No one else looks at all bothered. Do they not have jobs?

Gin offers up the remaining pancakes.

'Take one for the road, babe. Nothing absorbs Negronis quite like them.'

I grab two with my fist and stagger from the room. Then turn back in and say, 'Thanks so much for breakfast, I had a really good time,' and race upstairs to shower and change.

FIFTEEN

I arrive a sweaty, panicked half an hour late – which is every-body else's normal arrival time – and head straight to the coffee machine, trying to avoid the hubbub in the kitchen. But Jacob's appearance last week has caused my invisibility cloak to slip.

'There he is!' grins Marc from Front-End Development.

'Our fave fabulous writer!' grins Mark from Back-End Development, next to him.

As often happens, they're dressed near identically in black, with black caps and white Reeboks. They're a sort of hipster Tweedledum and Tweedledee. Double the intimidation for me.

'Hello, yes,' I say, grimacing, while pressing the button on the coffee machine for a latte and standing with my back to them.

It's not that I don't like my colleagues. They just make me feel like I'm in school. Tobbs hated it when I talked about them. He'd tell me they're a bunch of vapid hipsters. All fur coat, no knickers, he said. I said they're all vegan, so no fur coats at all.

'Your mate's actually pretty sick,' says Nadia from PR, hem-ming me in from the other side. She's dressed completely in neon pink today, including eyelids and acrylics. 'Stan'll be all over them.'

'Gross!' I shake my head.

'No.' She leans closer, in an unexpectedly candid gesture. 'Not "all over" like he is with the rest of us. "All over" like he can make money out of them, get traffic, subscribers, clicks, whatever. Apparently, LeSwann's been breathing down his throat because we're losing money every day.'

'Urgh!' I gag while adding my cursory two packets of artificial sweetener. 'Straight guys are literally *dégoûtants*.'

Nadia's eyes flare with the thrill of it. The shy little one's being bitchy, can you believe it?

'*Absolument*.'

At my desk, snippets from last night float up to me. 'You're so firm, like a breadboard,' I said to Zain as my hand slithered down his stomach towards his boxers. CRINGE. When he said, 'Want me to destroy you?' I replied, 'Yes, thank you.' This is the sort of thing you do at uni, not when you're twenty-seven and trying your best to be a functioning adult.

Sex still freaks me out so much. This intense, embarrassing, naked intimacy. All these movements you have to make seamlessly, and these sounds you have to make in the right way at the right time. It's a mindfuck. And before you know it, you've lost your boner and you wish you'd never started in the first place.

My stomach gurgles, as often happens post-latte. I head to the disabled loo, which I always go to because I get stage fright in the very audible stalls. But as I get to the door, I pause. There's a weird groaning noise coming from inside, like someone's struggling with a fat one. Maybe because it feels like the room is starting to spin sideways, or because I'm actually just a glutton for embarrassment, I shake the handle anyway, and the door swings outward.

In place of the toilet is Stan's white, spotty arse, hanging over the top of his tracksuit bottoms, thrusting again and again. I know it's him immediately because his cap is on backward, the 'Boss' lettering staring right at me. Two bronzed, muscular shins wrap around his sweaty back, and a huge bicep squeezes around the back of his neck. A set of cornflower-blue eyes lock with mine. They are wild with panic.

I pull the door to and race off to the men's, where I lock myself in the cubicle and deep-breathe for what feels like forever. As I head back to my desk, I hear Stan shout 'Snowflakes, assemble!' from the Brixton Skatepark. 'Or your P45s will be on your desks by lunch!' How wonderful he can still joke at a time like this.

People are meandering over, and in the crowd Callum tries to whisper something to me.

'Danny, it's not what it looks like, honestly.'

'He's the sugar daddy you want old-fashioned romance with?' I hiss back. 'He's married! And he's – urgh – *Stan*.'

Callum looks so torn up I almost feel sorry for him, but my reserves are low this morning, particularly when it comes to gay guys ruining other people's relationships with sex. Fortunately, Stan starts shouting again as we congregate on the edge of the half-pipe.

'Greetings, Woke Warriors,' he says, pressing his hands together. 'Another week, another opportunity to stretch the minds of our users wide open. But more on that later. First, I want to address the pink elephant in the room. Cal, come up here, bro.'

Callum sheepishly leaves my side and joins Stan's, where Stan's piggy hand lands on one of Callum's pert peaches. Nadia gasps and immediately takes twenty photos. The Marc/ks stare at each other. Callum gives a little wave, like he's marrying a royal.

'Yes, that's right, you frigid Tories,' Stan says merrily, almost – dare I say it – *proudly*, 'Cal and I are "homosexual lovers" now.' He does finger quotes. Callum couldn't look more uncomfortable. 'Yes, I am still married to Jane. Yes, it's very modern and probably illegal in most countries. And, yes, I'm sure you're shocked and appalled – and that, millennials, is the CULTRD way. The CULTRD "culture", if you will.' More finger quotes. 'And we need more of this attitude if we're going to smash our targets and win those awards.' He nods at Callum. 'Now go on, mate, sit down.'

Callum waves again to the crowd and dutifully returns to it. Nadia's open mouth has now curved up to a gleeful grin.

'On to Agenda Issue Two,' Stan trills blithely. 'Our failure, and what we're going to do about it. Robyn!' he whistles to the crowd. 'Pop yourself up here to explain the stats, there's a babe.'

The willow tree that is Robyn from Strategy emerges and positions herself on the other side of the graffiti wall, a safe distance from Stan. She always sways whenever he waves his arms, like his breeze is too much for her.

'Yes, thank you, Stan.'

'Stan what?' Stan says, grinning to his captive employees.

Robyn sighs. 'Stan Boss Man.'

Stan's laugh booms around the silent gathering. He points at the cap with both bacon-roll forefingers, then shakes his head. 'Just joshing. Go on, girl.'

Robyn's face, which already looks like it's been put on too tight, tightens further. A thin-lipped mouth forces a line of a smile.

'Thank you, Stan.' She coughs, and turns to the presentation now live on the screen: 'At CULTRD, our mission is to find the most exciting, unique people, communities and experiences in the U.K., and let our designated audiences know how they can access them. So, as you can see, subscriptions and unique page views have been dropping pretty steadily over the last . . . um, nine quarters.' Robyn's Norwegian accent lilts around. I always love listening to it; it's an ocean, and Stan's voice is the rocks. Flick to next slide. 'But dwell time has been good in some special areas.'

'Tell us about your special areas, Robyn,' Stan interjects in that 'I know I'm doing risky comedy' voice he's such a fan of.

Robyn coughs again and does not look at him.

'Yes, thank you, Stan.' Her knuckles are white around the screen flicker, and I swear to God her eyes flash red for a split second. Flick to next slide. 'Where we're seeing growth is very interesting. Users want to *feel* like they're part of a unique community or experience, that they are witnessing in the most honest way possible. People know when they're getting sold to nowadays.'

'Basically, we need weirder shit from absolute freaks that we can sell to hot, rich young people,' Stan interrupts. There is complete silence. 'Ha! Ha!' he belts. 'That's the corporate line from LeSwann, anyway. I obviously wouldn't put it like that. Nadia!' Nadia looks up from her phone. 'You must have some links with – I dunno – reformed terrorists?'

Her mouth falls open again. 'Yes, lots actually,' she says. 'My gran's in the Taliban, so.'

'Fuck, yes!' Stan cries, punching the air, unaware that everyone is struck dumb. 'And, Scudders, your fabulous drag-queen friend, we'd love to do something on him. ABSOLUTE STUNNER! Normal people don't know people like him. Cal could film a piece.' And he winks at Callum.

'NO!' someone wails. Everyone turns to stare at me. Oh God, it was me. 'I mean' – I try to recover – 'Jacob probably wouldn't do it. But – BUT – there's a protest next Friday, at the Russian

Embassy, about LGBT rights violations in Chechnya. I could cover that instead, maybe?'

Even though my boss is shagging my teammate, saying the letters 'LGBT' in front of a roomful of people makes my pulse quicken. I would never have said this in school – wouldn't have dared. Saying it now still feels like a 'kick me' sign I'm applying to my own back.

'There's the content ideas we need! Nice ones, Scudders!' Stan booms. I feel a swell of pride. The dare paid off. 'People love that faggy stuff these days. Mad for it. I know I am.' And the pride curdles to disgust.

———

For a while, we throw ping-pong balls at one another to help us think of under-represented communities to infiltrate, make videos and interactive maps about and then sell to wealthy urbanites. The balls are Stan's idea, obviously.

'You know who I'd actually suicide-bomb?' Nadia says when we're back at our desks.

'He just wants to be cool,' I say, glancing around, making sure Callum isn't back yet.

'He should be in prison.' Nadia's leaning in so close I can smell her lemony face cream. 'Can you actually believe he's our boss? I mean, is he even bisexual, or is he just doing it because he thinks that's what Gen Z are into?'

'My housemates would go ballistic about this,' I say, thinking about our conversation this morning. 'It's like corporate Pride to the max. Using marginalised communities to sell cheap hotel rooms and bottomless brunches . . . I'd love to win that British Journalism Award, though.'

'What?'

I realise I've said that last bit out loud.

'All right, lads!' Callum grins awkwardly.

'OK!' Nadia whistles, and leaves.

Callum watches her go as if in physical pain. 'Was it the terrorist thing?' he says to me. 'To be fair, she is kind of aggressive.'

'Um . . .' I consider. 'Probably just the tip of the iceberg, there.'

'Just the tip?' Cal says before thinking about it. He shakes his head, and changes tone. 'Dan, look, I'm seriously so sorry you saw us earlier. It's just, we were doing it for my OnlyFans.'

I hold up both palms and screw my eyes shut. I've really had it with gay people today — whether or not they actually are even gay.

'You do what you want to do, Cal.' *Just maybe not in the work loos, with our married boss.*

'Fabulous. Thanks, Dan.' He grins timidly. 'Ooh – also! – I can help you film that protest thingy if you want?'

'NO!' Oh God, I've done it again. 'I mean' – I try to backtrack – 'I'd like to get better acquainted with the camera gear, you know, as, like, a . . . learning objective.'

'Oh, righteo, then,' Callum flashes his teeth, bops his head and wanders off somewhere.

I actually can't remember the last time I saw him at his desk, and I realise I would love to punch him so hard. Him and Stan and Zain and everyone.

SIXTEEN

I walk from the bus in the rain and fumble with the front door keys for a while. All day has felt like a battle against the electricity in my head, the rumbling of the earth beneath my feet, and keeping it at bay has taken everything out of me. I'm absolutely shattered. Time for some Dolly in the bath, I think.

I stand on the inside of the door with my skull pressed up against the wood, wishing more than anything that my life was as it was before. As my breathing slows, a low, soulful melody replaces its rhythm. It's lolling down the creaking stairs with a gentle cadence, crawling deep from within the darkness of the house. It's Jacob practising the cello.

In typical Type A fashion, Jacob's talents don't begin and end at teaching, performing and turning epic lewks, they're also a Grade 8 cellist. It's one of the things that got them through growing up in Whistlecombe, I always think: being able to melt into the sound and drown everything else out.

Now I melt into it, and try to disappear.

Determined not to have a conversation with anyone, I tiptoe past the living room, keeping to the shadows. Light pools from the two arches across the faded terracotta and mustard-yellow tiles. I peep in. Gin and Ashraf are cuddled up on one of the sofas, projecting something onto the opposite wall. On it, a double-exposed woman in a black headscarf fastened with a large gold broach in the shape of a bow peers sceptically into the camera lens.

'This really is the best thing to wear for the day,' she's saying in a broad Long Island drawl. 'Mother wanted me to come out in a kimono, so we had quite a fight.'

I hold in a gasp of joy. It's my namesake, Little Edie Bouvier Beale. They must have decided to watch *Grey Gardens* after our conversation this morning. I don't know if this would have ever got a look-in at Luke and Laura's. I actually don't think I ever mentioned it to them, because I knew they'd just think it was strange. And obviously it was a no-go with Tobbs. He only ever wanted to watch 'serious' documentaries so afterwards he could tell you what was wrong with them.

A warm glow pools in me like the light, like the sound. They look happy, *really* happy. And the cutest thing? They're wearing matching lion and tiger onesies with the hoods pulled up, triangular ears sticking out. Maybe gay people can be happy together. Maybe it isn't a complete fantasy.

I creep along to the kitchen, and I can't help but smile.

———

For a while, I stand on the dim landing outside Jacob's door, listening. It really is the most wonderful sound, like a kind, sad voice humming through reeds. As the bow draws the piece to a close, I call, 'Are you decent?' through the door while semi-humping it with my chest. Trying to knock with an elbow and two bowls of pesto ravioli is harder than you'd think.

'Of body, but not of mind,' they call back.

The handle clicks, and it swings inward.

Jacob sits on a maroon conference chair in the middle of the room with the squirrel-red wood of the cello between the chest-nut brown of their slender thighs. Both gleam in the flickering light from the candles dotted around the room and the soft white glow of a Muji vaporiser dutifully spooling out steam from the desk in the wide, curved window.

Tonight they're dressed somewhere between a Victorian governess and a Tudor queen on her way to the gallows. From under their sharply drawn collarbone tumbles a mass of ruching and poufing in black silk with more than one tear. They are a haute-couture bin bag, with braids piled high in a bun and, amusingly, a pair of beige Ugg boots peeping out beneath the tattered hem.

'Did you make me tea?' they say.

I sidle in and close the door with my arse.

'In London we call it "dinner".'

Jacob returns the cello to her stand in one corner and relieves one bowl from my hand.

'You ghoul.'

They sweep over to the bed and rearrange the many patterned cushions for us to sit. I follow, propping myself up on Frida Kahlo's embroidered face.

No matter how many times I've been in here, Jacob's room always amazes me. You might first assume their boudoir would be an Aladdin's Cave, a chaotic treasure trove of fur coats and charity-shop oddities. But it's actually almost clinical, which, once you know Jacob well, makes perfect sense.

It's over the living room and shares its vast floor plan, with a grand bay window and peeling, ornate plasterwork. But that's where its similarities with *Grey Gardens* ends, because behind Jacob's giant persona are a hundred little elves scurrying around to make sure everything's in order. Three metal clothing rails line one wall, on which hang, in colour and type, Jacob's extraordinary wardrobe. Every item is labelled with a brown evacuee tag and sheathed in a plastic body bag to protect it from moths, moisture and anything else that might live in the crevices of this house. There's a separate shoe cupboard, and next to it a massive white IKEA shelving unit full of art and sewing materials. Various creations line the wall behind us: a papier-mâché bull's head, feathered carnival headdress, wings made from slithers of silver foil. Even the furniture, though distinctly not matching in anyway, has been painted white to provide a uniform background to the organised chaos. Jacob would never let something as pesky as a budget get in the way of a cohesive vision.

We chew away together.

'That was really beautiful, Jay,' I say. 'I've missed hearing you play.'

'Thanks, Danielle. And thanks, Debussy.'

'*De bus*sy?'

'*Oui*.' Jacob sighs deeply and stares at the opposite wall. 'He always calms me down. I've had a bit of a day.'

'Oh, shit. How was the seminar?'

Jacob tries to make a face, but their mouth is full of molten cheese and cherry tomatoes.

'It honestly never ceases to amaze me how people with all the money and education in the world can still be so utterly narrow-minded.' They swallow down said mouthful before continuing. 'And these people want to be *artists*. They talk about breaking the rules, changing how we see the world and all that, but when it comes down to it, they don't actually mean it – not *really*. They want to put themselves out there only when it's safe; they don't have the commitment to really *be* their art, to really challenge what people think with the way they live. Whereas *I'm* committed. I *am* my art, I *am* what I say I am and what I believe. But the difference is, I've never had a choice. They can opt in; I can't opt out.'

As they're speaking, they're getting angrier and angrier. In fact, they're saying it like it's my fault. Am I just reading too much into it? Or have they realised something, like they're embarrassed to have me in the house?

'Well, you could try,' I say in a half-joking, half-not-joking voice.

Jacob stares at me. Their elegant eyes are thick with rage. I immediately regret it.

'Everyone's always trying to take who I am away from me. Much like you did last night.'

For once, I'm not being anxious for no reason – they are annoyed at me.

'Jacob, I – I . . .' I stutter. 'I wasn't trying to take who you are away from you. I was just . . . just an absolute state. I dunno. I'm not proud of myself.'

'*Proud*?' Jacob spits the word. 'No, no, you are *not* proud of yourself, Danny, and that's the problem. Do you realise that was the most important night of my life? And you were just heckling me the whole time? It made me feel like I was back at school, when Basic Laura and Rory McClure would shout shit at me across the playground. Except this time it's my best friend, who's supposed to be supporting me.'

'Fuck, Jay.' I reach forward and grab their hand. They flinch. 'I'm so, so sorry. I really didn't mean to do that. I'm just shit at everything at the moment.'

But Jacob's not done.

'And then you came home and rode Zain Porowski!' They laugh. 'Bloody hell, that must have been a real shame sandwich.'

'Hey, that's not fair.'

Jacob pulls the hand away and crosses their arms.

'Do you even remember what you did?'

'Ummm.' A few blurry images swim back to me. 'I got everyone Negronis. Then did I pole-dance with a middle-aged woman called Jill?'

'Dill,' they say flatly. 'The late-night bouncer. She's a herb enthusiast. Anything else?'

'Ummm. Was there some guy looking after me . . . ? Black guy? Yay high? Dressed as a policeman.'

Jacob purses their lips. 'Nope. That was *my* guy.'

'*Your guy*?'

'Yes, dickhead! I do have a life outside of your drama, you know?'

'Yeah, no, I know that—'

'And Angel D is *such* an angel!'

'No way is his name Angel D?'

'Yah. Angel Delight.'

'Shut up.'

'Shan't.'

'Shut up are you dating a guy called Angel Delight?'

'Well,' Jacob says, bristling, 'we've only been on a couple of gallery dates. I haven't had anyone look at me like that in – forever. You cis gay guys aren't very open to a goddess such as I.' They pause, then reconsider. 'I was actually going to introduce you to him, but then you were – you know – being you.'

I swallow hard. This wounds me more than it should.

'You haven't told me about him.'

Jacob looks tired, resigned.

'And yet he knows all about you – since your *performance*. He was actually kind of horrified this was who I'd been talking about.' They puff up their chest and do a deep Jamaican accent: '"Man really had it in for you."'

'Oh God.' I bury my head in my hands. Tears are pricking my eyes. 'Oh God, I'm sorry, Jay.'

I blink them away, and look back. Something about their expression has changed. There's a haughtiness to it, even a cruelness.

'I still got an email from the programme director at the Southbank Centre, though.'

I blink a few more times.

'Wait – what?'

Jacob casually plays with a loose braid.

'Yes, well, he just said he was in the audience and my performance really spoke to him. He wants me to devise a new work for this Instagram Live series they're doing next year.'

'Jay!' I cry. 'That's amazing!'

They throw the braid over their shoulder.

'Well, I am a very strange and extraordinary person, Danielle.'

'You are, you really are!' I squeal with embarrassing eagerness.

Sated, Jacob smiles, and this smile flips my mood upside down. They knew this before I came in, so why did they test me? Just to punish me? Just to exert some power over me? Even in these tender moments with their oldest friend, is Jacob still performing? 'I *am* what I say I am' bitterly repeats itself across my mind.

They reach forward and pat me a couple of times on the thigh, like an uptight teacher letting you know your parents' divorce isn't the end of the world.

'So tell me about Mister Mistress of East London?' There's still a tone to this, but I ignore it. 'Was he as good as everyone says he is?'

I gag.

'It's so gross, isn't it? That Ashraf and me have been with the same guy.'

Jacob cackles, and it's full witch vibes.

'I'm afraid there's a lot of that, babe. The East gays are like horses on a carousel – each one gets ridden for three minutes by someone. Then the ride stops, and someone else gets on.'

'Vomit. If Ashraf had said he'd been with Tobbs, I just . . . It makes me feel sick just thinking about it.'

'I don't think creepy little journalists are Ash's type, to be honest. Plus, him and Gin have been a thing for a while now.'

'He wasn't creepy!'

'He was though, wasn't he?'

'I dunno – maybe.'

Jacob puts an arm around me and squeezes. The black silk rustles against my ear. *Shhhh, shhhh.*

'You know, Little Edie,' they say in quite a different voice, a more motherly one, 'you're on the cusp of a great new life. No Tobbs, no Basic Laura, just us and Nina and anyone else you might like . . . and that I approve of, of course. Don't look back, look forward – maybe towards Melania's mate, that little art-school twink?'

'Raj!' I remember with fondness. 'Yeah, he did seem nice. But I don't know if I'm really ready for—'

'Hush, now!' Jacob's holding a finger up to my lips. 'The pasta's getting cold.'

'Oh, right, yeah,' I say and we both eat in silence.

I cling to the bowl like it's a lifebuoy. I feel so massively un-tethered at the moment, and this has made it worse. Though we sit thigh to thigh, a gulf has opened between us.

SEVENTEEN

I don't see Jacob much for the rest of the week. Melania says they're busy with their residency, and with Angel D, but I can't help feeling like they're avoiding me.

I both mind and don't. For someone who's always the talk of every room they enter, it seems pretty rich to have a go at me for dealing with my break-up by getting drunk and being uncharacteristically loud. All the same, I hate the thought of them bitching about me to their new guy. Are they having lunch in the RCA cafeteria right now, discussing why they're even still friends with their bland friend from primary school? The idea of it makes my stomach turn.

And another thing at the moment: I keep suddenly crying. Anything could set me off. Callum puts some flowers from Stan in a jar between our desks, and away I go to the loos to have a sob. Or Stan himself says something gross about Robyn from Strategy's 'perky' campaign assets, and off I dart to the Grime Music Studio to weep snot into the turntables.

Having been a grade-A student all through school, and always doing my homework the night it was assigned, has set me up well to complete Nina's task. When I feel a strong emotion or thought, I write it down:

Thursday 8th November
- *Impending feeling of dread isn't so bad today, which must be good?*
- *Really miss Tobbs a lot. Like A LOT. But also feel relieved to be away from him. Weird/confusing.*
- *Not comfortable in house yet, but probs won't be for ages. Feel uncomfortable in whole body actually, like it's the wrong size.*
- *Can't believe I had sex with Zain! Feels gross but also kind of cool???*
- *Jacob is narking me off. But probs just me feeling weird about everything ATM.*

I am actually warming to life in the house. It's so different from anything I've ever experienced. It's sort of like a weird gap year, where you move to a hostel crammed with people you'd never normally speak to. The housemates keep inviting me to do stuff like yoga and life drawing in the living room, with Ashraf modelling. But I've made excuses and gone up to my room instead, because it's a bit too full-on. I have to be 'on' all the time around them. Plus, these tears aren't going to cry themselves.

Being around other gay (although I suppose I should say 'queer') people is itself a whole thing. The other day, Melania came out of the middle-floor bathroom and was like, 'Whose's douche is this? I'm using it.' I had to google what you actually specifically do with a douche, because it turns out it's not just French for 'shower'.

But(t) it's not all butt stuff. Gin and Ashraf are really cute with each other, and seeing them work out in the living room and make meals together kind of breaks my heart. Me and Tobbs never did stuff like that. I always wanted to, but he hated being in the flat together. He only wanted to go out for breakfast, and never, NEVER wanted to watch a movie with Laura and Luke. He didn't even like sleeping over. He said he got sleep paralysis if he wasn't in his own bed.

I ask Stan if I can work from home on Friday, and he says, 'As long as you don't spend the whole day wanking, Scudders!' And for once, he's not far off. Something has wakened in me. Something I've never let out before. Instead of fearing someone touching me, like I've always felt, I'm craving it. Maybe Zain opened the gate, as it were.

On my lunch break, I download several hook-up apps. I've never been on them before. Tobbs and I met on Guardian Soulmates, which seemed the least terrifying of all the options.

'It's just sex,' I say as I scroll, reminding myself how every other gay guy is constantly having fun casual sex and this is just me being typically uptight again.

It amazes me, though, how frankly people state things about themselves:

ANON MASC 28
Door unlocked, c*m & go, no chat.

SUCK NOW 47
Married man looking to suck all night. Can't accom cos of the wifey & kids 😩

LAURENCE 52
Gentle but curious community gardener seeks E15 tap dancing tutor. Happy to pay in cash or have recently completed my Level 5 Indian head massage training.

One guy, maybe a little younger than me, is standing on a beach next to a short, middle-aged woman with curly grey hair. They look similar; she must be his mum. His profile reads:

C*M-DRUNK GUTTER SL*T 24
Filthy piggy down to f*ck raw. No d**k pix, no action.

I watch traffic go past on the road outside, wondering what would convince me to upload a picture of Mary and me, and then a description like this. To avoid any parental weirdness, I've used my LinkedIn profile picture, which is me in a pale-blue shirt, smiling at the camera like I've just done a fart and I know any second now you'll smell it.

I continue to scroll. It's like shopping. Except, instead of a lovely new calathea, you might get someone the same age as your father knocking on your door and actually have to call him Daddy. The phone vibrates a few times, and I nearly drop it. I flick to the DM interface: I'm getting messages already.

Hi
Hi
Hi
Hi m8
6 here playing

Hey gorgeous, into fisting?

How old r u? 63 here but into younger.

I click the screen to black, feeling bleak. Modern romance. It's not exactly Austen, is it?

Who'll want you? a voice says in my head. Whose is it? Tobbs's? Zain's? Mine?

'Piss off,' I say aloud, and go back to the app.

During this time, someone not too bad-looking has pinged me a couple of photos and a 'Hey'. He's a blond guy, maybe in his late twenties, narrow features but kind of cute. The two first pictures are of him in a pale-blue shirt (tick!) in some kind of office. The last one is him shirtless in a tropical jungle. I part my fingers to zoom in. Pretty banging bod, which instantly makes me freak out. *Why would he speak to you? You're skinny-fat, not some Adonis.*

Seven eleven, seven eleven, I say to myself, shutting my eyes and breathing.

I look at the message again, the yellow words burnt into the black interface.

Hey, Mr! How's your Friday going?

He's written.

I take a deep breath, and type back.

Hey! Busy but good thanks

He types back immediately.

Oh haha! Nose to the grindstone, hey?

Kinda yeah

Need to relieve some tension? 😉

I feel some electricity spark, thankfully not in my head this time.

Yeah

175

Maybe

Wanna come over?

I stare at the message for a while. My chest is thumping. It's *that* easy. It's like Deliveroo. How weird that we can just order each other like this.

I don't reply, but then he sends through his location. It's three roads away.

I'm Klaus BTW 😌

My fingers shake as I reply.

I'm Danny

Nice to meet you Danny

Likewise

So, you coming over?

After a little bit of groinal topiary and some, *e-hem*, strategic personal hygiene (not involving the douche), I head down the stairs, feeling like I'm descending further into a murky pool with each step.

The kitchen is around behind the stairs, a sort of long room with a big table and more condiments on every surface than you can imagine. It sounds like most of my new housemates are in there, and, for some reason, I feel the need to sneak out. I make a dash for the door and pull it shut ever so gently.

—

Klaus told me to message on the app, rather than ring the bell, so I stand there outside the red door trying to stop my head from shaking, typing 'I'm here' into the black-and-yellow screen. Joining in with the nice electricity in my pants is my old friend the electric forehead fingers. The stomach is also swirling, which worries me, given the scenario.

Klaus had *not* told me his house was undergoing renovation, and several builders are clambering around scaffolding and going back and forth, yelling to each other in Polish, while Carly Rae Jepsen plays loudly from one of their phones.

'Hallo,' one says gruffly, bringing out some smashed-up bricks from the back and lobbing them into the skip on the pavement.

'I'm Klaus's friend,' I say. 'From uni.'

'Alex,' the man says, pointing at himself.

'Yes,' I say. He goes back around the side of the house.

A few more bars of 'Call Me Maybe' play. A few more bounces of my knee occur.

The door swings inward.

'Is that my chicken jalfrezi?'

Klaus appears in the doorway in a pair of Nike sports shorts and a baggy blue 'NHS at 70' T-shirt. He's taller than I expected, and even handsomer – which *never* happens, I'm led to believe. A cute cluster of light-brown freckles pepper his nose and cheeks, and he's slightly sunburnt across the forehead. He squints at me, and even this is endearing.

'Ah no, that'll be next, then.'

'Sorry,' I say. 'You can't eat me.'

He stares at me blankly, then lets out a laugh that sounds more like a sneeze. 'Aahh-*choo!*'

I feel my face colour. 'I didn't think about that before I said it.'

'No,' he says, laughing, 'you didn't. But I'll still let you in.' He turns back into the hall. I waver on the welcome mat. It says 'Hi, I'm Mat!' on it. 'I promise not to eat you,' Klaus says from the hall.

'Oh yeah. Thanks.'

I go in and close the door.

He leads me upstairs. What I see of the house is lovely, more adult and put-together than the Centrefold. It's all grey-blue walls and actually framed pictures that aren't weird and vaginal. There are cheese plants and bookcases with actual books in them. The several bedrooms he leads me past all seem to have colourful, charming quilts and shagpile rugs on white exposed boards. There's even a tabby sunning itself on a double bed in the master bedroom.

His room, like mine, is on the top floor, though it's larger, with a slanting roof and a big arched window that lets in a lot of light. Beyond it, I can see the scaffolding, a flap of plastic hanging in the calm air. This room, too, looks like it belongs to a real adult – there's a palm tree next to the desk where a series of medals hang from a clothes peg, and several nicely framed pictures of him with family and friends grinning in a variety of balmy locations. I recognise one as the picture he'd sent me – only it has a woman who must be his mum in it. He's done the wise thing and cropped her out. Weirdly, a sense of comfort floods my body – he's a decent guy.

'I love your plants,' I say. 'That parlour palm is a bit dry, though.'

Suddenly his hands are on my chest.

'So nice of you to come round,' he says, kissing me. 'I haven't seen you before.'

'I just moved here,' I say, trying to negotiate kiss and conversation at the same time. 'I used to live South, so.'

'Ah, the Southerner's first foray into East London!' His accent is maybe Dutch or German; I can't work it out. 'How are you finding it?'

'Pretty good, I s'pose.'

He pushes me back onto the tasteful woollen blanket across

the bed, where I fall as rigidly as a corpse. His mouth tastes freshly of toothpaste, but with an aftertaste of something tangy, like Orangina. His hands are now sliding up under my T-shirt.

'Well, maybe we can make it memorable.'

His tongue is in my ear. Now it's in my mouth again. Now it's circling my chin. Now it's licking my cheek like a cat lapping up milk. I lie as still as possible, unsure how to react to what's quickly becoming a lie-down bath.

'What do you like doing?' he whispers through the saliva in my ear.

'Like – everything.'

'*Everything*?'

'Yeah.'

'I'm excited; you Brits are usually so restrained.'

'My granddad's Scottish, so.'

'I'm really *kinky*.' The word alone makes me think of the porn I'm too afraid to click on. But it also adds to the arousal. I've gone beyond the boundary.

'Oh yeah?' I'm getting into it now, trying to redirect his mouth back to kissing me instead of licking me. He pulls off my top and gets stuck into the armpit. My strategy is failing.

'Yeah,' he breathes hungrily. 'I'm into all sorts.' And away go my jeans and boxers. At some point, he's also taken his off. How has he done this during all this licking? 'But, of course, the dream would be for you to take a dump on my chest.'

I start coughing manically. 'Of course!'

He sits up and glares at me. 'What, you're not into scat play?'

I try to stop coughing, looking at him quizzically. 'Like – jazz?'

Klaus rolls his eyes. 'Oh, just fuck me, then.'

'OK.'

This is harder than you might think. Or, rather, no hardness at all. From this point on, every time he touches my dick, it gets softer and softer. At one point, it basically turns into an innie. Though clearly frustrated, Klaus doesn't give up, and manages to suck it to completion. The whole experience is both mortifying and kind of hot, and afterwards I lie in the tangled sheets, staring at the ceiling, while he goes next door to the bathroom to get a towel.

'Hallo,' comes a voice from the window.

'JESUS CHRIST!' I cry, pulling the tasteful blanket over my distasteful mess.

'No,' grins the builder kneeling on the scaffolding. 'Alex.'

EIGHTEEN

My second visit to see Nina feels only slightly less uncomfortable than the first. What's she going to uncover this time, huh? The little archaeologist just digging, digging, digging away. What happens if she hits the drains?

'So, Danny,' she says, readjusting herself in the squeaking chair after I've given her a brief rundown of this week's shenanigans. Black bob on point today, mixed up with some black high-waisted slacks and a black satin blouse. Intimidatingly put together again. 'Last time, we discussed your anxiety, your relationship with Tobbs—'

'Not that we have to worry about that anymore. I'm very much into single life now.'

Nina shifts her head from side to side. From the road, an ambulance's siren shatters the relative quiet.

'We still have some more work to do there. It was quite damaging for you, I think.'

I think of Tobbs's unkempt hair as I ran my fingers through it, him flinching. His grey-blue eyes darkening to brown. His stupid teenage/middle-aged wardrobe that I loved. His mouth kissing mine, smelling of smoke.

'Yeah' is all I say.

'And then with Zain, was it? The builder guy from—'

'No, no,' I interrupt. 'The builder just *happened* to be there. Klaus, the guy, was . . . Actually, I don't know what his job was. Something well paid.'

'Right. Klaus.' Nina nods.

'And Zain was just, like, a whole different *thing*.'

'Understood. Let's stick with Klaus for now. You described the way he licked you and wanted you to defecate on him, but you didn't, is that correct?'

'I did actually let him watch me pee,' I say. 'Afterward. Just in the loo. I got stage fright, though, and he had to turn on the sink tap to get me going.'

Nina's head bobs as if this is the most reasonable thing in the world. 'And how did that make you feel?'

'Not gross, exactly. Just . . . uncomfortable. Like, I didn't get anything from it.'

'Did he force you to do it?'

'No, he was super-polite. I just, sort of, felt . . . obliged.'

Nina is nodding furiously. The hands are clasped around the knee again.

'Right. Right. Right,' she says with some urgency. 'So you didn't want to do it for you, but felt *obliged* to do it for him?'

'Yeah.'

'And did you agree to the licking?'

'Well, he just kind of did that before I realised what was happening.'

'But the defecation was too far?'

I settle her with what I hope is a 'bitch please' look. 'No shame if people are into that, but yes.'

'And how did you feel – *do* you feel – afterward?'

I shift about in the seat. Here come the knee trembles. 'I kind of – erm – nearly had a panic attack, I think.' She's looking at me so unflinchingly I'm embarrassed. 'Afterwards. I felt kind of funny. But I sorted it out, it's all good! I had a bath and did some deep breathing. I'm fine now!' I smile, to reassure her.

The shadow of a smile passes briefly across her little face. 'That's great you recognised the feeling and were able to self-soothe.'

'Yeah, I s'pose so.'

'What does it feel like when you have these panic attacks?'

'Well.' More shifting about, looking towards the window. 'I don't know if they are panic attacks, exactly. They've only happened a few times.'

'How many, would you say?'

'Just that one time at the station, really.' Lies. All lies. 'And maybe a few other times, I can't really remember. I sort of get foggy around it.'

'What does it feel like when it's coming?'

'Oh.' I wasn't expecting this. Talking about them makes me feel like they'll hear, like they're hiding in the walls and floor waiting to contort the building, break into the room and squeeze the breath out of me.

You're not dying. These problems are nothing to her. Stop being so pathetic.

I close my eyes and breathe for a few seconds.

'Danny?' I hear Nina's voice. 'Is it happening now?'

I open my eyes and smile. 'No. No. Just – erm – thinking about them.'

My blood is pumping in my ears. It's really like they've been summoned by an incantation.

Now Nina is smiling in a kind, gentle, real way. She doesn't believe me one jot.

'Can they come on just from thinking about them?'

I swallow.

'Not usually.'

'When do they usually come on?'

I think hard. As stupid as it might sound, I've actually never thought about this before. They always just take me, and then I have to deal with them. I've never sat back and really tried to see any links.

'I got them a lot with Tobbs,' I say, tentatively. 'And sometimes at work. Often with my family – Christmas is probably the worst. I always end up having to go and have a bath or a walk just to calm myself down on Christmas Day.'

'And with Zain?'

'I don't really remember, to be honest, so I think we're fine on that.'

Her smile broadens. 'We've all been there.'

And we both laugh. That's a relief.

'Danny, remember last week we talked about "boundaries"?'

'Yes,' I say, swallowing. 'Sorry for calling you so many times, by the way. I was . . . not doing so great on Sunday.'

'That's fine, Danny. But think about when this builder – I mean this *guy*, Klaus – asked you to do something you didn't want to do, and how you reacted.'

'I laughed.'

'But that was you asserting your boundaries.'

'I don't know if it was. I didn't really understand what he was talking about.'

'But then the licking and the urination, that was him overstepping your boundaries.'

'Well, I let him do it.'

'Exactly!' Nina basically shouts. Just the excitement on her face is enough to make me jump.

'Wait, so you're saying I should have said no? I was just being polite.'

'But you didn't want to do it.'

'It was no skin off my back – although, no, I wasn't exactly into it.'

'And with Tobbs, did you ever tell him about the aspects of his behaviour you didn't like?'

I twist my thumb in the palm of my other hand.

'Um . . . not really. To be honest, sex as a whole makes me uncomfortable. I never know what to do with my body. I normally just try to pretend it isn't happening. Except with Tobbs, I was mad about it with him – not that I got it.'

'Was there a time with anybody else that you enjoyed?'

'Um.' I swallow hard. 'Well, Tobbs is the only guy I've *really done it* with, you know? Like, *properly done it* – until this week. I've just tripled my numbers.'

'Congratulations.'

'Thank you.'

We smile at each other. She's actually great.

'Have you had other sexual interactions – with men or women?'

I think hard. I don't want to go down this route. It's a surefire way to make the earthquakes rumble towards me, to fill this room with thick, black dread.

Nina is smiling very gently.

'You don't have to tell me, if you don't feel comfortable, Danny.'

I inhale very loudly and suddenly.

'No, it's fine.' The leg's going. 'There were a couple of guys at uni I sort of had something with – nothing major, mostly alcohol-fuelled. And I gave a hand job to this guy at one of

Jacob's parties once. His name was Quaid. He had a pet ferret on his shoulder the whole time.'

'A pet ferret?' Nina is blinking.

'Its name was also Quaid.'

And now she's trying not to laugh. She takes a breath, and composes herself.

'Anyone else? When you were younger, for example?'

And here it is. The part I really don't want to discuss.

'Um – yeah. Back at home.'

Nina very visibly tries hard not to look as excited as she is.

'Oh yes?'

'This boy at secondary school,' I say, not looking at her. 'Billy Winters. Will, I mean. We, sort of, used to, you know – kiss and stuff, when no one was around.' I let out a huge breath and think for a second I'm going to cry. 'But he wasn't so into it, and then he told everyone, so . . .'

My voice trails off. I've been fixating on my knees this whole time but now look up. Nina is looking at me very sadly. No twinkle of a laugh left.

'That must have been very hard, Danny, to be betrayed like that.'

'No, no! It wasn't a betrayal. It was just like' – my eyes start searching the ceiling, as if there's an answer there – 'you know . . . It's school, isn't it? I mean, it was a whole thing. I had to come out of school for a couple of weeks, because the bullying got really bad. And I sort of stopped talking to Jacob as well.' I swallow very, very hard. 'Which was bad timing, because their mum had been really sick for a while, and then she died. And Jacob didn't know why I wasn't talking to them. But we became friends again – after a while. It's all good.'

Jacob's furious face is so present in my thoughts they might as well be in the room. It's not all good even now, is it?

Nina takes her time with this one. Silence in the little room. Cars on the road outside.

'Why did you stop speaking to Jacob?' she says eventually. I know that she already knows. She just wants me to say it.

I sigh, sounding more exasperated than I mean to.

'Because Jacob was so gay, I couldn't be seen with them after that. I wouldn't have survived. And I know now that it's wrong. Especially because they didn't really have any other friends. I mean, they had their older sisters, the twins, who they'd hang out with on lunch break, but not anyone in our form group. So I know it was rough.'

'Who did you hang out with?'

This really sounds like an accusation.

'Laura – my old housemate – and Rory McClure. Who was kind of a dickhead to Jacob. And to me, to be honest. But it worked, and people left me alone.'

'Did you ever speak to Will about it?'

'No. No, I didn't really speak much to him again, and then we went to different sixth forms.'

'What about Jacob?' she says softly. 'Did you ever speak to them about it?'

For some reason, I'm coughing now.

'Not really, no. We went to the same sixth form, in the next town – which was way bigger than Whistlecombe – and everyone sort of loved them there. I think it's because we were older. But, anyway, we started hanging out again. I don't remember how, exactly.'

Another lie. After it happened with Will, Jacob kept turning up at my house, and I'd tell Mum to say I was sick or out or doing homework. After a while, they stopped coming. We blanked each other in class, in the hallways. But I could always see them looking, this hurt expression burning into the back of my skull during Double English.

Eventually, we made up drunk at a school disco in the working men's club. We shared some Marlboro Reds by the wheelie bins. I actually can't remember if I said sorry. I said sorry about their mum, but not about dropping them. I'd gone to the funeral, but we hadn't really talked, just held hands in the pews. Mum and Dad were so happy to see them come around again, and even watched *The Rocky Horror Picture Show* with us one night. 'Funny old film, innit?' Dad had said, getting up from the sofa. We were too busy rewinding to the 'Sweet Transvestite' scene to disagree.

Nina is nodding sagely. 'Thank you for sharing that with me, Danny.'

''S'all right.'

'That must have been very difficult. Especially as you were coming to terms with yourself. These foundational relationships are very important, often setting up our expectations for future relationships. It sounds like this one with Will may actually have played into your relationship with Tobbs.'

I shrug. Sounds like a bit of a push to me.

'But isn't this just what it's like being with another guy?' I say. 'Like, it's not like a normal relationship, with, like, cuddling and dinners together and, like, trust. Guys just want to stick their dick in stuff and leave, don't they?'

'Do you want that from a relationship?'

I'm shrugging again. I can't seem to stop. 'No, obviously not. But I'm not exactly a, like, *proper* guy, am I? I'm not like "a lad", am I?'

Nina crosses her legs and stares directly into my soul. 'Danny, I'm not supposed to say this, but I think you need to hear it: two men can have an open, loving, trusting relationship where they both thrive. But they have to communicate their needs and listen to their partner's needs – and act accordingly. It's not about what gender you identify as, it's about emotional intelligence and wanting the same thing. Whatever happened in Tobbs's past affects his close relationships now, as do yours. He might not be able to have a mutually beneficial, functioning romantic relationship with someone. But let me assure you, there are many, many men who can.' She sits back and settles me with a different sort of look, like we're in a coffee shop. 'Stephie and I have been together for coming on seventeen years. It hasn't always been easy, but I still love her today as much as I did when we first got together.'

'That's lovely,' I say through a swallow. That lump is back in my throat. 'To be honest, Gin and Ashraf – two of my new housemates – are pretty lush together. It's actually super-sweet.'

Now Nina is back in therapist form.

'In your relationship with Tobbs, you put up with the bare minimum, making you feel anxious and unsure. And after you went to see Klaus, you came back and felt anxious and unsure. And do you know why?'

'Because I didn't assert my boundaries or whatever?'

'Yes, and also possibly because . . .'

She just stares at me.

'Because?' I look at her.

'Because . . . ?' she says again.

'Because I – because I . . .' I'm stuttering. I'm nearing something, but I don't want to go there. 'Because I don't think I'm worth it?' Our eyes meet. 'Because I don't think I deserve being loved and respected? Because of what happened with Will and school and everything?'

I gulp. I've never said that out loud before.

Nina is smiling kindly.

'Right.' She says this with such calm agreement, I don't feel so awful. 'And do you know why I think you keep your distance from your colleagues and dislike them so much – especially your boss?'

'Stan?'

'Yes.' Nina shifts her glasses up her nose. 'I think it might be because they essentially reduce you to a stereotype. You've made a life for yourself, a job for yourself, and here he is, demeaning you, making you into the very thing you've always feared being – a gay man. Do you think that could be true?'

'Well, I *am* a gay man,' I say, sniffing.

'Absolutely,' Nina agrees. 'But I don't think you've really explored what that means to you. I don't think you've really found your identity inside that.'

'Are you calling me a homophobe?'

'Do you think I am?'

'Don't shrink-talk me, Nina.'

'I'm afraid that's what I'm here for.'

'OK, fine!' I say. 'Maybe you're right. Maybe I don't believe I'm worth it or whatever. Maybe I don't speak up at work because I think people will just tell me to shut up. Maybe I just accept shit from Stan and Tobbs and Zain and Laura and Luke and everyone. Maybe I do that because, like you're saying, I just don't like myself very much. Is that what you want to hear?'

Nina is now very blurry. Nina is making my eyes sting. Nina is handing me a Mansize Kleenex.

I sob violently for an unclear period of time. Afterwards, the world feels stiller, realer. It's like I'm sitting in that room for the first time.

'OK?' Nina says, smiling.

'Yes, thanks.'

'Danny, you've had a big week. A lot has shifted in your life very quickly, and when this happens, we need to give ourselves time to process what's going on. It's wonderful you're trying new things, and moving forward with your life, but don't forget to take stock of what's just happened, because it'll come out one way or another.'

I blink at her. 'That sounds like a Stonewall Counselling ad.'

'Well, it is, I suppose.' She's very good, not rising to my snark. 'This is where journalling can be great. It gives you a space to reflect, outside of our sessions.'

'Yeah, I have actually started one,' I say, with embarrassing eagerness. She's right: I am desperate to please.

'You've done some great work today, Danny, truly. Make sure to take it easy over the weekend. Get enough sleep, write down how you're feeling.'

'What are you going to do?'

Her tiny eyes regard me shrewdly, with a little half-smile.

'You already know I won't be answering that.'

I realise I'm smiling back

'Worth a try though, innit?'

NINETEEN

Next morning, I write more bullet points in the Dolly Diary:

Sunday 11th November
- *Hate the idea of shagging some rando to get over someone who was actually important to you . . . but does seem to be working. I am a gross gay stereotype after all.*
- *Genuinely feel excited for new phase of life. Danny 2.0. The Danny no one knows, not even me.*
- *Still low-key scared of dying alone and never getting National Trust tea towel.*

Excellent progress here. Very chuffed with myself.

I put down the diary and pick up my phone, where I go to the album of Tobbs and me. I scroll through the pictures. In one swift movement, I leave the album, select it and delete it. Then I go into the Bin and *delete* delete it. Danny 2.0 is on the go.

It's 8.55 a.m., and I think everyone is still asleep, so I pull on a hoodie and tracksuit bottoms and go down to the kitchen and brew a coffee in a battered espresso maker with no handle. It's cold as hell in this house, and I shelter over the tiny stove flame as it cooks my coffee.

Next I search for milk. There are two fridges, I discover: one in the kitchen, next to a brightly coloured illustrated poster of a naked woman holding a fist high and the words 'PROTECT TRANS FREEDOM!' above it; and another in a sort of lean-to conservatory adjacent to the kitchen. This one stands next to a chest freezer that instantly reminds me of home: that's how Dad stores all the fish for the shop. The fridge holds five nondairy milk variants, and I'm reminded I'm still in London. I take oat, of course.

Sipping the coffee from what appears to be a hand-painted mug that's mostly purple and green splatters, I wander back into the conservatory. It's piled with dusty crap: maroon conference-centre chairs, tins of half-used paint, many a placard left over from a march, and bags and bags of 'sculptor's clay' all heaped in one corner. Plastic plant-pots litter every surface, including the greyed-out dusty Queen Anne tiles.

I go from pot to pot. Dry earth, cracked and thirsty for water. Withered, yellowed specimens. A few look salvageable. I hunt through the cupboards for a measuring jug or something, return with Ange's 'moon-cup' pan, and splash the plants with water. The glass of the windows and ceiling is all fogged up, meaning it must be somehow colder outside than in here. Holding hot coffee close under my chin, I lean over the chest freezer and wipe a portion of the windows clear.

I gasp. There's a door behind the conference chairs, and I clamber around them and slide the stiff bolts back. I have to put down the coffee, lean into the door with my elbow to force it open, and slip out through the narrow crack that forms.

I realise now that, in the year and a half Jacob's lived here, I've only ever been out into the garden maybe twice, both times at house parties, both times heavily inebriated. I've also just gone from my room to work all week, and not poked around properly, but now I can see out there is the most amazing garden.

Under a heavy, swollen sky that promises a storm is a tropical jungle. The conservatory opens out onto a deck with a table pockmarked with candle wax and a pergola above, hanging with dried-out vines. Some narrow wooden steps at the side lead down into a canopy of huge, glossy green leaves, spiky clusters of purple and pink, and palms growing taller than I've ever seen in this country.

My body weaves the thin path between the foliage. I stare all about. It seems to go on forever. I can't even see the sky anymore. If it weren't for the cold and the wintry lack of floral smell, I could believe I'm in Bali. A low pond hides under the giant rhubarb leaves of a well-established gunnera, over which darts an angry robin. He lands on the crinkly edge of the leaf closest and just stares me out. I'm in his territory. He's pissed off.

'All right?' I ask him. 'This would be incredible if someone put some work into it.' He just stares at me, then flits away into his kingdom. 'Bye, then!'

I turn back to the house. I can barely see it from here, just one white sash window halfway up a red-brown wall. In the window, however, is a naked woman. She looks down at me, pauses, then waves animatedly. It's Melania. She draws up the window and holds an arm around her breasts, which are stunningly white.

'Fuck, it's cold!' Her voice echoes to the neighbours' gardens. 'Found our little Eden, have you, Fresh Meat?'

'More like little jungle!' I call back.

'Bring me a coffee, would you, dear lamb? Black, five sugars.' And she shuts the window.

I look around the garden again, and head back inside.

I knock gingerly.

'Are you . . . decent?' I have to stop asking this.

Jacob is practising the cello again, and its melodic, rolling notes thread up through the house. Is Angel D in there with them? I wonder.

The door swings open. Melania is in a faded pink silk bra that looks like it's from a *Playboy* spread in the seventies and some voluminous men's boxers in a yellow Bart Simpson print. Her eyes are outlined in thick black, and her lips are bright, vampiric red, matching her cheeks.

'Is this an angel I see before me?' she says.

'Oh, w-well,' I stammer, 'I wouldn't exactly say that.'

'Not you,' she says, taking the coffee. She sips it and goes, '*Ahhhhhh!* Well, come in, don't make my lady parlour cold.' I shuffle into the room. She slams the door behind me.

And lady parlour it is. I've never been in a room that looks more like the set of *Moulin Rouge*. Everything is a battered antique. Everything is draped in something else. Pink ostrich feathers sprout behind Venetian masks lining one wall. Make-up powder dusts every surface – at least, from the vanity table covered in compacts and brushes, I assume it's make-up powder. By the window, an influencer ring-light sits on a black tripod. If she does YouTube make-up tutorials, that'd really tie this whole thing together perfectly.

Melania takes a sharp sip of coffee and swans over to the mauve velvet stool at the table. She seats herself, and turns to me with evident enjoyment.

'I'm just doing a subtle day-look. Please, recline on the chaise.' She points to a dusty, rose-coloured chaise longue under the window. I sit on it uncomfortably and sip what's left of my coffee. I've never seen so many pink and purple cushions on one bed. Somewhat bizarrely, over them hangs a framed poster of a red five-pointed star with a golden hammer and sickle inside and the letters 'ZKS' underneath in gold.

Melania catches me looking in the mirror. She seems to be painting her nose.

'For my country,' she says. 'I want never to forget the hardships my mother and *babica* went through – plus, people don't expect it.'

'Who looks after the garden?'

A ghost of bemusement flits across Melania's face.

'She looks after herself. The way we all must.'

'I can't believe Jacob didn't mention it to me. They know how much I love plants.'

'Perhaps Jacob is busy with other things.' There's a slight edge to her voice.

'What do you do for work?' I ask, trying to make sure she realises I'm interested in her, not just myself and plants. 'You told me what everyone else does, but not you.'

'Isn't it obvious?' In the mirror, her eyes flick to the ring light, then to me. 'I'm a cam girl.'

'A . . . a what?' I ask, although I realise as I say this that I know what she means, which is good, because she ignores me anyway.

'Just for money,' she clarifies, 'while I am completing my master's in international finance – how I know Raj! Before he left for another course, the traitor.'

'Right, right,' I say, mimicking Nina for some reason. I don't really know what else to say about this, so I change subject again. 'Do you ever miss Slovenia?'

'I miss my family. I miss real, genuine *kremna rezina* – so delicious! But' – her reflection smirks at me again – 'I have never been so cold in my life as in this country!'

'Cold? Really?' I say. And I am literally shivering.

'Yes! I miss the warm! English people do not know how to build houses. In summer: too hot. In winter: too cold. And always damp! Why are they always so damp?'

'I – I dunno.' I feel personally responsible for the failings of my nation's architects.

'Titty always said I complain so much about houses,' she goes on. 'Moan, moan, moan, she said. Put on a jumper. Always telling me to put on a jumper. Why should I hide this beautiful body from the world?'

'*Totally.*'

'One thing I do not miss about Slovenia is the women.' Now she is shading in her cheekbones. It's quite captivating to watch, really. 'All so pretty, pretty – and I love a butch dyke. And I cannot hold their hand without getting punched by someone's dad – always someone's dad! At the butcher's, and a man comes past in a suit and hits you. They want women kissing only on their phone screens when their wife's asleep, not when they are purchasing their pork.'

'That sounds familiar,' I say. 'In my hometown, you can't so much as look different without someone yelling something.'

'Is that why you dress so boring?'

Our eyes meet in the mirror.

'I – I . . .' I don't have an answer for that.

Melania turns in her seat to look at me properly. 'I am bloody-hell sorry! I do not mean it this way.' She chews her bottom lip as she tries to find the words. 'I mean: when I came to London, I got a whole new wardrobe – except this.' She strokes the cone-like silk of the bra. 'This is my mother's. I mean: I knew I could be the person I always wanted to be here. The *real* me. Not the fake me I had always been.' She turns back to the mirror and tuts at herself for biting her lip. She goes back in with the lipstick. 'Not that Titty cares one way or another way that is a different way.'

My eyes are looking into my now empty coffee cup. I think about Zain looking down at me. Cool Zain, with his sheen of perfect urban queerness. I think about Tobbs and his complete rejection of that, of everything. I think of Jacob and their larger-than-life persona. And then I think of me: Danny Scudd, the guy you'd never pick out of a crowd. The guy who barely sees himself in the mirror.

But I don't want to be that guy anymore. The guy with no 'boundaries', as Nina keeps saying. I want to evolve, I want to learn. As I think this, I get that strange, vertiginous feeling of falling. It's thrilling and scary all at the same time. And perhaps this time I want to fall?

I look up again, feeling some new power pulse in my veins. And the start of what might be a plan.

'Mel, do you know any good clothes shops round here?'

Melania turns from the mirror and looks directly at me. The gleam in her eye is palpable.

'I do, Danny Scudd. I do.'

TWENTY

It seems to take Melania less than three seconds to change into a leather miniskirt and a fringed leather biker jacket – still with the silk bra beneath – and rally the troops. Ashraf is plucked from his morning protein shake, Gin from their yoga, and before I know it we're waltzing down Cambridge Heath Road, four abreast, arms linked. I feel like I'm in *Sex and the City* – on acid. People's heads turn and stare, but it could just be because we're filling up the entire pavement. Or it could be because they're thinking, Queers, as vividly as it says across the bonnet of Jacob's car. My forehead sparks, but I try to breathe it out. *This is who I want to be. This is who I want to be . . .*

'Too big?' Gin says, holding up a dangerously large translucent purple dildo. At first I don't realise what it is, because we are, as far as I'm aware, in a vintage-clothing shop. Turns out, beyond the black velvet curtain at the back is a sex dungeon. East London never fails to surprise me.

'Um, for whom?' I say over the rack of furry coats and jackets I'm leafing through.

Gin leans forward and bops me on the nose with it. I try my best not to recoil. Why are people always doing this?

'For you, of course.' They grin like a little sex pixie. 'We gotta loosen you up somehow.'

I sigh and stare at the ceiling. 'Is it really that obvious that I'm this, like, uptight virgin who can't drive?'

'You're a virgin?' Ashraf gasps from the harness corner.

The owner, an elderly gentleman in a turquoise Chinese dress, doesn't look up from his battered Proust paperback. Still, I glance around self-consciously. Is there a place in this world I truly belong?

'No, not really,' I say. 'I just feel, you know, like—'

'Square and vanilla?' Gin suggests helpfully.

'Try these on!' Melania says, thrusting a stack of extremely patterned clothes into my arms. 'And then see how Virgin Mary you feel.'

'Please, don't bring my mother into this,' I say, to blank faces. 'Never mind. I'll just . . .' I head into the little changing booth.

What follows next is a montage any teen movie would be proud of.

I try on at least fifteen outfits, which Melania delights in styling and amending. She even forces me to walk out into the shop for every other customer to pass comment on. The owner – whose name we learn is Raven – eventually puts *Swann's Way* face down on the counter and turns up the music – 'One Way or Another' by Blondie – and I really feel transported to the films Jacob and I used to binge-watch while drinking Dad's warm Stella Artois. He even starts cheering as the later outfits are revealed.

I try on all sorts, including, but not limited to: leather trousers and a velour shirt, giving Angel from *Buffy* realness; baggy combats and an oversized heavy-knit orange jumper, *à la* the TLC era; and some workman's trousers and a varsity jacket, both in black, which makes me feel incredibly Zain. All I need now is the shaved head and earring.

This last outfit causes a series of 'oooh's around the shop, where there is now a small audience.

'I love, love, LOVE this look!' Melania cries, jumping up and down, clapping her hands. She's gone full-lesbian Cher Horowitz.

'Danielle Scudmore,' Gin says, doing their best RuPaul Charles, 'we love your new monochrome style, but this lewk had us asking, "Why's it gotta be black?"'

I tug at the front of the jacket in the mirror.

'I dunno. Is it really "me"?'

'It is if you want it to be,' trills Melania. 'Remember what I told you about when I came to London? This is the same for you – although you have already been here many years.'

'But I can't just . . . change, like this, can I? What will people say?'

Gin laughs. 'What people?'

'I dunno.' I shrug. 'Work people?'

'Trust me,' Melania says, combing my lank hair back from my forehead, 'no one cares what you look like. Everyone cares what *they* look like. No one is thinking about you. Everyone is thinking about themselves. Have you ever cut short your hair?'

'Um, not since I was a kid.'

'You look rocking, mate,' Ashraf says, grabbing me around the waist from behind and, really out of nowhere, giving me a peck on the cheek. 'Ever think about getting an ear pierced?'

I twist around and stare at him. 'I was actually just thinking that, yes.'

'Bonzer.'

I look at myself again. The jacket swamps me a little. I don't

201

look like a cool jock, I look like a kid in his older brother's clothes.

'Guys, I dunno. I'm not, like . . . brave like you are. You all have such awesome looks and, like . . . lives. I'm just this shy little guy from Whistlecombe.'

'What's a Whistlecombe?' asks Ashraf.

'It's all about the attitude, Danielle,' says Gin, taking a few slow struts towards me, then moving straight past me and striking a pose in front of the mirror. 'Fake it till you make it, bitch.'

I scrunch up my nose. 'Is that true, though?'

'The massive task of our lives as queer people is to unpick the parts of ourselves that are truly us and the parts we've created to protect ourselves,' Gin says to the mirror, with sudden, sage-like wisdom. They turn around and smile at me. 'Read that in a tweet once.'

'That's what you're doing now.' Ashraf nudges me with a cheeky grin.

'Is it?'

Melania claps her hands again. 'This is *just* like that consumerism-wet-dream movie *Clueless*!' She regards me seriously in the mirror. 'That film made me queer.'

'Same,' intone both Ashraf and Gin, followed by peals of hysteria.

I laugh along, but I can feel my chest tightening. I think about Nina sitting in that chair. Is it the change that's challenging, or is it just plain wrong for me? How are you supposed to know the difference?

But, too late, Melania is dragging my new wardrobe over to the till, where Raven is excitedly DJ ing from an ancient record player. The opening bars of 'Believe' by Cher filter through the shop, and I wonder if there ever were a gayer moment in the history of the world. What would my parents say if they saw me now?

'So it's decided,' Melania says, spinning around from the counter. 'To the barber's . . . though not Dick's.'

———

By the time Jacob emerges from their room in their kimono, my 'coming out' party is in full swing.

'Danny, Mary and Joseph!' they gawp from the living-room archway.

'Jay!' I scream, from where I'm leaping around on the sofa, bashing the Chinese lanterns like they're piñatas. 'Jay, come and dance with me!'

'With all of us!' cries Melania from the other sofa, where she and Ashraf are doing the same. From the window, Ange chain-smokes, thumbing through the playlist and tutting.

They float over and ascend the sofa.

'What have you done to my sweetest of angels?' they gasp, running both hands across my freshly shaven skull.

'He's gone punk rock!' cries Ashraf, handing a blunt to Melania.

'And an earring!' Jacob screams. 'You've pierced my baby!'

'Oh, Big Edie, don't be so dramatic!' I say in my Little Edie voice, though it's slurring.

Jacob just stares at me. It's hard to imagine anything shocking them, and yet here it is. Slowly, a smile perks up the corners of their mouth.

'Oooh, gurl! Shock me with that deviant behaviour!'

'Do you love it?' I say, now in my best attempt at Paris Hilton.

They shake their head, still in disbelief. ''Tis a sight to behold, indeed.'

''Tis I!' I cry. ''Tis I!'

'What a day you've had,' Jacob says.

203

'What a day *you've* had!' cries Melania. 'Or day *and* night, I should say.'

Jacob looks tired, I realise, not their usual effervescent self, but also rather pleased. They purse their lips as if they have the biggest, most scandalous secret they're about to tell.

'Well, yes, it cannot be denied, Angel D and I have had *quite* the twenty-four hours.'

'Who?' I ask.

Jacob gawps at me. 'Angel Delight, Danielle. I told you all about him, remember?'

'Right, right, right,' I say in Canadian.

'New look, new brain, huh?'

'Bit harsh.'

'Look, sweet sangria, I think I'll go to bed and read.'

'No! No! No!' I go in for a hug, but elbow them in the ribs instead. They step backwards off the sofa and nearly fall.

'Bloody hell, Dan!'

'We're gonna do karaoke!' I scream, right in their face. 'Come on! You love karaoke!'

I grab them by the hands and jump up and down even harder. *They're just jealous. They aren't the centre of attention for once. I am. The new me. The real me.*

'Who wants slagtinis?' calls Gin, bringing in an assortment of mugs on a baking tray.

'Me!' cries everyone.

Jacob takes one and eyes me.

'OK, fine! But just one little baby tipple.'

—

The night starts to dissolve into a series of laughing faces and looming vagina paintings. I feel everything drift mercifully away. All these horrible feelings that have been plaguing me, the worries that I'm too this, too that, not enough, not anything.

At one point, Jacob and I are back on the sofa, both holding the karaoke mics as the lyrics to '9 To 5' are projected on the wall opposite.

When the chorus hits, we all go mental, and I honestly can't remember the last time I felt such all-encompassing, ecstatic joy. Before I know it, the others have gone to bed and it's just me and Jacob lying on the floor, sharing a joint, surrounded by cushions and a few of the fallen lanterns.

'I've gotta say it, Dan, you're fitting in really well here,' they say, blowing smoke rings.

'Well, I'm good at that, aren't I?' I say to the spinning ceiling. "Fitting in."

'I'm not gonna lie, I was kind of worried.'

I twist my head towards them. 'What do you mean?'

Jacob takes a long toke, and hands it to me. 'I offered you the room to help you out, and then I worried it was all going to be too much for you.' Their eyes flick up and down my entirely different-looking body. 'But I see now you're adapting *gloriously*.'

Smoke fills my lungs, and I cough violently. I see what's going on. They've got another bloke now, so they can afford to be bitchy to the one that's been hanging around since forever. I hear Nina say 'boundaries' in a stoned echo.

'Do you not want me to be here?' I say, perhaps more sharply than I'd meant to.

Jacob sits up and takes the joint away, in a motherly gesture that fills me with rage.

'I didn't say that, did I?'

Now I'm sitting up.

'Do you still like me?'

Jacob turns their head to the archway that leads into the hall. They take a quick, sharp toke, then look back at me.

'Danny, you are, and have always been, my best Judy.'

'That's not what I asked you.'

I'm trying to read Jacob's expression, but there's currently two of them. Both look unwilling to have this conversation.

'Let's get you to bed.'

They put their arm around me to pull me up, but I shake them off. Jacob looks stung, like I've slapped them.

'Are you still angry about what happened in school? When your mum died?'

I only hear how bad that sounds after I've said it.

Jacob takes three deep breaths before replying.

'Danny, I don't know what you've been talking about with Nina, but I know you're going through a tough time. I'm not angry at something that happened a decade ago.' They go to grab me again. 'Now, let's get you to bed.'

I shake them off again and clumsily get to my feet.

'Stop treating me like a child all the time. I can look after myself.'

As I say this, I lurch into two of the Chinese lanterns on the floor and trip into the sofa.

Jacob stands with infuriating serenity. They've always been able to hold their drink better than me.

'I'm taking you upstairs and I'm getting you the moon-cup pan.'

TWENTY-ONE

For the first time in a long time, everything is good.

Monday, I go into work late and hung-over again, just like everybody else. I don't even remember having a go at Jacob until I get off the bus at Oxford Circus, and then the regret gets lost in the crowd. I get several comments about the hair and earring, but all positive ones.

'It's Danny, bitch!' one of the Marc/ks says to the other, before high-fiving me. Unexpected. It's the one with the 'c'. He has slightly less perfect teeth.

Nadia from PR presses the latte button for me as I struggle with the coffee machine in the kitchenette.

'You feeling as shit as me?' she says, grinning.

'Yeah, fucking dying,' some voice says out of me.

She leans in and squeezes my arm with her white-tipped acrylics. 'Just gotta make it through another day in this shit show, then back home to catch up on *Drag Race,* right?'

'Right, girl?' I say back. AND THEN I SNAP MY FINGERS.

She giggles and slopes off, and I realise they think I'm one of them now. I'm no longer the nervy, quiet, hard-working Danny Scudd with the limp hair. I'm the slightly more interesting young media professional Danny Scudd, who has lots of friends who he gets drunk with on the weekend, who makes poor sexual decisions he might joyfully discuss with careless abandon on the corporate half-pipe, who can have 'banter' with his colleagues about how many pills he popped on a Sunday night. I'm visible for the first time to them. I'm the gay guy they always wanted me to be. And maybe, just maybe, I like it.

Despite the hangover, I'm super-focused on my job. I whizz through edits of 'The Vegan Condom Brand You HAVE to Try' and 'Eat My (ski p)Ass: Sex on the Scottish Slopes'. Where I would have once read these pieces with scorn (and possibly jealously), now I feel like a worldly-wise older brother, bestowing my boundless knowledge of conquests and boozing to the wide-eyed eager first-year students the algorithm will send these articles to. *Teaching the children,* Jacob would say. *Little Edie goes large at last.*

It reminds me of when I made a 'newspaper' on the back of utility-bill envelopes as a kid, *The Whistlecombe Whisperer.* I thought that was so clever. 'SPOTTED: Mrs Riley from next door on mission along seafront. Suspicious? I THINK SO!' 'Stripey Cat: Is he yours? Watch out for his claws!' I'd put in headlines and write in messy columns with a smudgy biro, then staple it all together and run down to the shop to show my parents. The whole time, I'd have this buzzing through me, this energy to just keep doing it, while the rest of me sank away. And now I have it again. Only this time it stays with me after I've finished work, too. It's ever-present. The pulse of change.

I'm doing it, I write in the Dolly Diary. *I'm finally learning how to live. How to really live!!!*

Tuesday, I try out the baggy combats with my usual pale-greeny-blue T-shirt and get even more compliments. Stan actually stops the Weekly Trend Alert! meeting to announce that it's me, I am the trend alert. My bones tremble as everyone stares and claps, but in kind of a nice way. More like the wave machine at Center Parcs than the waltzers at the county fair, which always makes me feel sick.

At five-thirty, a time I always worked beyond, unlike anybody else, Nadia comes over to my desk and says, 'Stan, Callum, Robyn and a few of us are going for a drink, if you fancy joining?'

At first, I don't know what to say, and then I say, 'Gimme five minutes. Meet you by Reception,' and actually do that, rather than making an excuse to get away.

The group of ten or fifteen or so of us head into Soho and sit in a booth in a bar they apparently rent every Tuesday evening.

'Jägerbombs!' cries Stan. 'On the company card, of course!'

Much to my own surprise, I cry 'Yeah!' along with everybody else.

'You're a strong boy, come and help me with the drinks,' I hear Stan say to Callum, who's next to me. He bounds off with him. In the dim red light, I see Stan squeezing Callum's perfectly tight, round arse. The whole thing feels off. Why would Callum even consider him?

'*So* happy you're here,' Nadia says. 'We've never really got to know each other, have we?'

I can't take my eyes away from the two of them at the bar.

'No,' I say. 'But I have the feeling we're going to get on famously.'

Nadia squeals and claps her hands.

I'm doing it. I really am doing it.

In the house, we do yoga in the mornings, and one night even haul some of the clay out of the conservatory and, under Gin's instructions, make pots together, which Jacob takes into the art school they're teaching at this week to fire in the kiln. We line them up on the kitchen windowsill, behind the sink, like an odd little gnome family portrait. Mine is the teenage daughter in her mother's heels, we decide.

Whenever Jacob and I have argued in the past, we've normally talked about it, hugged and got over it − then watched one of our go-to movies. But we don't talk about my 'outburst' on Sunday night. Instead, there is a crackle in the air between us when we speak. It's almost like we're play-acting as ourselves − a game in which we both know something is amiss but we can't let on. Gradually, we loosen up. Wednesday night, we watch *Showgirls* in the living room, and quote every other line until we're both howling.

Thursday, I take a deep breath and go the whole hog, wearing the workman's trousers and varsity jacket. As I walk along Oxford Street from the bus, someone actually whistles at me. At least, I think it's at me. I turn to see, but miss them. When I get into the office and sit down, Callum stares around his computer at me.

'Not being funny, Dan, but you honestly look fit as.'

'Oh, this old thing,' I say, mimicking Jacob.

'I'm just saying I would. If you weren't my line manager, obviously.'

'That would just be too far,' I say, rather nastily.

'Exactly!' Callum laughs.

This must be what it's like to be famous.

———

That evening, I try explaining what my new place is like to my parents over the phone, but in the end I just give up and describe what era the house is from, which Dad corrects me about.

'No, sounds more 1880s to me, lad,' he says, the noise of a stadium cheering in the background. 'Watched that programme about the Victorians on Channel 4. Definitely sounds 1880s.'

'Oh, Joe, I'm sure the boy knows what era of architecture his own house were built in!' Mum scolds.

'He in't no architect,' Dad says, chewing the soggy chip leftovers.

'Is it nice living with Jacob?' Mum goes on.

I consider.

'Yeah, mostly.'

My foot is tap-tap-tapping against the duvet. With this increased energy I have, I've actually started putting things away in the room. The plants have positions on the desk and chest of drawers; Dolly is up. I pick at a jagged nail on my ring finger. Even though I'm feeling better than ever, I'm biting them again, like when I was younger.

'What about the other flatmates?'

Trying to explain who each of them is to my parents just isn't worth the hassle. Even describing what they do for money might cause Dad to choke on those chips.

'They're nice. We've been doing lots of things together, like yoga, movies, that sort of thing. We're having a Christmas party in a few weeks actually. They've been really welcoming, which is good, because it's helping me get over Tobbs.'

'Yes, well,' Mum says tartly, 'with all this excitement, you won't want to come home to see your poor, old, dull, decrepit parents this festive season, will you?'

'Mum, it's the middle of November, for Christ's sake.'

'Don't you take that tone with me, Daniel. I birthed you, remember?'

'Funnily enough, no.'

'I'm just checking that seeing us won't interfere with your entertainment plans.'

'The party's *at the start of December*, Mum.'

'I know how long these urban discos go on for, Daniel. I read the news.'

'I'll be back for Christmas, Mum.'

'Who you calling decrepit?' Dad says suddenly.

'*Shhh*, Joseph! Your lad's talking,' Mum says. 'And we have to cherish these few moments he lets us have with him, our one and only offspring.'

'I'll see you in a month. Bye, Mum.'

'We could be dead by then, Daniel.'

—

Friday morning, I'm woken by screams.

Instantly panicked, I rush from my room and peer down from the top landing, fingers gripped tightly around the wooden banister. The Centrefold is one of those Victorian villas with the stairs in the middle of the house, lit above by a slanting skylight, the rooms spilling off on multiple landings and half-landings. I'm on the top floor, along with a bathroom and a small attic room completely rammed with junk.

A few steps down is Gin and Ashraf's room, from which the screams are emanating. Their door is open; the pastel-pink, blue and white beaded curtain hung from the frame is moving slightly, as if from the power of the noise.

Cautiously, I creep down the warped stair treads, and linger outside the curtain. I'm getting slightly more confident in the house, but it still feels like I'm a guest here.

'Fresh Meat!'

Through the curtain, the two of them appear to be wrestling on the ground, half dressed. Oh God, I've just managed to get involved in some sex thing, like a batshit little perv.

'S-sorry,' I stutter, and turn to flee.

'Don't be, mate!' Ashraf calls. 'Come on in!'

I've often wondered when the moment would finally come that I'm presented with an orgy. In gay world, they seem to be ten a penny – certainly if we believe the gay sex-education tool of hardcore pornography.

With a sinking sense of acceptance in my stomach, I part the strings of plastic beads and enter. At least this will be a good story to tell my colleagues on Monday.

But it's not all leather harnesses and red bondage rope. Instead, it's more like the back room of a dry-cleaning and clothing-alterations shop. Black-and-white half-finished garments of various sheer fabrics hang from walls and ceiling and are draped over a large workbench under the window, which also features what must be an industrial sewing machine. Sharply rendered charcoal dress sketches are tacked messily to any free wall space, along with various photos of Ashraf: moody 1950s-style headshots; grainy stills from footage of him stomping the runway; and some glossy, quite erotic ones of him climbing out of a lily pond.

The designer and the model lie at my feet, entangled in each other, grinning up at me.

'Get this monster off me, Fresh Meat,' Gin cries, reaching out a hand. I oblige, and pull them free of Ashraf's giant, muscular form. Ashraf protests and tries to pull them back down, but they kick him off. 'You BEAST!' they screech. 'You'll ruin my latest collection.'

Ashraf leaps to his feet and straightens what he's wearing: a short calico tunic with angular shoulders, currently inside out, black dogtooth stitching marking seams.

Gin swivels to me in their black satin dressing gown, clawing their bowl cut neat with both hands.

'He says he wants to walk in my show, and then he doesn't take rehearsal seriously. Typical man!'

Ashraf takes Gin by the waist and kisses them on the top of their head. 'That's me.'

Close up, I can see two dark scars running under Ashraf's pecs. He sees me looking and flexes everything. Gin rolls their eyes.

'Four and a half years ago now,' Gin says.

'And still as happy as the day I had it done,' Ashraf says with a grin.

Gin softens, and leans in to kiss him on the shoulder. 'And just as sexy.'

'Sorry,' I say again. 'I didn't mean to—'

'I don't mind you looking, Fresh Meat.' Ashraf drops his arms and puts one around my shoulder.

'He loves it, actually,' Gin says, turning and going to the worktable. 'And let's hope everyone loves *him*.'

'Have you got a show coming up?' I ask.

Gin is now flipping through a selection of fabrics on the table, sighing. 'Trying to. I just can't find the right space for it. Everything in this city is so fucking expensive.'

'What about the house?' I say.

'That's what I keep saying!' Ashraf hits me with the back of his hand so hard I nearly topple over.

'Who'll come here, though?' Gin says, clearly not for the first time. 'It's a crack den.'

'You could live-stream it as well as invite people,' I say. 'And tweet influencers and things like that.' I'm suddenly embarrassed. They haven't asked for my opinions. God, I'm bolshie these days.

Gin slinks back towards us like a fashion Morticia Addams and gazes at me with real fascination. Without make-up, their face is very pale and delicate, but with a hard edge to it.

'I forgot you're a media professional.'

'Well,' I start, 'not really.'

'It's so exciting to meet one of Jacob's friends from home — isn't it, Ginny?' Ashraf says, his arm still around my neck.

Gin sinks down onto the messy bed, which is just a mattress on the floor surrounded by scraps of fabric.

'Absolutely,' they say. 'Jacob always paints their hometown as this real hellhole. I can't imagine what it was like growing up there.'

'It wasn't a war zone or anything,' I say in Tobbs's voice. Then I check myself, and try again. 'I mean, it's not, like — interesting. Or fun. Or, I suppose, very accepting.'

Ashraf's arm is growing heavier as I grow smaller. I don't know why I feel the need to defend a place I, too, spent my teenage years fantasising about escaping from. Jacob and I would comb through the websites of London universities, deciding where we would both apply. We had a pact we would get out at the same time, the same month. In the end, his dad drove us up together on the same day, them to Central Saint Martins, me to UCL.

'I imagine Jacob's always been the same?' Gin asks.

I laugh. 'Pretty much.'

'Bet you had some mega-barneys over the years?' Ashraf says.

I crane my neck around to look him in the eyes. 'No, actually. Why would we?'

'Because Jacob always has to be the centre of attention,' Ashraf says. He doesn't say it in an unkind way, just a factual way, like we all know it. I swallow. All the same, hearing someone else say it feels dangerous. It makes me want to defend them.

'I suppose so. After their mum died, everything was thrown up in the air.' I don't add that they were ghosted by their best friend for months as well. 'I think they just got sick of being

215

bullied and decided they'd scare away other people before they had the chance to be scared themselves – you know?'

'They haven't scared Angel away yet,' Ashraf says in a naughty little voice.

'Or me,' I say flatly. A look passes between the two of them that I don't like.

Gin rises again and approaches. They rest both hands on my freshly shaven skull. I am totally ensconced by the two of them.

'You're not the person we thought you were, are you, Fresh Meat?'

Why does everybody treat me like a child? It's really starting to wind me up. And what makes them think they know Jacob better than I do? We've known each other inside out for years. Just because I'm new to this whole mad world of exaggerated queerness doesn't mean I'm somehow on the outside of my own friendship. My skin vibrates.

'I mean,' I say, 'I've only been here a few times before, so maybe you don't really know me.'

This is the sort of thing I'd say to Nina, but not to anybody else.

My breath catches in my throat.

Have I been rude? Have I ruined it already?

But they just laugh. Ashraf releases me and puts his arm around Gin instead. They look at me like fond parents.

'Anyway,' Gin says brightly. 'Fancy some pancakes?'

TWENTY-TWO

A little later, Melania and I clatter down the stairs into the hall. She is in what can only be described as a Soviet swim-instructor ski suit, in triangular panels of purple, green and yellow, with a white fur hat covering her short locks. I'm entirely in camo, with black Doc Martens and a little black beret, looking pretty fucking hardcore, if you ask me.

'My little Erin Brockovich is all grown up!' Jacob's voice sings from the living room, where they're eating cereal from a giant Sports Direct mug in their cherry-blossom kimono with rollers in. Things seem almost normal between us.

'You know it!' I call back, checking I've got everything I need in my bag: camera, rain mac, notepad, sensible mid-morning snack, enormous rainbow flag.

'Smash the patriarchy!' Ange yells from the kitchen, followed by several 'Yeah!'s from the others.

'We shall take down the Cold War bastards,' Melania says, as she applies tomato-red lipstick at the hall mirror.

Jacob raises their fist in a Black Power salute.

'Do it for the browns and the queers, Little Edie.'

Behind Melania, I adjust my beret in the mirror.

'Well, today I'm kind of doing it for the Chechnyans,' I say.

'Do it for the brown and queer Chechnyans, Little Edie.'

'I don't know if there really *are* any brown Chechnyans. Wait: am I allowed to say "browns"?'

Jacob stands up, moseys into the hall, and kisses me on the forehead in a matronly manner.

'No, queen.'

'What about blacks?'

'Noooooo, queen.'

'What about yas, queen?'

'No, queen.'

'Really? But Ilana says it on *Broad City*!'

Jacob glugs down the milk at the bottom of the mug and pats their rollers.

'It's cultural appropriation from African American vernacular, dodo.'

'Shit,' I say, heaving my backpack on. 'I'm just not *woke* enough to be a journalist.'

Jacob shrugs. 'You're a white liberal. Don't beat yourself up about it.' They slap me violently on the arse. 'And *definitely* don't say "woke". Now, go do it for those brown Chechnyan queers!'

—

On the Tube journey over, Melania and I chat about all the other political 'actions' she's taken part in: a 'funeral' in Trafalgar Square about oil-company sponsorship of the National Portrait Gallery; a 'lock-on' at the Houses of Parliament around funding cuts to LGBT+ housing; a 'tits-out parade' down the Mall to 'show Queen Elizabeth how it's done', whatever that means.

'Ange got completely naked on that one,' she says, giggling at the recollection. 'Full foof to Buckingham Palace.'

I half listen, but am mostly preoccupied with my own thoughts. This whole thing feels unreal. I keep catching myself in the dark window of the Tube carriage as it screams between platforms. I look like Che Guevara, or a cooler Greta Thunberg. But it's me. Me! Danny Scudd from Whistlecombe!

My two main thoughts I wrote down in the Dolly Diary earlier, are:

- *Bet the protest's going to be huuuuge! Hope I can get enough coverage with work camera and voice recorder on my phone.*

And:

- *Fuck you, Tobbs. Who's the real fucking journalist now?*

We climb out into the freezing air at Notting Hill Gate and spend twenty minutes wandering around before we find it, and when we do, I double-check, with a middle-aged lesbian couple in matching rainbow woollies, if this is it.

'This isn't, like, just the start of it or something?' I ask. 'And there are a hundred thousand people round the corner?'

'Nope.' They shake their heads and point at the white palatial building that forty or so people are gathered in front of, waving rainbow flags and cardboard placards painted with pink triangles and slogans in Russian and English. There's a small camera crew stood around, drinking coffees, and some armed guards chatting away happily enough. I follow their fingers: A sign on the brick wall around the building says 'EMBASSY OF THE RUSSIAN FEDERATION.'

'Oh.'

'Fifteen thousand people clicked "Attend" on Facebook,' a wizened, bearded old man next to them volunteers. 'But this is a fairly good turnout for a weekday.'

'Oh.'

'Not everyone is as free and single as us,' Melania says, somehow making it sexual.

'You a journo?' the old man asks.

'Yes.' My chest swells. 'Yes, I am.'

'For who?'

I swallow. 'CULTRD.'

'That *Vice* knock-off?' one of the rainbow couple says sceptically.

'We're one of *Time Out*'s Top Fifty Art and Culture Apps, *actually*,' I say, almost convincing myself.

'Aren't they the one Debs says is too try-hard?' says the other.

"Like a creepy uncle," the other replies with finger quotes. Then turns back to me, smiling. 'That's our daughter.'

'We're all about inclusivity,' I say. 'So . . . who's the person organising this?'

'It's self-organised,' says a youngish girl with a tight green fade and a pink triangle painted on her face.

'TITTY!' Melania screams from next to me.

'ANIA!' the green-fade girl screams back.

'This is your Titty?' I blink at Melania.

'She's not my Titty anymore,' Melania says back, drawing herself up to her full five foot two and staring at the girl like a viper ready to pounce.

I stare at Titty, who does not look as I had imagined – the fourth Railway Child – but is in baggy combats and an oversized black puffa jacket and has gold rings the whole way up the outside of both ears. She is squat and sallow-complexioned, and does in fact fulfil Melania's taste for a 'butch dyke'.

'If Dick is here, I will kill him with student Oyster Card!' Melania threatens, waving the little piece of blue plastic at Titty, who doesn't look the least distressed. Beside us, the older couple watch with utter glee.

'Oh, Ania,' Titty sighs. 'When will the dramatics end?'

'When you stop causing them!' Melania shouts.

'It was behaviour like this that pushed me away,' Titty goes on in the same patronising tone.

'Hey!' I shout. 'I'm getting a really hostile vibe from you, Titty, and that's not what the LGBT community is about. Now, don't you speak to my friend like that!'

Both Melania's and Titty's eyes widen.

Oh my God, I'm shouting at a stranger in defence of someone I've known five seconds. And I don't seem to be able to stop.

'We're all here to fight for our brothers and sisters in Chechnya,' I go on. 'Let's – erm – try to band together around that, OK?'

'Yes, Titty,' Melania says, still waving the Oyster Card. 'Try banding together for once.'

I turn to Titty, who looks so shocked that a crimson blush has crept up her neck and darkened her chicken-flesh-coloured face. My instinct says to apologise immediately, but I hold my nerve. I must keep on track. I cannot fail at my first assignment.

'So, then, who's in charge?' I say, trying to steady my voice. 'I need to interview them.'

'No one's in charge,' Titty says after a few seconds. 'All our actions are self-organised.'

The lines in my forehead furrow into canyon-deep crevices. 'Why are you talking like the Queen?'

'This protest is a non-violent direct action,' she says. 'That's what it's called. *We* are LGBTs 4 Chechnya, the activist group organising it.'

I don't know how, but I just know from the way she's saying it that it's spelled with the number 4.

'Ohhh,' I whistle. 'So you're an organising member?'

'*Everyone* here is. We *all* organised it.'

I root around in my backpack, spilling folds of rainbow flag, organic flapjack and my sludge-green mac. The middle-aged couple watch with fascination. I point the camera at Titty.

'Do you mind if I ask you a couple of questions on the record?' Yes, I just said 'on the record'.

Melania grabs the camera. 'Why do you have to ask *her*?'

'Well, I have to ask someone, don't I?' I shake her free of it.

'You might want to turn it on first,' Titty says, smirking. At least Melania's ex is also a twat.

'Right. Right.'

I fiddle around with it.

'No, that's the "Power" button,' she says, then takes it from me and flips out the little rectangular window. 'Here you go.'

'Thanks. OK, so I'm going to start recording now.'

'Brill.'

'OK, I'm going to start recording now.'

'Yep. Heard you the first time.'

'Hello, I'm reporter Danny Scudd, and I'm here on the sixteenth of November in Notting Hill, London, to witness activist group LGBTs 4 Chechnya as they fearlessly protest against the country's recent "gay purge".'

'Thrilling intro,' says Titty, crossing her arms.

'Don't you ruin his life as well!' shouts Melania.

I make a face behind the lens.

'What do you want me to do?' Titty goes on.

'In-tro-duce your-self,' I mouth loudly.

She sighs. 'Hi, I'm Titty McGuffrie, and I'm a founding member of LGBTs 4 Chechnya. Oh, and here's one of the others. RAJ! RAJ!'

Well, this is the point I was low-key dreading, wasn't I. Because coming over and hugging Titty is Raj.

'Sorry I'm late, Titts,' he pants. 'It took me ages to get this right.' He waves a hand at the lopsided upside-down pink tri-angle painted from forehead to chin.

'Don't worry, we haven't started yet,' she says.

'What's going on?' He looks directly into the camera. Fuck me, he's absolutely gorgeous. Now I remember him vividly from Klub Klutch. 'Getting papped again? *Classique Tittwah.*'

'For a budget version of *Vice*,' volunteers one of the couple.

'It's one of *Time Out*'s Top Fifty Art and Culture Apps!' I snap, letting the camera fall from my face.

Raj blinks at me.

'Oh, *wow*,' he says. 'It's *you*.'

'Hi,' I say, with an awkward wave.

'Mr Break-up, I barely recognise you.' Raj grins, taking in the new me. 'How's your head?'

'Haven't had any complaints,' I say without thinking.

'Raj!' Melania sweeps in and hugs him tightly, all the time staring lethally at Titty.

'All right, babes!' he says. 'Didn't think you'd come, consid-ering' – he looks briefly at Titty – 'you know.'

Melania's stare at no point breaks from Titty.

'I will not let wicked women stand in the way of my commit-ment to social justice.' Then she softens and is all giggles with Raj. 'Plus, I thought it would be nice for you to say hello to my new Fresh Meat housemate while he is sober. Doesn't he look handsome?'

My face is throbbing hot. I know it's going red.

Still, Raj says, 'Damn! You scrub up good in that activist costume!'

'I know,' I say in this phantom voice that possesses me more these days.

Titty looks from me to Raj.

'Grindr?'

'No, no!' we both say quickly.

'We haven't fucked,' I feel the need to add.

'OK,' Titty says, nodding.

'Not everyone fucks as easily as breathes,' Melania adds.

'Well, I'm glad you're both here,' Raj moves on seamlessly, not at all fazed by how gut-hollowingly uncomfortable this entire conversation is. 'Especially given how you were the other night, mister.'

'Yeah,' I say. 'I know I was a mess. I'd just—'

'Been dumped. I know.'

'Drunk too many Negronis, I was gonna say.'

'Yeah. That, too.'

'But I'm over it now. I'm a new man. And thanks for looking after me; it was nice of you.' And we have a cute little exchange of smiles.

'He's all about saving the planet now,' Melania says. 'Not destroying lives.'

'Look.' Titty is clearly getting bored. 'We need to start.' She nods towards a few people finishing off pink triangles on one another's faces. One of them, I notice, is a drag queen in a long silver-blonde wig and an orange Guantanamo Bay-style jumpsuit.

'Wait!' I chirp up. 'Can we just finish the interview?'

Raj is making signs at the drag queen. He turns back to us. 'One minute.'

I bring up the camera and realise it's been recording this entire conversation. Once I work out how, I'll delete the hell out of this shit.

Raj tries to wander off, but Titty grabs him by the arm. 'Stay here, please,' she snarls.

He rolls his eyes. 'Fine, Mother.'

'So . . . I'm here with organisers from activist group LGBTs 4

Chechnya,' I say, my voice cracking with embarrassment. 'Can you please just tell us about how you're supporting LGBTQIA Chechnyans today?'

'Chechens,' Raj says flatly.

'Excuse me?'

'People from Chechnya are called Chechens, not Chechnyans.'

'Right.' I swallow hard.

'We're showing solidarity with our LGBTQIA brothers and sisters in Chechnya, who are being beaten, abused, rounded up and incarcerated by state-sanctioned police, in the worst gay purge we've seen in Europe since the Nazis. We want to show the Russian government – and the world – that we will not stand for it, and we will not rest until every LGBTQIA person can live freely, openly and honestly. LGBTQIA rights are human rights!' And he and Titty both raise Black Power fists, which confuses me, but I decide not to bring it up.

'Cool; thanks, Raj,' I say, feeling so red in the face I can barely look at him.

'Raj!' calls the drag queen, in a surprisingly broad Scouse accent. 'Now!'

Raj nods. He stares straight into the lens. 'Wanna be part of history?'

I drop the camera from my face again, and nod.

He reaches out and takes my free hand. 'Come with me, mister.'

'Would you mind just . . .' I hand the camera to one of the middle-aged couple and mime a filming action at her. She stares at me like I'm a lunatic.

'You go, Dan-Coco!' Melania cries, clapping her hands together wildly.

Titty rolls her eyes as Raj leads me up to the closed gates of the Russian Embassy. Through the bars, the two armed guards

225

stare at us with a mixture of amusement and contempt.

'Everyone!' Titty shouts. 'Join hands!'

In a rehearsed rhythm, the small crowd lines up parallel to the wall, each holding hands with the person next to them. I feel my free hand clasped in a powerful grip. 'Hiya, babs,' says the drag queen in a gravelly voice, winking.

'Ready, everyone?' calls Raj. 'And die!'

There isn't enough time to process what he's saying before I'm pulled to the ground. My head hits the pavement with a smack.

'SHITFUCK!' I yell.

'Shhhh!' hisses the drag queen.

Everything is suddenly very still and very quiet. I can hear the rumble of traffic passing by, the caw of birds overhead, the thumping of blood in my ears as it potentially works its way out of the fracture in the back of my skull. Next I hear the electronic whispers of camera shutters, and the slow tread of feet walking past.

A woman's voice I recognise from somewhere is speaking: '. . . activists have staged a mass "die-in" in front of the Russian Embassy, here in West London, to send a message to Vladimir Putin's government to put an end to the so-called gay purges happening across former Soviet territories . . .'

She's from the News, I realise. The real, actual BBC News. We're on TV, maybe live. *I'm going to bleed to death live on national TV.* My head lolls towards Raj and presses against his chest. My excited heart is beating in time with his. *That's pretty cool.*

———

'Danny!' Someone is shaking me by the shoulders. 'Danny, get up!'

Raj's beautiful face comes blearily into view. The crooked

branches of leafless trees stick out from his head like a thorny crown.

'God?' I say, in Madonna's voice from 'Like a Prayer' on *The Immaculate Collection*.

'Get the fuck up, Danny.'

I pull myself up, rub my head. No blood, thankfully.

'What happened?'

'You fell asleep.'

'What?'

'You fell asleep on national news.'

'You're kidding.'

'I am not.'

'Fuck.'

'Yeah.'

'Shitfuck. Are you annoyed?'

'It's not really about me, Danny – but yes.'

People are milling around. The blonde news reporter is still talking to the camera a little way off. The drag queen is chatting to Titty, making punching movements with her fist. The middle-aged couple sidles over with Melania, who is still shooting daggers at Titty. They hand back my camera.

'Got your forty winks on camera,' says one of them.

'Give you even more kudos,' says the other, and they wander off, cackling like witches.

I put the camera in my bag. Raj is staring at me.

'Look, I'm really sorry, all right,' I say. 'It's been a really weird time for me, and I guess I'm just knackered . . . or concussed.'

He crosses his arms and continues to stare at me. I shift uncomfortably. He really is *very* handsome. Pretty deep-brown eyes, thick little eyebrows, pouty, defined lips, and just the right amount of stubble fuzzing a long, square jaw and a slight bum chin, which on him looks bizarrely sexy. The nose ring winks at me, like it wants to give me a second chance.

'Give me your phone,' he says.

'What?'

'Give me your phone.'

I clutch at the pocket that contains said phone.

'What are you gonna do with it?'

'Gimme!' he demands.

I reluctantly hand it over.

'Unlock it, please.'

I do as I'm told.

He types something in and hands it back.

I blink at it for a few seconds.

'What's this?'

'It's my number, dum-dum.'

'Why have you given me that?'

'Because, Mr Danny Break-up, you might not have much stamina as a protester, but you're certainly a very strange and extraordinary person.'

'*Cabaret*!' I squawk. 'You've seen it, too?'

'Just because I'm an activist doesn't mean I don't have Netflix,' Raj says, giving me a flirty little flick on the chest.

I stare at where he's touched me. Then I stare at his face. His beautiful face.

'Gimme a text; we'll go out for a beer sometime.'

I continue to stare. I am potentially still half asleep. Potentially dying from a brain aneurysm.

'OK, then,' he says. 'Nice to see you again. Bye, babes.' He hugs Melania, who has been watching from nearby. 'Don't worry about Titty – seriously.'

'I never worry about people beneath me,' Melania snaps.

Raj stares at her with a cheeky smile.

'Totally. And you' – he's looking at me again – 'you drink in moderation and get enough sleep.' He pats me on the shoulder, and walks off towards Titty and the drag queen. 'Psyched to watch the interview!' he calls back with a grin.

'Work *and* a date from a protest?' Melania says as we wander off towards the Tube station. 'Capitalism in action!'

TWENTY-THREE

'Here's to Fresh Meat!' Gin cries, raising a little brown mug of some kind of rum-and-tequila cocktail Ange has brewed up. 'First of Her Name, Journalist Extraordinaire, Date-Getter of Beautiful Boys, Former Wearer of Boring Blue Shirts—'

'Hey!' I shout.

'And Mother of More LGBTQ-Plus Representation! Cheers to you, girl!'

'Cheers!'

I clink assorted receptacles with my new housemates. Ashraf nudges me with his huge breeze-block arm. Melania smiles broadly, like a Persian cat.

'So glad you are here, dear lamb,' she says. 'And excited for you to digivolve into strident political agitator cursing Soviet states for all their evils.'

'To kicking off!' cries Gin. 'And pancakes!'

'Yeah,' Ange agrees, swigging her drink. 'Another posho to mess up the kitchen.'

I smile back at them all, and feel something I've maybe never felt: popular, cool, powerful. The thought of Zain looking at me snarkily flashes across my mind, and I feel so superior, essentially indestructible. Then, the way the brain likes to taunt you, an image of Tobbs replaces it. But, instead of my stomach turning and twisting into doubt over how I handled the whole thing, I feel different: deeply, deeply relieved to be free of him. I have a new life now, and it doesn't include him.

We're sitting in the cramped little kitchen because, if we have the oven on and the door open like a drawbridge, it's the warmest room in the house.

'I *was* pretty iconic,' I say to my audience, my fans. 'Felt well chuffed.'

'And he protected me from the evils of Titty,' Melania says. She's smoking one of her pastel-pink cigarettes with the gold filter. 'Sometimes I wish we never met at the LGBTQ event at Orientation Week all those months ago. Although, obviously, then I would not have met Raj, who is second wonder of queer world.'

'What's the first?' Gin asks.

'Jacob, obviously,' she says, waving a hand to where Jacob sits on the table in a Vivienne Westwood-style shredded tartan dress, a yellow Big Bird jacket and a pair of neon-orange wedged Spice Girls trainers.

'Unless Danny's taken my crown,' they say, causing everyone to laugh.

'Danielle is certainly coming for the role,' Melania goes on. 'He fell asleep on BBC News at protest *and* got a date with second wonder of queer world.'

'Bloody waste of space,' Ange mutters over her shoulder at the counter, where she's making more drinks. Everyone ignores her, as I'm realising is often the case.

'Ooooh!' Ashraf pummels me in the thigh with his Adamantium knuckles.

'So – when are you gonna see him?' Gin says, leaning in. How are they still only in the sheer dress?

'I dunno,' I say. 'Like – whenever. I'm not bothered, really.' Raj's lovely, slightly lopsided smile glows in my memory. There's something just so *good* about him, I can sense it. 'Can I have a cigarette, Mel?'

'Of course, lamb.'

Melania passes me the svelte box and I pull out a pastel-green one. They are all different colours, all with gold filters. She lights it for me, and I cough so hard Ange passes me a jam jar of whatever she's made, which I swig back in one go. It tastes like creosote.

As the coughing subsides, I lock eyes with Jacob, who is gazing at me with a steady, lightly condescending look.

'Smoking now as well as dating?'

I thump my chest and look back at them. This energy coursing through me bursts out of my mouth.

'Oh, I'm sorry, I didn't realise I needed to ask permission.'

The radio is playing, and its blurring background electronica is suddenly vividly present. I can hear every beat as the chatter goes silent. Even Ange looks awkward, in her leopard-print dressing gown and scarlet urban turban. She tops up Jacob's mug with more creosote, which they swig, also in one go.

'I'm just enquiring, babe.'

Usually, this would be the point where the guilt kicks in. My brow would spark, the ground would shake, and I'd apologise. But on this occasion, I just feel angry, and even more sure of myself.

'I don't make comments about you and Angel D, do I?'

At this, Melania literally gulps.

Jacob steps down from the table and smooths out their dress. Something about how measured and controlled they look, how they aren't rising to me, makes me even angrier.

'Danielle, you should absolutely go on a date with that gorgeous queer brown crusty activist student if you want to.'

'Well, thanks for the blessing.'

'And smoke if you want to.'

'I will, thank you.'

Out of the corner of my eye, I see Gin and Ashraf glance at each other uneasily.

'Anyway, angels' – Jacob stands, still with maddening calmness – 'I'm off to see my own gorgeous queer brown student.'

'What's he a student of?' Melania asks.

'*Moi*,' they say, and waft out.

I stare at the dark space where they had been standing. I actually hate the way they always do this: hold court, then flounce off. Always in control, always the centre of attention. Well, now I'm the centre of attention, aren't I? I'm the star in my own life and in our little society here. I'm not the shy kid Jacob still has me pinned as, following them around the Methodist church day centre. And if I want to go on a date with a gorgeous, kind, morally driven guy like Raj a few weeks after my break-up, I will, fuck you very much.

'Well, that was awkward as shit,' Ange says, and for once everyone fervently agrees.

'I'm going to text Raj,' I say, then take another puff on the cigarette, cough, and waltz from the room, leaving a trail of blue smoke behind me.

———

I go to my room and try to unpack some more of my things, but I'm so annoyed by Jacob I keep pausing, a book or Dolly vinyl in my hand, and staring into space. Even some more bullet points in the diary don't quieten it:

Friday 16th November

- *OK so Jacob is WELL narking me off. We've been friends since we were four years old. We went to preschool, primary school, secondary school together, sixth form together. We did our A-levels in the same sports hall. We've lived a lot of life together, but they've always been the star, and me the supporting role. I love Jacob a lot, but maybe moving in with them wasn't such a great idea.*

- *Jacob has always told me I need to change my life, take control, etc., but now I'm actually doing it, they still have to make it about them. They've always been like this. Screaming and dancing. They suck the air out of every room. It irritates me. Can't something be about me for once? Why does Jacob have to be like this ALL. THE. TIME. So in your face? So fucking extra? So fucking faggy?*

I can't get rid of the thoughts, so I go into the bathroom, run the water and climb into the piss-green seventies tub. It's only mid-afternoon. I have a while before Nina. My hands are shaking so much I have to deep-breathe before I can even turn the taps. It enrages me that Jacob's snogging their new bloke while I fight off yet another panic attack.

Little Sparrow or *Backwoods Barbie*? I scroll through the Dolly albums I have stored in my music library. I'm about to click on 'Better Get to Livin'' when a message comes in at the top of the screen. It's all in capitals, and I don't recognise the number, so I click on it. It's just a short message, and then a link to a YouTube video:

OMG DANNY! YOU'RE FAMOUS!! 😊

The link takes me to a video titled *Gay Rights Activist Falls Asleep Live on News*. To my horror, I recognise the blonde reporter from earlier, who is speaking to Titty in front of the gates of the Russian Embassy. Behind them, most of the pro-testers are on their feet, milling around with banners and signs. In the space between the two women, centre-screen, is me, still lying on the pavement. Beside me, Raj is looking down, clearly speaking, although we can't hear him. Then he's kneeling next to me. Then he's shaking me. Eventually, my arms and legs spasm, and I slowly sit up. The fucking camera actually focuses in on my bewildered face, even though the two women are still speaking. I'm blinking, staring around. It really looks like I've had the most wonderful nap.

The footage freezes, and the word 'BUSTED' appears across my face in blocky capitals.

I play it again.

And again.

And each time, I can feel my brow lighting up like a circuit board. The water in the bath trembles, white waves lapping towards the edges and spilling over. I feel sick.

Another text comes in from the same number.

It's Raj, BTW ☺

I stare at the message, trying to think rationally.

Then I type back:

Fuck no, this is awful!!!

No it's not!
You're a meme!
My goal in life is to become a meme

Mine is to stop being a complete moron all the time

OMG it's not that bad, Danny!

**It actually got the protest on the front page of BBC News,
so it was a good thing**

You wouldn't be saying that if it was you

It IS me

Shitfuck!
Have I embarrassed you in front of all your activist mates?

LOL Danny, no, it's fine
Don't worry so much
People will forget about it by Monday

You think?

I know!
ANYWAY
When can I take you for a drink to drown your sorrows?

I dunno
I'm kind of busy being the new Louis Theroux

Haha!
Oh, playing hard to get, are ya?

LOL, as if

Next Thursday then?

                    Sure you want to be seen with me?

I'll come in my balaclava

                              Perfect

See you then
   ☺

I drop my phone onto the bath mat and sink low into the water with my eyes closed.

Goodbye, credible journalism career.

Hello, potential new boyfriend.

TWENTY-FOUR

'. . . And then, it was all over the news. Which was really shitty, because it's actually a really important issue, and also being there felt really amazing, like I was really part of something, you know? It's crazy – sorry, *wild* – but I feel like this is the life I was meant for, you know? Like I've self-actualised at last. I've finally worked it out.'

Nina sits across the room from me, blinking placidly.

She leans in. 'Danny, I think it would be good if we used this session to go a little deeper than we've gone before. Especially since I've noticed you seem a little . . . *different* from last time.'

I look down at myself. I'm wearing black patent Doc Martens, the baggy combats and an oversized T-shirt with Marilyn Manson's naked white female body across the chest from the cover of *Mechanical Animals*. A thick bicycle chain sinks heavily against my neck and into my clavicles. It's just a thing I'm trying.

I look up at her, not mentioning it.

'Didn't we do that last time?'

'Not really. We discussed some earlier experiences that might have started patterns you're still in today, but I think it might be useful to go further – particularly to understand your anxiety.'

My knee is bobbing up and down like anything today. I sort

of can't concentrate; my mind keeps rushing around, catching the edges of thoughts, then falling off them again.

'OK.'

'You seem a little *agitated* today,' Nina says carefully. 'We can maybe wait until next week, if you'd prefer.'

'I'm not agitated,' I say reflexively, holding my knee still with one hand. 'I'm just sort of psyched up, you know? Like, I'm really embracing my new life, the new me, and it's giving me all this energy – I didn't even need to go on a juice cleanse.'

'I see that,' Nina says with a kind, sad, gentle compression of the lips that isn't quite a smile. 'You're certainly trying out new experiences and seeing which you like, and which you don't.'

'Because I'm in control now,' I say.

'You always were, Danny,' she says, and somehow this feels like a read. She coughs, possibly also realising this. 'Now, let's go back a little, to before you moved to London, to when you were still living at home in – what was the name of the town? Sleepy Hollow?'

'Whistlecombe,' I say firmly.

'Oh, right, right!' Nina says, and looks a tad embarrassed. 'Sorry, we just watched that last night. Of course, Whistlecombe.'

'I mean, it is kind of like that, to be honest. Except by the coast, and instead of a headless horseman, the true terror lurking down the country lanes is my dad's driving.'

Nina does that thing again where she tries not to laugh, crushing her hand into a fist and holding it to her mouth, as if she thinks I won't notice.

'Right. So . . . you've described this feeling to me' – she glances at previous notes she's made on the clipboard in her lap – 'the electricity around your forehead, your bones rattling, and the ground shaking.'

'It sounds so ridiculous when you say it,' I remark, in a sort of scoffing voice, like I'm too cool for it.

'It doesn't sound ridiculous at all, believe me,' Nina says with a knowing look. *You should hear what some of the other psychos say to me*, I imagine she's thinking. 'Can you remember a time before you felt these sensations?'

I shrug. 'Dunno. Maybe when I was really little.'

'Elementary school?'

'Yes.'

'Can you remember the first time you felt the electricity?'

I gnaw on my bottom lip. Images float up from the murky depths, things I haven't thought about for a long time.

'Well, there were a few times, maybe, at secondary school. Like when all that stuff happened with Will, and everyone started calling me a faggot.' I swallow immediately after I say the word, and swig from my bottle. I brought my own water this time, in anticipation of a dry mouth. 'I had it when I tried to go to sleep when I was off school for a bit. When I heard the phone ring. When I'd be in class and realise I was crossing my legs.'

Nina frowns. She looks down at her crossed legs, then back up at me.

'Why crossing your legs?'

'Because . . .' I feel ridiculous saying this too. 'Because if you cross your legs it means you're gay. But I'd always do it without thinking. And then sometimes people would notice and call me out on it. I know that's stupid, but there were loads of other things like that. Like never having a limp wrist, making sure your index finger was the same length as your ring finger, which it isn't.' I wave my hand at her. 'And not having a piercing in your right ear – that's the gay ear.' I tap the thick silver hoop sitting in my right lobe. 'Well, here it is. Turns out, I am, in fact, gay.'

Nina is nodding like anything. 'How would you describe yourself as a teenager?'

'Shy. Almost completely silent. Basically invisible.'

Wow, I said that pretty easily.

'And as a young man?'

'The same – until now.'

'So, Danny,' Nina says carefully. I can tell she's trying not to put words in my mouth, while also desperate to do it. 'You learned to play a role, the role of a straight teenage boy – is that fair to say?'

I shrug again. 'Well, of course. What else are you supposed to do if you don't want to get lamped every day?'

'And when would you say you stopped playing that role?'

'When I came out, I suppose, at uni. Although, obviously, I'd told Jacob before. They basically shook it out of me – well, literally, actually.'

'So did you change your behaviour then? When you came out at university?'

I'm staring at my knees again. I never cross them, I realise. It's just a habit. I never do it.

'I don't know,' I say, and, in all honesty, I don't.

'Danny, do you know what anxiety is?'

I look up at her like she's a complete idiot.

'Yes, Nina. It's when you're worried you left the iron on but you've already gone out, and then you're all, like, "Shit, I've burnt the house down!"'

'Right.' She laughs, even though I said that super-curtly. 'Sort of. Although, generally, the iron wasn't left on at all. Anxiety is our body's fight-or-flight reaction to feeling in danger. When this happens, our brain floods our nervous system with cortisol, which can cause many of the physical symptoms you've been describing. The problem is, we humans learn patterns and then stick to them. So, if you learned you were in danger at one time, and you're in a similar situation, your body might assume you're in danger now, and create the same symptoms.'

'OK,' I say slowly, actually listening properly for the first time this session. 'So me pretending to be something when I was younger could still be making me, like, stressed out now?'

'If you think you're in the same situation.'

'Like at work? Like with Tobbs? Or Zain? Or Laura and Luke?'

'If that seems to fit.'

I sit back in the chair, which makes the fart noise, but slowly: a long, sorrowful fart.

'You know, Nina, when I was with Tobbs . . .' I say, and see the exasperation in Nina's eyes – *Not him again!* 'Jacob kept telling me to focus on what *I* wanted, rather than what I thought *he* wanted me to want, if you know what I mean.'

'I do. How did it make you feel when they said that?'

I pause. Now is a moment. A moment to tell the truth.

'It's just . . .' I stutter, feeling on the edge of a precipice again, 'I know this sounds crazy but . . . doing stuff just for me has always felt, kind of – *selfish*.'

Nina's eyes widen. She leans in. This is what she wants.

'Yes, yes! How do you mean?'

I swallow hard. Something about this room, about who I become in here, brings out these words, bypassing the usual filter, the usual fear.

'Well, I dunno, it's, like, when I've been home alone – my old home – I'd never make a nice meal just for me, I'd just have pesto pasta or cereal. But when Laura and Luke were in, I'd often make a nice big meal for us all. I'd spend ages looking up recipes at work, and go to these weird little shops that sell, like, pickled Brussels sprouts and deer placenta and things.'

'Yes, yes!' Nina says, on the edge of climax.

'And at work, I normally just say yes to everything, and it feels good. I feel like I'm being useful. But then, when I have the time to pursue my own projects, I never do. It feels just not important, like, secondary to what everyone else wants. I actually think I only like plants because they, sort of – *need* me.'

'Right. Right!' Nina essentially screams. 'And you told me you'd wanted to be a journalist when you were younger?'

'Yeah, and I tried really hard at it at uni, spent a couple of years doing internships and temp work, and eventually got this job at CULTRD. But then, when I met Tobbs, it all vanished. All I could think about was him: getting stuff for him, doing things for him. It's like everything I wanted for myself just vanished. Isn't that mental?' I look at her. 'Sorry – *unusual*?'

Nina sits back, looking as pleased as a little piggy rolling in mud.

'I think what you might have just realised is the crux of the issue, Danny.'

Both my knees are bouncing. I'm watching them so I don't have to meet eyes with her.

'I only think I'm good enough if I'm doing something for someone else?'

Nina nods encouragingly.

Saying this feels like I'm finally putting voice to a deep truth I've always known. 'Because I've always tried to please people by being someone else, not who I really am, because I'm scared of how people will react to who I really am. And doing that all the time is stressing me out, making me *anxious*.' Now my eyes rise up to meet hers. 'That's it, isn't it?'

'I think you've got it.'

My chest is heaving; spots dance in front of my eyes. My blood is rushing through my whole body.

'So – what do I win?' I say.

Nina sits back and grins broadly, but with no teeth.

'Your freedom, Danny.'

———

Outside, on the street, there's a stillness. The buzzing is silenced for a moment. It's rained during the session, which I hadn't noticed at all. The pavement glitters, and the headlights passing streak the darkness.

I decide to walk home. It's about half an hour, but it feels good to be out in the world. As I walk, I notice things: two girls stumbling along with a bottle of gin; a group of guys in a late-night barber's dancing to a music channel on in the corner; a homeless man with one eye closed by a dark-blue bruise.

The world is a weird place.

I walk, staring at my boots as they get splattered and stained. Somewhere inside me, in my chest, I can feel something rising. What is it? Is it sadness, more tears?

No, I can feel it building. Building after being quiet for so many years.

It is violent, it is uncontrollable.

It is rage.

TWENTY-FIVE

All night long, the fire burns inside me. I barely sleep, but I don't care. The electricity of anxiety has mutated into a skin-fizzing, bone-shaking anger. How crazy that I've been pushing all this down, hiding it in plain sight for – how long exactly? My blood pulses with it. I am awake – *properly* awake – for the first time in years.

Scenes race through my brain, so vivid I can almost reach out and feel the texture of the football stitching as Rory McClure kicks it at my crotch, shouting 'Danny Skid Mark! Danny Skid Mark!' I can taste the Haribo on Will Winters's breath as we kiss between the branches of the yew tree at the bottom of Jacob's dad's garden. Haribo and weed, which is what he had led me there to do, allegedly. I can hear Jacob shrieking along to 'Time Warp' from the house, where their sixteenth birthday party messily rages. I feel how magical it felt, how special, how true, and how ours it was. I hear his shy little giggle, the blush on his face so dark I can see it in the faint yellow light from the kitchen windows.

Then, just as fast, I feel the shame across my forehead, the pulse in my neck, the tightness in my chest, as everyone looks at me differently. The whole school becomes one giant, judgemental face. Laura walks past me in the hallway with Rory. She stifles a snort behind her hand. I'd forgotten that snort, though I'd replayed it in my head for years and years. Everyone is clustered by the whiteboard in my form room. I see them scatter like falling May blossom as I enter. I hear the chairs scrape against the floor. Hear the awkward tap-tap-tap of Mrs Andrews's sensible court shoes coming down the hallway towards us. I sit. I look over to where Will Winters sits. I see the familiar shape of the back of his head: delicate fair hair, quite a flat skull. His head is dipped down. He's writing something intently.

I look at the whiteboard. I read the words written on it in jagged red capitals: 'DANNY SKID MARK IS A FAGGOT.'

I hear Mrs Andrews's high, angry, worried voice from the door: 'Wipe that off – *now*!'

I hear the phone ring when I'm at home, in bed already at 5 p.m. I hear Mum knock on the door. I hear the lump in my throat as I try to make some gabbled explanation. I hear that phone ring every night for years to come. And, every time I do, I feel the electricity spark across my forehead.

—

Because I can't sleep, I try to write in the Dolly Diary. I write 'Danny Skid Mark is a faggot' over and over and over again.

But that does nothing to diminish the buzz, so I start thinking about work, about everything I have to do, about how differently they're all treating me now. They never even talked to me before I changed up my style to look more like them. What do any of them even know about me? I mean *really* know?

Nina's voice enters my head just as powerfully as my teen memories.

Why is it that they don't know anything about me? Is it because they don't ask? Or is it because I don't share? Is it because

I hide inside a shell of something I'm not? Is it because I'm lying to all of them? Is it because I'm lying to myself, and have been, for over a decade?

Maybe, I think.

Jesus Christ, I'm always on the fucking fence.

Just pick a side, Danny Skid Mark. Have you been lying to yourself, or not?

Yes. Yes, I have.

It's always just been automatic. Agreeing with people, whatever they say. Going along with things, not really knowing what I don't want to do. Not really knowing what *wanting* to do something even feels like.

Do I even want to be a journalist, or did I just do well in English class?

I turn a page in the diary and start another list:

- *Do I like Dolly Parton?*
Yes, I definitely like her. Here You Come Again *is the greatest album of all time.*
- *Do I still want to be a journalist?*
Yes. I want to tell amazing people's stories.
- *And the plants?*
What's more beautiful than a calathea triostar?
- *What about pale-blue shirts?*
Pretty insipid, TBH. Too boring to even hate.

And yet hate my usual uniform I suddenly do. Never again will I wear those stupid clothes. I've always made myself invisible. Well, not anymore. They'll know who I am today . . . even if I'm still working it out.

———

'Out of the way, bitches, a star is about to be born!' I shout to the queue of phone-scrolling, beard-fiddling, quietly chatting hipsters in the lobby.

Every head flicks up. Every pair of eyes widens, then narrows. I stomp past them with my oat-milk latte, straight into the lift. I can hear my breathing coming loud and fast. My shoulders are heaving. My phone buzzes. *WHO THE HELL IS IT*? Whoever it is, is going to get it in the neck.

Uncle David and Auntie Denise definitely coming for Xmas Day now David's had his flashing anklet off. Be very upset not to see you. LOL Mum

Despite being told on numerous occasions, both in text and IRL, Mum still thinks 'LOL' stands for 'Lots of Love'. It gives her messages even more of a sarcastic tone. But on this occasion, it really fuels this whirl of anger I'm in.

Yeah, ofc Mum! Love you XXX

I text back rabidly.

Heads continue to turn as I storm to my desk and throw off the furry, yellow Big Bird jacket I've taken from Jacob. My colleagues are looking, but I don't give a shit. I slump languidly into my chair, like I own fifty-one per cent of this damn company. Even though these leather trousers might squeak and strain around the crotch, I stick my Doc Martens up on the desk. One of the chunky silver rings I've borrowed from Gin catches on the floral embroidery of Melania's long-sleeved sheer shirt. It's too small, and I can only do up two of the buttons, but something about it makes me feel like Dolly, gaining sovereignty over the glitzy Liza number from Halloween. *Fuck you, Laura*, I think as I turn my computer on.

And that's when I see it. An A4 printout taped to the monitor. From it, my face stares back, with bleary eyes and a dopey waking half-smile. Blocky white text reads: 'WHEN HE DOESN'T PULL OUT.'

The edges of my vision become watery. The ground is unsteady. My brain is gripped by a vice-like pressure. I don't have to guess who did this.

'Morning, boss!' Callum yawns, sliding into his chair opposite. He glances at me with a fearful smile. 'Or should I say Mr Celebrity Boss.'

I don't reply immediately. Instead, I breathe deeply with my eyes shut. When I open them, Callum looks just as tentative and just as amused.

'Is it . . . everywhere?'

'Honestly, Dan, I can't believe I work with a real-life meme. You're bigger than Grumpy Cat.'

I pull the A4 sheet from my screen and slowly tear it in half, staring Callum straight in the face.

'Stan's well excited about all the different bits we can do on it. He was telling me last night at the Ivy. "Gotta grab these opportunities the way you grab an intern" is what he said.'

I stare at him with such violent hatred, it really is a testament to his limited intellect that he doesn't notice.

'Did he?'

Right on cue, Stan lumbers past. He leans in and gives Callum such a grotesque, wet kiss that my stomach actually turns. As he does, he winks at me, then wanders off again. I can see the disgust on Callum's face as he wipes the slobber from it. Then he catches my eye, and smiles.

'He's dead good to me,' he says.

The anger and indignation in my veins are alive with electricity. This is the world, isn't it? All of us using one another for our gratification one way or another, but nothing is meaningful. Stan creeps on Callum, and Callum lets him because – why? Attention? Money? Daddy issues?

Either way, I can't bear it anymore.

I click open a new email to Dying-Swann-HR and write the subject line: 'Formal Complaint Re: Creative Director'.

From the half-pipe, Stan yells, 'Right, Callout Culture Cunts, let's see what you've got this week!'

I click 'Send'.

———

'Great idea, Mark, loved that,' Stan booms. 'No one's done a POV from the perspective of a Jack Russell before. Really *niche* concept – but where's the oomph? Where's the WTF factor? If it ain't shocking, people ain't flocking. Anyway, who's n ext?'

'Me!' I say, pushing through Development and Design. 'Me, Danny Scudd. I have an idea.'

'Aha! Scudders! Can we have a hand for our resident sleeping beauty!' An excitable clap runs around the half-pipe. There are several whistles. 'Shame you can't see your trendy new threads in any of the GIFs. But you know what they say?'

'Never wear a cap the same colour as your face?' I retort, plugging my laptop into the graffiti-wall screen.

A shocked but secretly delighted laugh meanders around the crowd. Stan's marble eyes follow it uneasily.

'Ha ha, good one, Scudders. Good one,' he say, laughing, and punches me in the shoulder, a little harder than usual.

The presentation is ready to go. I spin around.

'Hi, everyone. What a time for me to finally do a presentation, huh? Well, maybe it's the perfect time, actually.'

'Goowan, Harry Styles!' someone yells, probably one of the Marc/ks. More, less cautious laughter.

'I'm going to assume you've all seen the photos and footage of me going around at the moment?'

'Yeah, there's a whole piece on UNILAD about it,' Nadia yells.

'And *The Guardian* tweeted it.' That's willowy Robyn.

'This is why we need to do an exclusive right now!' Stan says, clapping at his own voice.

'Yeah, well,' I go on, 'this is what I wanted to talk to you guys about. Just this sort of thing.'

I take a deep breath, and descend into the PowerPoint I worked on obsessively all day yesterday.

'"Drink the COOL-aid, join the CULT". That's our brand proposition' – I look around at the blank faces of my colleagues – 'and doesn't that make you fucking sick?' There is a collective inhalation of breath, followed by delighted laughter. I do not turn to look at Stan. 'What does it even mean?'

I press the clicker. A grainy photo of a bunch of long-haired men in white robes pops up. They're all grinning, with dead eyes.

Clickety-click. Now an image of Homer Simpson being sworn into the Stonecutters.

'What does that mean to us as a brand with significant visibility?'

'Everybody get down on their knees and worship Stan!' the other of the Marc/ks yells.

The laughter gets louder, and more cathartic. Something's happening. People can sense it – the Untethering.

'Well,' I say, 'we could do that, but I'd suggest this instead.'

Callum is standing at the back, gnawing on the nail of his pinkie finger, looking worried as hell. We meet eyes for the briefest of seconds. The electric fingertips formally known as Anxiety, now accepted as double-platinum recording artist Gay

Rage, strike a violent chord in my forehead. But this time, it's not crushing, it's thrilling.

Clickety-click-click.

A grainy photo of me and Jacob sitting on the quayside in sunny Whistlecombe. We're both in our emo phase. They, of course, pulling it off better, looking pretty punk rock. I look almost exactly the same, except with a chain hanging from my skinny jeans rather than around my neck.

'When I was a teenager, life always felt like it was elsewhere. Life happened to people on MTV. Especially' — my voice trembles — 'as a queer kid, I never saw anyone like me. I never felt part of "the cult". All I knew was that I had to not be me, and instead be as much like everyone else as possible.' The Marc/ks eye each other knowingly. 'Now, our digital resources are so vast, what we crave, more than fame and glamour, is authenticity — someone who seems like you, who feels as you feel. Less of the ridiculous, clickbaity stories we've been told people like, more of the raw honesty of those experiences.'

The room is silent now. People are listening, genuinely listening to me.

Further clickature.

A photo of Stan, red-faced and half dressed as Father Christmas at last year's Christmas party, falling towards us, mouth and fur-trimmed jacket open, revealing his large, pink, hair-covered stomach. The laughter bursts out hysterically. Callum continues to glare.

'It's unpleasant having people laugh at embarrassing photos of you, isn't it, Stan?' I turn to him, all smiles. His cap no longer matches his face, which is dark, thunderous crimson. 'Now imagine you're part of a minority and have been victimised your whole life for the thing you're getting laughed at on a massive platform. Well, that's what we do, isn't it? We trade in getting clicks by offering up vulnerable people for the slaughter.'

'Hang on there, Scudders!' Stan interrupts. 'We shed a light on marginalised people to give them visibility.'

Clickety-click-click.

Headlines from our most recent stories fill the screen: 'Flexible Muslim Burkini Model Opens Tantric Yoga Parlour – and You're Invited'; 'Here's Where the Man with No Arms Buys his "Handy" Meat Alternatives'; 'Don't Panic! This Trans Woman's Only Sneaking into Your Bathroom to Freshen it Up'.

I turn back to my colleagues. Then to Stan.

'No, we don't. We're profiting from them. And not enough, from the sound of things.'

Stan's Adam's apple bounces in his throat.

I see everyone's expression change. Never have they heard me speak like this to anyone.

'Whoooa there, Scudders, don't be like that.' Stan puts his hand on my shoulder. He smiles, trying to mollify me.

'My name is Danny,' I say to him. 'Not Scudders.'

An actual gasp goes around the crowd.

I fix them with a smile any crocodile would be proud of.

'Wouldn't you love to come to work every day and not feel like your soul is getting sucked out of your arse by creating content that actively damages people and society, just for profit, and give a platform to those people to tell their stories and champion their businesses? Make work we can all actually be proud of?

'I live with a group of the most amazing people, from all over the world, all talented and unique. Each with their own story to tell. Each with small businesses we could support and gear our subscribers towards – rather than point them to the Hilton and the Ivy.'

As I say this, I stare Stan straight in the face. In my peripheral vision, I see Callum biting his nails down to the quick.

'Sounds like a sick idea!' Nadia shouts, while filming.

'Harry's got a point!' say the Marc/ks simultaneously.

'The management culture here is toxic!' I can't see who that was, but it sounded like Robyn.

The mood in the room has changed. The revolution is here, and it will be live-streamed.

Stan hovers next to me, eyes darting about his army as they dissent.

'Come on, Scudders, it's all just for fun, isn't it? We're just trying to make people laugh, get them to read something funny and edgy. You don't have to take things so seriously. We're not the news.'

'No,' I say, and I can hear the bile in my voice. 'We are most definitely not the news. Although, with your behaviour, I'm surprised you haven't ended up on it.'

The gasp that echoes around the half-pipe is my greatest achievement to date.

'Oh, come on, you lot!' Stan cries. 'It's all just a bit of fun, isn't it?'

And now the room is silent. Stan steps back a few paces, glancing at Callum, then at me. But he's not going to get any sympathy there.

'The time is over when corporations can steal from the vulnerable and profit from it,' I declare, thinking how I absolutely have to tell Raj about this moment. 'Either you move with it, or it leaves you for dead.'

Stan gulps, making his temples shudder, causing the "BOSS" on his cap to bob up and down.

'I mean, yeah,' he says finally. 'Let's run with your idea, Scud— Danny – and see how it goes?'

I grin at him, feeling power swell in my veins.

'No problem, Boss Man.'

TWENTY-SIX

Winter is here. The nights are darker. The air freezes and fills with sleet. Every shop window is starting to twinkle with little lights and glitter with scattered snow and baubles. We saunter ever closer to my least favourite time of the year: Christmas.

Despite my mother's constant reminders, it's hard to think about it right now, I'm so busy with all my new work, and seem to be texting Raj all the time. Callum edits the footage I took from the march into something salvageable, and I write an article to go along with it, titled 'Why We Should All Be LGBTQ+ Allies', and push through to donating to LGBTs 4 Chechnya at the bottom of the page. It gets the most views we have on any article that year. But the Marc/ks inform me it's probably because people want to see if Sleeping Meme Guy does anything else stupid. All the same, I feel proud of it. While I'm rushing around between meetings, drinks with the team and the house. I don't think about the email I sent to HR, not even once.

The house is a whole thing in itself. There's never something not happening. The other night when I got home, Ange and Gin were in the second-floor bathroom, using the bath to ferment two bags of cooking apples they'd found on the street. Ange sat on the loo saying they were making 'proper East End moonshine'. As she said it, she flicked ash into the swirling, piss-coloured liquid Gin was stirring with what I pray to God wasn't the douche.

'I'll bring you some in bed,' she said, with a grin.

Another night, I came back to discover a group of people Melania said were Buddhists sitting in a circle in the living room, chanting and chiming a little bell. They continued until well after midnight. The house was vibrating with the sound of it. It was sort of magical, but also just a lot.

Even if I could sleep, I wouldn't get a full eight hours; the front door is constantly slamming, shaking the walls of the house.

It is always slamming.

It is never not slamming.

And it's SO COLD. Melania was right. I'm worried that if I could actually fall asleep I might die in the night.

I can't tell if I like life in the house because it's exciting, or if it's starting to get on my nerves, or if I'm just generally agitated at the moment. I do feel well and truly integrated, though, which is worth it all.

One night in the living room, we're just, you know, *chilling* – drinking some possible moonshine and passing around a joint – and the subject of my presentation comes up. I can't remember how exactly, but, next thing I know, I'm showing it to all of them on the projector – all of them except Jacob, who's out with Angel D again. It's kind of funny how I haven't even met him properly. I did bump into him coming out the shower in just a towel a few days ago, and he was absolutely gorgeous, but that's about it. Considering we're best friends, it's weird how Jacob's keeping us apart.

Or maybe not so weird. I mean, didn't I do the same with Tobbs . . . ?

'Is Marx's work you do. If Marx was a meme,' Melania says from the floor, where she scribbles content ideas on the inside of an opened-out box of Shredded Wheat with a pink highlighter. 'You are bringing down entire capitalist system from within.'

'You know, I read *On Palestine* last night,' I say. 'When I couldn't sleep again. Turns out that whole situation is fucked.'

Gin's and Ashraf's eyes flick to each other. They're crouched over the breeze-block coffee table, working on a joint spider diagram on a scrap of calico with fabric pens. Somehow I've turned this into a brainstorming session for my new content series.

My leg, which once only shook when I was most nervous, is now in a constant state of movement. It just has to be active. The foot is tapping. Or, when I'm seated, the knee smack-smacks against the palm of my hand, which is often thrumming its own tune. It used to be Jacob who was the busy one, a comet shooting across the night sky. Now it's me who can't sit still.

'Check this out, cunt,' Ange says from the corner, where she's painted words across an old vagina canvas. 'Reckon this'll win you that bullshit award.'

I walk over. She's scrawled 'CAUSE CRIMINAL DAMAGE' in scarlet acrylic.

She stands back and puffs on her cigarette.

'An oldie but a goodie,' she chuckles.

'I just feel like you're not taking this seriously, Ange,' I hear myself say. The air in the room freezes dead. People do not answer back to Ange. She is this sort of messy, semi-malignant force in the house, like a poltergeist. And you don't want to anger it. 'This is a *real* chance to create *real* change. Don't you want to be represented? Don't you want your voice to be heard?'

Ange throws down her paintbrush and storms from the room.

'EAT SHIT, YOU POSH FUCKERS!' she screams. Her

bedroom door slams, and the muffled opening guitar chords of 'Break Stuff' by Limp Bizkit play.

'You know, my family is actually very poor,' Melania says, doodling away, absolutely unfazed.

I'm more agitated. The rate of hand slaps to thigh per minute has gone up by fifty per cent or more.

'Yeah,' I say. 'Mine, too.'

'I have an idea!' Gin cries, raising up their fabric. 'We could do a full-on Queer Revue, right here, in the house. Jacob could perform, Ash and Mel could model my latest collection, and we could live-stream it across your company channels and then push them to our websites with a message to support independent queer creatives! And we can do it when we normally have the Centrefold XXXmas Party, so all the usual suspects will be coming anyway. Wouldn't that be iconic?'

I blink at them for a hot minute.

'*I* gave you that idea!'

Gin gazes up at me like they're going to cry. Ashraf puts his arm around them. Who is this person I'm becoming?

'Maybe we're done with the brainstorming session for now, mate?' he suggests.

'Come on, you guys!' I say, possibly shout. 'Don't you want the world to know who you are? Don't you want them to listen to you at last? All your lives, you've been told you're nothing. Now's your chance to prove to them you *are* something!'

The three of them stare at me like I'm crazy. I cough and look at the floor.

'I mean, it's a good idea, though, Gin. We should totally do it.'

———

That night, I can't sleep again. I lie in bed, my body vibrating. I've forgotten what it is to relax, so I unpack the last of my stuff from boxes. The room seems to be even messier by the time I get back into bed again and do some deep breathing. I don't even consider listening to Dolly in the bath.

At some point, Jacob and Angel D came back, and honestly went for it ALL NIGHT. Jacob, as you might imagine, is not the kind of person to be silent in the sack.

Oh no.

Jacob is a screamer.

But a screamer if the screamer is screaming in an opera. It has this incredible cadence to it. It builds. It's really quite spectacular, and I even recorded the sound on my phone. Well, it would be spectacular if it hadn't been at 11.30 p.m., 2.43 a.m. and 5.22 a.m. There was then another crescendo in the shower at 7.30 a.m., meaning I had to use the other bathroom. The other bathroom only has a bath. This bath was full of the nostril-tingling, rancid acidic-apple smell of the pavement-bag moonshine. I washed my face, pits, balls and dick in the sink, sighed into the mirror at my puffy eyes and tired cheeks while Pavo-fucking-rotti closed their greatest performance yet.

It's Thursday at last, mine and Raj's date night. He texts me: "*Excited to see you later, Miss Fame!* 😏" But how the hell am I supposed to be on form when I've had no sleep? The anxiety prickles at my brow. I text back. ***Can't wait!!!!!*** 😀 😀 😀

And he does a smiley face and an 'X'. I pause, then put an 'X', too. Gosh, it really can be that simple.

I add another list to the Dolly Diary, opposite the last entry:

Thursday 22nd November

- *Am really smashing life. Am an icon, and am the moment.*
- *Have crazy energy to do everything. Probs cos am now high-flying media professional and all-round sickening legend. Can't sleep though.*

- *Am hardcore activist for political change! Want to say I can't believe it, but I can believe it because am now Danny 2.0.*
- *Jacob still pissing me off, NGL. But don't have time for their ridiculous drama ATM.*

I sit back and stare at what I've written. Then at the page opposite, where I slag off Jacob. Even a fortnight ago, this would have felt like a betrayal. But it doesn't now. And maybe I'm fine with that.

'Mad?!' a voice gasps from the doorway.

Jacob is standing there in their kimono with two cups of coffee and a cinnamon-and-raisin bagel covered in a metric ton of marmalade. It's like they know I've been thinking about them and have been summoned.

Death Becomes Her ranks as our second-favourite movie to quote, after *Grey Gardens*. Luckily, a blonde Madeline Ashton-style wig is near. I don it and turn to them with open arms.

'Hel!'

Jacob blinks at me. 'No, I wasn't doing Meryl,' they say. 'I was asking: have you gone mad?'

'Oh.' I pull off the wig. 'No, I just wanted to make the room look nice. I was thinking, what if Raj comes back here and it's this weird, empty room with loads of boxes? He'll be like, WTF, this guy moved in weeks ago and hasn't even unpacked.' I laugh, kind of manically. 'He'll think I'm absolutely mental!'

The Uggs shuffle in. The bum goes to the bed. The knee goes over the other. The hand comes out with the coffee.

Jacob hands me the coffee and gazes around the room as if it is our hometown, hit in the night by a hurricane.

'Dan, I think you might be going through the Seven Stages of Grief. This is the Eighth Stage: Interior Destruction.'

Here they go again, acting like they know more about me than I do. Immediately I'm riled.

'Maybe I like it like this.'

'Danielle.' Our eyes meet. 'I know you've got a lot going on right now, but the Centrefold is a house of love and respect, and you've been – how do I say this – rather a she-devil recently.'

I sip the coffee. I hate the way Jacob evades personal issues by taking the moral high ground. They always want to be the bigger person offering advice to the little people, never being called out on their own bullshit. This morning, their narrow, angular face is tired, sad-looking, and this weakness makes me bolder.

'You just don't like that you're not the centre of attention anymore.'

They're about to take a bite into the orangest bagel ever to hit the London performance-art scene, but it pauses mid-air.

'I know things have been a bit iffy between us since you moved in, Little Edie, but that's not what it's about.'

But I'm on a roll.

'It really gets on my nerves that you still call me that.'

'What?'

'Little Edie.'

'What the fuck, Dan? We always call each other that. It's like our "thing".'

I put the coffee down.

'We're not in Whistlecombe anymore, Toto.'

Jacob looks at me in a way I can't quite work out. Somewhere between hurt and angry.

'You know what today is, don't you?' they say.

I think, briefly.

'Thursday.'

'It's my mum's birthday.'

I swallow hard. I'd completely forgotten. Every year since she died, I've joined Jacob's dad and sisters for a meal where we remember her. It used to be at the pub the family always went to in Whistlecombe, but the last few years it's been in London, or in Bristol, where the twins live with their boyfriends.

'Oh, shit, Jay,' I say. 'I'm sorry, I forgot.'

Jacob is sitting very rigidly.

'I came in here to ask you if you wanted to come this evening. Dad and the twins are in town. We're going to that French place in Piccadilly.'

'Well . . .' I can feel my lip contort, and Jacob sees it. 'It's, just, I have this date . . .'

Jacob stares at me so darkly I can almost feel them stabbing me in the heart.

'No problem. I'll ask Angel instead. He's still downstairs, so.'

I'm not looking directly at them now, but at the Dolly Diary, which I've just realised lies open between us. As casually as I can, I flip it closed.

Jacob's eyes flick up from the bedazzled cover.

'I had this great idea for work yesterday,' I say, in a high, different voice – the kind my mum uses after she and Dad have had a fight and she still wants him to take the bins out.

Jacob pauses before replying.

'Did you?'

'It's for this new series I'm running. We're going to do a Queer Revue in the house and live-stream it across CULTRD's channels, then push viewers to everyone's sites, and I was wondering if you wanted to perform?' Jacob just blinks at me. 'It'd give you and your work loads of visibility, as well as everyone in the house. It'll be really good for everyone.'

Jacob remains silent.

'Sure,' they say eventually. 'Whatever.'

They get up and go to the door.

'Thanks, Jay!' I call weakly.

Jacob pauses in the doorway, then ducks out through it.

TWENTY-SEVEN

Despite my recent sassy, gives-no-fucks demeanour, I sit at the high table in the cool under-a-train-tunnel East London bar fiddling with my beer glass like it's an executive worry-toy.

Since I spoke to Jacob, my brain has frazzled, and the ground has shaken at several points, which I noted down in the Dolly Diary:

Instances of Heightened Anxiety

- *Explaining my concept for the Queer Revue to a roomful of my colleagues who are now my 'project team'.*
- *Getting home and having to sit on edge of the bed while deep-breathing.*
- *Trying on outfits in front of Melania.*
- *Deciding on an outfit: sheer white T-shirt with red rose appliqué, high-waisted, stone-washed jeans, and the white Converse ('capitalism classic, like U.S.A. distilled,' Melania said).*
- *Leaving the house.*
- *Getting the Overground.*
- *Every stop on the Overground.*

- *Getting off the Overground.*
- *Approaching the bar.*
- *Entering the bar.*
- *Waiting in the bar.*
- *Seeing Raj pushing open the glass door, seeing me, smiling, waving and approaching between the man-buns, blunt fringes, topknots and undercuts.*

I slam the diary shut, slide it into my backpack, and rise to greet him.

'Hey there, mister,' he says, giving me a firm, self-assured hug.

He's dressed in his uniform of baggy black T-shirt and high-waisted black Levi's, only this time with an army jacket thrown on over the top. We look sort of like we've been dressed by the same stylist, which I count as a win. He smells strongly of Fresh Man Smell, which makes my insides tingle as we embrace.

'Hey,' I say, with no flirty qualifier.

'Sorry I haven't been able to meet sooner,' he says, sitting down and shrugging off the jacket. 'Things have been so hectic ever since the action.'

'Natch,' I say coquettishly. 'I got you a beer already.'

Raj looks at me like I've said something in Esperanzo.

'What did you say?'

'*Naturally.*' I hear my voice crack. Is this experience more nerve-racking than just turning up at a random Dutch guy's house and sidestepping getting shat on? Quite possibly.

'Oh!' Raj laughs. 'Obvie! Sorry, didn't realise you were so down with the kids.'

I try to lean in alluringly, but can't find anywhere for my elbow to go so end up moving back to how I was.

'Well, I'm a very strange and extraordinary person.'

'Ha ha!' Raj laughs again. His laugh is such a lovely sound, it's got all of him in it, so full and genuine. 'How are you, anyway? Ever since stepping into the light of stardom?'

'Oh, you know, just fucking up neoliberalism while hanging out with celebs.'

'She's a champagne socialist now?'

'More of a radical queer Marxist,' I say, with no irony whatsoever.

Raj can't stop laughing. 'Natch!'

'We put out the video and article about the protest, and it did really well.'

'Oh, shit, yeah!' Raj says with genuine enthusiasm, eyes glittering excitedly. 'I'll have to take a look. Although, really, you're the star attraction.'

'Oh my God, don't!' I smack myself in the face. 'Most embarrassing moment of my life.'

'I honestly see that meme everywhere. I can't believe it's you. It's so cool!' Raj rubs me on the arm excitedly.

I'm thrown; I really don't know how to react. Tobbs never said stuff like this, excited-for-me stuff, even at the beginning.

'Well, not as cool as you,' I say, pushing a beer-damp coaster across the sticky table with my forefinger. 'I mean, I don't work as an activist, I just fell asleep on TV. I'm not changing the world like you.'

'Yeah you are. You're doing your bit, that's what counts.' He smiles. My chest flutters. My stomach swirls. 'And anyway, I don't work as an activist, I just do that in my free time because I believe in it. By day, I'm doing a master's in criminology and work in a bar round the corner. The glamour.'

'Wow, amazing,' I say. 'You know, my ex really wanted to report on more crime stuff – well, that and, like, conflict in the Middle East. He kind of wanted to do everything, I think, which always made me feel kinda—'

Raj leans in, making the tea light between us flicker. He puts his hand softly on top of mine.

'Look, Danny, I know you've only recently been broken up with, but you're on a date with me, not with your ex.'

He says it kindly, but it still feels like a bullet to the gut.

'Yeah, I know,' I say, and see him frown. 'I mean: sorry.'

'If you're not ready, that's cool,' he says, squeezing my hand.

Oh yeah: boundaries. It kind of blows my mind that you can just say this to someone. I would *never* have just said this to Tobbs.

'No, no – I am. I just . . . Sorry, I'm just being an idiot.'

Maybe I'm not cut out for this dating malarkey. Suddenly what I'm wearing feels like an ill-fitting costume, what I'm saying a script for a dodgy BBC sitcom. The urge to get up and run away is pretty strong. Is this what Tobbs felt like the whole time we were together? Maybe he didn't not-like me, maybe he was intimidated by me? No, wait, that can't be it – can it?

'You're not an idiot, you're far from an idiot,' Raj says, not breaking eye contact for a second. He studies me with a curious half-smile. 'But you are very different from the person I thought you were when I first met you.'

'Yeah, well, you know,' I say vaguely, 'I'm like an iceberg, me.' What the fuck am I saying?

'Totally!' He laughs again.

'And I'm just trying new things at the moment.' I shrug.

He sees my discomfort and kindly sidesteps it, but I can see he's thinking things he isn't saying. I honestly feel like my heart is bursting.

'So.' He coughs. 'What are the latest crazy capers happening in your madcap journalistic existence?'

'Um . . .' I consider, trying to think of anything he might want to hear. I decide not to mention everything going on between me and Jacob. No one wants to hear how much your best mate is pissing you off, do they? So, instead, I say, 'Well, Stan, my straight married boss, is having an affair with Callum, the twenty-two-year-old junior videographer.'

'Fuuuuuuuuck!'

'Yeah. I caught them. Literally, caught Stan with his trousers down, and, my God, you don't want to see that.'

'Whoa, how come?'

'Honestly, it must be the spottiest ass in apps.'

'BA-HA-HA! How did this even unfold?'

'Well, I went to use the disabled loo because I, like, you know, like the privacy. And walked in on it: the thrusting, spotty arse of Mr Boss Man. Glistening with sweat. And inhumanly white.'

'Quite poetic, really.'

'Then, afterwards, Stan announced it to the whole office as this edgy thing they're doing, but it really seems like he's taking advantage of Cal. Cal is this, like, super-buff gym bro. I can't tell what's going on.'

I take a glug of beer.

Raj is looking at me seriously

'It's the power imbalance, isn't it? Is Cal just going along with it because he thinks he has to? Do you know if Stan's done this to anybody else?'

'I dunno. But it really made me angry. Kind of because of the protest, actually.' This'll get me brownie points. 'And I sort of staged a coup, because CULTRD publishes so much shit and pushes people to big brands that don't support LGBT people or any other minority group but gets money off the back of our content regardless. And Stan is just parading around the office taking the piss out of everyone for being gay or Muslim or a woman, for Christ's sake. He's everything that's wrong with our culture. So I humiliated him in front of the entire workforce, and now I can basically do whatever I want.'

I sip my drink. Mic drop.

Raj stares at me with his mouth slightly open. 'Wow, you've had a real awakening.' He sips his beer and looks away.

'Yeah, I have!' I agree emphatically. 'Before, I knew *nothing*. But now I know what I didn't know – you know? And I know we have to bring creeps like him down.'

Raj regards me carefully. He takes a moment before he replies. 'That's super-awesome, Danny,' he says slowly. 'But you need to be careful with the anger. We queers take in so much of it from others, it's easy to become it, and just project it back on the world. But it doesn't really get you very far.'

I blink at him blankly. This was not the reaction I was hoping for. I thought that this would be a unifying anecdote, that Raj would realise how similar we are: kind and principled and not afraid to fight for what we believe in.

'Also, I'm doing a live-stream event at ours this week. It's a Queer Revue.' I adeptly change topic. 'Everyone in the Centre-fold is involved. It'll be iconic.'

'The Centrefold?' Now that lopsided smile is coming back.

'That's what we call the house,' I say. '"The Commune" wasn't as catchy.'

Raj blinks at me, then bursts into laughter.

'You crack me up, Danny,' he says. 'Your life is seriously like a sitcom or something.'

'Everyone says that.'

'Have you ever considered putting pen to paper?'

'I have started writing a diary, actually – not that it'll ever see the light of day.'

'I'm intrigued.'

'Don't be,' I say in Renée Zellweger's Bridget Jones accent. 'Everybody knows diaries are full of *craaap*.'

'I bet yours would be a bestseller.'

Then Raj takes both my hands, leans in and kisses me. If there are other people in the bar, I can't hear them. His lips taste amazing. My whole spine is melting. I'm swallowed by the kiss, although, the entire time, this nag swirls in my stomach. My body is vibrating, like I'm in a rattling train carriage, rather than a hipster bar.

'Raj?' I say afterwards.

'Daniel?'

'I think I need to take this slow.'

'You know this is only our first date?' he says, laughing.

'Yeah, I know. I just. Sorry. I just want to be straight up with you.'

'Don't worry, I've got it. You're kind of an open book, you know?'

'Am I?'

'Well, you're not exactly an international man of mystery.'

'S'cuse me, I just moved from South London to East London. Pretty adventurous, if you ask me.'

'Ha! Totally! But, yeah, we can just be chill, take it easy. No sweat.'

He smiles at me again. I smile back. There's more kissing. The swirling feeling mixes with the electric brows and this intense desire to keep kissing him, to mould with him, to never leave him.

'Actually,' I say cautiously, 'can we just go back to yours, please?'

He laughs extra hard this time. 'So much for taking it slow!'

'We don't have to, like, you know . . .'

'Fuck?'

'Yeah.' I bite my lip, stare into his eyes. He's a kind man. I can trust him. 'We can just, like, cuddle or something.'

Raj doffs me across the head gently with a fist.

'Danny Scudd, you're a real sweetheart, do you know that?'

I shrug. 'I don't really know much about myself at all, to be honest.'

His palm is on my cheek, warm and comforting.

'We don't have to do anything you don't want to do, OK?'

'Thanks,' I say, trying to breathe my way through all the sensations going off in my body. 'Because, otherwise, that would be rape.'

His glassy, hazelnut irises shrink to nothing.

'And you've got quite the sense of humour.'

'Have I?'

'Let's go.'

'OK.'

Raj leads me through the darkened streets, sparsely scattered with wrapped-up figures darting between supermarkets, takeaway places and home. I don't feel the cold, just the warmth of his hand in mine. Tobbs and I never held hands. I always felt too scared to. Whether I was scared of people seeing or of him, I'm still not sure. But walking down the street with Raj makes me feel powerful, like I'm floating, like if someone shouts something I'll be able to take them on. Raj seems completely oblivious. As we wait for the lights to change, he even leans in and kisses me, just like that, no biggie. Fucking hell, is this what a healthy relationship feels like?

—

His flat is a sixth-floor ex-council situation with two other activist-y people who are out at an 'advocacy thing'. His bedroom walls are almost totally hidden beneath cereal-packet placards daubed with thick acrylic slogans – 'PROTECT OUR

TRANS SIBLINGS!' 'BLACK AND BROWN IS BEAUTIFUL!' – and *Buffy the Vampire Slayer* posters.

He goes to the kitchen to make two cups of chai tea while I lie on his bed, over the covers, and do seven-eleven breathing. Why am I freaking out so much? He's a good guy. He's maybe the best guy I've ever met. So moral, so kind. It's weird, because I feel excited and under threat at the same time. Something to talk to Nina about . . .

'Mama Singh's finest tonic,' he says, padding in in socks and placing the cups on the bedside table, next to a copy of *Becoming* by Michelle Obama. The aromatic odour fills my nostrils, and I do actually feel more relaxed.

He lies down next to me and puts an arm around my waist. He kisses me gently on the cheek.

'You OK?'

I continue to stare at the ceiling. 'Sometimes I get kind of . . . overwhelmed. Sorry.'

'Don't be silly! You don't have to apologise. Plus, our community suffers more from mental-health issues. I get really low sometimes.'

'I'm not Indian.'

He gives me a *Really?* look. 'I meant the LGBTQIA community.'

'Oh – oh yeah, totally.' God, I'm such an idiot. My head is on fire.

'And I was born in Luton.'

'Yeah, shit, sorry, I didn't mean—'

'I know, I know, it's OK.'

'Sorry. I'm just another stupid white gay guy trying to be woke.'

Raj considers this. 'You are. But I'm into it.'

He leans in to kiss me, but I scrunch my eyes shut.

'I love Buffy, too,' I say, and tentatively open my eyes. He pauses, a little way away from my face. 'And I love Dolly Parton. Did you know Dolly Parton was actually an executive producer on *Buffy*?'

Raj settles back on one elbow. 'I did not know that.'

'I know, right,' I go on, for some totally unknown reason. 'She's uncredited. It's just another of her many talents.'

'She's certainly got a lot going for her.'

'And her and Buffy even share the same birthday – 19th January. Can you believe that?'

Raj settles me with a gentle, no-nonsense look.

'Danny, if you don't want to do this, you can just tell me. I don't mind.'

My whole body feels like it's being drawn into some storm at its core. Is that true, though? Can you really just say that?

'No, no,' I say. 'I want to. I just feel kind of – I don't know.'

'Look, let's just—'

Raj squeezes his arm around me, pulls me in close so our bodies touch the whole way down. I roll into the little spoon. We lie there for a bit. I can feel the heat of his breath on the back of my neck, where my pulse is gradually slowing down.

'Was the ex that bad?' he says, not in an intruding way, but in a curious one.

'Um,' I say, 'I don't know. I don't think I was happy with him, but I didn't really know it. I don't think I've been happy with any of the experiences I've had with guys, to be honest. There was this boy at school I had a thing with, but it got out, and then everyone started bullying me, even though I was the quietest kid ever already. It was pretty bad.'

'Oh, Danny.' He squeezes me tighter. His hand is in mine, his chin in the bowl of my collarbone. I hear his heart melting in those two words. Am I pulling moves on him? 'Sometimes it's hard to ask for more, especially when we're used to having less.'

I don't say anything back. Is that true? Is that why I didn't tell Tobbs I didn't like the way he stared at every other guy? Is that why I let him say those mean things to me?

Awkwardly, I shuffle around so we're face to face. The tips of our noses are touching. All I can see is his face, ending at the earring. His breath is warm and wheaty from the beer. I kiss him gently on the mouth.

'Sure?' he says.

'Yeah,' I say.

He kisses me. I kiss him back, letting the thoughts rolling around my head spill out and away. He isn't fucking me around. There's nothing to be afraid of. I am just here, with him.

I take his hand and put it loosely on my belt buckle.

'Is this OK?' he says.

I nod.

And it is. It really is.

TWENTY-EIGHT

Something is jangling with metallic urgency.

Anxiety? Hidden teen trauma? Gay Rage?

My eyes pop open.

No, it's wind chimes.

Raj must have got hot in the night and opened the window, and outside jingle a line of metal panpipes. This is such a fortunate problem to have; at night, my new room is as cold as a tomb in Sunnydale.

My chest is heaving, and I'm covered in sweat, despite the slight breeze. My eyes find their way around the room, the placards, the *Buffy* posters.

It's OK, it's all OK.

I'm in this warm, comforting space. Everything is good here. It feels *right* to be here.

Raj's arm is flung across me. His face still buried in my neck. I feel the gentle, rhythmic heat of his unconscious breathing. I'm the little spoon, although, during the act itself, I had been the top, which is unlike me. I got so nervous that we just snogged for ages until things started to, e-hem, *get going*. He was really nice about it all, obviously.

It's a whole world away from being with Tobbs. I honestly

can't believe how different everything about last night was. I always thought getting a new boyfriend would be like getting a new job. Like, maybe the toilets and kitchen are in different places, but, once you sit down at your desk, it's essentially the same.

But I'm wrong. *Everything* is different.

I can just say how I feel to him – I mean *really* feel, which is not something I normally experience beyond Jacob. Certainly not something I experienced with Tobbs. But Raj has made it all seem so fucking simple. I can't believe it. I was always on edge with Tobbs, never sure how he'd react. Everything seemed to centre on him, on the way he was feeling right then, or might be feeling. With Raj, I actually feel (whisper it) . . . safe.

I only ever bottomed for Tobbs, and when that happened, he never looked at me – he always had his eyes closed. It gave me the impression he was doing his duty, performing what was required of him to make it some semblance of a relationship. Was he like that with the other guys he hooked up with? Or was that where the real passion was, the real excitement?

Lying here, with the wind chimes making their tiny pixie tinkles, I think about how much has changed over such a short period. I hear Nina's voice, what she said about poor Tobbs. If she's right, it's not his fault. He's struggling the way we're all struggling – just like Zain; just like Callum, maybe even. *What's Tobbs doing?* I wonder, a dull pang rising in my stomach. I know it's weird, but I still miss him. I miss his patchy beard and the mess of his eyes. I hope he's doing OK.

Raj inhales deeply and rubs his nose against me. He smacks his lips. Squeezes me around the middle. Kisses me absent-mindedly on the neck.

'Morning, mister.'

My mind flicks back to the present. His eyes are fluttering open. They have green eye-gunk in the corners, but for some reason I can't keep the smile out of my voice.

'Hey.'

'What's up?' He kisses my neck a couple more times.

'Nothing. Just thinking how nice this is.'

He nuzzles me. 'It is nice, isn't it?'

'Tobbs hated doing anything like this.'

Raj's lip contorts. As it does, my stomach twists. *Shit, I fucked it up again*.

'Dude,' he says, and I know this warning voice, 'can you just try to leave him out of this?'

'Shitfuck. I'm sorry.' Instantly, the electric hands are here, squeezing hard. 'I don't know what's wrong with me. It's just, I dunno, I've never really—'

'Done this before?'

Raj wedges himself up on his elbow. His thin gold chain is caught in his chest hair. It's really hot.

'No, yeah, I mean, I have done this before. As in, had a boyfriend.'

'*Wow*, I'm your boyfriend now? I thought you wanted to take it slow?'

'No, no, I don't mean that!' Now I'm sitting up, gesturing with my hands, feeling like my heart is beating faster than it ever has. 'I mean, just, like, either I've hooked up with guys or been in a relationship with one. I've never, kind of, dated – really. It's all . . .'

I trail off.

Raj has his knees up, his arms around them, and is staring out the window. The chain is shifting in the chest hair. He's trying to keep his breathing calm, but failing.

I put my hand on his arm gently. 'Raj.' And my voice is so

277

little. 'I'm really sorry. I know I'm not good at this. It's just, you're so nice and I feel so . . .'

I trail off again. So? I don't know. I don't really know how I'm feeling. The moment of calm is roughed up by my busy mind, pushed aside, torn apart.

Raj puts his hand on mine and squeezes it. He looks at me with his beautiful brown eyes. They're sad, conflicted. I can feel the floor dropping out of the room even before he speaks.

'Danny, I don't think this is going to work.'

My forehead is alight with electricity. I'm dizzy, sick.

'I just think we might be at different stages.' He's saying it in a very kind, gentle voice, which makes it even worse. He's doing everything Tobbs couldn't do. 'You're not over your ex – you already know that, along with half of London. But you're also just discovering who you are. You need to go out there and work it out.'

'Can't we work it out together?'

I hate how pathetic my voice sounds.

He squeezes the hand again. 'No, Dan. You've gotta do it for yourself. It wouldn't work out between us, you'd see. We'd both be unhappy. Trust me, I've done this before.'

I sniff hard and glare at him. 'Now who's talking about their ex?'

'Don't get sassy with me, mister.'

'Stop calling me "mister". I hate it.'

The hand retracts into a pair of crossed arms.

He just stares at me.

I just stare back.

'You should probably go,' he says after a while.

I disentangle myself from the bedclothes and bend down, scrabbling for pants and socks. I pull on my boxers.

'I have to get to work now anyway, so.'

'Great.'

When I'm dressed, I stand in the doorway. He's still sitting in bed, arms crossed. He's impossibly gorgeous. Fuck everything.

'I'll just let myself out, then.'

'OK, Danny. I'll see you around.'

I turn and head for the stairs, then swing around and poke my head back into the room.

'You know what? Wind chimes are really fucking annoying. Why would you have them outside your room? It's not Glastonbury.'

———

Staring at the tracks in the icy rain as the trains screech past, jolt to a stop and howl off again, I think, *This is it, this is finally the moment I kill myself. And it's on the District Line, the worst fucking line.* Afterwards, people will say I died as I lived: slow as fuck and constantly breaking down.

How have I managed to fuck up things with the first good guy I've ever been involved with? I've been trying – really trying – to be different, to be a better version of myself, but it's not working, there's no hope for me. I can't have relationships. I'm too fucked up, and I don't even fully understand how. Just the way Tobbs is fucked up and bullied me. Just the way Zain dismissed me. Is there hope for any of us?

'You all right, mate?' My head turns from the track to a large man with a worried smile. He's wearing a navy-and-red TfL jacket with a name badge: Ali. 'Wanna come inside and sit down for a minute?'

'No.' I cough. 'No, it's fine.'

'Havin' a bad day?' he says.

'Something like that.'

'They're the worst.' And we both share the sad smile of all humans who feel like absolute shit.

I get on the next train.

I wouldn't really have done it.

—

I beep into the office, readying myself to be a media professional, but it's deserted. My Converse scuff warily between rows of unoccupied desks. One single, solitary skateboard rolls across the half-pipe, and a pair of VR glasses occupy two leather beanbags, like the players evaporated mid-game.

There's a low hubbub in the direction of the Council Estate Rec Room. If anything exemplifies my loathing for this company, it is this room. It's essentially the boardroom, but with exposed breeze-block walls covered in graffiti, and wheelie bins turned into chairs around a concrete ping-pong table. Spoofed Banksy rats make spray-paint appearances on said table, chasing after spray-paint balls and skip merrily across the tops of the white 1960s metal window frames.

One of the scuffed red board doors is ajar, and I slip through it. Inside, the entire workforce is crammed in tensely. This is odd. Even when things are serious, there's still an element of bullshit conviviality to proceedings.

A woman with a grey bob skilfully highlighted blonde and eyebrows more arched than those of a suspicious governess is standing in front of the 'ironic' yellow street sign that reads 'UNAFFORDABLE HOUSING', gesturing gently, yet firmly, as if letting us all know someone has died. Out of character with everyone else in the room and the room itself, she's decked out smartly in a flashy black corporate trouser suit and tasteful, minimal gold jewellery. It's deeply unsettling.

'Who's that?' I whisper to the guy in front of me.

He turns. Fuck me, it's Callum.

'Sophie . . . *Lewisham*?' he says, crunching his brows together.

'You mean Sophia LeSwann?' I say. 'The CEO of Dying Swann PLC.'

'Got me again, Dan.'

He turns back around. That's weird – his eyes are red.

I strain on tiptoe to see as much as possible past his general bulk.

'. . . and after all his many . . . *eleven* months of service in the company, we're sorry to have to say goodbye to such a valued member of our team. While we at Dying Swann PLC foster innovation and risk-taking in our staff, there is a line, and Stan unfortunately crossed it . . . on multiple occasions. And' – leaning her weight on one hip, with a conversational flip of the forearm – 'as a woman in business, I must encourage you all to come forward if you have any more evidence of his *inappropriate* behaviour. It's only then that we can stop men like this taking advantage of senior positions. On a different note' – now the tips of her fingers meet before her in a triangle – 'where is Danny Scudd?'

A terrible tightness compresses my body. I'm certain I'm going to faint. Everyone turns to stare at me. Gingerly, I raise a hand.

'Here,' I squeak.

Sophia looks around the room as if she's accepting an award.

'Can we all just give this man a round of applause? Most. Viewed. Post. Of. The. Year,' she says, with a dramatic pause between every word. 'We haven't seen a piece of content perform this well in – I don't know how long. And spawning a widely used meme on top of that, well, it's a media dream. How long have you worked here, Danny?'

'Three years.'

'Ah, excellent! You know, Danny' – leaning in, conversational – 'the higher-ups loved your piece so much, we wondered if you'd like to step in as interim creative director, while we interview for Stan's position?'

I am speechless, which must look funny to her, I realise. I am, after all, a punky-looking young queer who just wrote a successful article about a protest and spawned a ridiculous meme. Not the sort of person to get tongue-tied when receiving praise.

'Sick,' I say. 'Yeah, I s'pose I can do that.'

The room erupts into laughter. Sophia actually claps. I can see she's trying to smile, but very few of her features move. It's kind of eerie.

'Fantastic!' she says. 'This is just what Dying Swann PLC wants to see coming from this room, from these creative brains. And this is the kind of content that rivals other media hubs, and builds our reputation. If you're asking yourself what video shall I make next, what article shall I write, what cultural event shall I live-tweet? Just think: What Would Danny Do? Can we have another round of applause, please?'

It happens again, this time with whoops. Everyone is looking and smiling, not looking and judging. They are genuinely happy for me, for themselves, for what it means to be working somewhere with even a glimmer of purpose buried in the deep heap of bullshit.

My skull is buzzing as we walk back to our desks. People I've never spoken to before are slapping me on the back and saying well-dones. I should be feeling elated, but instead I'm filled with unease. *You deserve this*, I think. *You deserve this*. But it doesn't push the feeling away.

I'm walking behind Nadia and Robyn and catch their conversation.

'Pretty rich, her marching in in her Dior suit and suddenly having morals,' Nadia says.

'How much did she embezzle from her dad's company?'

'It was legitimately millions.'

'Hence why she was so happy about the uplift in page views.'

'And ad revenue.'

'At least we can put out better stuff now Stan's gone.' Robyn sighs with relief. 'You know, I always just tell people I work at "an app", because otherwise they'll look it up and read some of our headlines back to me, and I just can't bear it.'

'You think it'll be better now?' Nadia laughs. 'Under Mr Sleepy McSleeperson? It's just more of the same, isn't it?'

Either they worry someone else will hear or they actually sense my presence, because they both turn and stare directly at me, horrified.

'I am *not* like Stan,' I say and turn to walk away. But the Rage takes me, and I fix them with a smirk. 'Don't make me get rid of you next.'

TWENTY-NINE

'. . . And it felt so weird, because everything was going so well, and now everyone's acting like I'm some kind of monster. Like the way Raj looked at me – I can't stop thinking about it.'

Both knees are pumping up and down, so I cross my legs aggressively and stare at Nina. She is blinking as I talk. I've just spewed out everything for the last half an hour without so much as a break for air.

'Maybe Raj wasn't so great after all,' I continue when she says nothing. 'I mean, who has wind chimes outside their bedroom window? That's just not practical. So, actually, I think that's a real red flag. I've definitely dodged a bullet.'

'You think the wind chimes are a red flag?' she says, and I hear her tone, as much as she tries to disguise it.

'Well,' I say, battling with myself, 'not just them, obviously. But there were loads of things. I think I had just fantasised about him so much while we were texting, in reality he just didn't live up to it.'

'What didn't he live up to?'

'Well, you know.' I'm moving around a lot in the seat, making many a little fart noise. Nina's getting on my nerves tonight. This whole thing is a waste of time. I could be sorting out stuff for the shoot next week.

'He's so . . . sanctimonious,' I say eventually. 'Like, he was really judgey of me when I was telling him how I stood up for myself against Stan.'

'Ah yes, the – what did you refer to it as' – she looks at her notes – 'the "CULTRD Shock" moment.' She chuckles. 'That's funny, Danny.'

I barely hear her, I'm in such a rage.

'Thing is, I wasn't just standing up for myself! I was standing up for everyone against him, against what he represents.'

Nina resettles her expression back to that of A Serious Listener.

'And you're saying they weren't' – she picks her next word carefully – 'grateful?'

'Exactly!' I shout. 'I'm doing what they all want, and they're not even grateful. Everyone hates Stan, so I got rid of him. And that was the right thing to do. Old Me would never have done that. But I have a duty to protect everyone in that office.'

'Why is it your duty, specifically?'

I hate it when Nina asks me these stupid questions.

'Well, isn't it everyone's duty to call out evil when they see it?'

'Would you call Stan's behaviour evil?'

'Yes! It's an abuse of power!' I say.

Nina mulls this over.

'Certainly Stan does sound like he transgresses boundaries of propriety with his staff. But I wonder, in this specific instance, did you speak to Callum about it?'

'He'd just apologise for him,' I say immediately. 'He's an apologist.'

'How do you know that?'

I go to answer, but realise I have no words.

'I just . . . know what it's like,' I say eventually. 'To feel powerless when you're with someone.'

'Do you know that he feels powerless?'

I swallow hard.

'No.'

We are both silent. I've got used to these lapses in conversation, even found solace in them, but this time it's annoying, too, like everything here.

'Have you been journalling?' Nina says.

'Yeah. A bit.'

'Has it brought up anything surprising?'

'Yeah. No. I don't know, really. I actually don't think it's for me. It's kind of stupid.'

I look at her right in the face as I say this. She only slightly raises her eyebrows.

'Danny, you do seem extremely agitated, increasingly so in our last few sessions—'

I cut her off. 'Well, that's because I'm self-actualising. I'm finally not putting up with everyone's shit, and being my true self at last.'

Nina looks down at her notes, then back at me. She's dressed more casually this evening, in a plain black T-shirt, black jeans and black Converse. Even this irritates me, like she can't be bothered to dress nicely for me anymore.

'You're certainly releasing years of pain,' she says.

'I'm not in pain, Nina, I'm angry,' I snap. 'And don't I have a right to be?'

Nina licks her lips and folds her notebook closed. She leans in, looks over the top of her glasses.

'Absolutely, Danny. It's a completely rational response. However, I worry it's being channelled towards the wrong sources.'

'I thought there was no right or wrong, just what's acceptable to me?' I laugh at her, and I can hear it's cruel. '"Boundaries", Nina?'

Weirdly, Nina almost smiles.

'Yes, absolutely,' she agrees. 'But again we come to this question that what's acceptable for you might not be acceptable for others. Your relationship with Jacob, for example, sounds like it's going through a difficult patch?'

I look at her. She's really pulling all her shrink tricks to catch me out this evening. But I'm not falling for it.

I sit back in the chair, my arms stretched out, like a bad guy about to tell her how she only has three minutes and fifty-eight seconds to defuse the bomb strapped to her underwear.

'Jacob's always been the centre of attention. Always. Everywhere we go, people always say, "Oh, wow, who's your friend?" They always remember what Jacob said, what they wore, what they're working on. I've always been their sidekick. Their boring friend. Well, I'm not anymore, and they don't like it. And maybe that's OK.'

Nina's posture doesn't change. She nods, and I sense some sadness in it.

'It is usual and healthy for relationships as long as yours to change as you both change—'

'We haven't changed! Not since we were four years old. I've always been the shy one who Jacob comes to when there's no one else around. And they're the fun one who takes my mind off whatever's going on with me. Until now. Now I'm different. They're still the same.'

The nod is in full flow. 'You say that, Danny, but it actually sounds like maybe you've both changed, and now the dynamic between you is having to shift. Does that sound fair?'

My legs are trembling again. My whole body is taut, like a washing line. And now I feel it wobble in the wind.

'They've got Angel now, so what does it even matter? Not that I'm allowed to meet him.'

'Ah, yes, interesting!' Nina is loving it. In this moment, I hate her. 'You have mentioned how you kept Tobbs and Jacob apart, because you were worried how each would react to the other. It sounds like maybe Jacob is doing a similar thing now.'

My hands go to my knees to keep them still. 'Why would they be doing that?'

Nina makes one of those smiles where the lips compress together, as if eating themselves, as if apologising for something. She says nothing.

'Because Jacob's embarrassed of *me*?' I say. 'Is that it?'

Nina puts her hands together. 'If you think it might be.'

'As long as they don't fuck up the Revue next week, I don't care. I deserve this job, and I don't want them to ruin it for me.' As I say this, the ground jolts.

'I think you do care, Danny.' Nina's vanished lips turn into a sad smile. 'Jacob's one of the most precious people in your life; don't alienate them.'

We stare at each other. My heart is beating so fast it's almost coming through my chest.

'I think we're out of time,' I say, looking at the little clock.

'Oh yes,' Nina says. 'You're right.'

THIRTY

The Centrefold is alive with people. And, for the first time, I don't stick out like a sore pee hole.

In fact, I'm in the middle of it all, wearing a pretty sick camo-print two-piece, black beret and sunglasses, even though it's night-time and we're indoors. But they work. No one can see how stressed I really am. I appear cool, in control. Everyone keeps asking for my approval on everything: 'Where do we put the tripods, Danny?' 'Do the VIPs go in the front row?' Everyone except one person.

'Where the fuck is Jacob?' I scream across the cluttered kitchen, which has become dressing room for the models and command centre for the production team.

Callum pokes his head out into the darkened hallway, which is lit only by strings of white, ghostlike lights. There must be nearly a hundred people out there, some quite prominent across the arts and media. I pressured everyone in the house to pull their strings.

'Can't see 'em, boss,' Callum calls back. 'But that bloke from *Vogue* is here.'

'*No!*' Gin screams, stabbing Melania with a pin as they fix her into a fluttering black gauze gown. 'This is the greatest night of my life!'

'Does not mean you can murder the models,' Melania snaps.

'We need to start,' the Marc/ks say to me. Somehow they've got involved in the tech side. 'Subscribers will be tuning in to the live stream at eight.'

'Shitfuck. OK, let's go ahead,' I hiss. 'Callum, don't just stand there, go and fucking find Jacob. They're meant to be opening the show!'

Callum almost replies, but thinks better of it and ducks out into the crowd.

'You really have become benevolent dictator,' Melania observes.

'OK!' I clap my hands three times. 'Let's do it, people!' The room erupts into applause. 'Remember: tweet and 'gram the shit out of this on your own channels, but make sure to @ us.'

Melania and Ashraf lead the other models out, followed by Gin, who fusses with taffeta collars and netting sleeves. The Marc/ks and I sneak out into the hallway, and stand in the shadow of the archways. The production crew have built a small stage between them for the performances, festooned with similar dim lighting, the floor hidden by a swirling white carpet of dry ice. It's all part of Gin's aesthetic. The crowd is split like the Red Sea, sitting on all the conference chairs we gathered from around the house. Their low hubbub goes silent as the first chord booms from the corner speakers. In the bay window, Ange controls the decks. I see the whites of Melania's eyes before she steps out. This is genuinely the most thrilling moment of my life.

She strides out onto the catwalk, lit starkly by a sudden burst of light, making her appear to float on clouds. It also makes it apparent how see-through her dress is. Everyone claps. Flashes from cameras go off as the beat sets in. Melania turns at the end of the runway and blows a kiss. Next to me, her image is reflected on the monitor in Mark's hand.

'Ten thousand viewers already,' he says, and my chest is tight. Where the fuck is Jacob?

Behind Melania, Ashraf struts out in his tunic, looking like an ancient Olympian. Without warning, he drops into a squat and starts voguing through the ankle-height smoke. The crowd goes wild. On Mark's screen, I see hearts of every colour proliferate in the bottom right corner. Melania twists around and joins him in the dance, and the other models filter in. Ashraf bites his lip and backflips back towards us. Everyone screams.

'Boots the house down, Mama, yes, Gawd!' someone cries. Is that the bloke from *Vogue*?

'Boss.' Callum is at my side. 'I can't find 'em!'

'Fuckssake, Callum!'

'I'm sorry, Dan! I just dunno where they are!'

'Why are you so fucking useless?'

Callum's bottom lip trembles, and I realise I might have gone too far. I'm about to apologise when the music is cut short. I glare at Ange, who looks confused, rather than her usual furious.

A strange silence fills the room. Then, in a truly spectral gesture, from somewhere high in the house, we hear the soulful draw of the bow against the cello. It spools down the stairs, like liquid. Next it's coming from the speakers, filling the room, building, rising.

Heads turn. The models pause in their struts.

And there they are.

Jacob is wafting down the stairs in a billowing gown of white and gleaming gold, corseted and hugely collared, like the spirit of a Jacobean Rihanna. Their braids are intricately styled skyward, laced with golden thread and pearls, resembling a crown.

Across their eyes is painted a jagged stripe of silvery-white, like a scar.

They step past me, under the arch, and onto the stage, where they bow low to the audience, their diaphanous skirt flowing about them. Everyone goes wild, some people leaping to their feet, clicking their fingers.

The spotlight illuminates their face as their eyes glance about. Something about their movements puts me on edge. They aren't their usual effervescent self. A microphone is set up on a stand already, and they grasp it with both hands.

'Good evening, sweet angels,' they croon, somewhat sorrowfully. 'Welcome to the first annual Queer Revue. Brought to you by CULTRD – actually.' They snap the microphone out of the holder and put their hand on their hip. 'Fuck that. This is everything I hate. Corporate events. The commercialisation of Pride. The commodification of queer black and brown bodies for profit that they never see.'

The room erupts into further applause.

'Fuck the landlords!' someone screams.

'People love this,' Mark says, looking up from the screen with a grin. 'They love edgy content.'

I hear my stomach as it twists itself in knots. The feeling of dread creeps back towards me. *Edgy content.*

'Ange!' Jacob commands. 'What we talked about.'

Ange fumbles with some buttons, and a projection of a black woman's face, huge and smiling, fills the wall behind Jacob, dwarfing their statuesque frame. Flowers adorn her hair, and her smile is infectious.

'Queer people today have our freedoms because of black trans pioneers like Marsha P. Johnson,' Jacob declares, every sequin on their bodice glittering. There's actually something quite *Bram Stoker's Dracula* about them. Or even Glenda the Good

Witch. 'Activists who fought with their bodies and minds for our liberation. And now that same movement is being co-opted for profit. Like the ancient god Saturn, capitalism eventually eats its own children.'

To this, there are only a few scattered claps, and one whoop, which I suspect is Melania. Though some of these people would regard themselves as radical thinkers, most are media professionals like me, people who spend all day in meeting rooms doing exactly what Jacob is denouncing.

'Uh-oh,' Mark whispers, flicking through the comments as quickly as they appear. 'Here come the trolls.'

My bones shake with that horribly familiar feeling. Any second, the brow will spark.

'And so, my babies,' Jacob continues, as the smiling face fades into another image, 'here's a poem I wrote recently. It's called "Eulogy".'

From my awkward angle, I squint at the projection. I can't work out what it is. It looks like two kids sitting on a wall. Then the fingertips have me in their grasp: it's me and Jacob in our early teens. The same picture I presented at work a week ago.

Jacob clears their throat. Their eyes gaze darkly out across their congregation.

'Once I had a mother
Once I had a friend
Once I had a lover
But all good things must end

Once we were in prisons
Some of us still are
Once we fought for freedom

Now we dance in bars

Once I was alone
And now I am again
They sold off my identity
They sold off my best friend.'

The room bristles with pin-drop silence. The fabric floating around Jacob's neck and shoulders shudders, winglike, as if preparing for flight. A white, rhinestoned acrylic goes to the eyes, and I see they're crying. A lump rises in my throat.

They turn and step down from the stage, and rush past me into the darkness. I try to reach out a hand after them, but they're gone. The image of us fades into a pink triangle on a black background with a fist raised at its centre. My throat contracts. Now I'm going to cry.

Slowly, clapping filters around the room. It grows, until everyone is on their feet, whistling and shouting praise. Ange shrugs and starts to play the thumping electronic music again. The models commence their movements.

And I couldn't feel worse.

———

It's hard to tell how long I've been sitting in the top-floor bathroom, with the bottle of gin, ignoring the constant knocks on the door and the comments through it: 'You must be brewing up a steamer in there, mate!' The performance part of the evening is over, and the heavy drinking has commenced. I slurp back another mouthful of the £9.99 paint stripper and gag. *What's happened to me? What have I become?*

At some point, I'm drunk enough to head out onto the top-floor landing. It's rammed with people, none of whom I recognise, except one who might be a famous YouTuber.

'You're alive, then?' a guy in a harness with a yellow mullet says to me before sliding past into the bathroom, followed by a friend with a Mohawk and dimple piercings.

'Yeah, I'm alive!' I shout back, after they've already shut the door.

Steadying myself against the wooden banister, I peer down into the long drop of the hall. Every step and every space on the three landings is filled by someone in a wild outfit clutching a paper cup, a bottle or a can. Smoke drifts up and collects in the skylight, tinged with various flavours. For some reason, I take out my phone, open the company Instagram and start filming.

'This is what it's like for young creatives today!' I slur. 'Those people just went in there to take drugs and have sex. Those people work for *Vogue* and are sniffing something off a key. Don't you wish you lived this life?'

I stumble downstairs, where the hall is already trashed. Dirt, broken cups and fag butts are ground into the chequered tiles. The front door is open, with the pulse of the bass stretching out into the crisp winter air. The weed-addled front lawn is filled with people in denim and leather, smoking and drinking and laughing super-loud. Two girls in baggy hoodies and no evident trousers stand on the roof of the Pride Mini, holding on to each other while trying to pose at the same time. Smoke shoots from their mouths, steam rises from their bodies – ghosts flitting upward in the amber glow of the street lamps. A third, with a bald head, photographs from below. Oh my God, it's Titty!

The living room is a mass of sweaty people, none of whom I recognise in the neon strip light someone has propped up on the mantelpiece. Appearing to be naked except for a top hat, Ashraf is deep into his set in the curve of the bay window. I lean against the archway and try to focus my eyes. I spot Gin,

Ange and Callum in the centre, going absolutely crazy to the music. With them is someone else I recognise: Raj!

My heart beats noisily in my eyes, overpowering the music. He's dancing with such freedom, throwing his skinny limbs around. All three of them look devoid of their humanness, mindless almost, while simultaneously completely embodying it. They're free, they're alive, they're really alive.

I'm still filming, I realise, and I narrate this scene.

'Every queer person fucks each other. No one gives a shit. It's just sex, innit?'

The ground shifts as I watch them. I've got to get another drink.

When I fall into the kitchen, a room also thick with people, I'm relieved to see there's booze open on every sticky surface, amid limes and bottles of Coke and tonic water. I find a full bottle of gin and pour a big one into a china gravy boat in the shape of a curious squirrel that looks mostly clean. I neck it and immediately refill it.

'Danny! Danny!' a voice cries from the conservatory. It's Melania.

She pushes through the strangers with little regard and wraps her arms around me, kisses me on the mouth. Her breath is gackily sweet. She draws back, keeping both hands on my chest.

'My darling lamb. Where have you been hiding? You're the talk of the town!'

'You mean Jacob is,' I slur.

Melania scrunches up her forehead. 'Why are you filming?'

I poke my phone directly in her face.

'I'm an investigative journalist now, don't you know?'

She grabs the phone from me and fiddles with it.

'You've been streaming this on your company's Instagram!'

I snatch the phone back.

'It's edgy content!' I say ironically.

Either she doesn't reply or I stop listening, because now, looming behind her, as though materialised from dark matter, is a black silhouette I recognise all too well.

'Hi, Danny,' it says.

'Oh Jesus!' I splutter.

'No, this is Zain!' Melania trills. 'He's my new favourite! We've been chatting about astrophysics and also anal beads. He is a glorious man.'

'Is he, though?'

'This party is sick,' Zain says with weird, awkward brightness. 'The whole place is actually pretty wicked.'

I stare him full in the face. His eyes flutter, and he sips from his Red Stripe. I can't tell if he's being serious or just goading me again, so I say: 'Yeah, it is. It's the fucking coolest place in East London. With the coolest people, too, who are just, like, super-nice and not arseholes.'

'Oh, sweet nicotine!' Melania embraces me, then glances back at Zain. 'He is a stunning lamb. I would marry him if he had a firm pair of tits.'

'Titty is actually here,' I say to her, and the room is spinning.

'WHAT?' Melania screams, causing the general chatter around us to halt. 'I shall find the witch. I shall pour water on her?'

She strides away, knocking into several people and spilling one girl's beer. But she's out of here.

Zain and I stand opposite each other, not speaking. The music pumps irrepressibly. I can't breathe. He is evidently drunk as well, because eventually he waves the hand with the can in it and knocks me on the chest.

'You know, Danny, you're actually a really interesting guy.'

'I know.'

My vision is blurred, but I swear I see him blush.

'I didn't give you credit before. You're full of surprises.'

I mimic him by waving the curious squirrel and poking him in the chest with it, very aware that Raj is just in the next room.

'Well, maybe you shouldn't be so judgemental of people,' I say, and my brain is so alive with electricity, I'm certain my head will explode. I suddenly spot Jacob propped up by the bar, which is actually just the kitchen hob covered in cooking pans full of ice and beers and bottles, and use this as my opportunity to escape. 'Anyway, nice chatting, babe.'

I float towards them, feeling pretty smug about this seamless getaway. From behind me, I think I can hear someone saying, 'Danny? Danny!' but it's hard to tell what's what now.

'Oh, look who it is.' Jacob waves a can at me, their eyes almost totally closed, their ethereal appearance comedically at odds with the scummy surroundings. 'My best friend in all the world, who would never sell me out to further their own career.'

I don't quite catch what they're saying.

'Huh?'

'How did my performance go down with your subscribers?'

'They loved it,' I say, trying to find my phone to show them the live stream.

'And what about you? Did you love it?'

I'm trying to fully comprehend what they're saying, but my mind is so muddled, I can't make the links between the words.

'I love you, Jay,' I say. 'Whatever's happened between us, I love you.'

Jacob sways back against the hob. 'You just don't listen to me, do you?'

'What do you mean? All you ever do is talk.'

Jacob stares at me, and I really think they're about to punch me. When they speak, I flinch.

'You're ringing.'

'I'm sorry?'

Jacob sticks their hand in my pocket and pulls out my phone. 'Answer your damn phone. It could be Mary.'

I grab it away from them and just stare at it. I don't understand what I'm seeing. With shaking hands, I answer it.

'Tobbs?'

For a few seconds, all I can hear is panting. No, not panting. Crying.

'Tobbs?'

'Daniel?' His voice is broken and ghostly.

'What is it?'

'Daniel.' Big pause. 'Daniel, I'm sorry I'm calling you, I just – I've got no one else to call, and you're always so . . .'

Jacob watches intensely as the music and people around me fade. The longer the call goes on, the more sober Jacob becomes. By the time I hang up, they look completely compos mentis.

I stare at the black screen of my phone, then at Jacob.

'Danny,' they say. 'What's wrong?'

THIRTY-ONE

For such a small car, the Pride Mini is surprisingly hard to park.

In the end, Jacob leaves it in a disabled space and limps ridiculously as we walk past a row of doctors smoking and a security guard on the phone, laughing.

'This feels kind of . . . not cool,' I whisper to them as the glass doors slide open.

'Do you want to see him or not?'

'I thought you'd have been morally against this sort of thing?'

'I could have a hidden disability.'

In the voice of Mae West, I say, 'Honey, ain't nothin' about you's hidden. *Ohh*!'

They raise an eyebrow. 'Don't start with me, Dan.'

Watching Jacob walk through A&E in six-inch Perspex stripper heels, the glittering gown floating behind them, is more surreal than usual. There's definitely an *Angels in America* vibe.

Turning heads is just part of the Jacob experience. You get used to it. But in the starkly lit clinical oblongs of Reception, Corridor A, and the East Wing, green- and blue-clad staff, patients in wheelchairs, visitors in flocks like anxious birds, all stare with unbridled wonder. I suppose you would do, if you came in expecting to see your nan and instead were confronted by Naomi Campbell dressed as Elizabeth I.

As usual, Jacob doesn't even notice. Or, if they do, they don't show it. Their full ass smiles at me as they waltz ahead, like two Ferrero Rochers bouncing up and down all the way to the governor's ball. I swim after them, as in a dream. Everything is strange now. Anything could float towards me down these underwater passageways. If an octopus crawled past, doffed its cap and smoothed its curled moustache, I think I'd just nod back and say good evening.

A hand is in mine. It's Jacob's.

'He's in here, Little Edie. The Victoria High Dependency Unit.'

I don't know how to feel or reply, so just comply.

'OK.'

They look at me steadily.

'Dan, are you sure you're up to this?'

I swallow.

'Yeah.'

'You don't know how you're going to react. He had a massive impact on you, and this is likely to be . . . disturbing.'

'I'm a big boy, Jay,' I say.

Jacob doesn't say anything, so I turn and push the heavy door open.

'Over there,' says the nurse, a small, stout middle-aged woman with a name badge that says 'PAMMY'.

We follow her finger to the corner bed.

The ward is dim, the few lights from screens and bedside lamps illuminating the unconscious faces of other addicts. It's like walking through a morgue. One man, who's lying flat on his back like a corpse, has a white patch taped to his cheek, but even as he sleeps, you can see how torn up the mouth is.

Another, a lady full of tubes, is so bruised around the face I almost can't tell if she has a nose or eyes at all.

One other nurse shuffles noiselessly from bed to bed. A low buzz filters around the place, like someone's left the phone off the hook. It all smells of vinegar, but maybe I'm just thinking about Mum and Dad and how I should definitely call them in the morning and tell them I love them.

Jacob pulls their gown about them. Their eyes are wide, unblinking. Their heels tap-tap hesitantly.

There he is.

There's a drip in his arm and a pipe in his nose. He is pale, with dark rings under his eyes, his dishevelled hair even more dishevelled, but he's still him. Handsome. Stubborn. Sad.

Jacob stands at the end of the bed. They nod at me, but I don't need any prompting – I'm already standing over him, watching him breathe. I'm about to say his name when his head rolls towards me and his eyes flicker open.

'You came!' he croaks. He sounds happier than I've ever heard him. 'You look different.'

I pull up the plastic chair, which squeaks nastily on the laminate floor.

'I came.'

He tries to smile, but his lips are so cracked he winces and then grimaces them shut. His head turns to the end of the bed, to where Jacob is standing over it, like an angel on a Victorian grave.

'Jacob,' he says.

'Tobias.'

Jacob gives me a look and takes a seat some distance away. They cross their legs, nod at the nurse and start thumbing through their phone.

Tobbs tries to sit up. For a bit, I fuss with pillows and the bed sheet and say things directly from my mother's mouth. When he's settled, I sit back down. One hand fiddles with the other as he tries to meet my gaze. He has tape, too, I see, just like the corpse man, only it comes from around the back of his head. Tobbs sees me looking and rubs both his eyes.

'Split my head open.'

I shuffle in my seat.

'How?'

'Sure you want to know?'

I swallow. That vinegar taste is overpowering.

He answers for me. 'I mean, it's not like I spared you the details before.'

Maybe I don't want to hear. Maybe I don't want to know.

'How?'

'Passed out by Vauxhall Cross. Came to with a homeless guy staring down in my face. He said, "Too much partying, bruv?" But I couldn't say anything back. I didn't know what was going on. I'd been in that sauna for – I don't even know how long. I couldn't remember *not* being there.'

He starts sniffing and blinking a lot.

'The guy helped me up, and I went and sat with him under the arches. He had this whole little set-up there. A bed, some clothes, some meth, which he offered me. I still couldn't speak, so I just shook my head. I'd taken too much G already. He gave me some beer. He sold things he'd got out of dustbins. There was a pair of brogues, a handbag without a strap and a dead pot-plant. He was saying the wound on my head looked pretty bad, but then things started to go blurry, and then, next thing I knew, I was here.'

Now he's crying, lines spilling down his face. I reach for his hand and take it.

He looks at me full in the face.

'Boyo, I must have been fucked by a hundred guys in that place, but every single one of them I pretended was you.'

My eyes crush shut. My whole body buzzes. I'm going to be sick. *Seven eleven. Seven eleven. Seven eleven.*

I try to carry on in a flat, neutral voice, like a doctor, but it just comes out sounding haunted, empty.

'Did you use protection?'

'I don't know. They put me on PEP anyway.'

'OK,' I say, nodding slowly. 'OK.'

We sit there for a while, listening to the buzz of the equipment. From the little office by the ward door, the nurses are suppressing giggles. It sounds like they're watching a funny video on one of their phones. Someone across the ward starts coughing uncontrollably, and Pammy appears and slopes over. Eventually, it stops.

'Do you hate me?' Tobbs says after a while.

I don't answer immediately. This doesn't feel like the time to lie.

'No,' I say eventually. 'Not exactly.'

He rubs his messy eyes. They're very dark now. Any light they had held is gone.

'I know I'm fucked up,' he says, sniffing. 'I know I'm a waste of space. I'm not asking you to get back with me. You're too good for me anyway.'

'Hey, hey, don't say that.' I can't believe he's saying this. He always acted like everything I did was extremely below him, trivial, inconsequential. I hear Nina's voice in my head, explaining things I just hadn't understood. 'You're not a waste of space. We all find it hard trying to fit into a world that isn't made for us. Then trying to fit into gay world, which is all about sex and nothing about intimacy—'

He is nodding and nodding, and then he is crying. Crying like I've never seen another person cry. I get up and cradle him.

I kiss his hair, which is matted and smells of chlorine and sweat. Out of the corner of my eye, I see Jacob sitting up straighter in their chair and looking, wondering if they should intervene.

After what doesn't seem like very long at all, the other nurse, an older black lady with an orange bob, comes over and tells us to go outside or keep it down, because we are disturbing the other patients.

We keep it down.

Jacob appears at my side, genie-like, and produces a violet silk handkerchief. I take it, hand it to Tobbs and look back to Jacob to thank them. They are already back on their chair, scrolling, scrolling, scrolling.

I rub Tobbs's forearm as he blows his nose, gets his breathing down a bit.

'The fucking makes it all go away,' he says after a while, not really to me, to the ether. 'The bleakness. The nothingness. The feeling that I'll never be good enough. The feeling that I don't deserve it. It just makes it all go away for a bit. But it always comes back.' He looks at me with a hollow, pleading stare. 'I was trying, with us. I really was. I just couldn't get to that next place – in my mind, I mean. I've always looked after myself.'

'I know,' I say, swallowing. 'I know that now.'

'I know I couldn't open up to you. But that doesn't mean I didn't care about you.' More tears. 'Danny, I fucking loved you. I *do* love you.'

And tears from me.

For a while, we hold each other, shaking silently. I hear the feet of the nurse threaten to come near, but then decide otherwise and go back to the video on the phone.

There seems to be no time, no air, no world beyond this ward, beyond this bed. I hold him by the shoulder and look him in the eyes.

'Tobbs, you're not alone. You were never alone. We're all in this together, OK? As queer people, we've got to look out for each other.'

He gazes at me with the saddest look I've ever seen. He's completely vulnerable, stripped of his protective layers. I'll never forget it. The blue is coming back to his eyes, though. It isn't completely gone.

'I'm sorry I couldn't make you happy,' he says. 'I just, I just—'

'You're not ready yet,' I say.

He looks like he's about to contradict me, then decides there's no malice in this, and nods slowly in agreement.

'You'll get there. It'll just take time.' I put my hand to his face and think of Raj. 'If it makes you feel any better, I'm not there, either.'

'This is the real gay curse,' he says. 'It used to be AIDS. Now it's emotional distance. We're all so fucked up, we can't connect with each other.'

'That's not true,' I say, thinking how this is exactly what had broken us up, and what had prevented me and Raj from getting any closer. 'We can all get there. We just have to unlearn the things we've been taught. We just have to love and look out for one another.'

Tobbs leans forward and kisses me on the mouth, very tenderly. Our entire time together rushes back to me as his cold, dry lips brush mine. It's like in a movie. It makes me dizzy.

He sits back, with his hands in his lap.

'Thank you,' he says, 'for everything. I've never felt as close to another person as I did with you. You're really amazing.'

I can feel the tears coming again, so I tip my head to look at his knees. When I look up, something has resolved in him.

'I better get some rest,' he says.

'You can call me whenever.'

'I know.'

—

'If he calls, do *not* answer the phone,' Jacob says as we walk back towards Reception. 'Now let's get out of here. I fucking hate hospitals.'

I now also feel sober, or at least level to some degree. I can tell, because the ground is unsteady, the feeling of dread is creeping closer.

'So I should just let him kill himself, should I? I should just let him get fucked by random guys off their tits on GHB, get AIDS and die, should I?'

Jacob is suddenly in my face. They're angry as hell.

'Danny, Tobbs is *not* your responsibility. He's *not* your boyfriend. He made you so unhappy. You've helped him out. That's enough.'

'Oh, easy for you to fucking say. You've never had to deal with anything like this.'

Jacob leans back from me with their hand to their chest, their mouth open in disbelief.

'*Excuse me?*'

'I don't need a lecture, OK?'

They look around the empty hall as if there's an audience.

'So I drive you down here to see your emotionally abusive ex who's ODed on G after a three-day sex bender, give him my favourite fucking silk Versace handkerchief, and now I get shit?'

'I'm just saying I don't need this right now.' My bones are trembling from within. The zaps across my forehead are coming thick and fast.

'Oh, bitch!' they shout, their voice echoing all the way to Westminster. '*You* don't fucking need it? What about what

307

I need?' A twelve-year-old doctor with a greasy fringe is fast-walking towards us with his hands in his pockets. Jacob opens their arms to them and shouts, 'A girl's got needs, am I right, doc?'

'Damn straight,' the doctor says back without breaking his stride. He continues past us, into the darkness of the corridor behind.

A rage – or maybe a panic – is bubbling up in me that I can't control. I look at Jacob, basically naked in their glittering gown.

'Why do you have to be like this all the time?' I say in a horrible, breathless voice. 'So fucking attention-seeking? So fucking—'

'Faggy?' Jacob cuts me off, as if they were expecting it. 'Why do I have to be so fucking faggy all the time?'

'No, that's not what I mean—'

That familiar vertiginous feeling is taking over. I clutch the wall with both hands to stop me toppling over as the floor rumbles.

'Yes, it shitting is.' Their finger is in the air. It's waving. 'I saw what you wrote in your diary – the diary that I gave you. *Why does Jacob have to be so fucking faggy all the time? They suck the air out of every room and make everything about them*—'

'Jay, I—'

But they are in full flow now as spots dance before my eyes, as my chest constricts so tightly I feel like I'm drowning.

'You know how much I've been doing for you? I listen to you go on and on about these guys I can see immediately aren't right for you, and listen to you moan and moan about your lovely, living parents, who might say the wrong thing from time to time but would do anything for you. And the worst thing is, you think you've had it hard, don't you, Danny Scudd? You think you've had the hardest time of it, and you think I'm just doing this all for attention, like always. Well, I'm not. This is me, it's always been me. You hid at school, just like every other coward. No one had to know your truth. But I couldn't, could I? I was the massive black faggot with the dead mum who couldn't hide for anything. You know how hard it's been for me? It's hard every fucking day, Danny. And then' – their voice wavers – 'you think you've found someone who likes you for you, someone who finally gets you, accepts you, and then you're completely honest with them, and they fucking drop you, because even in a community of outsiders – I'm still the outsider.'

'I'm not dropping you, Jay—'

'I DON'T MEAN YOU!' they scream. 'Not everything's about you, Danny! I mean Angel. I have my own fucking life with my own fucking problems. He fucking dumped me, on my mum's birthday – a day that you forgot, because you've got completely obsessed with being cool and edgy. And you've posted all this shit from the Revue, I looked just now, saying how everyone's getting high, because you think it's provocative, because you think it'll make people like you and you'll feel less alone. Well, this is going to fuck up my career – did you think about that? If the Tates see this?'

'That's not fair!' I try to shout, but I'm totally breathless, and it barely comes out at all.

'And never, not since we were four years old, have you supported me when something goes wrong in my life, because you always think people are after *you*. Like when Mum died, and you just disappeared. It's just like then. I might be fucking faggy, but you're fucking self-involved. I don't even know who you are anymore. Do you even know, Danny, huh? Do you know *anything*?'

'Jacob,' I try to say, reaching for them. 'Jacob . . .'

309

The corridor is warping, crushing inward as though in a giant fist. Any air left in these underwater halls is gone. The electricity courses through my body, bending my bones in terrible contortions, making my blood flow backward.

Next thing I know, I'm looking up at Jacob, my back against something cold and hard. I'm on the floor. I can't see properly. Everything is spotty. Then Jacob is around me, holding me.

'Fuck's sake, Danny,' they're saying. 'Why am I always looking after you?'

PART THREE

PART THREE

THIRTY-TWO

That night, everything changes. Something in me short-circuits. I can't really explain it more than that. My brain just goes kablooey.

Apparently, Jacob drove us home and put me to bed, where I slept for thirteen hours, despite the party still raging around me. The next day, I was sort of a zombie – but, then, everyone was. All the same, I called my parents, crying, asking if I could come home for a bit, and crept out without saying goodbye.

My clearest memory is sitting on the train with my cheek slumped against the cold window, watching the frosty countryside slide past. After what felt like no time at all, the crisp, pale farmland and bare, twiggy hedgerows gave way to the distant curve of the coast under the brittle grey sky. Huddled against it were the whitewashed, slate-roofed houses of Whistlecombe. It felt like pulling into a memory.

My parents were there at the station to meet me, which isn't usual. Even Mum looked fretful, despite the new blonde dye job for the party season. Dad helped me with my bag, even though it's not my back that's damaged. I went straight to bed, where I stayed solidly for a week. Periodically, one of them popped in with a cup of tea or a funny concoction meal – mini–barbecue

HENRY FRY

sausages with plain spaghetti and pre-grated Parmesan – which I sipped or nibbled at but never finished.

One day – though I couldn't tell you which, I assume it was a Monday – Dad comes in, sits on the edge of the bed, strokes my hair and says, 'Shouldn't go back to work yet, lad,' then calls the local GP surgery and holds the phone to my ear while I answer questions as a 'temporary patient'. They give me a phone appointment half an hour later and, just like that, sign me off work for a month with 'stress', which is weird, because I don't feel stressed. I don't feel anything.

All the same, I text a photo of the note to Callum – seeing as I have no direct line manager anymore – and tell him to forward it to HR. He sends back a voice note saying, 'Oh my God, Dan, honestly can't believe this! But fair play, though. When I get stressed, I just have a few big nights out and let off some steam and it sorts me right out – have you tried that?'

I've slept a lot. In between, I've watched the light move across the ceiling and down the wall, which is oddly mesmerising. I haven't spoken much, and, when I have, it's very slowly, like I'm learning how to do it again. My brain is similarly slow, no longer darting around all over the place, like the electricity really has been cut off. Normally, I would have worried I'd had a stroke or something, but the part of my brain that used to worry about everything is silent. No more shaking bones, no more feeling of dread, no more electric fingertips across my temples, no more second-guessing everything I say or do.

Everything is the same, but different. I don't know how to describe it. It's like I've lived my whole life in a room that I've only ever gone into in the morning, with the strong, bright morning light. And now, for the first time, I've stepped into it in the late afternoon, and the shadows are longer, the shapes of

314

the legs of the chairs are different. It's disorientating, uncanny, and I don't think I can ever go back into it in the morning. The whole feeling of life is different. I am different, really different, at last. Just not in the way I'd wanted to be.

I've listened to so much Dolly. People are always surprised by how much emotion her songs have. They think of her as a big-titted, campy icon – which she is – but she's also an incredibly gifted singer/songwriter who really understands the human condition. I mean it. I've listened to 'Cologne' over and over. It's a sort of 'answer' to 'Jolene', from the perspective of Jolene. It's super beautiful.

I text Nina and say I'm sorry I missed our session last week, which I only realised when I was texting her to cancel this week's. We talk briefly over FaceTime.

'Danny, it sounds like you've had quite a significant emotional episode.'

'Do you mean a nervous breakdown?'

She freezes. Or maybe pauses.

'If that's helpful for you to call it that, yes.'

'How very 1950s-housewife of me.'

'Most people experience a difficult period of mental health at some point in their life.'

'It does genuinely feel like I've lost my mind.'

'Is that frightening?'

'No. It's not anything. It just is.'

'Do you feel safe?'

'Yeah. My parents are looking after me.'

'That's great.'

'Well, you haven't had their cooking.'

We both smile.

'Rest up, Danny. Speak in a week.'

———

I lie in my tiny, cluttered childhood bedroom, staring at the ceiling. This is what I used to spend every night doing: wondering when I could escape. It's not changed at all. There's the Avril Lavigne poster, next to The Killers, next to the front cover of *Playboy* magazine from October 1978, featuring the one and only Miss Parton, black bunny ears tufting out of her curly locks as she straightens a bow tie and beams. I think Dad had given me that one in a well-meaning gesture of male bonding.

Next to that is a cut-out of Teri Hatcher and Dean Cain from the newspaper weekend supplement. I remember saying I wanted to be a journalist because of her, but I mostly watched *Lois & Clark: The New Adventures of Superman* because I couldn't stop staring at Clark when he pulled his shirt open and revealed the red-and-yellow spandex 'S' beneath. There are still the same plastic stars stuck to the slanting roof, which light up in the dark. Mum got them for my sixth or seventh birthday, and me and Jacob would lie in this bed and stare at them as we fell asleep. Jacob would always say they could see a shooting star, but I always missed it.

Then there's the little bookcase next to the wardrobe, full of all the adventure stories I devoured. With an impossible amount of effort, I slide off the bed and crouch down in front of it. On the bottom shelf are all my newspapers handmade from the backs of envelopes. 'JELLYFISH TERRORISES HARBOUR,' one headline reads in felt tip. Under it is a pencil illustration of said terrorist, smiling benignly.

Beneath that are a series of green ring-bound notebooks, five or six of them. These are the diaries I kept between the ages of about fourteen to eighteen. I leaf through them. The tone veers dramatically from utterly banal to deeply troubling:

Got the new Dolly album today from Smiths. Had to save up two weeks' pocket money from helping Dad in the shop. Can't wait to listen on the AMAZING NEW IPOD Mum and Dad got me for my 16th. Will would like it. Not that he'd admit it. I keep trying to catch his eye in English ever since THE EVENT, but he won't look at me. When I think about it, I feel sick and just want to die. Wish I could talk to Jacob about it but I just can't. I keep going down to the beach and just want to walk into the sea . . .

It upsets me more than it should that the diary I wrote when I was sixteen is in better prose than the diary I'm writing at twenty-seven. I remember *wanting* it to be good. Not for anything other than it just being good. I regarded it as the testing ground for honing my journalism skills before I went out into the wide world beyond Whistlecombe, a world that seemed so full of adventure and opportunity.

What would this sixteen-year-old think of me now? He had the strength of his convictions. He had dedication and drive. When did he lose that? I can't blame Tobbs; he just put the nail in the coffin. Was it Will? Was it Jacob?

No.

It was me.

I did it. I let it slip away, the way I let my entire identity slip away from me. And then I tried to claw it back, but somehow got it all wrong, and hurt everyone in the process.

My throat violently contracts, my hands go to my face, and I sob and sob and sob.

—

'Christ alive!' Mum screeches, pressing the anti-bac spray to her navy apron, across which is printed 'FISHERS OF MEN, EST: 1962.' 'I thought you was the ghost of Old Alf, then. Don't you frighten me like that, Daniel!'

I step down onto the orange tiles of the shop, and see it's mercifully empty except for my parents. Old Alf is Dad's deceased dad, who ran the shop before him, and whose dad was a fisherman. The Scudds have a long history based entirely around cod and mackerel – until I up and left to have a nervous breakdown.

'Don't start, Mary. He's barely arisen,' Dad says from behind the counter, where he's nibbling chips straight from the fryer and playing a football game on his phone. I've long given up wondering how he doesn't burn himself. 'You all right, son of mine?'

My dad is a short, squat, bald man of incredible pinkness. He has no evident neck or wrists, but does have a tattoo of a mermaid on one forearm and a ship battling the waves on the other. He also has a pair of half-moon reading glasses from Boots that usually dangle on a red cord around his neck; though now they balance on his pug-like nose as he smiles at me. He is a kind, gentle man and generally a wonderful father.

I slump down into one of the blue metal chairs bolted to the floor.

'Yeah, all right.'

'We was worried you'd died,' Mum says, as she goes back to spraying and scrubbing the fish-themed laminate table cover in front of me. The spray gets into my mouth and I cough, causing her to frown at me like I'm making a statement.

Somewhat unnervingly, the white eyes of a grinning reindeer peep over the top of her apron, stretching across the entirety of her bosom, distorted and bizarre in contrast to her steely expression. She always wears this jumper for the weeks preceding Christmas, seemingly every day, then, on the day itself, with matching plastic reindeer earrings.

'Nope, still alive.'

'I wish you'd at least come down for meals,' she continues.

'Leave the lad alone, Mary!' Dad says, looking over the tops of the glasses.

Mum waltzes over to the counter in her neon-pink Crocs and places down the spray bottle and blue cloth heavily, so the glass rattles in its casement.

'Joseph Reginald Scudd,' she says, 'if you take that tone with me again, I'll throw that stupid phone of yours into the fryer, then there'll be no football for you until the new year.'

'Still got Sky,' Dad says, as unbothered as always. 'No good matches till January, anyway.'

Dad enjoys small talk for an average of two minutes, but generally isn't one for a lot of chat. Sometimes, however, these moments of wit slip out, hinting at a richer inner life we seldom see.

Mum interlaces her fingers on the countertop. Her nails are painted burnished gold, as they are every December.

'And do you want to enjoy the Christmas meal your loving wife has painstakingly slaved away over for weeks, or are you happy with leftover bream?'

Reluctantly, he clicks the phone to black and moseys around the counter, still chewing the chips. He wraps Mum in an embrace and kisses her on the lips with a loud *mwah!*

'Oh, wife! Oh, goddess! You are a culinary angel sent by the Lord himself! What did I ever do to deserve thee?'

Mum slaps him away, looking to the door in case a customer should that moment enter, catching them, a couple of thirty-seven years, in embrace. The scandal! Unlikely, given the storm that has whipped up outside, painting the harbour greyer than usual and causing the thick clouds to slug-slide across the wet bowl of the sky.

'Get off, you silly old bugger!' She pats her pixie bob and regards me brightly. 'How's work, then, Daniel?'

I'm lucky, given the nature of my sudden arrival, they haven't already commented on the usual things: (a) my lateness, (b) my 'urban' fashion choices. But still I cannot escape the inevitable (c) career. At least they're too scared to ask about the dreaded (d) my love life. Generally, I try to fend off any questions about any of these, or send one up as a sacrificial, multiple-choice lamb.

I sigh. I can't be bothered with the usual games. I'll just give them the truth.

'My straight married boss has been shagging my gay twenty-two-year-old colleague in the work loos, and I walked in on them at it, so I got him fired for sexual misconduct.'

Silence.

'But I did get a promotion.'

'Oh, that's brilliant, love!'

'There's my boy!'

Typical.

I decide to push it a little more.

'My ex-boyfriend is also in hospital from a drug overdose, Jacob hates me, and now I guess I've had a breakdown.'

I look up at them and do jazz hands.

Mum makes a face like she's just about to say something, her mouth a round, preparatory 'O', but instead closes it. Then, almost as quickly, opens it again and says, 'Now, Auntie Denise and Uncle David are coming for Christmas lunch, so you better be feeling perkier by then.'

There's silence again. The wind outside is really battering the windows. From the quay, the harbour bell is chiming in what feels like the end of the world.

'They've let Old Dave out,' Dad says in a very measured voice. He pads over and heaves himself into the seat next to me. In one of the many sweet little actions he does, he takes both my hands in his and sets them in his lap, like he's warming them.

'It weren't a real crime,' Mum says imperiously. 'He were actually himself the victim of a crime. The bastard he sells the car parts with was crooked, and the police got him on a technicality.'

'Oh, right,' I say, swallowing hard. That's the end of the love-life discussion, then. I feel the usual mix of relief and anger – they just don't want to hear it.

Old Dave is Mum's younger brother, whom she has spent her life defending, despite him making every possible bad decision and being a complete and utter bellend. I doubt anyone is as crooked as Old Dave, whom I secretly call Uncle Dickhead. The thought of seeing him and his wife Denise in the next few weeks, having to fend off their questions and opinions, is almost too much to handle.

'You won't cause a scene this year, will you?' Mum shoots me a warning glance.

'Like when I told him not to use the n-word?' I say back.

'You know what I mean.'

'I can't promise anything.'

'I've put a lot of work into Christmas Day, Daniel. Please, do it for me – you can make it my Christmas present.'

I stare at her incredulously.

'I actually haven't got either of you presents.' My voice cracks. 'Sorry. I've been kind of . . . *floopy* recently.'

Dad rubs my hands together and smiles up at me with his encouraging, lipless Pillsbury Doughboy smile. 'Don't matter, lad,' he says. 'You're the present.'

'Hmm,' Mum tuts. She sprays the counter and wipes it fiercely.

—

For an hour, I help them with a few tasks around the shop, including my favourite: meticulously spooning the salt from the big bag it comes in from the wholesaler into the six shakers we have on the countertop and two tables. Mum doesn't like it to be poured, in case it spills.

After that, the rain lets up a bit, and there's still an hour or so of light left, so I take Dad's yellow mac and head out for a walk. I came back to Whistlecombe last in August, when the town feels very different. It's full of tourists, families wandering along the harbour wall with ice creams, taking photos on the narrow spit of shingle beach as the sun fades the colour from the few remaining fishing boats. In winter, it's a deserted Victorian ghost town. You can almost see Dracula's ship approaching on the solid, crushing, salty waves.

Trying to avoid the fierce wind rolling in across the Bristol Channel, I tread carefully through the slippery cobbled lanes, shielding myself between the narrow stone and limewashed houses. I just pray I don't bump into anyone and have to have small talk about how my life is going in the big city. All I want is some time alone at my favourite spot in town.

It takes me a while to find her. 'The Pregnant Witch', Jacob and I used to call her. I move around the circular pool, which splutters with the rainwater spilling through the high, circular eye above, running my hand across the various shapes we used to name, until I spy her.

She sits just left of the 'altar', a raised podium at the back of the largest of the caves that form the Whistlecombe shell grotto. In the centre, the pool glows azure blue from the shaft that opens to the sky above, illuminating everything with an eerie, submerged light. You can almost see the shadows of the Victorian tourists that visited here in the 1890s.

The witch's main body is a round, grey cockle shell, which

protrudes from the concave wall like an engorged belly. Her hands are whelks and her feet periwinkles, and the hat is a twizzling auger shell, pointing back coquettishly. I can't remember who coined 'Pregnant Witch', but at one point it was on everyone's lips almost as much as 'Phantom Logger'. She was always our favourite of several figures that really could be anything. There's the Worrisome Jockey and the Engorged Monk, but none had our heart the way the Pregnant Witch did.

I sit down on the slate bench next to the pool and look at her. My heels kick against something that rattles: empty beer cans. It's good to know the local kids are still getting smashed in here. Things never change in Whistlecombe.

Wandering to the grotto after our parents have fallen asleep in front of whatever Harry Potter movie is on is Jacob's and my Christmas tradition. Normally, the little run of underground caves hidden in the cliffs – encrusted with shells, almost invisible when you're strolling just outside in the seaside gardens – fills me with warmth and comfort. Today, it's like a tomb. I hug myself. It's colder in here than it is out in the rain.

I miss Jacob, I realise. We were each other's anchor in this town. We looked out for each other – Jacob more vocally than I, it's true. But even after everything that happened with Will – the bullying, me distancing myself from Jacob, Jacob's mum – we had come through it. And maybe this was just another one of those moments? You can't be friends your whole life without taking a good look at it, can you? Without noticing the other person has changed? Without noticing you've changed?

Jacob was actually the person who convinced me to go for the job at CULTRD. It looked so cool in the job description.

'Think how awful it was for us, Little Edie,' they said as we scrolled down the applicant criteria. 'In Whistlecombe. The only two queer kids anyone knew. Think how you can speak to young people now. You can really make a difference.'

Of course, I had been too nervous to actually put any of my ideas forward like that, to put myself on the spot as the gay person in the room with the gay agenda. I'm not even sure I knew I was squashing that bit of me down.

All teens lie to their parents. But if you're a queer teen, you're forced to lie about everything about yourself – to them, to your friends, to the whole world.

'Oi, lad, what you listening to?' Dad would ask.

'Green Day,' I'd say.

TRUTH: Britney's *Blackout* album.

'Oi, boy, want to come to the game?'

'Can't. Got after-school club.'

TRUTH: I want to dance around to 'Lady Marmalade' in Mum's shoes and pearls while you're out.

'Oi, boy, why doesn't young Billy Winters come over anymore?'

'Got too much coursework.'

TRUTH: Got stoned at Jacob's sixteenth and noshed me off in a bush and now won't look me in the eye.

Suddenly you're telling all sorts of lies where you don't need to. Things like, 'No, I haven't seen the dustpan and brush – GOD, MUM.'

TRUTH: I had, it was in the hall where it always was. It had just become a natural reaction to lie.

I spent my teenage years fancying boys I knew would never fancy me back. When Will showed an interest, no matter how sporadic or confusing it was, I felt grateful. I felt lucky that anyone was looking at me the way I looked at them. And I felt that way with Tobbs, too, I realise. Grateful that his horrible behaviour was channelled towards me, because at least it meant I existed.

My parents were mostly good about it, but I always knew I could never be too open with it. They *tolerated* it. They loved me *in spite of* it. It was a defect, but we needn't dwell on it. In fact, please never mention it.

I came out to them in the summer holidays of my second year at uni, with Jacob at my side, holding my hand. Mostly they were relieved Jacob and I weren't a couple, I think, which took the edge off. But afterwards not a lot changed. I still didn't really talk about any guys I liked, or any Gay Pride celebrations I went to. Whenever I mentioned anything remotely queer, I could see them clam up. I still did it – I still do it – but it always makes me feel on unsafe ground, like this could be the time they finally tell me to stop going on about it.

As a teenager, I wanted to be good at things. I felt like this would make up for it. It was better to be known as the clever try-hard than the faggot, I remember thinking to myself as I got another A* piece back about Macbeth's 'Out, brief candle' monologue. I watched what I said, how I said it, how I sat, who I spoke to. I acted pretty well for a long time, until all that stuff with Will happened. Then I took the shit, silently, until I could escape to London.

But then, even as an adult, I made myself acceptable. I didn't offend straight people. I was *all right* to have around, but never the life of the party. I wouldn't come on to you, because I was essentially sexless. I wouldn't fight you if you said something that was 'just a joke'. I didn't realise how exhausting the charade had become. I just did it, because I'd always done it. But that can't go on. That's very clear to me now.

I slip my phone out of my pocket to check the time. There's three missed calls from an unknown number and a series of messages.

Hey boyo, how have you been? Just ringing for a catch-up really. Be nice to hear your voice. T

I hear Jacob's voice in my head telling me not to answer Tobbs's calls. Or maybe it's my voice? Either way, I slip the phone away, say farewell to the Pregnant Witch and to the shadows that still hang about the grotto.

———

The dusk is blowing in on the tide. Yellow squares of light are appearing in the darkness, along with the orange glow of the few street lights along the seafront. I walk back without urgency, taking a detour past the cul-de-sac where Jacob lived with his dad, Amadi, the twins and his mum, June, before she died. Could Jacob be back for Christmas already? I could go and ring the doorbell, like I've done a million times, ask Amadi if Jacob can come out to play. Mum's right, of course. I know it's hard for them this time of year. I know I've been a shitty friend to Jacob, and not just recently.

As I peer over the hedge from the road, the light in the living room goes on. Amadi, now in his seventies, plods over to the window, perfectly illuminated. He peers out for a second, as if he senses my presence, and draws the curtains closed.

THIRTY-THREE

Christmas Day.

I always wake in the same way: first, a childlike sensation of joy; next, a teenage muddle of anxiety. It's like there's a snag on the door frame, and every time I go through, it catches the same loose thread of my jumper, ripping it just a little bit more. I didn't understand why before this year, but now I do.

Wrapped up in Dad's spare grey fleece dressing gown, I pad downstairs. Mum decks out our little terrace the same every year: plastic Christmas tree from the box room, and then swags of tinsel on absolutely everything. The smell of the fryer downstairs never really leaves, even with Mum cooking up lunch in the narrow kitchen out the back.

'Merry Christmas, love!' she trills from the stove, where she appears to be stirring the contents of six pots simultaneously. 'You gonna get dressed, then?'

'I was actually planning on spending most of the day completely naked.'

'Happy Son of Cod Day, lad,' Dad says; he pads over in his other grey fleece dressing gown and gives me a little squeeze around the shoulders. 'They'll be here soon,' he adds in a low whisper.

327

And they are. About an hour later. Old Dave bursts in and fills every space with his booming West Country voice. Denise follows up with confirmatory chatter, like she's his secretary. They bring presents. Mine is a pocket atlas. 'You like travel, don't you, boy? You in't never here, HA HA!'

We have some warm white wine in the living room, over the shop, then move into the conservatory out the back, which Mum has laid with the kitchen table, plates and glasses, crackers and two fan heaters they normally have behind the counter in the shop. I gaze out over the houses as they peter out, replaced by cliffs and rolling sea. The worst of the rain has passed, but the gorse bushes at the end of the garden are still getting tugged about this way and that.

'Cathy's about to pop any day,' Denise is saying. 'We couldn't be more excited, could we, Dave?'

''Nother yapping little 'un – bloody hell,' Dave says. There are no other babies in the family. 'You got anyone sprogged up yet?'

He's talking to me. My eyes turn from the storm-tossed cliffs to his pug-like face. He looks exactly like my mother if she lost her hair and drank so much her skin dried out, patchy and pink. A thick gold chain sags, rather like the tinsel, in the V of his pink polo shirt, tangling with the greying brown hairs.

I clear my throat.

'Nope, still a fairy.'

With a vacant stare, Dave smacks me hard on the arm.

'Never mind, I'm sure there's one on the horizon.'

'He's just got a promotion!' Dad intervenes.

'In *London*,' Mum adds.

'Well, I never,' Dave says in the same joyless charade.

'Still at the media company?' asks Denise. I don't know if this is because she's changed, or I have, but she looks like a perfect amalgam of Dave and my mum – only with twisted, discoloured front teeth she's always trying to hide. When I was a child, I always thought of her as very glamorous. But, year by year, she's seemed less exciting and cultured, and more parochial.

'Yes,' I say.

Dave has another swig of wine. I often think, if Mum wasn't in the room, he'd have thumped me on more than one occasion.

'That why you was sleeping on the pavement?'

Denise taps my arm excitedly. 'Oh yes, Danny! We saw you on the news!'

'I was awake most of the time,' I say, certain a 'but' is coming. 'It was just that one moment they chose to show . . . over and over.'

'Well, we're very proud of you.' Denise smiles encouragingly. 'What was the cause?'

'Gay rights in Chechnya.'

'Oh – right.'

We eat in silence for a while.

'What about that African whoopsie you used to hang around with?' Dave says out of nowhere.

Mum's cutlery clatters to her plate. The air tangibly leaves the room. Beyond the glass box, the wind whips harder.

'I don't know who you mean, Dave,' I say flatly, meeting him right in the eye. I've had years of this, and I won't take it anymore. The best thing is, for the first time ever, I don't feel afraid of him.

'Yeah, you do,' he says back, almost snarls. 'You used to flutter around together before pissing off to London.'

'Oh yes,' I say. 'You must mean Jacob.'

'Got a bloke's name? Wouldn't have bet on that.'

'*David*,' Denise says in a mollifying but still-pleasant tone.

'You still see him, then?' Dave continues. 'Or you too busy with your fancy writing job to keep up with our sort? Not that he's our sort. 'Course, you got a lot of them in London to choose from.'

'David!' Denise snaps. 'Stop antagonising the boy.'

'What?' Dave says to the room. 'These poofy liberals want that lot paying our wages now. Does your fairy mate pay yours?'

I set down my knife and fork very gently, and raise my chin so my eyes directly meet his.

'I am a liberal and a poof, Dave, that's true. And I'm not ashamed of it, as much as you'd like me to be. Jacob is one of the kindest, cleverest, most inspirational people I've ever met, despite the shit that's been thrown at them by small-minded bigots like you.'

'DANIEL!' Mum shrieks.

'And, incidentally,' I continue, 'the wages I'm paid come from a powerful woman and are more than you'll ever earn selling knock-off car parts.' And I sip my wine.

Dave's face has darkened to a violent puce. This is the moment when he finally smacks my lights out, I know it. And you know what? I'm cool with that.

'Dessert, I think,' Dad says, standing. His face is white and glistening, the eyes darting from person to person.

'Are you done, David?' Mum says, extending a hand.

Dave looks at her, not clocking what she means.

'The plate, David,' Denise says, fanning herself with a cracker. 'Blimey O'Reilly, it's hot in here.'

———

As is tradition, we go for an after-lunch walk around the harbour and along the seawall. It is fresh, bracing; the sun comes out from behind the clouds, painting golden strips across the ocean. I walk ahead with Dad, while Mum lingers back with Dave and Denise. It's been silently decided we must be separated until they leave.

330

'Why do we put up with him saying shit like that?' I say into my scarf.

'He don't mean it,' Dad says, looking out to the waves. There are a few other people dotted about up ahead, but the pebbly beach and scrubby incline are totally desolate.

'He definitely does.'

'Well, he's got a point. There's a lot more of *them lot* taking jobs what could be done by locals. Even the Co-op's got a foreign fella behind the till now.'

'Dad!'

'Well, there is!'

'What about Jacob? Are they "taking a local's job"?'

Dad's head whips to me with a look of horror.

'He's one of us.'

I decide now is not the time to correct him to 'they'.

'Why is Jacob one of us when the guy in the Co-op isn't?'

Dad looks back at the waves, sticks out his bottom lip.

'We don't know him, do we.'

'Is that how it works?'

Dad just shrugs, as if he, too, is mystified by it all. I try to start several sentences, but leave it. The selective nature of prejudice never fails to amaze me, even within my own father.

'Danny!' a woman's voice squeals over the long, drawn-out yawn of the wind.

Coming towards us, as though from a memory, are Laura and Luke. They're wrapped up and red-faced and with another couple, both of whom are in green waxed jackets and Hunter wellies. A chocolate King Charles spaniel runs out towards us and starts jumping.

'Laura!' I bark back. I'm genuinely happy to see her. 'Merry Christmas! Dad, you remember Laura Clifford from school?'

'Soon to be Laura Yeates,' Laura says, holding up the hand

with her giant diamond ring on. 'And just as soon to be Mama Yeates.'

'You're up the duff, too, are ya?' Dad says, completely ignoring the fact that Laura wasn't in our previous baby conversation.

'Twenty-two weeks!' she says. She smiles at me tentatively. 'Danny, how are you?'

'Yeah, all right.' Now isn't the time to go into it all.

'Great to see you, Dazzer!' Luke says, smacking me on the shoulder.

'Merry Christmas, Danny,' says the man next to them. I squint but can't quite work out who it is.

'Is that Young Billy Winters?' Dad says, suddenly much more animated, going in to shake his hand.

The dog is still jumping at me. The sun is in my eyes. The woman has long dark hair, the mirror image of Laura's. They could be sisters. The man has flyaway blond curls and long, rather gawkish features. As he smiles, I catch a glint of pale light off an impressive snaggletooth. I recognise that snaggletooth. It grazed the end of my penis many years ago.

'Oh, Will, lovely to see you!' Mum cries, joining our halted little gathering, embracing him and the woman. Her register immediately alters, which is what always happens when she's talking to someone in a waxed jacket. 'And this must be Andrea! I heard your news – how wonderful! When's it due?'

Andrea puts her hand across her belly. 'We've just had our twenty-week scan,' she says, smiling.

'And . . . do you know?' Mum says in a game-show-host voice.

'Yes, it's a little girl.'

'Oh, fantastic! I do love a girl!'

'We haven't seen you round these parts for a while?'

This is Will talking to me. He hasn't properly spoken to me since Jacob's sixteenth-birthday party. How mad that I've been thinking about him so much recently. It seems almost indecent when there's no way he's been thinking about me.

I squint at him but barely recognise him. To fill the void, the image of teenage him with ironed-flat fringe and black, square-framed glasses, clumsily trying to unbuckle my skater belt, fills in.

'No. I've been living in London for the past few years. Went to uni there and just stayed.'

'Escaped this little place?' he says with a laugh.

'Yeah, exactly.'

'Who'd stay here? It's all racists and homophobes!'

'Totally!'

'And there's nothing to do.'

'No, nothing!'

'Might as well just all kill ourselves!'

'Absolutely!'

We both laugh manically and I realise the others are joining in.

'We're just back, catching up with our faves,' Laura says. 'And to see their lovely new homey-womey.'

'Oh yes, the one by the high street. Margaret told me it's lovely, just lovely!' Mum chimes.

'Yes, all in and decorated,' Andrea says. 'Just in time for an appearance from this one.' Again the hand to the belly, the triumphant, fertile hand. 'So lovely to meet you at last.' Now she's talking to me directly. 'I've wanted to meet you for years. Willy won't shut up about you.'

I blink at 'Willy'.

'Well, it's been a long time,' I say non-committally.

'Come on, then,' Dad says, as he always does, suddenly getting bored of a conversation he instigated.

'So lovely to see you, Will!' Mum croons. She hugs him and Andrea. 'And lovely to meet you, Laura and – what was your name, sorry? Gosh, you're a big lad, aren't you? That child'll be strapping!'

Then we're embracing, all seven of us. I don't feel the bulk of Dave and Denise, so imagine they're sitting this one out.

'So glad you're doing well, Danny-boo,' Laura says. 'See you at the baby shower.'

'Definitely!' I say. Something else I've forgotten about, clearly.

'Nice to catch up, Danny,' Will says from the other side, squeezing my arm. 'See you around, yah?'

———

I say I need to lie down and digest, and go to my room for the remainder of Uncle Dave and Auntie Denise's visit. Everyone agrees the meal was wonderful, but filling, and lets me go. After I call 'NICE TO SEE YOU!' through the door in reply to Mum yelling 'They're leaving!' up the stairs, I gradually creep down and pick at the cold plate of meats and veg left over. Turns out I still have room for more. I join my parents in a line on the sofa, where they are watching *Love, Actually*, Mum with a cup of tea, Dad with a beer.

'Sorry I made a fuss again,' I say.

'Yes, well.' Mum is gazing fixedly at Martine McCutcheon's junior staffer charmingly ballsing up her introduction to Hugh Grant's prime minister.

'Dave's a bit of a prick though, in't he?' Dad says with a wicked side smile. 'Should be called Uncle Dickhead, not Uncle Dave.'

'JOSEPH!'

Sometimes I really feel like my father's son.

'Well, this is the thing . . .' I start. I have a prepared speech. This isn't exactly like coming out all over again, but there is something similar about it. 'I just wanted to say: I know you love me, and I love you, and you are wonderful, supportive parents, but I just was wondering: can you maybe . . . try a little harder, like, with the gay stuff?'

After a pause, Mum says, 'What do you mean, love?' very, very reluctantly.

'I mean . . .' I actually know what I mean, for the first time ever. 'I mean, like, with Dave spouting off, or when I talk about a boyfriend or going to Pride or something, I know it's hard for you to hear, because I suppose I'm not the sort of son you thought you'd have and I'm not living the sort of life you thought I'd live – I mean, Christ, *I'm* not living the sort of life I thought I'd live – but I just . . . I need your support with this. It's really hard being a gay person. It's like you have all the normal stuff to negotiate, and then there's this extra layer of stuff that you're not even aware of to begin with, but it's everywhere, it's part of everything you do.'

'Don't have to be,' Dad says quickly.

'No, that's what I mean, Dad,' I say. 'It *does* have to be. Or, rather, it *is*, whether I like it or not. I've spent a lot of time feeling ashamed of myself, hiding who I am, trying to be different, and I think I'm only now really working out who I am and what I want, and . . . and I need you to support me with it, rather than try to push it under the carpet the whole time, because, believe me, *I've* been trying to do that for years, and it doesn't work.'

Dad's hands are around mine again, kindling them. He looks at me with his kind, droopy, worried eyes. He did the exact same thing when I came out to them all those years ago. They were nice, accepting, they said they loved me. But then it was never discussed again.

'Oh, love,' Mum says. She's put down her tea and is looking at me. Her eyes are wet. Something one rarely witnesses. 'We knew you was different, ever since you was a little boy, running around the house shouting, "I'm Dolly Parton! I want to be the town trash!" I don't know why you young people get so upset about these things. All we want to know is that you're happy with someone – anyone at all, we don't mind. They could be a Martian or a Jack Russell for all we care!'

'I'm not going to shag a dog, Mother.'

'Oh, you know what I mean!'

'I'm not asking for special treatment. I'm just asking for *normal* treatment – even if you don't think I'm normal.'

'Of course we think you're normal!' Dad shouts all of a sudden. 'We love you, you silly boy! We're proud of you, and we love you for who you are!'

'Yes, love,' Mum says, less certainly. 'You don't need to worry about that.'

Now even she is hugging me, smelling powerfully of some dreadful, cheap perfume.

'Thanks, family,' I say hoarsely. 'Sorry for being, like, *heavy*.'

'Oh, don't be silly!'

'Don't need to apologise!'

'I love you both very much, you know.'

'We love you, too.'

And I'm holding on to them both, crying so hard I can't believe it.

—

'Thank you for being so wonderful,' I say at the station a week and a half later.

'That's OK, lad,' Dad says, patting me on the shoulder. 'We know you're under a lot of pressure with the new job and new digs.'

Mum is fiddling with my floral collar, huffing.

'You're always welcome home, Daniel. As long as you don't start something with your uncle every time.'

'Mary!'

'I wasn't "starting something", Mum; he called me a "poofy liberal".'

'Oh, look, now I've gone and set you off again!'

'You haven't "set me off", Mum,' I say, although she has. I'm feeling pretty wobbly now that I'm on the precipice of returning to my real life. After clawing to get away from my old life, now all I want is to stay here. It's a miracle we haven't murdered one another after a whole month, really, but maybe that's 'growth'.

'Now, listen, lad,' Dad says, eyeing me squarely. 'You mustn't be melancholy. You've got everything going for you.'

'Speak to Jacob if you feel low,' Mum orders, nodding towards the train. 'He's always cheery.' She shakes her head. 'He or she.'

Dad leans forward and kisses me on the top of the head. This is something he's done since I was little.

'You know we love you, lad,' he says in a shaky voice. 'Now, just you concentrate on loving you.'

Mum and I both stare at him like he's unzipped his skin to reveal an Illuminati overlord. Him trying to normalise saying 'I love you' really is a radical act.

'*Joseph*!' Mum breathes.

Dad just nods and pats me on the arm. 'Go on, then.'

'OK. Bye, then,' I say, waving, despite them being directly in front of me. 'Thank you for a lovely Christmas.'

'It'll go without you,' Mum warns.

I climb on board and sit down. The parents stay where they are, both waving, Mum tight-lipped and anxious-eyed, Dad smiling dopily.

The carriage jolts and starts to move off. They continue waving until they and the station vanish into nothing.

A lump rises in my throat. I am lucky to have them whatever

they say or do, I know I'm lucky. And a massive part of me doesn't want to go back, back to the life I've messed up. It wants to stay, to be swaddled and misunderstood by them, fed battered cod and chips, having ambiguous small talk with my primary-school crush and ex-landlords. Part of me just wants everything to stop, so badly.

But I can't have that. I can only move forward. And I'm determined to do it this time, to be the person I am at last. It's not enough to stay here, live a half-life like Will. What even is the deal with him and his wife? Was it a phase he had with me, or is he hiding who he really is now? Is he living the life I would have lived if I'd stayed in Whistlecombe?

'Sometimes we have to give ourselves closure,' I hear Nina's voice say in my head – although I could have read that on Instagram instead. But she's right, I'll never know probably, and I have to find a way to be OK with that. Just like with Tobbs. I've got to find a way to put it behind me.

The instructive lyrics to 'Dump the Dude' come to mind – the words of another great modern philosopher. I'm lucky to have these wise women in my life. Between Nina and Dolly, I think I've got things covered.

As the countryside slides past, I take out my phone. Two more missed calls from an unknown number and some texts.

Boyo I understand if you don't want to see me, but at least answer. I just want to see how you're doing. T

I select the messages and delete them, then scroll Instagram, Twitter, check my emails. Then, just because I haven't looked at it since I hooked up with Klaus, and as a small act of rebellion against my ex, I open Grindr and flick through the meagre local offerings.

Nearest guy: five miles away.

Lots of middle-aged men. Some squaddies who look like they'd murder you. A few thin-faced twinks claiming to be eighteen. I worry about them when I see them. Gay world is a scary one to get inducted into, and there's no one there to check on you.

The *GRRRIII!* sound lets me know I have a message.

And another.

And another.

I go into the message section. They're from a blank profile, six miles away.

Nice to see you the other day sexy 😊

Then a photo.

It's fucking Will.

THIRTY-FOUR

The door slams shut behind me. The hall is silent. It feels like a decade since I was last in this house.

I peek into the living room, the kitchen and even the conservatory. I head up the stairs, expecting to hear voices from bedrooms, but there's nothing. I pause on the second landing. There's light spilling from an ajar door: Ange's room.

After knocking gently, I poke my head around. The room is exactly as I had imagined it: a messy bed, and then everything else is giant paintings. Literally, crammed everywhere. They cover the desk by the window, line every spare bit of wall, are piled up against the radiator – a potential disaster right there. The floorboards are splattered a hundred different colours, and on them sits Ange, cross-legged, in paint-stained navy overalls, her hair hidden beneath a leopard-print wrap, painting yet another giant vagina. This one, I note, appears to be giving birth to something decidedly non-human. Somewhat incongruously, Enya plays.

The floorboard I'm on creaks, and her head spins around.

'Fucking shit! Yous scared the tits off me!'

'Hey, Ange.' I wave limply.

She jumps to her feet, walks over and embraces me with

incredible tightness, oblivious to the paint she's pressing into my black puffa jacket.

'Where you been, then?'

'Erm – I sort of had a mental breakdown and went to stay with my parents for a bit.'

Ange just sticks out her bottom lip and nods, like this is a perfectly normal thing to say.

'Good to get a time-out from all these posh twats when something like that happens, innit?'

'You should have met my old housemates.'

She ignores me. 'Not that they're here.'

'Yeah, where are they?'

Ange cocks her head at me, then, as if understanding, nods again.

'Jacob ain't spoken to you?'

I feel like I'm being caught out.

'No.'

'Ginny and Ash fucked off to Japan. Mel went to stay with that bird of hers. And Jacob's been with their family.' She looks at me with a firm but surprisingly kind glare. 'They was pretty hurt.'

I fiddle with my thumb.

'Yeah. I know. I want to make it right.'

Ange glares at me another two beats, then spins around and goes back to her painting.

'I ain't got no family,' she says over her shoulder. 'Well, I do, but they ain't a fan of dykes, so I don't see 'em, even though they're closer than any of yous lots' are. Every year, everyone goes back to their family. But not me.' She turns and stares at me. 'If I had a friend like Jacob, I'd do everyfink I could not to lose 'em – know what I mean?'

My eyes are stinging. More tears. Turns out, Ange can

actually talk some pretty good sense.

'Yeah,' I say. I wipe my eyes. 'Do you want a cup of tea, Ange?'

—

The phone rings six times before I answer.

'Tobbs?'

'So you're not dead?' That familiar stern tone sends a shiver down my spine.

'No.' I sort of half laugh. 'How are you doing?'

'Oh, you know – also alive.'

'Tobbs, I know I said you can call me, but actually, I don't think you can.'

The hum of the line is loud.

'I hear what you're saying. But the thing is, boyo, well, I . . . I've actually started seeing this shrink, and she told me to start journalling—'

'Nina Leibovitz?' I interrupt.

'What?'

'Nothing. Never mind.'

'Anyway, I've been reflecting on our relationship, and I wanted to reach out and tell you how grateful I am to you. You were the only person who came to see me that night in the hospital, and it really made me . . . really made me think about everything, about, you know, the way I was with you . . . about the way I am. I'm really sorry, Daniel. I know I'm a complicated person, and maybe you just weren't the right guy to get that. I should have realised you weren't really up to the job. So . . . sorry.'

I'm in my room, standing at the window, staring out at the minimal traffic, at sleet now spitting over everything. I've thought about replying to his texts over the last month, about checking on him, but I just couldn't bring myself to do it, because deep down I knew he'd be the same, as much as I'd always wanted him to be different. Now it's like I'm hearing him for the first time, the way everyone else has been hearing him all along.

My palm is flat against the cold glass. It burns. 'Listen, Tobbs, you can't call me anymore. You were a twat when we were together. Like, really selfish and narcissistic. I know you were struggling, but so was I, and it doesn't give you a free pass to be an arsehole.'

'Whoa, boyo, where's this all coming from—'

'But, also, I just accepted it. I didn't challenge you – I didn't know how to. I thought that kind of unhappiness was just how it had to be. But it isn't.'

Again that loud line.

'That's not a very nice thing to say.'

'No, it isn't.' I'm amazed by how calmly I'm saying all of this. 'But I need to say it. You said a lot of not very nice things to me, too, you know?'

'Daniel, I really just wanted to—'

'Tobbs.' I bite my lip. 'You can't call me again, OK?'

'OK, boyo.'

'I'm glad you're getting help. Look after yourself.'

'Sure.'

'Bye, then.'

'Bye, Daniel.'

——

'. . . And I actually said to him, "Don't call me anymore" – can you believe that? I don't think I've ever said that to anyone! And it wasn't in, like, a mean way, it was just in, like, a factual way, like: I won't put up with this anymore. You'd have been well proud of me, Nina, seriously.'

Nina is gazing attentively, hands clasped around the knee. How long have I been talking this time?

'And it made me realise how I'd always just accepted this supporting role in Tobbs's life, in our relationship, and it's just like I've done with Jacob! Well, until everything at the hospital, when my brain essentially imploded. But Jacob's right, they *are* always looking out for me. And I *am* self-involved and think everything's about me, and they come back tomorrow, and I just don't know how to rectify things – like, have I ruined everything between us forever?'

Nina is not blinking. The pause between us is as pregnant as fuck. I draw breath to keep going, but she gets in there first.

'Danny, let me stop you.'

I stare at her. In a move I haven't seen before, Nina TAKES OFF HER GLASSES, lets them dangle from her hand against the black jeans of her shin, and looks at me – properly looks at me, like: Right. In. The. Soul.

'These are all great realisations – really, really great. And it's great you took the time away when things got too much, to recuperate and think. You've been through a lot in the last few months. What has happened to you is your body and mind saying, "I can't take it anymore." It's a wake-up call, telling you to take things slower, be kinder to yourself. You need to listen to it.'

I nod. I nod a lot. It's funny, her saying this even a month ago wouldn't have made sense. Now it does, perfectly.

'I understand. I mean, I did go full Bertha?'

'I'm not sure I get the reference.'

'From *Jane Eyre*. You know, madwoman in the attic.'

'You're not mad, Danny.'

'Good thing I didn't have any candles, really.'

'Absolutely.' I see her smirking. I'm still funny, even if I'm also mental.

'So what happens now? What should I do?'

Nina sits back and returns the glasses to her little nose. She looks a bit agitated today, a bit frazzled. She's wearing a new pair of black patent brogues that look box-fresh. Old me would have made a joke about them, tried to work out who had given them to her. To be honest, I do still wonder that, but it doesn't seem like the most important thing.

'You know I can only advise you,' she says. 'But I'd suggest we keep going with these sessions for a little while, though not forever – endings are important, and therapy needs to end. It's important you don't try to address everything all in one go, or we might end up in a boom-and-bust cycle.'

'Bertha versus Jane.'

'If you like. You need to take this recovery slowly. After everything that's happened, I think now is the time for healing. Do nice things for yourself: have long baths, read, relax. Treat yourself to something you love. If you're feeling up to it, why not write down how you feel about everything that's happened? You can even talk it through with a trusted friend. Jacob, maybe – or maybe not. Think hard about how you *really* feel about everything.'

'Well, that's what I'm saying. Jacob's back tomorrow.'

She considers a moment. Something twinkles in her piggy black eye.

'OK, I'm going to set you some homework.'

'I thought I was supposed to be relaxing?'

'It's a suggestion.'

'You said the word "homework".'

A smile tugs at the corner of her lip. 'Right, right. You won't be marked – think of it as a fun challenge.'

I stare at her.

'Nina, I thought I was the one who'd lost my mind, not you?'

She laughs, a big laugh, like I'd made her do before. But this time I don't feel the same sense of victory. I don't even feel that sense of achievement I usually feel when I make someone laugh, or when someone says I've done a good piece of work. Instead I feel a warm glow, like we're sharing the feeling.

'You haven't lost your mind, Danny.'

'So what's my "fun challenge"?'

'Jacob has been your most important friend throughout your entire life. They understand you in a way few do, but they have been finding your behaviour recently a little too much, and vice versa – is that fair to say?'

I swallow but don't look away.

'Yeah, I think so.'

'Your relationship has shifted; it'll never be as it was. But this is a wonderful opportunity for honesty, and for deciding how you want your friendship to be now and in the future.'

'So you're saying: talk to them?'

'I am. As honestly as you can. Which all starts with being really, truly honest with yourself, without judgement – which I *think* you can do now?'

She says this kindly; she's not mocking me.

'I hope so.'

'You can. I'll see you next time.'

She smiles. She's a nice woman. She does like me, I decide.

'OK.'

'Look after yourself, Danny. You've been through a lot of very real pain. Take it easy.'

THIRTY-FIVE

Welcome back Mother darling

Sorry, who is this?

Some dickhead who wants to say sorry

I don't know her

Seriously seriously Jay, can I invite you to tea?

It's 11am, bbz

Tea as in ☕ not as in dinner

Maaaaaaaaybe

Jay! Can you just come down to the conservatory please?
Like only if you want to I mean

???

The little glass shack behind the kitchen

LOLLL CONSERVATORY! SCUSE ME QUEEN OF SHEBA

And dress as Big Edie

Plot twist!

I know

OK fiiiiiine
See you shortly Mrs Bouvier Beale

XOXO Gossip Gay

———

'Treat yourself to something you love,' Nina said.

'Take it easy,' Nina said.

Create an elaborate apology meal for your best friend,— Nina didn't say, but I surmised.

Which is how I've come to be standing in the 'conservatory' in a fur coat and floral headscarf, surrounded by all my houseplants.

Jacob stalks in from the kitchen, chin held queen-mother-ly high. They straighten their floppy hat and horn-rimmed tortoiseshell glasses, pull their baby-blue dressing gown tightly around their vintage lingerie. A long grey wig falls around their shoulders, held back from their face with kirby grips in a perfect facsimile of Jackie O's aunt. How on Earth do they always manage to pull it out of the bag at a moment's notice?

'You look like the cat's pyjamas,' I say in my finest New England drawl.

They regard me coolly. This is the first time we've seen each other since that night.

'Don't I look like a girl who has everything?'

'I'll have to start drinking. I can't take it.'

They peer around the spread of rugs, cushions, stuffed toy cats, mismatched vintage plates, teacups and saucers I've amassed from around the house. I've covered the chest freezer with two cream-coloured shag rugs that I borrowed from Melania and have topped with parlour palm, cheese plant and the few plants already in there that I've managed to revive. I'd tried unsuccessfully to procure a gramophone from a charity shop (which you think you'd be able to find in East London), but instead opted to play Cole Porter from my phone – it does its job to drown out the sound of the two fan heater hidden in the greenery. The windows are fugged white, making it feel like we're inside a *Gatsby*-themed cloud.

Jacob spreads their arms wide in the doorway. 'Yes, this really is the best outfit for the day.'

'Tea for two, Mother darling?'

They waltz in with a hand held out limply before them. 'As long as you haven't got it confused with giblets for the cats.'

'The pâté's here.'

We sit. I pour two cups of lukewarm Earl Grey. It seems appropriate. Outside, we hear a woman next door screaming, 'But you didn't ask? But you didn't ask?' It's just a quiet Sunday in our East Hampton mansion.

'Well, this is really something, Dan.'

'Jacob!' I hiss. 'You're supposed to be in character!'

'Don't tell your mother what to do, Edie.'

I pass them a cup and saucer printed with an especially lurid take on Wedgwood, and sigh.

'But thanks. It's not really enough to say how sorry I am, but it's a start.'

Jacob doesn't respond. We sip our tea. There's an atmosphere between us, a taut, silent thread.

'Did you know Big Edie died of pneumonia?' they say suddenly, like this was hot off the press, not news from fifty years ago.

'Of course.'

'And Little Edie of a heart attack?'

'No!'

'Call yourself a fan.'

'I'm more of a fan than Drew Barrymore.'

'Lord, why did they bother with that remake?'

'She actually wasn't *terrible* . . . to be fair.›

'Jessica Lange was amazing in my role.'

'A literal, actual icon.'

'Agreed.'

'Cake?'

'What sort?'

'Tesco's Finest.'

'No, thanks.'

'It's gluten-free lemon drizzle.'

'OK. One slice.'

I leap up, race back into the kitchen and run around looking for a knife; I return with a sheathed samurai sword that's mounted above the stove. I don't stop to wonder where all the knives are – Ange was staple-gunning them to her bedroom door a couple of days ago. I awkwardly cut a slice and flop it on its side onto the chintzy little plate I have ready. Jacob and I chew in silence.

'Tart,' Jacob says as they chew.

'What you call me?'

'Harh-harh.'

More chewing.

'Jay.'

'It's Mother darling, remember?'

350

'No, Jay, listen.'

Jacob delicately places their plate down on the rug, smooths out their dressing gown. They're even wearing oversized skin-coloured tights, bunching in rolls at the ankles. Their attention to detail never ceases to amaze me.

'I haven't' – this is harder than expected; the Tesco's Finest cake crumbs are lodging in my throat – 'I need to apologise for – well, for everything.'

Jacob picks up their tea and sips.

'Yes. I think you do.'

Jacob is looking at me seriously. The costume now gives them a sage-like quality. They look wizened, weathered, wise – not that I'll say that right now.

'You were right, that night in the hospital – you *are* always looking after me.' I take several deep breaths. 'You've always looked after me, ever since primary school. And you've always had a lot going on – being queer, mixed-race and gender-non-conforming in our town, I mean, I know it wasn't easy.'

'*And* six foot four.'

'And with your mum and everything.' Jacob's Adam's apple shifts in their throat. I meet their eyes. 'You were always the strong one. You're still the strong one, and sometimes I get jealous about that, and sometimes it makes me feel smothered or, like, infantilised, or whatever, because everyone's always acting like I can't do anything for myself, and it makes me really angry, actually, and then I feel guilty, because you're just doing it to be an amazing friend, but it makes me feel like I can't grow, can't develop – not that that's an excuse, because I've been an arse to you, and what I wrote in the diary that you even gave me, and you really are the most genuine person I know, and all the things I said I don't like about you are actually the things I love about you. Like, I'm jealous of those things, and that day of the Revue, what you said made me realise how I'd been making you feel and how shit of a friend I've been to you, and I fucking hated myself for it.'

There, I've said it. I'm out of breath, but I said it.

Jacob is eyeing me very carefully. They're clearly finding this as hard as me.

'I had to make you listen somehow, didn't I?'

'Yeah. I'm sorry.'

'You kind of became everything you were saying you hated – corporate Pride, all that stuff. Did you realise you'd basically turned into your vile boss?'

'I didn't – I was kind of . . . on one, wasn't I?'

'Yeah. It was actually quite scary seeing you like that, Dan.'

'I can imagine.'

'You were manic. You wouldn't listen to anything anyone said. You were totally self-absorbed.'

'Jay, I'm really sorry, I honestly didn't know what was going on with me, or where it was going.'

Jacob sits up straight. 'I knew it was going to happen, babe, because I've seen it happen to a lot of us. It happened to me after Mum died. All the shit you've held inside all those years becomes too much, and then there's the last straw, and a bit of you explodes.' Jacob's hands go to their glasses. They take them off. Wipe them. Return them. 'And then things are never the same afterwards.'

I lean forward and put both hands on their knees in quite a strange gesture that feels bizarrely sweet and right.

'I'm so sorry I wasn't there for you with your mum, Jay. I was so scared. I did what I always do: I disappeared. But it was selfish. And you have no idea how much I hate myself for it.'

Jacob swallows and stares at the pile of conference chairs I haven't been able to disguise.

'I . . .' Their voice cracks. 'I'm not going to pretend it didn't hurt, Dan. I really, really needed you then. Just like I've really needed you now. But we were fifteen. We were both struggling with stuff. And I should have said, instead of keeping it inside all these years.'

'No,' I interrupt. 'I should have been the one to make it right. I just . . . I just buried my head in the sand, as usual.'

'Well, that's one thing we've got in common.' A look of deep knowing passes between us. Jacob takes an uncertain breath. Their hand is shaking around their teacup. 'I know I come off as strong, I know I'm "a big personality", but I find it hard to share this shit – even with you. Mum was always unapologetically herself, which wasn't easy in Whistlecombe as the only mixed family, let me tell thee, Danielle. When she was dying, I promised her I'd always be me, that I'd always bring colour and joy to the world. She's the one that taught me to sew, after all. And after everything that happened – with her, the bullying, you vanishing – I said to myself the last thing I'd ever do would be to shrink myself. Mum wouldn't want it. It's my defence; Nina taught me that. I've always done this character, so if people attack it, then they aren't really attacking me – and, fuck, do they like to attack it! But sometimes it's hard to tell which is the defence and which is the real you, you know? That's why it hurt so much to let Angel in and then be rejected. I was like, "Here it is, the confirmation at last. No matter how hard you work, you'll never be enough. No matter how much attention you get, it'll never shut the voice up that tells you you can't be loved because you're a freak".'

I'm nodding. 'It's like me going invisible, disappearing into the background. If it's not you, you can't be hurt. It's like Tobbs drawing away from me, shutting himself off.'

'And that's why I was so angry at him, at Tobbs.' Jacob is

looking back at me with fervour in their eyes. 'I could see the self-destructive streak in him, because I've been there, too, and I could see it sucking you in, and you just going along with it because you wanted it to work so badly. And then it happened with you, and it really took me back to that place when we were at school. It really stung, Dan, when you cut me out. I didn't understand. And I was too scared to share it with you, because I thought you'd leave me again.'

'Me leave you?' I could almost laugh. 'I thought you were bored of me? I thought you'd grown into this amazing adult, and I was still this shy little teenager inside. I thought I was embarrassing you in front of the housemates!'

'Well,' Jacob considers, 'maybe you did embarrass me on one or two occasions. I've always been the loud, fun one, and you've always been the quiet, thoughtful one, not the other way around. And maybe it made me feel out of control. Maybe I've had a hard time letting go of how we always were. You've changed *so* much, Dan. You've done things I never thought you'd do, and, honestly, I think I was jealous, and I'm sorry.'

I can't believe I'm hearing this. I'd spent so long thinking Jacob was oblivious to everything. Really they're just as tuned in as me.

'No, I'm sorry,' I say, realising I'm crying. 'Jay, you have nothing to apologise for. I'm sorry I've been like this. I've dealt with things really badly for a really long time. Well, no more.' I take both their hands in mine. They're still shaking. 'Will you forgive me? For being the worst best friend in the whole world?'

'You're not as bad as Carrie Bradshaw.' Now they're smiling. 'You'll always be my bestie, Dan.' They sniff again, run an index finger under their eye to wipe away the tear. 'I suppose maybe I need to open up more about these things. But it don't come natural to this all-natural gurl, you know?'

'And I always think you're so confident and can do and say anything.'

'We've all got our thing, babes.'

'I know. Maybe I can help you the way you've helped me?'

Jacob's eye catches mine. There's something wicked in it.

'You do love to talk about your emotions, so maybe you could give me a masterclass?'

I smack them with the sword's sheaf.

'Oi! More like a *mistress* class.'

'Mistress of *my* class!'

'Class dismissed, we have a mistress in our midst!'

'Miss-stressing me out!'

'Miss, when I grow up, I wanna be a mistress. I always top biology, after all.'

Jacob blinks at me.

'Why do you always go too far?'

'Apologies.'

'Finger sandwich?'

'Ooh yes, lovely.'

I pass them the plate of salmon-pâtéd bread.

'We're OK, though, Jay?'

''Course, you idiot,' they say, munching on down. 'And I promise to back off, stop smothering you.'

'No, I didn't mean—'

'I know, babe, it's OK.'

'You know I love you a lot. I'd honestly do anything for you.'

Jacob suddenly launches themselves at me. They embrace me hard, their firm, skinny arms all around my neck and ears.

'Love you, too, Little Edie. Madly. *Wildly*. Even if you are a very staunch character.'

'There's nothing worse than dealing with a staunch woman.'

'S-T-A-U-N-C-H.'

THIRTY-SIX

'You are good to go, dear lamb.'

Melania gives me a thumbs-up, which I can barely see behind the glare of the ring light. I cough, and look into the phone, where it sits, clamped into the tripod, recording.

'Hi there,' I say, my voice wobbling. I look at her again. She nods insistently. 'My name's Danny Scudd. You might know me as the activist guy who fell asleep on the News and became a meme. Well, that's me. Sleeping Meme Guy. I'm actually a content editor at CULTRD, a culture and listings app, and that was an assignment which kind of . . . went awry.'

Melania stifles a giggle. I can't help but grin. I suppose it is kind of funny if you think about it.

I cough again, and continue.

'So . . . the reason I wanted to make this video was really to apologise to everyone in my life over the past three months. I've had kind of a wild ride with mental-health stuff, and I know that's not an excuse, because I've really been an arsehole to everyone – especially the people I care about the most. But I wanted to publicly apologise, even though I'm kind of a nobody.'

'You are not a nobody!' Melania objects.

I feel my face heat up. But it's nice.

'Thanks, Mel. That's my housemate – one of the people I've been a dick to. On top of my best friend, who I've taken for granted. And my boss, who I got fired when I actually didn't know the full story and didn't ask the other person involved if it's what they wanted. Basically, I've been a total shit to everyone. It's not the person I ever thought I'd be, and yet it's who I became.'

I shuffle forward on the edge of the chaise longue, lean in. Unusually, the words are coming. It's like I'm in a session with Nina.

'See, the thing is: we all try to fit in, don't we? We all spend our whole lives trying to be liked, trying to be some perfect version of ourselves, and it's really easy to get lost in that, and to lose the you in you. I've just been on this hectic journey, where everything I thought I knew about myself turned out to be wrong. And then I tried to be someone else, and that really didn't work out. In fact, I ended up falling asleep on national news and getting headlines for all the wrong reasons – even if this lush guy I was sort of involved with said it didn't matter. Well, it does really, doesn't it?'

Melania taps her wrist. 'Keep it short,' she'd said before we started. 'People only watch titties for ten minutes before they cum. They definitely don't want to watch you cry for fifteen.'

'So I just want to say,' I try to wrap up, 'if you're going through a wild time: remember the people around you. Remember they're probably going through stuff, too. Remember how much you need them and they need you. You aren't all on your own in this. We all struggle, we all fuck things up, we all need each other to get through this life. Especially if you're from a marginalised community . . . like I am.'

I pause. I nearly stop there. But this is not the time to shy away from the truth. Now is the time to really face it, once and for all.

I take a deep, shuddering breath.

'I'm a gay guy, and I've found the journey to accepting myself – *really* accepting myself – longer, harder and more confusing than I'd ever thought. And I couldn't do it without my amazing friends and family and super-badass therapist, who really is a fucking fashion icon.' Melania clicks her fingers and I just know the microphone picks it up. 'There's no shame in feeling lost, in feeling alone, in feeling *shame*. There are people who love you just the way you are. You don't have to be perfect. I mean, you don't have to fall asleep on BBC News, either, but it's not all over if you do. In the words of one of our greatest philosophers, "Storms make trees take deeper roots". And if you open your eyes, you can see all around you is a forest of other trees.'

Melania is smiling at me. I smile back. Uh-oh, here come the tears.

'Anyway, I just wanted to say that. Hopefully, this'll help someone. Ciao for now.' I wave, and signal to Melania to stop recording. She leans in and taps the screen. I wipe my eyes with both hands. 'Was that OK?'

Melania folds her arms. For a minute, I think she's going to cry, too. Then she cocks her head to the side and does finger quotes.

'"Ciao for now"?'

———

Standing outside the office is weird. It's like I've been gone for an entire century. I've sort of forgotten how busy the streets are, how corporate a building it is.

Heading in is even worse. As the lift ascends the floors, the fist tightens in my stomach. I'm breathless, faint.

DOORS OPENING.

Weaving through the rows of desks is probably the worst bit. People I've forgotten existed look up, look back at their work, look again, then smile awkwardly, not quite meeting my eye. It makes me feel like someone's died (me?) and they don't know how to handle it. 'Nice to have you back, Danny,' a couple of them mutter to their screens.

I sit down at my desk, which is unusually clean on account of my absence. Spinning slowly in my chair, I survey the office; everything is as normal, as if I never left, and yet I am so changed.

Nadia waves from the bank of PR desks. I wave back, at which moment I notice the huge shoulder bulging out around the sides of the screen opposite. I lean around it. Callum is tensely crouched over his keyboard, nose about an inch away from his screen. His blond hair is messy, and he doesn't smell dipped in Lynx, like usual.

'Cal?' I say tentatively.

'Fuck!' he cries, lurching back from the screen and staring at me. 'Oh my God, Dan!' He leaps up, runs around and clutches me to his rock-hard titties.

'Cal! Cal!'

'Oh my God, sorry, Dan!' He releases me. 'I'm just so pleased to see you, aren't I? I've never been so stressed in my whole life. And I'm not lying.'

His eyes are shadowed and wired-looking. I notice three paper coffee cups messily encrusted with old foam around the tops, next to a pile of papers on his desk. It's still only nine-thirty; how long has he been in already?

Callum kneels down on the floor before me and holds my hand in an odd, childlike gesture.

'Gonna be honest, Dan, I'd forgotten you were coming back today. But I'm as cheesed as chips to see you.'

I frown at him.

'Do you mean "cheap as chips" or "pleased as punch"?'

Callum pulls the hand away and smacks me on the knee with it.

'Dan, I'd never call you cheap!'

I closed-lipped smile at him.

'OK.'

Apparently immediately forgetting how stressed he is, he crosses his legs, props up one elbow on one knee and rests his cheek in one palm, looking up at me quizzically.

'So do you feel better, now you aren't mental? Or are you still a bit mental? Do you mind me calling you "mental"?'

'Erm – I feel fine now, Cal. How have things been here?'

He runs his hands through his hair, but is also smiling.

'It's honestly been mental here, just so busy. I feel like I might have a breakdown, too! Things really picked up after the meme. Then there was that video you posted from the Revue. Everyone went crazy on Twitter about it. "Sleeping Meme Guy goes to a house party for the first time." I actually can't believe how much traffic it brought us. In fact, we're hiring a whole new content editor because of it.'

'Wait, wait, wait.' I hold up palms to him. 'So you didn't take that video down? From the Revue?'

'Oh my Christ, no, Dan!' Callum swipes me with his big paw. 'Everyone thought it was the funniest thing ever. They were like "Refreshing my phone to see what Sleeping Meme Guy will do next".'

I violently face-palm.

'So you're saying the biggest success of my career is essentially me fucking things up live on camera?'

More paw swiping.

'No, Dan! Everyone loves it. But you know what I loved?'

'Please don't say Stan.'

'The apology video you made! Honestly, Dan, I've never laughed so hard. The girl off-screen who's, like, negging you the whole time. Absolutely fabolus. Loved it! So did Twitter.'

I press my forehead into my hands and groan.

'Maybe I really do just need to accept I'm a complete and utter idiot.'

Callum rubs my shoulder with incredible force.

'You're not an idiot, Dan. You're, like, the cleverest person I know.'

I look up at him, and we both smile.

'Cal,' I say, trying to be as genuine as possible, 'I'm really sorry about all the Stan stuff. I should have spoken to you before going to HR. I made an assumption, and I shouldn't have done that. I'm sorry.'

'Dan, honestly, don't worry about it. I'm actually kind of glad you did it. It meant I had a proper reason to break up with him at last. You know he's like fifty-eight?'

I sit up straighter and look at him. Stan's definitely no older than forty.

'So – what was going on between you guys? If you don't mind me asking.'

Callum puts his head back and exhales at the ceiling.

'Oh, I dunno, really. He just started coming over to my desk and saying how nice I looked. And it's nice to get compliments, isn't it? And then he started texting me, and saying how good-looking I was and stuff, and – Dan, not being funny, the guys I normally go out with don't have a pot to piss in, you know what I mean? Personal trainers don't earn that much! But Stan took me out for dinners at posh restaurants and things, and I know he's not peng to look at, but he actually isn't that bad, so I was, like, fair play, and gave him the odd blowie and stuff. I know it was wrong going along with it, but I just didn't know what else to do, and now they've gone and fired him, and it wasn't all his fault.'

I tilt my head to the side.

'No, it definitely was.'

'But he said he'd give me a promotion. And I thought how else am I going to get one, I'm not Einstein like you, am I? He didn't make me do anything I didn't want to do. Well, I didn't *want* to do it, but it wasn't so bad. I mean, it's just sex, isn't it? And I really, *really* wanted a new Switch.'

I put my hand on his shoulder. 'Cal, it's not your fault. He was in a position of power. He took advantage of you.'

'Whoa, Dan!' Callum stares me in the eyes. 'I'm not, like, a "victim of abuse". Guys are always after stuff like that, it's just what they're like. How else am I supposed to get them to like me?'

Callum is recounting this with such sweet openness, any feelings of superiority towards him vanish. He's just another insecure gay guy – how had I never realised this before? I was so busy being jealous of him, and making myself feel better for being cleverer than him, that I'd missed that inside we probably aren't as different as we first appear.

Just like Tobbs, I think in the same heartbeat. He said all those things to put me down because he felt threatened by me. He didn't have any friends, so he put down mine. He thought his writing work was bullshit, so he said mine was, too. He was afraid of the intimacy I wanted with him, because the love he'd been shown had wounded him so deeply.

A wave of affection floods from me to Callum. I want to hug him . . . but maybe I won't.

'Cal, you don't ever have to do anything you don't want to do just because the other person wants you to – trust me, I've learned that the hard way.'

Callum rubs his elbow with the opposite hand. He looks at me meekly.

'It's hard not to sometimes, though, isn't it?'

'Yeah.' I smile sadly. 'It is. But we've gotta try.'

'You're a better boss than him anyway.' Callum grins naughtily. 'Especially given you got us nominated for that award.'

I just blink at him.

'Sorry, what?'

'Yeah, that journalism award.'

I keep blinking.

'You're gonna have to fill me in there, Cal.'

'That's what Stan said,' Callum says immediately, then shakes his head. 'Sorry. Basically, they nominated the whole Meme drama series. They said it was like a meta-take on the news cycle or something. Like a perfect parody, I think.'

I stare into space. Not exactly doing Lois Lane proud, like I'd always planned.

'Oh my God, so they think it's all a joke. They think me trying to be a serious journalist is a deliberate spoof of journalism in the Web 2.0 era?'

Now Callum blinks. 'Um – yeah. And we get to go to the awards ceremony. I'm gonna splash out and get a Marc Jacobs blazer.'

I consider this unexpected turn of events. 'Well, it's a start, I guess.'

'Oooooh, girl!' comes a voice over my shoulder.

The Marc/ks are gliding past, both in maroon.

'Guess who's back in the house!'

'And looking fly as fuck!'

I glance down at my First Day Back from Having a Mental Breakdown Lewk, which is something between my old and new wardrobes: black jeans, white Converse, a white tee and Jacob's billowing eighties silk shirt over the top. I do look pretty good, it can't be denied.

'Hey, Marc,' I say with a little wave. 'Hey, Mark.'

'Shit! How are you feeling, Dan?'

'Yeah, OK. You know, just . . . catching up on things.'

'Totally.' They exchange glances. 'We're glad to have you back. There's been hardly any drama since you left.'

'But now maybe you can fall asleep on TV again.'

One nudges the other. How can I still not work out which is which?

'Actually, your little award-nominated piece is bringing in new gays already,' he says.

'Like, subscribers?'

'No.' He frowns. 'He's in the Grime Music Studio now. He's been waiting for, like, fifteen minutes.'

'Oh, bloody hell!' Callum jumps up and starts rummaging through the pile of papers on his desk. 'I'd forgotten about him! Dan, are you ready?'

'For what?'

Callum stares at me like I'm an idiot.

'For the interview, Dan.'

'What interview? Cal, I just got back.'

Callum clutches the bits of paper to his chest.

'For the new junior content editor.'

'ANYWAY, good to have you back, Danny!' the Marc/ks say in unison before floating off together.

I smile and nod. 'Thanks, Marc. Thanks, Mark.'

Callum is now pacing towards the Grime Music Studio, very red in the face.

'Come on, Boss Man!' he calls back.

I leg it after him into the little blacked-out meeting room where I know for a fact at least four different members of staff have had sex. Callum is already seated at the table, which is decked out exactly like a studio mixing desk. A band of blue neon runs around the edge of everything, including the ceiling, the table and all four chairs. It gives it the air of a public toilet, rather than a high-end music studio.

'This is Danny,' Callum says as I sit down next to him. 'Our interim creative director. He's pretty fit, isn't he? Like, for a boss.'

'Thanks for having me,' says the media grad across the table from us. 'I'm JC.'

'Hi, JC,' Callum and I intone together.

I hastily flick through the crumpled pages in front of us – JC's CV and covering letter – to make it look like I've read either.

'So, JC, you're applying for the role of . . . ?'

'Junior content editor.'

'Right!' I say, channelling Nina. 'I see you've got lots of experience. Wow, interned with the BBC last summer. Published on *Vice*. Amazing. Cool. Rad.' Now I'm turning into Stan. Gotta rein that in. 'And what attracts you to the role?'

Despite being an extremely handsome young man, JC suddenly looks shy. He brushes his fringe to the side and adjusts the collar of his shirt, which is a crisply ironed blue number. Something about him jolts me into my own past.

'Well,' he says in an embarrassed voice, 'I was inspired by the LGBTQ-Plus comedy series you guys are running. I've never seen something done like that, where it was both ridiculous and relatable without ever being insulting to the people you were interviewing.' He nervously glances at me. 'I loved that you played this clueless character as a window into these worlds. It was such a clever move – sort of like a more hapless Louis Theroux. And you played it so well, you should be an actor.'

'Yes, well' – I cough – 'that was the whole strategy behind that.'

'Dan's a, like, actual genius,' Callum chips in.

'And that apology video?' JC goes on. 'Such a great spoof that also has heart. It was silly, but it was also *real*. Just the opposite of all the stupid, in-your-face corporate Pride content companies put out when they really understand nothing about actual queer people and our struggles. There's so many LGBTQ-Plus people who don't feel like they belong in queer culture, and it's so refreshing to see them given a voice – especially if they don't belong in straight culture, either. Like, my parents are from Jamaica, right? So they weren't really down with the whole trans thing to begin with. It's been a journey, but we've come through it. And I'd love to be able to help others through it like that.' He sniffs and looks at us with lovely hope in his face.

On the edge of tears again, I say: 'I'm so happy you liked it. It'd be great to get your opinion on the upcoming pieces in that series, given that it's just been nominated for a British Journalism Award.'

'Oh, wow, amazing!' JC beams. 'Yeah, the tone of the content was great. And I *loved* that epic non-binary artist – JJDiaspora? They gave me life!'

'They're actually coming to the awards ceremony with us.' I grin. 'They just don't know it yet.'

'That's ace. They are super-iconic, a really inspirational character.'

Suddenly everything is right. I am exactly where I'm supposed to be. And so is JC. Everything is going to be all right. For him, and for me.

'They absolutely are,' I say. 'And that was a great answer, by the way. In fact, I have a feeling you're going to answer all of these questions really well.'

JC smiles.

'I hope so.'

THIRTY-SEVEN

'I'll take your coat,' Simone says, in the strange, infantilised voice I just know every single girl in the flat will be using today. 'Laura will be *so* happy to see you, Danny. Oh, wow, don't you look snappy!'

'Thanks,' I say, watching her search for space on the coat rack by the door I used to walk through every single day. I smooth down my shirt and tie. 'I've got this *thing* I'm going to after, so.'

'Ooh, Mr Popular!' She's still searching.

'I can just put it on the back of the bathroom door,' I offer.

She dips her head at me, remembering that I used to live here.

'Right, right.' She hands it back to me and regards me with a serious, motherly glare. 'We were *so* sorry to hear about you and the BF, Danny.'

'Oh, it's fine. That was a while ago now.' I wave a hand; it feels like another life. But I don't like the use of the term 'we'. How many of them have been talking about this, exactly? 'We weren't right for each other, so it was for the best.'

'Well' – Simone takes my arm and leads me from the hall into the living room – 'you know who we've always thought you'd be great with?'

I don't have to ask, of course, expecting to see his perfectly chiselled face as we emerge into the gingham-pastel haven. But, mercifully, I don't see him, just a lot of girls in what at first glance appears to be the same mid-calf-length dress in slightly different prints. They are all chatting and gasping and pawing at one another and the tiny knitted jumpers and socks they've brought as gifts.

'Danster!' bellows Luke, who's sitting on the arm of one of the sofas with his legs spread impossibly wide. He's in jeans and a navy rugby shirt – presumably because Laura hasn't allowed him to actually have a game on, so this is the only way to allay the separation anxiety.

'Hi, Luke.'

He wraps his massive, hard body around me in a classically firm bro-hug. I have my coat over my arm, so cannot reciprocate; I am merely absorbed. Still, our penises press together.

'How's it going, fam?'

'Yeah, all right. You know.'

'Oh, sick, sick!'

He's grinning at me with a slightly manic twinkle in the eye, and I realise he's actually relieved to see me.

'Brought you guys a little something.' I hand him a bottle of prosecco wrapped in gold paper.

'Thanks a mill, mate,' he says, and pops it immediately.

I look around. I hadn't thought the flat could get any twee-er, but I was wrong. Joining the white, heart-shaped affirmations are pastel-coloured bunting and some shiny blue balloon lettering over the stove that spells 'BABY BOY'. I am the only other birthed male visible, and Luke is clearly struggling with it. These girls probably don't have a lot of rugger chat.

'Danny-boo!' Laura coos from the sofa, where she sits resplendent, surrounded by the girls, like the Virgin Mother with the farmyard animals – if the Virgin Mother had been taken in at a Chiswick gastropub rather than a stable. She's in a lemon dress with a lot of ruching around her significantly engorged nunga-nungas and a pale-pink cardigan that can clearly no longer close. Her stomach is absolutely massive. I can't help but imagine Luke's giant spawn doing press-ups in there, ready to explode into the world at any moment, shouting, 'PILE ON!'

'Hey, Laur.' I lean in to kiss her. She smells overpoweringly of baby powder. 'You look amazing.'

'It's the sweat,' Luke proffers from behind me.

'Lukey!' Laura scolds. 'I'm "glowing".'

'She is,' Georgia says sternly from across the coffee table. 'Hey, Danny! Haven't seen you in a while.'

'Hey, Georgia!' I smile back awkwardly. 'I've had, like, a lot on with work and stuff. Actually, tonight I've got this award—'

'Aren't you going to put your coat somewhere, Dan-Dan?' Laura says, folding a hand around my forearm. 'Then you can get a drinky-wink. We've got oodles and oodles of Nosecco!'

'Party!' I say, to which no one reacts. 'I'll just—'

I head off towards the bathroom, passing the open door to the bedroom I lived in for five years. I pause. It's been transformed into exactly what a baby boy's nursery would look like if you could buy it all from the Boden catalogue. There's pale-blue pirate wallpaper, a selection of picture books propped up on the windowsill and, in the centre, a vast white wooden crib. I can't suppress a giggle: above it is a mobile of wooden rugby balls. Evidently, Luke has had *some* input into the well-being of their child.

The bathroom door is closed, so I push on it gently, getting horrible flashbacks to work. It opens slowly, and I tentatively step in to find someone sitting on the loo.

'Shit, sorry!' I say and jerkily turn to get out ASAP.

'Fuck, Danny!' It's Zain, of course. 'I'm not taking a shit. It's OK!'

I turn back around and chance a glance. He's not. The toilet seat is down. He's just sitting on it. In his uniform black sweat-shirt, jeans and white Reeboks.

He looks up at me AND ACTUALLY SMILES.

'Thank fuck it's you. I just needed – you know – some time away from it. Hey, shut the door.'

Oh, so he's actually just relieved I'm not someone else. That follows.

I linger on the threshold, wondering if this is some kind of trap. But I turn, close and lock the door, and hang up my coat on the hooks.

I really don't know how to approach this. I try a stab in the dark.

'Are you . . . sick?'

'Nah.' He looks over to the bath, the pile of flowery towels piled neatly next to the drying rack. 'It's just a bit *intense* in there.'

For a second, I try to work out how to play this, before I realise I don't need to play anything any way anymore, I just need to react the way I feel. This is really a whole new way of being I'm getting used to.

'Too much baby chat?'

His lips erupt outward in what I can only assume is a sort of frustrated laugh. He's glad to be understood by someone.

'Too much baby chat, man.'

'That's why I came a bit late,' I say. 'I don't think I could do a whole afternoon of it.'

'I got here at one,' he says, rubbing his shaven skull. 'It's been three hours of "And will he board?" and "Will he play

371

rugby?" and "You must be so thrilled!" How thrilled can you be? It just makes me feel so—'

'Alien,' I say.

His eyes flick up to me. We stare directly at each other for a solid four seconds. His eyes are dark, almost as dark as Nina's, though less piggy.

'Yeah: alien.'

'No one knows quite how to talk to you about it?'

'Yeah! Whereas everyone else is like "Oh, me and Sim want two, because one always turns out weird," and then they're like "I know, right?"'

'I think I'd rather be at one of our house parties – and that's saying something.'

'Hey, your Christmas party was sweet, man. I had a great night.'

'Yeah.' I think back to what was easily the worst night of my life. 'I'm sorry I was kind of a dick to you.'

'Nah, nah, you were cool.'

Zain looks at me again, then down at his hands, which loosely fiddle with each other between his knees. He even looks a little embarrassed. Maybe he isn't just some stone-cold narcissist; maybe he's just doing the same protective actions we all are. Maybe his defence is the sheen of coolness. And maybe I'm just getting past that.

'Hey,' he says awkwardly, 'I meant to say to you that night, actually, I'm really sorry for getting at you the morning after we . . . you know?'

'Got drunk and fucked?' I say.

He starts coughing violently. 'Yeah. I was just in a really bad place with the break-up, and I think it sort of set me off—'

'Hey, it's fine. I get it. I've been in kind of a bad place for a while, but finally come out of it.'

His eyes look at me, and there's real anxiety in them.

'I think you're actually really cool, Danny. Like, I think we could be good mates.'

I smile. I genuinely cannot believe I'm having this conversation with Zain Porowski.

'Just because we're both gay doesn't mean all we can do is fight or fuck.'

He laughs. 'Feels like that sometimes, though, doesn't it? Being gay, I mean.'

'Yeah, it does . . . But it doesn't have to.'

'Totally.'

I lean back against the door.

'How's stuff with you?' he says.

'All right, you know. I'm actually pretty nervous. I've got this awards ceremony to go to in a bit.'

'Sick! What ceremony?'

'The British Journalism Awards.'

'Fuck! No way!'

'Way.'

He grins, actually grins, a broad, genuine smile, and I see he's got a slightly discoloured left front tooth. He's not so perfect, after all.

'You surprise me every time I see you recently.'

I shrug.

'You too.'

And we smile at each other. Part of me is still on guard. Why is he being so nice? Is he just relieved to be talking to someone that feels the same as him? Not that either of us would have admitted that before.

'Look.' He leans in, looks serious and shifty. 'So Laura didn't want anyone drinking at this baby shower because she can't, but here's the other reason I came to hide out in here.'

He slides a hip flask out of his jean pocket. I nearly scream. It's a hot pink laminate one printed with a face I recognise as well as my own: Dolly!

'You're a fan?' he discerns from my expression. I nod. 'Same. Rufaro actually got this for me. He's not around anymore, but Dolly stays. You like gin?'

'Is Dolly's hair closer to God than mine?'

'And you're funny, too. I really underestimated you.'

Sort of a backhanded insult, but I decide not to bring him up on it. Instead, I sip Dolly's fiery nectar.

'You know, if you liked the Revue, you should come round for one of our barbecues. The garden's amazing.'

I hand Dolly back to him. He takes a swig. 'Sounds sweet. Thanks, Danny.'

I smile. 'You're welcome, Zain.'

He raises Dolly high. 'To friendship!' And necks the last of it.

All of a sudden I leap from the door, because there's a thundering at it.

'What are you boys up to in there?' cries Simone, with audible glee. 'We don't want any more babies today!'

Zain looks at me, and we both crack up.

—

The rest of the shower isn't actually too painful. Laura and I have a chat and a hug, and I leave just at the right time. Zain is stuck with Luke by the sink and mouths 'Nooooo!' as I wave and slip out the door.

I've never been to an awards ceremony before but anticipate it'll essentially be like MTV's Video Music Awards. To be fair, the venue is wildly fancy – Old Billingsgate Market, a building on the Thames that looks like a Venetian palace.

I leg it from the Tube to meet my date outside. And there they are, lingering halfway up the entrance steps, posing for pictures. They're in a sheer, floor-length golden gown, teamed with the golden Belle gloves, throwing their braids back over their glossy shoulder, now reaching past their arse and fading from black to gold. They're clearly loving every minute of it, looking like the most glamorous alien stripper you've ever seen, and I don't even feel jealous.

'There's my Adonis!' Jacob waves their bejewelled silver swan purse at me as I leap up the steps to join them. They kiss me on both cheeks and grin. Metallic make-up, too, of course – the Jacob signature. 'Don't you scrub up well?'

'What, this old thing?' I say back to them through a static grin. The suit I'm in consists of a leather biker jacket and matching trousers, both painted on in wild pink flames, lips and pointed teeth. The shirt and tie are in the same bright pink. Thank you, Melania.

We pose for several photographs together, and even though there's no flashing bulb lamps, like in Hollywood movies, I still feel dazzled.

Inside, we find our table with Callum, Nadia, the Marc/ks and JC, all of whom look incredible. The Marc/ks are in matching designer suits, of course. There are actual waiters with trays of free prosecco, and round tables with our names on them. There are actual chandeliers. There are even actual journalists I actually recognise and respect. Some famous correspondent I half recognise presents something presents something – I forget what, though, because that prosecco is going down nicely on top of the Dolly gin.

'Here we go, Dan,' Callum whispers to me as we clap onstage the presenter of the Outstanding Contribution To LGBTQ+ Culture Award. I recognise him: it's the hunky BBC LGBT correspondent who i've Googled numerous times. I just nod at him. I'm pretty drunk, not just on free booze, but on everything. A rumbling shakes my bones, and my whole body tenses.

Oh no, not now. Not at this moment!

I thought I'd beaten it. The earthquakes, the electricity.

But as I put my hand to my stomach to calm my breathing, I realise it's not fear or anxiety. It's excitement.

'Now onto the award that champions our new LGBTQIA-Plus platforms,' says the hunky correspondent to the room. 'This award is for a news site, app or campaign that's pushing our culture forward to where we want to be, showing the true representation and diversity within the queer world. So, without further ado, I'm proud to say this year's award goes to . . .'

'Get me a towel to wipe off my chair; that journalist is hot,' Jacob whispers from my other side.

'Jacob!' I slap them on the wrist, and then the sound that follows it is truly deafening.

I'm not sure what's going on. Everyone is all around me. Callum's mouth is wide open, right in my face, yelling, 'Oh my God, Dan, we did it!' Then next thing I know, the correspondent's face is in my face, grinning his stunning smile and shaking my hand. I'm looking down at the room of round tables, at the hundreds of journalists clapping at us.

'Oh my God, I honestly can't believe it. I wanna thank the academy, my mum . . .' I'm hearing Callum's voice echo around the massive space, marred by a wild amount of feedback. 'But I mean, really, the whole thing was Danny's idea – even though I did do *a lot* to help, not gonna lie.'

Suddenly a microphone is in my hand, and I'm staring out into the room. The electricity sparks across my forehead, and I see myself as a child, making that mini-newspaper, imagining being here, among all these incredible people, having to say something meaningful, and the electricity feels for the first time like a power supply I can tap into, not one I need to turn off at the mains.

'I . . . I used to be scared of everything,' I say into the black lattice of the mic. 'Scared of getting it wrong. Scared of looking like an idiot. Scared of really being me. But, over the last few months, I've discovered what it really means to live truthfully, and to be supported by – and support – other members of your community. And, in doing that, I've discovered you don't have to be perfect, you just have to be you. So – this is for everyone who's ever felt like they're still figuring it out and getting it wrong along the way. Thank you!'

And the room erupts into clapping. Someone at the table right in front of us even stands up and whoops. Is that Louis Theroux? I look to my left and see Callum and everyone, standing at the podium, raising up this ugly Perspex award, flanked by gorgeous correspondent and his massive chest basically popping the buttons off his shirt with each breath. Then I look to my right, and see my best friend in all the world, the glittering Oscar themself, Jacob.

Their Belle-gloved hand is in mine. They squeeze it.

'You're a winner, baby,' they say, and I've never seen them look prouder in their life.

'We all are,' I say back cheesily.

'Gross.'

We sit back in our seats and watch as they play various clips of me unconscious on the pavement, and how it multiplied across the internet, Raj talking into the camera about fighting for others, Melania and Ashraf voguing the house down boots. Jacob's face appears more than once, and when they look straight into the camera and say, 'Once I had a mother, once I had a friend . . .' I press my head against theirs and hold their hand so tightly, the tears of everything that's happened pouring down my face.

These amazing people in my life have been so brave for so long. After everything that's happened to me, can't I do the same? Can't I be brave?

THIRTY-EIGHT

Sunday 19th May

Things I've learned about myself recently:
- *I actually have a personality*
  News to me. Turns out, as much as you try to repress your true self, it explodes out at some point, so better to accept it earlier. If there's one thing I've learned recently, it's you really have to take the time to look at yourself. REALLY look at yourself, and sit there and say, 'This is who I am. Maybe it's not perfect. Maybe I don't even like it. But this is what we've got to work with.'
- *I'm not over all the stuff with Tobbs/guys in general*
  It's complicated, and that's OK. His revelation in hospital that he still loves me and found opening up so hard is something I'm still thinking about. Stuff with Will has scared me. It's shit that stuff that happens to you when you're little can fuck you up right into adulthood. Nina calls it 'the work'. Jacob calls it 'the Untethering'. Makes me realise how lucky I am to have Dad and Mum and Jacob. And my new friends in the house, who actually are becoming friends now. When I next get involved with a guy, I need to really think about

what I want, and if I think they want what I want. Also to look out for those red flags, instead of picking them up and waving them.

- *The anxiety is here to stay*
  Hard truth to swallow TBH. Don't like to think of myself as having a 'generalised anxiety disorder', but is also helpful maybe. Nina says the important thing is to stay 'present', to 'observe' how I feel in my body when things 'trigger' me. Will probs always be a part of me, but can learn to manage it better – have baths, sleep well, not get involved with wrong sort of guy for me . . . But mostly listening to how I feel in certain situations or relationships; otherwise, Bette Midler will reappear and zap my brains again.

- *Yeah, I fucked up*
  Even though it feels like it was another person saying and doing those things, it wasn't. It was me. Was on the verge of a breakdown, yes, but was still cruel and selfish, especially to Jacob. Our friendship is different now. It's evolving as we evolve. Think we were both scared of things changing, but you can't stop things changing, you can only react well or badly to them.

- *No more wasting time*
  I've spent the last fifteen years living a half-life. Have missed out on so many things. Not all my fault it's happened that way, but is my responsibility to do something about it, and a lot of it will be hard work. But, as Dolly says, if you want a rainbow, you gotta put up with the rain. From now on, am going to live my life, not hide from it. I CAN be brave. Danny Scudd is in the waiting room no more!

I look up from the Dolly Diary.

I'm sitting on the decking in the garden. Next to me, Jacob

lounges on three conference chairs, reading Audre Lorde in their kimono. It's the middle of May, one of those crazy hot spells that lasts for less than a week and makes you wonder if global warming isn't actually so bad after all. In two days, the world has gone from grey, cold winter storm shaker to balmy hipster terrarium – at least, it has in our house. I've spent an alarming amount of money on new gardening equipment, and this is where I've been all weekend. I'm already excited to get into bed early and watch a BBC drama tonight.

I've been digging up weeds while Ashraf stands by the pond in that funny crunch pose you see bodybuilders do, leaning forward with both arms bent, one behind and one in front. He's in only a pair of startlingly white Y-fronts, his chestnutty skin glistening in the heat, sweat trickling down every muscle. Before him, Gin sits on a blanket with one of the big bags of clay from the 'conservatory', sculpting a smaller version of a man who already looks like one of Rodin's bronzes. Fast-paced Slovenian spills from the open window of Melania's room, where she's speaking to someone. Distantly, 'Girl' by Destiny's Child plays. It is a perfect moment in our queer little world.

Queer.

My CULTRD-branded biro hovers on the page.

This is a word I've always shied away from. Not just shied away from, but been afraid of, I realise. That and all the words of its ilk. Gay. Faggot. Homo. I've always hated them, hated myself by association. I even hated it when queer people used them.

And now?

Now I feel calmer about it. I am queer, what's the big deal?

I close the diary's cover, and look around at my handiwork. Not being funny, but I've done wonders for this garden. It's coming back to life in the most amazing way. I've been lost in it for hours, making notes in the diary about what other plants I can buy. I've even cleared a spot to grow some vegetables. Now's the perfect time for regrowth.

My phone sits on the table between Jacob and me, and I pick it up and scroll through messages.

'Shit, Laura's had the baby! A boy . . . called Ethelred.'

Jacob looks up over the rims of their triangular Gucci sunglasses.

'Gender is a construct.'

I give them a look.

'You know what I mean.'

'I'm not being a bitch. Tell her I'm happy for her.'

'I absolutely will not.'

They blow me a kiss and lie back. 'You know, I have this theory about heteronormative society.'

'Uh-huh?'

'It's mostly just making cheese sandwiches and taking the bins out.'

'Ha ha! Brutal!'

Jacob sits up again. 'It is, though, isn't it? They always go on about how obsessed we are with gender. *They're* the ones obsessed with gender. "Be ladylike," "Be a real man," "Don't act like a girl" – they're literally addicted to policing gender. It must be so exhausting for them. That's why they get so angry at us for flouting the rules and living fabulously, because they've put these intense restraints on themselves.' They lie back again and sip the latest batch of moonshine from the Charles and Diana mug. 'Well, I, for one, refuse to be restrained.'

I digest this for a moment. A few months ago, I would have said something like 'I don't know, Jacob . . .'

Well, I do know now, because I did put intense restraints on myself without realising, and now it feels so good not to.

'You know, Jay,' I say, thinking out loud, 'it never occurred to me to think of being gay as anything other than a defect from being straight. Like, it was only ever a condition you had to work out how to live with. But, you know what, it's actually got its own things going on – like it's so fun, and it's definitely made me more empathetic.'

'Now that you're being more empathetic to yourself,' Jacob interrupts.

'Right. I'd just never thought of it that way before.'

'What did I tell you about rainbow matter?'

'Don't be smug. I hate it when you're smug.'

'And I love it when you can actually tell me how you hate it.'

'Boundaries, Big Edie.'

'Boundaries, Little Edie.'

I go back to weeding the garden. It gets so hot I take my shirt off – something I don't think I've done in public since I was fourteen. Ashraf whistles, which makes my face heat up, but it also feels kind of good.

After a while, I hear giggling from the conservatory door. I glance up, and I freeze.

Raj is standing on the decking in his black jeans and T-shirt, watching me work. I haven't seen him in months, not since the night of the Revue. Beside him is Titty, in tomato-red dungarees. I wipe the sweat from my forehead and wave a cautious hand. Melania comes out with four beers and kisses Titty on the mouth. What a day this is. Before I know it, Raj is wandering over and handing me a beer. Even though he's seen me naked, I scrabble to get the top back on.

'You don't have to,' he says, with his kind, lopsided little smile.

'I never take my shirt off in public normally,' I say, panting, as it gets stuck on my head.

Raj gently manoeuvres it so my head slides through the hole.

'You should,' he says, locking eyes with me. 'You look fit.'

'Ha ha, thanks.' Oh God, I'm giggling nervously. To deflect, I lean in and whisper, 'What's going on with them?'

Raj glances behind, at where Titty and Melania are now cuddled up on my seat, chatting to Jacob.

'Oh yeah, I know – scandal!' He laughs. I'd forgotten what a lovely sound it is. 'Apparently, they've been texting ever since the Revue night, and are giving it another go.'

'No more Dick?'

'No more Dick.'

Our eyes meet, and we crack up. He leans in and rubs my shoulder.

'You all good, now? Mel said you had a hard time.'

My dirty Converse scuffs the soil I've been digging up.

'Yeah. It was a whole vibe.'

His thumb and forefinger caress my collarbone ever so slightly. 'Was it the gay stuff?'

Now my mouth is as dry as the soil. 'Yeah,' I cough.

'Gets us all, whether we like it or not. Everyone's gotta have their reckoning.'

I look up at him.

'Have you?'

'Yeah.' He laughs again. 'A couple of years ago. It was pretty messy. Took a whole load of drugs, dropped out of the course Mel and I were both on. Took me a while to come to terms with things, you know? Especially with my family—'

'Hard relate.'

'Haha, exactly! That's why I recognised where you were at when we were, you know—'

'*Involved*?'

Now we both laugh. His hand drops from my shoulder to my

waist. The thumb rubs my love handle, and it tickles in a really intimate way. We just smile at each other for a few seconds. He really has the loveliest face I've ever seen.

'No dogging in the daytime, please!' Jacob shouts from the decking.

'We'll be back later, then!' I shout in reply, and everyone laughs.

'Dear lamb!' Melania calls to Raj. 'We've got to get to that gig.'

'OK!' He leans in and hugs me very tightly. Then steps back. 'I'm proud of you, Danny. Let's go for a drink again one night . . . if you fancy it.'

'Yes!' I say too fast. 'I mean: yeah, that'd be cool.'

He laughs, and the three of them vanish into the house. After we hear the front door slam, I come and sit next to Jacob again. The air bristles between us.

'He's a nice boy, isn't he?' Jacob says after a while.

'Jay, remember our talk,' I say in a fake-stern voice. 'Our talk' has now become code for 'back off'.

They hold their hands up in surrender and we begin to cackle like a pair of old witchy aunts on the porch of our crumbling New England mansion. Then I go in for a hug.

'I'm not him, you know?' they say.

'I love you, Jay.'

They peer at me with a smile.

'I love you too, Dan.'

'Look at us, communicating honestly.'

'Nina would be proud!'

I pull Jacob up and we dance around, singing the words from Tina Turner's version of 'Rolling on a River'. From the garden, Ashraf and Gin start clapping along. We build to a big finish and hold each other's hands aloft. We embrace again. They really are the *most* strange and extraordinary person I've ever met. We've been through a lot, hurt each other a lot, but really they are the true love of my life, my best friend, forever.

I get back to the garden. The others stay out a little while, before going in to make dinner. Gin's making vegan lasagna. I dig and dig, until I need to grab the hoodie and pull it around my shoulders, which are already aching from sunburn. I sit by the pond, watch the flies dart across it. The city feels so far away. The mania I'd felt last year feels so far away, and yet it's stored in me, it's a part of me and my story.

Something disturbs the palm tree overhead, and I look up. The aggro robin is sitting on one of the green, dagger-like prongs, regarding me as suspiciously as usual.

'All right, robin?' I say.

It stares at me, then flits off again.

Maybe it's not angry, I think, the leaf it was on still bobbing from its departure. Maybe it's just unsure what to make of me. Maybe it's just eyeing me up, working out if it can trust me or not, if I'm a threat. It doesn't know I've only recently turned my indoor botanical skills to the outside. But I think we'll get along.

I pick up my trowel, rub my shoulders in the crisp, cooling air, look around at the garden as it comes back to life, and head inside for dinner.

ACKNOWLEDGEMENTS

So many people have supported me through the creation of this novel (as well as the many, many other books that'll never see the light of day), and I'll always be grateful to those who believed in me right from the beginning.

A shout-out to all my different families: my birth family, who have been bemused by me since Day One, but supportive nonetheless. My loving, intelligent, joyous boyfriend Adam, who at this point can probably recite as much of the novel as I can. My London Writer's Award family, particularly Bobby Nayyar and Ruth Harrison. It's so incredible to be on this journey with people who truly share your passion and with whom to celebrate your collective successes. My extended Flodden family, who I wouldn't be without, particularly when producing a naked calendar. My family of wonderful friends all over the world; you've always been there for me, even when we're thousands of miles apart. My professional family: my brilliant agent Hayley and the team at Madeleine Milburn, my editors Charlotte, Jesse, Bhavna and Anna – and unofficial editor and literary icon, Clare Bullock – and the talented teams at Orion, Ballantine and Doubleday.

And lastly, my ever-growing queer family. Growing up, I felt

387

like the only one who was different, like an alien wearing a human suit. But the more of you I meet, the more I realise we're connected through so many similar experiences of shame and alienation. But that doesn't mean our lives have to be shameful and alienated. The pain we've felt can become what connects us, what creates understanding, support and love. We never have to be alone again if we take the time to seek out safety and work on ourselves – and what fabulous selves we are! We really are each other's family.

XOXO GOSSIP GAY

CREDITS

ORION CREDITS

Henry Fry and Orion Fiction would like to thank everyone at Orion who worked on the publication of *First Time for Everything* in the UK.

Editorial
Charlotte Mursell
Sanah Ahmed

Proofreader
Jade Craddock

Audio
Paul Stark
Jake Alderson

Finance
Jasdip Nandra
Afeera Ahmed
Elizabeth Beaumont
Sue Baker

Marketing
Helena Fouracre

Contracts
Anne Goddard
Humayra Ahmed
Ellie Bowker

Editorial Management
Charlie Panayiotou
Jane Hughes
Bartley Shaw
Tamara Morriss

Production
Ruth Sharvell

Sales
Jen Wilson
Esther Waters
Victoria Laws
Rachael Hum
Anna Egelstaff
Frances Doyle
Georgina Cutler

Publicity
Alainna Hadijgeorgiou

Design
Charlotte Abrams-Simpson
Joanna Ridley
Nick May

Operations
Jo Jacobs
Sharon Willis

thinking about them (and wish we were friends). A very relatable journey of self-discovery'
RADHIKA SANGANI

'This is the modern gay novel, with the sass of a drag queen and the wisdom of a queer elder.

Henry Fry was longlisted for the PRH Write Now scheme in 2016 and won the Literary Consultancy's Free Reads Award for new LGBT+ voices in 2017. In 2019 he was a recipient of the London Writer's Award programme and his words have appeared everywhere from national magazines, sites and apps to toilet cubicle walls. He has performed as a spoken word artist at events featuring Ed Sheeran, Kate Tempest, Dean Atta (and more) and is currently a writer and designer at Greenpeace. *First Time for Everything* is his first novel.